Eden Falls Montana — Book 2

When MIDNIGHT STRIKES

RILEY SKOV

WHEN MIDNIGHT STRIKES

Copyright © 2024 by Riley Skov

All rights reserved.

No part of this book may be reproduced, distributed, or transmitted in any form or by any means, including photocopying, recording, or other electronic or mechanical methods, without the prior written permission of the author except in the case of brief quotations in a book review. Thank you for respecting the rights of the author.

This is a work of fiction. Names, characters, places, and incidents are the product of the author's imagination or are used fictitiously. Any resemblance to actual events, locales, or persons, living or dead, is coincidental.

Edited by Red Adept Editing.

Proofread by Red Adept Editing.

Also by Riley Skov

EDEN FALLS MONTANA SERIES

When Shadows Fall
When Midnight Strikes
When Secrets Kill

For you, Mom.
For all that you have sacrificed for me.
For teaching me resilience.
For always picking up the phone.
For being everything I needed you to be.
I love you.

CHAPTER 1

PAIN SLICED THROUGH MY TEMPLES. I closed my eyes for just a moment, not daring to block out my surroundings any longer than that. If I showed that I was in pain—showed any weakness at all—things would get so much worse.

Under its own power, my index finger tapped out the slow progression of time against the cheap pressed wood I was chained to. I'd been there for hours, in that exact position. My shoulders ached, my neck was stiff, and my legs longed to move—to stretch out and carry me far away from that dismal place. I squinted against the artificial light burning holes in my retinas. It seemed impossibly bright against the darkness that permeated the rest of the room, causing the pain in my head to pulse even stronger.

Sensing that I was about to lose my grip on my careful self-possession, I closed my eyes once more and took a deep breath through my nose, and as I slowly released it, my eyes drifted open. No longer feeling in danger of losing control, I glanced around to ensure I hadn't drawn any attention.

The two women to my left still sat with their backs to me, though their rolling office chairs were angled toward each other to better facilitate their constant chatter. A third woman, still with plenty of bloom in her rosy cheeks and smooth features, sat across from me in profile, as she, too, was turned in a manner that allowed her to take part in the conversation with the others.

"That man can slide between my sheets *anytime* he wants to!" one of the women to my left said with a cackle, and the other nodded in appreciation.

I rolled my eyes then caught myself, quickly schooling my features. In desperate need of distraction, I glanced at the phone sitting in obstinate silence on the left side of my desk. *Ring, you stupid thing.*

The dispatch center had been unusually quiet, even by the standards of our sleepy town. We'd had the usual grievances early in the day—the elderly citizens calling in to complain about kids walking across their lawns on the way to school, newspapers being swiped and thrown onto roofs, Mr. Finnigan watering his lawn in nothing but his underwear and boots even though we'd had plenty of rain and could forego such endeavors.

I leaned back and placed my hands on the back of my neck, squeezing and pinching in an effort to alleviate some of the tension. If my headache got any worse, I would soon be seeing ten screens instead of five. To the far left of my workstation, the monitor that worked our antiquated phone system was a blank blue screen at the moment, with the exception of the on-screen buttons around the perimeter. The three monitors in the middle of my setup showed all of our current calls for service, for both fire and law enforcement, a series of maps, and a list of on-duty personnel and their current locations. To the right, the monitor that operated all of our radio frequencies jumped to life every now and then when an officer got bored enough to initiate a traffic stop or pedestrian contact.

Our dispatch center operated differently from most in Montana. Instead of dispatching for the entire county, we were hired by and dispatched solely for the town of Eden Falls. Though it meant less funding and therefore working with some outdated equipment like our phone system, I loved that we were a *part* of the department and able to more intimately serve the town in which we lived.

And though I cherished Eden Falls, I had to admit that on days when I was forced to do nothing but listen to the gossip and man-drooling machinations of my partners, I missed dispatching for a larger department with a higher call volume.

"Seriously, though," Meredith, one of our more venomous dispatchers, said with a pout, "I know Gabe is crazy about Alex and everything, but if he ever felt the need to add a little more spice to his life, my door is always open."

"You mean your *legs* are always open!" Blair, one of our supervisors, replied with a flip of her raven hair. She had it cut in an angular bob that fell just past her jawline and suited her superior attitude.

"You should talk!" Meredith shot back. "You'd be on your back, across this desk, in a heartbeat if Trevor came walking through that door right now, wanting his way with you."

Blair snickered and eyed her cuticles. "Pleeease, we'd need something a lot sturdier than this shitty piece of wood."

Ugh. I wasn't sure how much longer I was going to be able to listen to those two unravel their fantasies in detail. That kind of behavior gave all dispatchers a bad image. It was hard enough to attain the respect of the field units without the likes of Blair and Meredith painting us all as a bunch of glorified badge bunnies.

I'd been on shift rotation with the two of them for more than a couple of months, and to say that I was enjoying my job a lot less lately was an understatement. The truth was I'd been struggling for a lot longer than that. For whatever reason—perhaps I'd unwittingly pissed off the fates—no matter what I did to avoid Blair's shift, I somehow ended up on her watch nine times out of ten. The supervisors always rotated shifts in a predetermined sequence, so it should have been easy to avoid her. But of course, with my luck, despite that I had seniority over most of the staff, either my shift bids were ignored because of "department needs," or Blair inevitably made a trade with one of the other supervisors.

Regardless of how it went down, I would once again spend another four months having to deal with her vitriol and the black cloud she brought to every shift.

Every time I allowed myself to think about how the department had put a woman like that in a leadership position, my blood boiled, and it took all my willpower to keep from throwing my headset down and telling Blair to stick it up her self-loving ass. So in the interest of keeping my job, I put my head down, focused on my work, and did my best to block out Blair and her brown-nosing cronies.

With nothing else to keep me occupied at the moment, I clicked into one of my screens, pulled up my department email, and said a silent prayer that the correspondence I'd been anxiously awaiting would finally be sitting in my inbox.

I rubbed my tired eyes, trying to get them to focus on the bright screen. The dispatch center had no windows, and most of the dispatchers liked to keep the room dark. The stark contrast between our screens and the environment made the ache of my eyes so much worse, but in true dispatcher fashion, I kept my mouth shut because it wasn't the kind of place where you voiced your disapproval unless you were the queen bee.

My eyes ran down the endless string of emails. Aside from BOLOs, a flyer about an upcoming department barbecue, and an online training I needed to complete, there wasn't much of interest. Disappointment landed heavily in my gut. I had applied for the vacant supervisor position more than three weeks ago, but so far, I hadn't heard anything. But I was pretty sure the gossip about my applying had already made the rounds. Blair, who had never been shy about showing her disdain for me, had been even more caustic lately, ensuring that I was well aware that if *someone* she didn't think was a good fit were to apply for that position, she would do everything in her power to block the promotion.

That wasn't exactly a surprise. I'd known when I applied that I would have to contend with her, but I put my hope and faith in the powers that be, choosing to believe that, in the end, they would make the decision that was best for the department, even if it meant they would have to deal with fallout from Blair.

The dispatch center was in serious need of change. Morale was terrible, thanks to the proverbial mean girls who had the run of the place. Relations between the public and the department were strained due to the typical cynicism that naturally developed in a field like law enforcement. And our dispatchers were in desperate need of further training to better support field units and the public. Those were all issues I planned to tackle hard and fast if I were promoted. And the best part of all —there was never more than one supervisor assigned to a shift, so I could say goodbye to Blair as a shift partner once and for all.

A giggle from Julia drew my attention back to the room. At twenty-two, she was our youngest dispatcher. She was a sweet enough girl by nature, but she'd fallen in with Blair and Meredith, mostly as an unwitting mascot, and I had noticed a change in her. She had been so excited about working Dispatch as a profession when she first started—eager to learn everything she could to become one of our best. But eventually, she became more interested in fraternizing with the badges than she was in keeping her focus on her skills and advancement. I let my eyes settle on her, taking in the intricacies of her features, and noted the way her light-brown hair fell to her hips when she was seated at her desk. Her eyes matched her hair, and her body still possessed the litheness of a trim figure that hadn't yet fully developed into womanhood.

Julia nodded eagerly as Blair made the suggestion that they all meet up at Rustlers after work. Meredith smiled in a knowing way, her chubby cheeks turning her black eyes to slits. "You planning on finally having your way with Trevor?"

Everyone knew Rustlers was a second home for Trevor. I wouldn't have been surprised if he spent more time at that bar than he did at his actual house.

Blair shrugged as though she hadn't yet decided. "You can't

just give a man like Trevor what he wants. You have to play hard to get. Make him work for it."

I could have sworn I felt dust forming between my molars as I ground them together. Trevor Ryan was *the* last man I wanted to sit there and listen to those harlots lust after. The mere mention of his name was enough to set my teeth on edge. I didn't consider myself a violent person, but never had someone evoked such homicidal desires in me as that man had.

And who the hell does Blair think she's fooling? Everyone in the department knew she had been throwing herself at Trevor ever since she started working there. For reasons I didn't care to fathom, Trevor, despite his man-whoring ways, had never taken Blair up on her desperate offers.

Resting my elbows on my desk, I placed my fingers on my temples and rubbed hard enough that I thought I might drill down to bone.

"How about it, Quinn?" Julia's lilting voice cut through my internal monologue about why I needed my job.

My eyes flew open, and I sat up straight. Unaccustomed to being included in the conversation, I was struggling to get my bearings. I looked from Julia to Blair and Meredith, who were clearly as surprised by Julia's invite as I was.

Blair recovered first. "I'm sure Quinn would rather sit at home alone. She doesn't get out much." She smiled at me with every pore oozing bitchiness, daring me to start something with her. *Wouldn't she just love that?* Starting a fight with my supervisor in the middle of Dispatch. That would be a surefire way to ensure I didn't get the promotion.

I returned my attention to Julia, who genuinely appeared oblivious to the dynamics of the room, and smiled. "Thank you for the invitation, Julia, but I've already got plans."

She nodded and pressed her lips together, her eyes reflecting a hint of disappointment. Damn, I hoped that girl woke up one day and realized how much better she was than the women whose heels she was chasing after.

Riiinnng.

My hand shot to my phone and snatched up the receiver. Grateful for the intrusion on the awkward situation that had developed, I glanced at my call screen. The call was on the nonemergency line. "Eden Falls Police Department. How may I help you?"

A rich timbre poured through the line, smooth and languid like the smoke from a post-coital cigarette. "I'm calling to report a body."

My fingers, in the process of opening a call-taking screen, froze and hovered over my keyboard, but it took only a millisecond for my brain to come back online. "What's the location of the body, sir?"

"About ten miles outside of town. Northwest."

I glanced at my call screen to check the caller's location. When I saw that the latitude and longitude weren't populating correctly, I clicked the refresh button.

Nothing.

"Sir, can you be more exact? What road are you on?"

His chuckle was almost imperceptible. "I'm not on a road. But it wouldn't matter if I was. The body is in the woods, near the river."

I paused for a moment, finding his phrasing strange.

Again, I tried to get the call to geo-verify. Still nothing, not even the caller's name.

The line was silent but had that quality to it that I could tell it was still open. If he was near the river, I should have been able to hear the water. "Sir?"

"Yes?"

"Are you still on scene with the body?"

"No."

Though I was grateful I didn't have a hysteric caller on my hands, the man was a little *too* calm. Something in his tone wasn't sitting right, but I couldn't pinpoint it.

"How did you access the area where you found the body?"

"A forest road, 3758, I believe it was."

I quickly turned my attention to the monitor on which my maps were displayed. With a few clicks of my mouse, I located the road he'd provided. I squinted at the screen, zooming into the area that would have been about ten miles outside of town. "Sir, was anyone else around when you found the body?"

"No."

"Did you see any landmarks or anything distinctive that could assist officers in finding the location?"

"Hmm." The line was silent for several moments. "There was a lot of trash on the ground. It looked like the area enjoys a good deal of activity."

I knew exactly the place he was describing. The locals referred to it as Tweaker's Cove because the addicts went there to get high and avoid contact with the cops. Normally, a location that far outside of town would be in the sheriff's jurisdiction, but several years ago, the county and Eden Falls had come to an agreement that EFPD would maintain jurisdiction over that particular area because the people causing problems there were locals, and it was closer to our department than any of the sheriff's offices.

Finally having a location, I entered it into my call-taking screen and sent the information through to Blair, who was working our main police radio. At least that would allow our officers to get rolling that way while I tried to get more information.

"Sir, are you certain the person you found was dead?"

"Yes."

"How can you be sure?"

More silence followed. When he finally answered, he spoke as one would stroll. "She wasn't moving. Her eyes were open and vacant. She had clearly been through a terrible ordeal."

I waited for him to continue, but he offered nothing further. Everything about the situation was raising flags—he was calling from a phone that I couldn't get a lock on; I was having to drag the information out of him; and he spoke in a nonchalant way, as though we were sitting across from each other, enjoying a coffee. My instincts were telling me the man hadn't just *happened* upon the body. Still, if he had gone to the trouble of dumping the woman in the middle of the woods, he probably wouldn't call the police to tell them where to find her. But it wouldn't be the first time a criminal narced on themselves.

I took another deep breath to keep my voice even despite the annoyance bubbling up beneath my skin. "What do you mean, 'she had clearly been through something terrible'?"

"I'm sorry, miss, but I really must disconnect now. Your officers will know what I mean when they locate her."

My stomach tightened. I *had* to keep him on the line. Whether he was involved or not, the officers needed to speak with him. I had a reputation for being good at gaining cooperation even from the most difficult callers and prided myself on being able to acquire information others couldn't. If I let the guy off the line without getting even a name and callback number, I would consider it an egregious personal failure.

"Sir, just one more moment, please. I just need your name and phone number so that officers can get in touch with you."

"Don't you have my information on your screen?" I had heard those words often enough from callers, but the smile in his voice as he said it told me he knew very well I didn't have a scrap of information on him."

"No, sir, if you could just—"

The bastard disconnected. And I had no way to call him back. I hung my head for a moment, a sense of defeat, heavy and suffocating, draping over me. Lifting my eyes to the call-taking screen, I gently tapped my fingertips on my keyboard, enough for the keys to make a slight clicking sound but not enough to actually type anything.

Blair activated the mic on her headset, using the large pedal beneath her desk. When she was through speaking, she raised her foot, a loud *thunk* as the pedal returned to its starting position echoing in the still room. Trevor's static-covered voice came in reply, informing us that the units were making their way up the mountainside where the body allegedly rested.

I kept my eyes on my screen as I continued to contemplate the call. My gut was telling me I hadn't simply been speaking to a good Samaritan, and I was tempted to include that information in the call notes. Still, being calm and a bit strange wasn't a crime, and it certainly wasn't enough for me to point the finger at someone based on a three-minute conversation. Besides, I had no name, no address, and no phone number. The guy might as well have been a ghost.

With a sigh, I moved my mouse around until it landed on the exit button of the call-taking screen. At the end of the day, my job was to obtain facts and provide them to the field units. It definitely wasn't to speculate about those facts and those who provided them.

I glanced at my map and watched as the GPS locators on the police cruisers marked their progress. Trevor and Gabe, minutes away from their destination, were leading the pack up a winding road. I had a feeling they were in for a very long day.

CHAPTER 2

Trevor

REBECCA TATE. My eyes swept over the body for what must have been the fortieth time. She lay face down, and various scavengers had already begun to relieve her bones of their flesh, but with her head turned to the side and her big blue eyes staring right at me as I crouched in front of her, I knew with certainty that it was Rebecca.

A cold drop of water landed on my forehead and traveled down my temple before I wiped it away. We'd had steady rain throughout the night, and though the rainfall had stopped hours ago, the trees wept with the remnants of the storm. The weather certainly hadn't done us any favors. Between the critters and the elements, I just hoped we had enough evidence left to nail the bastard who'd done this to her.

"Well..." My partner, Gabe, stood across from me on the opposite side of the body. "Judging by the bruising around her neck and the petechiae, I'd say it's likely she was strangled to death."

Still in a crouched position, I nodded but didn't take my eyes from Rebecca. I gently tilted her body just enough to examine the livor mortis, which told me she'd been there for several hours. "I doubt she died here," I added to Gabe's hypothesis, turning my head to examine the area around the body. "There are no signs of a struggle. No dirt that's been disturbed. No broken branches on shrubs or trees. No blood spatter." I returned my gaze to the deep gouges across her back and thighs. Whatever she had been beaten with, her wounds were incredibly deep. There would have been a lot of spatter.

Gabe nodded, his lips pressed into a thin white line. He had known Rebecca too. In a town as small as Eden Falls, it was easier to count the people you didn't know than the ones you did.

I stood and shifted my weight back and forth a few times to get the blood flowing in my legs again. Hooking my thumbs over my duty belt, I eyed my partner. He ran a hand along the back of his buzz cut, his dark eyes fixed on the gashes across Rebecca's body. If it weren't for the haunted look on his face, I would have thought he was simply assessing the evidence further.

"What is it?" I asked.

He looked up from the body but kept his hand on the back of his head and blew out a deep breath. "When I was deployed, one of our guys was captured." Though he was still looking at me, Gabe's gaze grew distant. It was apparent he was seeing something I couldn't. "He was tortured and killed, and his body was left where we were sure to find it. It was a way to torture us, too—showing us how we had failed to protect one of our own and how he had paid the price."

I furrowed my brow, waiting for him to continue, but he just stood there with that glassy stare.

"Where are you going with this, partner?" I asked.

The vacancy in his gaze vanished, and he was once again with me, in the middle of the woods, standing over a body. "The way she looks," he began, nodding toward Rebecca. "She reminds me of that."

I looked down at the body again. Someone had obviously wanted to cause her a lot of pain before she died.

Squaring my shoulders, I refocused. If we were going to ensure justice for Rebecca, we had to set aside our personal feelings and approach the crime scene like any other—concentrating on the evidence.

"All right, brother, what are we thinking?"

Picking up on my cue, Gabe visibly shifted back into investigator mode, raking his gaze over the body and the surrounding area once more. "I doubt this was done by a stranger," he began. "She and William are one of the wealthiest couples in town, so that's a good motive for a break-in gone wrong, but a burglar wouldn't have taken his time with her. It would have been quick and clean."

I nodded and picked up where he left off. "She's dressed in a teddy, so it's possible she was in bed when the attack happened." The flimsy black garment was so shredded that it was barely hanging on to her frame. She had clearly been wearing it when she was beaten. I scratched the stubble along my jaw. "While we're on the subject, that's not exactly the kind of thing you wear when you're sleeping alone. Why haven't we heard from her husband?"

Gabe's eyebrows rose. "He *does* travel a lot. Maybe he's out of town."

I looked around the perimeter but saw nothing but dense trees. "Yeah—or we're going to find his body out here too."

Gabe shook his head. "I doubt it. Someone from his office would have called in by now if he hadn't shown up for work this morning."

I canted my head. That was a valid argument. William Marshal was a high-powered corporate attorney who spent more time at the office than he did at home, which brought to mind another possibility. "What if she was seeing someone?"

Pursing his lips, Gabe rested one hand on the butt of his holstered sidearm. "It's definitely possible." After a moment, he added, "You think her husband could have done something like this if she *was* having an affair and he found out about it?"

I only had to contemplate the question for a moment. "Nah. He's too refined. Not his style." I held my hand out. "Now, *hiring* someone to kill her? Yeah, maybe. But again, a hired gun wouldn't waste his time toying with her. He would just kill her quickly and get the hell out of there."

We fell into silence, allowing our theories and the evidence to percolate and filter through our brains.

Finally, I said, "We need to start by tracking down William. She's been dead long enough that it's suspicious that we haven't received a missing persons report."

Gabe nodded.

"Besides, if he wasn't involved, he still needs to be notified of her death and questioned further."

"All right." Gabe indicated to the crime scene folks that they could move in and do their thing. "We should also start pulling her phone records and financial statements. Questioning friends and family. Find out if anyone had a bone to pick with her."

Standing shoulder to shoulder, we started picking our way over the low-lying shrubs and fallen tree limbs.

I gave Gabe the side-eye. "So... when are you planning on notifying William?"

"Ha!" A grin broke across Gabe's face, some of the heaviness of the past hour lifting. "Nice try."

"What?" I tried not to smile, knowing he knew exactly what I was trying to pull.

"When I agreed to handle that drunk girl who barfed all over herself and kept ranting about the aliens who impregnated her, you said you'd handle the next shitty thing that came up. *This*"— he pointed toward the ground—"is the next shitty thing, partner."

I didn't even try to suppress the groan that rumbled from my chest. Notifying a guy that his wife was not only dead but that she'd been *tortured* to death, only to then turn around and interrogate the poor bastard, was beyond just a "shitty thing." But fair was fair.

As I stepped over another fallen branch, my black boots shone with moisture and quickly became covered in leaves and pine needles. A loud yawn escaped my lips, and I scrubbed a hand down my face, trying to banish the need for sleep.

Gabe glanced at me out of the corner of his eye. "Late night?" he asked with a smirk, indicating he already knew the answer.

I grinned. "Yeah. That chick from the bar was a real freak. Kept me up half the night."

Gabe shook his head. "Don't you ever get tired of the endless carousel of women? Try sticking with one woman long enough to actually build something worth having. It's less exhausting."

I laughed as if the idea was ridiculous. "Why? So I can be whipped like you?"

Gabe's tone sobered. "There's a difference between being whipped and being devoted. Alex is everything I could ever want or need in a woman, and I'll shout that from the rooftops all day long."

His long strides allowed him to keep up with me as I gradually gained speed, trying to outrun the conversation.

"I was damn lucky to find her," he continued. "That's worth more than a lifetime of easy lays."

My grin slipped just a bit before I managed to put it back in place. "Alex is a great woman, brother, and you know I love her. I'm just giving you a hard time." I clapped him on the shoulder. "But what you two have isn't for me. I don't do serious. Gets too messy. Women get too clingy. I'm not looking for anything more than a good time."

"Yeah?" Gabe raised his eyebrows, and I could tell by the way he said it that he was getting ready to pull out a big gun. "What about Annabelle Murphy?"

Ah, shit. Really? I knew exactly where he was going, but I schooled my face and played dumb. "What about her?"

Gabe stopped and grabbed my arm, forcing me to face him.

"You dated her *all* through high school."

I looked past him into the woods, scanning the landscape without really seeing what was there.

Gabe wasn't deterred. "Despite the fact that you had practically the entire female population of the school, including *teachers*, panting over you, you never strayed or even looked seriously at any of them as long as you were dating her."

In an attempt to lighten the mood, I rolled my eyes. "Damn, dude, that was a lifetime ago! And she was fucking *hot*. Not to mention pretty kinky." I waggled my eyebrows and grinned.

Snorting, Gabe shook his head—something he did a lot when we were together—and resumed the trek to our black-and-whites.

"So," I said, shifting gears. "You up for some pool after work? I have a feeling I'm going to need some booze, babes, and billiards by end of watch."

Gabe laughed. "Sure. But only a few rounds. Alex and I are going to have a night alone after she and my sister are done planning that damn masquerade thing."

I let out a belly laugh and punched my partner in the shoulder. "So Liz conned your woman into helping with her latest community shindig, huh?"

"Yeah, well, it didn't take much effort. She and Alex are thicker than thieves. One calls, and the other answers." Gabe spoke as though annoyed, but the smile in his eyes proved he loved the life he was building with Alex.

The truth was I was happy for Gabe. He deserved the love of a good woman like Alex. Though I would never have thought in a million years that the two of them would end up together, considering how much they antagonized each other when they first met. I guessed that passion was what kept the home fires burning.

Not wanting to think any more about home fires and long-term relationships, I let my mind return to the murder investigation that had landed squarely in our laps. The day had started out on such a high. Gabe, Alex, and I had been at the bus stop, seeing Jace off as he left for the Marines. No sooner had the taillights of his bus faded than the call for a body dumped in the woods had come through my earpiece.

I didn't know Rebecca well, but she was part of our community, and the thought of any woman dying the way she had—scared and in pain—took my blood beyond a boil. I was going to catch the asshole who'd done this to her, and I would personally see to it that he suffered as much as possible.

CHAPTER 3

Trevor

I LEANED OVER THE TABLE, the cool wood of the cue stick gliding through my fingers as I lined up my shot. The sound of drunken laughter and billiard balls clacking together became a dull roar around me, the smell of nicotine and cheap perfume assaulting my nose but barely registering. I was too focused. Everything faded into a blur of color and activity except for the one thing I held in my sights.

Narrowing my eyes, I slid the wood through my fingers a few more times and ordered myself to concentrate on the eight ball across the table. I could feel my buddies' eyes on me and knew they were wondering what the hell was wrong with me. I was usually an ace when it came to pool—racking 'em and sinking 'em faster than most could keep up with. Tonight, I was lucky to sink one in three.

Sensing my focus was slipping again, I hastily drew back the cue stick then sent its tip slamming into the white ball that was *supposed* to end the game. Instead, the ball spun out of control and missed its intended target by what might as well have been a mile. I rested my hands on the rail of the table, pinning the cue stick between my palm and the chipped wood. Hanging my head,

I released an aggravated breath and braced for the shit I was about to catch.

I raised my eyes and glared at the object of my distraction, who was sitting thirty feet away at a high-top table. Long, dark curly hair fell down her back and shimmied with every movement. Though it was too dim in the bar to make out the color of her eyes, I didn't need to see them to know they were glowing like honey in sunlight. She tossed back her head and laughed at something the smug asshole sitting across from her had just said. On his face was pure satisfaction, and I wanted nothing more than to slap his smirk right off.

I should have taken the shot from a different angle—one that didn't put Quinn right in my sights. Realizing I'd been staring at her long enough to draw attention, I straightened and swaggered over to the railing that surrounded the pool tables. As I half sat, half stood against it, twirling my cue stick mindlessly between my fingers, I glanced around the room, partially to avoid eye contact with the guys and partially to scope out my options for the evening.

Rustlers had been built on levels, something I appreciated most about the design. The middle of the room sat at ground level and was filled with a dance floor and a bunch of high-top tables. From the main entrance, a long bar sat along the wall to the left, and a stage, raised about three feet off the floor, sat on the opposite side of the spacious room.

But my favorite place in the bar was right where I was sitting —on the elevated dais opposite the main door, where all of the pool tables were situated. From that vantage point, with the side entrance to my right, I could see everyone coming and going and most of the activity in the room. Eden Falls might be a small town, but we had a criminal element that ensured a cop never wanted his back to the door.

Looking around the room, I had no shortage of come-hither glances coming my way, many of them from women I'd rolled around in the sheets with before. My eyes landed on a leggy blonde who took her invitation one step further. Sitting at a nearby table, she turned her body to face me and slowly opened her legs so that I could see everything her tight miniskirt was barely concealing. I held eye contact and gave her a small smile. But a familiar voice, as sultry as a Florida summer night, slammed into my ears and drew my attention back to Quinn. She was laughing—*again*.

As I eyed the wavy-haired Ken doll she was with, the muscles in my jaw tensed. I rarely saw Quinn outside of work, which meant I rarely saw her out of uniform. I got the impression she didn't get out much. She was way too serious to have a good time on the regular, but damn if she didn't look good in those tight jeans and that royal-blue tank top. But what really made it hard to look away was her thousand-watt smile. If I was being honest with myself, that was what really pissed me off about the guy she was with. He was getting all of her smiles and making her laugh. All I'd ever gotten out of Quinn was a scowl.

"Ha-ha! Yes!"

I whipped my head around to Carlson, who had just sunk the last of his and Nash's pool balls.

"We kicked your ass, Ryan!" Carlson said, calling me by my last name, as we often did at the department.

I smirked. "Don't get used to it, Pee-Wee. You're still learning how to use your stick."

Nash and Gabe tried to hide their amusement as Carlson's face turned a satisfying shade of scarlet. The kid was one of our younger officers and as cocky as hell. He had the chops to be a great cop, but some of us veterans made it our mission to knock him down a few pegs so that it could happen.

Before we got into another pissing match, I jerked my chin at him and gave orders to rack the balls for another round. While Carlson went around and retrieved the pool balls from their pockets, Gabe leaned against the railing beside me.

"Did you get in touch with William Marshal?" he asked.

I nodded. "He's been out of town on business since Friday.

That's why he didn't notice Rebecca was missing. I called his office to confirm his travel dates."

"When was the last time he heard from her?"

"Yesterday. They spoke in the afternoon."

Gabe's brow furrowed. "That means they went twenty-four hours without contact. No matter how busy I was, I'd never go twenty-four hours without checking in with Alex."

I snickered. "Yeah, well, that's because you and Alex can't keep your hands off each other. According to William, he and Rebecca were having a lot of problems."

"What kind of problems? The kind that could drive a husband to murder his wife?"

"No, my gut is telling me he wasn't involved in her death. They both travel a lot for work, and they'd grown apart. Rebecca had brought up the idea of divorce a few times, but he said she mentioned it again right before he left for this trip and seemed more serious about it than she had been before." I rubbed my eyes, finally feeling how long the day had actually been. "According to him, they had a long talk and decided they were going to try to work out their issues. He said he'd already talked to his boss about reducing his travel, and they were able to come up with a new arrangement that would allow him to be home more, which the boss confirmed."

Carlson finished racking the balls before he took off toward the bar to grab another round. As I tracked him, my eyes locked on Quinn again when Carlson crossed in front of her. The jealousy that ripped through me every time I looked at her enjoying herself with Peter Pan suddenly dissipated when a young dishwater blonde I had seen at the gym with Quinn on countless occasions walked up to their table and planted a kiss right on Pete's smacker. She then moved to Quinn and gave her a tight hug before taking a seat between the two.

She's not on a date.

The feeling of relief was way stronger than I would admit or give any attention to.

"Hmm." Gabe braced his hands against the railing behind him, staring at the floor as though he was trying to wrangle all the thoughts flying through his brain. "So, that brings me back to questioning whether there could have been a lover."

Tilting my head from side to side, I contemplated the theory. "It's definitely possible. Maybe that's why she was more serious about the divorce this time—she wanted to run off and be with this other guy." I scrubbed the side of my face, rough stubble scratching my palm. "Then Rebecca and William have their heart-to-heart and decide to give their marriage another go. She tells her lover it's over. He goes into a rage and kills her."

"Given how personal the attack was, it wouldn't surprise me if it was someone close to her." Gabe pulled his lower lip between his teeth and shook his head. "That was *brutal*. This was someone who hated her and wanted her to experience a fuck ton of pain."

I couldn't argue that. In all my time on the force, I'd seen people do some pretty callous shit to one another, but outside of the violence related to the Serpents, our local motorcycle gang, I had never seen anything of that magnitude.

Having reported everything I'd been able to dig up, I tossed the metaphorical baton to Gabe. "How'd you do? Find anything interesting?"

He straightened from the railing and turned to face me, leaning on his pool stick. "I spoke to Rebecca's assistant. She had the day off, which explains why we didn't get a call that Rebecca was missing."

Like her husband, Rebecca was an attorney. She'd left William's firm a couple of years back to start her own practice handling high-profile divorce cases and ran the business from her home office.

"I was also able to get a warrant for Rebecca's and William's cell phone records and their financials," Gabe continued. "I've already sent the request for both. With any luck, some of that information will start trickling in within the next day or two."

I scoffed. "Yeah, and without luck, it could take a lot longer."

Wondering what was holding up Carlson, I glanced at the bar. When I did, I found the leggy blonde still staring at me, one elbow draped over the back of her chair in a way that put her tits front and center. There was no misreading the invitation in her blue eyes. A night of distraction with no strings attached was exactly what I craved, but even as I pictured going home with the nameless pinup, my eyes wandered back to Quinn. She reached up with both hands to gather her curls then pulled them over her shoulder. The action highlighted her toned arms and drew my attention to the delicate curve at the base of her neck. I pictured what it would be like to put my mouth on that neck, her soft skin pressed to my lips and the feel of her pulse growing faster under my tongue as her body melted into mine.

The growing constriction of my jeans told the story of who I really wanted to take home, but the voice in the back of my head reminded me why it was never going to happen, so I did what I always did and settled for a different kind of interaction with Quinn.

I grinned at Gabe and waggled my eyebrows. "Wanna see Quinn go *Exorcist* on me?"

He glanced at her then rolled his eyes, returning his attention to the activity around the various pool tables. "You ever going to actually *do* something about that woman?"

I frowned. "What do you mean?"

Playing dumb wasn't my forte, and Gabe's expression indicated he was thinking the same thing. "How long have we known Quinn?"

I shrugged, pretending I didn't know that it had been a little more than five years since I'd met her when I was a rookie cop. I had just passed my one-year probationary period when she was hired by the department, and I would never forget the first time I saw her. I'd gone into Dispatch to pick up some paperwork I'd asked them to print and hold for me. My eyes had found her the moment I walked through the door. She had her long hair in a bun. A few curls had escaped and cascaded down from the rest.

She was wearing her uniform, black slacks and a navy polo that had an embroidered shield over the left breast with Eden Falls Police Department scrawled underneath. She glanced up from her workstation when she heard me enter the room, and my first glimpse of those honey eyes and rosy cheeks was the only time a woman had ever made my gut do a somersault. But when I'd smiled at her and really turned on the charm, her expression turned stony, and she ducked her head. It caught me off guard, mostly because I was used to getting my way with women. I *definitely* wasn't accustomed to them full-on blowing me off. From that moment on, I'd restricted my interactions with Quinn to annoying the hell out of her. I flirted and teased and ruffled those pretty little feathers, but that was where it stopped.

Gabe raised his eyebrows. "Uh-huh. It's been five years, and in all that time, you've never once made a move on her." He shook his head and ran a hand over his dark buzz cut. "What I can't figure out is why a man who has never been afraid to approach a woman—a man who goes home with a different woman practically every night—would be so damn terrified of Quinn."

I jerked back, laughing. "Terrified? I'm not terrified. I'm just not interested in starting anything with Quinn."

"Mm-hmm." Gabe looked away. Clearly, he wasn't buying what I was selling.

"Seriously. It's fun to get under that ice-cold skin of hers, to get her to actually show some kind of reaction, but Quinn's the kind of woman who expects a guy to make all kinds of commitments."

"Yeah, Heaven forbid a woman expect a man to be faithful and want to spend time with her for reasons other than just sex."

I rolled my eyes. "Look, I'm not knocking the whole relationship thing. It works for some people. It just doesn't work for me. I already told you—I don't want anything but a good time."

Gabe's expression grew sober, and he looked me dead in the eye. "Yeah, well, a good time isn't going to be there for you when the shit hits the fan and life kicks you in the nuts."

Carlson finally returned with the next round of beers and not a moment too soon. Gabe was poking at things I didn't want to think about. Sure, none of the women I spent time with were the kind of woman a man could count on when the chips were down, but that wasn't what I was looking for. I didn't need a woman to lean on. I needed a body to get lost in. And that was all those women wanted from me too.

Carlson held out my beer. I downed half of it then went to the table to break the balls. Before leaning down to line up my shot, I rolled my shoulders and head, trying to knock loose the shit I had gone there to escape. I was done thinking about women beyond which one I was taking home that night, and I was done thinking about the case. The medical examiner and the companies Gabe had reached out to would likely provide new information for us in the morning, and I hoped to hell we would soon discover that this case was a one-off, because the alternative just wasn't something I wanted to consider.

CHAPTER 4

Quinn

I PLAYED with the skinny straw sticking out of my short glass, distracted by more thoughts than one person's brain should hold. Half-melted ice cubes clinked together, but it was barely audible above the din of Rustlers on a Thursday night. The weekend was near for most, and I could feel the anticipatory energy buzzing through the growing crowd. Too bad I couldn't join in that excitement. The weekend for everyone else wasn't the weekend for *me*, which was just one of the many joys of shift work.

Normally, I wouldn't be at a bar on a night when I had to get up for work the next morning, but after the day I'd had, the last thing I wanted was to go home to an empty house and spend the evening ruminating over Blair and the dispatch center. So when my best friend had texted and asked me to join her and her husband for drinks, it was an easy yes.

"Hello?" Shelby waved her hand in front of my face. "Earth to Quinn."

I looked up from my watered-down drink to find Shelby and Josh watching me, worry in their eyes. Sighing, I leaned back. "I'm sorry, you guys. I was just thinking about work."

"You're *always* thinking about work."

Shelby didn't mean it as a dig. She'd been genuinely

concerned for a while about how much work had been stressing me out.

I smiled flatly. "You're not wrong."

Josh hooked his arm over the back of Shelby's chair and leaned forward. "What's on your mind this time, Quinn?"

My eyes darted between them as I contemplated how much to say. I didn't want to be *that* person—the one who was always whining and complaining about the same thing. Still, it was sweet of them to be concerned about me, so I didn't want to brush it off either.

I waved a hand. "It's just difficult sitting in that dispatch center all day with the women I work with. I thought I left high school behind when I graduated, but clearly, the song has it right."

Josh scrunched his forehead. "What song?"

Shelby clucked in exasperation and answered for me. "'High School Never Ends,' Bowling for Soup."

Josh nodded, playing along like he actually knew what we were talking about. The poor guy had to do that a lot. Shelby and I had grown up together. We were practically sisters, usually knew what the other was thinking, and often finished each other's sentences. We listened to the same music, and when we were in school, we'd joined the same clubs and played the same sports. We even went to college together and shared a dorm room.

When Shelby and Josh had met and fallen hard for each other, he pretty much got a two-for-one deal, but he'd never made me feel like I was a third wheel—the opposite, actually. From the start, he'd always made sure I was aware that there was an open invitation to join them whenever they got together. That was how he'd won me over. Any guy who let his girl's best friend crash their dates because he knew how much they meant to each other was worth hanging on to.

I smiled and tried to get it to reach my eyes. Shelby could always tell when I was faking. "I'm fine, guys. Really. Just tired."

And that was the truth. I was very, *very* tired—of the long hours, the caustic work environment, of waiting to hear back about the supervisor position, and of worrying that this was what the rest of my life was going to be like.

Josh nodded, buying my canned answer. Shelby, on the other hand, watched me with eyes that said, "I'll let you get away with that excuse now, but you and I are revisiting this issue later."

"Excuse me for a minute, ladies," Josh said, getting up. "Nature calls."

Just as he left, Shelby's phone pinged. She snatched it up from its face-down position on the table and fixated on whatever had just come through.

I took a long swallow of my cocktail. Tequila and tonic burst on my tongue, followed by the subtle hint of lime. Setting the glass down on the black cocktail napkin, I allowed my eyes to roam the bar for the first time that evening. Usually, I kept my eyes to myself because I didn't want to give men the impression I was open to being approached.

A flash of movement pulled my gaze to a table in the far-right corner. A plump woman in her mid-forties dressed in tight jeans and a black see-through shirt with a red bra underneath had just slipped right off her bar chair. She was laughing hysterically and clearly didn't care that she looked ridiculous. The man sitting with her, who was equally drunk, got up and placed his arms under her armpits and was struggling to lift her from the floor.

I shook my head, thinking that that was exactly why I had never allowed myself to get drunk, even in college. Actually, *especially* in college. My mother had told me too many horror stories about young girls who had gone out, gotten drunk or been drugged, and were sexually assaulted. My fears and warnings of the same to Shelby hadn't kept her from constantly trying to get me to go to parties with her, but I had been committed to staying in my bubble, where it was safe.

No longer interested in watching the growing spectacle of the couple in the corner, I let my gaze continue to wander. Nearly every table was occupied. The only empty space was the stage, where live bands often played. Rustlers usually reserved that kind of entertainment for the weekends. Every other night, the patrons kept the old neon jukebox against the wall near the restrooms playing until well after last call.

A sudden uproar from the billiard tables made my head whip around. Only then did I notice several of the officers with whom I worked were gathered for a game. Not surprisingly, Garrett Carlson was puffing out his chest and high-fiving Nash as he loudly pronounced their win. With his sandy-blond hair and flushed cheeks, Carlson had a handsome look about him that was spoiled by the jut of his chin and the constant challenge in his eyes. As far as I was concerned, arrogance could ruin the appeal of even the handsomest of men.

Case in point was the object of Carlson's gloating. My gaze skipped to Trevor, who was standing with his pool stick across the back of his shoulders, his wrists looped over either end to hold it in place as he tilted his head back, closing his eyes in frustrated defeat. The lighting was dim, but a yellow bulb enveloped by a lime-green plastic shade hung above every pool table. Anyone else would have looked horrendous in that light, but even lime-green and yellow accents couldn't stunt the beauty of Trevor's Adonis-like features.

As much as I hated to admit it, he was hard not to notice. He stood well over six feet and was sculpted from granite, but his powerful physique was only part of his appeal. Somehow, despite the long winter months in Montana, Trevor always had a sun-kissed glow about him that set off the varying shades of gold in his tousled locks and the vibrant blue of his sky-colored eyes. Though he kept his hair short on the sides, he wore it longer on top, and as he lowered his chin to glare daggers at Carlson, a few stray pieces fell over his brow. The man seriously belonged on the cover of *GQ*.

Without meaning to, I swept my gaze across the bulge of his biceps and along the contours of his chest as he continued to hold the pool stick on his shoulders, the fabric of his thin white T-shirt straining against the assault. My eyes dipped to his tapered waist and continued their descent to fitted blue jeans that left nothing to the imagination. Only when a conspicuous throat clearing from my right shattered the spell did I realize what I'd been doing and was horrified.

Heat flooded my cheeks, both from shame and embarrassment. I couldn't believe I'd actually been *ogling* Trevor Ryan. I scrunched my face and slammed my eyes shut, taking a moment to collect myself before turning to Shelby with what I hoped was an innocent smile.

The corners of Shelby's mouth and her eyebrows rose in tandem.

"What?" I snatched my drink and attempted to take a casual sip but failed as my mouth missed the straw—twice.

Shelby's grin grew until I could have counted all of her teeth. She nodded toward Trevor. "Be bold, Quinn. Make a move."

I puckered my mouth to show that I found her suggestion absurd then went back to trying to capture my stupid straw and finally had to resort to holding it in place so that it couldn't dance away again.

Shelby's elbow bumped mine. "Quinn, I haven't seen you look at a man like that in..." She looked at the ceiling and pursed her lips. "Actually, I don't think I've *ever* seen you look at a man like that." Her lighthearted chuckle had a tinkling quality that reminded me of wind chimes in a lazy summer breeze.

I slurped the last of my watered-down drink before answering. "That's not what I was doing. I was just wondering what was going on." I canted my head toward the pool tables. "I work with those guys." I met Shelby's gaze, expecting that that was explanation enough, but the rise of her eyebrow and the bob of her head said otherwise.

I sighed deeply, not wanting to get into that conversation again. I didn't have the energy. "You know I'm taking a break from dating and that even if I weren't, I don't date cops. Especially *that* cop."

Shelby snorted. "A *break*," she said, placing the word in air quotes, "means a short interlude. Five *years* is practically enough to get your chastity belt back."

I folded my arms on top of the table and stared at my empty glass, contemplating how it could have been a metaphor for my life lately. Then I shook myself from the doldrums of self-pity because that wasn't true. My life might have been lacking in certain areas, but it wasn't empty. I had Shelby and Josh, and though my mom didn't live nearby, she and I talked regularly, and she rivaled Shelby as my biggest cheerleader. I needed to stop acting like a victim for decisions *I* had made.

I opened my mouth to feed Shelby another line about how I was happy with my love life, but a bunch of screeching and deep laughter drew our attention back to the pool tables. Both my annoyance and my eyebrows hit the ceiling when I realized the cause of the ruckus.

Trevor was pinned between two women, a leggy blonde in a miniskirt and a petite redhead who looked barely legal. The two women were reaching across him to claw at each other while his partners—with the exception of Gabe who stood off to the side, shaking his head—laughed hysterically at the debacle. Trevor was just beginning to get a handle on things, using his infamous silken tongue to soothe the women's ruffled feathers when I turned back to Shelby and lowered my chin, pinning her with a hard stare. "That is exactly why he and I will *never* happen."

She shrugged sheepishly and chuckled. "Sorry."

I shook my head, still fuming over the fact that those women, like my salivating partners, gave us *all* a bad name.

"Okay, so maybe you don't go for that guy," Shelby said. "But, Quinn, it's high time for you to get out onto the playing field again."

I didn't answer, choosing instead to look straight ahead at the empty stage.

Shelby sighed and leaned in. "Quinn." She waited until I set my stubbornness aside and turned to look at her. When I did, I saw that the challenge had left her eyes, and only earnest concern remained. "You've got to learn to trust yourself again. If you hold on to the pain of your past, you're going to miss out on all of the wonderful things you *could* have."

Her gaze held mine. I was incapable of looking away. The swirl of brown and green accented by flecks of gold had stared me down in a similar manner many, many times before. Usually, I knew how to answer her. Sometimes, I didn't. At the moment, I simply couldn't respond, not because I didn't have an answer but because it was the same one I'd given her every other time she'd broached the topic. No matter how many times I tried to explain why I couldn't get past more than a couple of dates with a man, she just didn't seem to understand. It was one area where Shelby and I were too different to speak the same language.

I finally broke eye contact, indicating that I was done with the subject, and looked to my left in time to see Trevor descending the stairs from where the pool tables sat, one arm around the blonde, the other around the redhead. Both were tucked into his sides and beaming up at him as they made their way to the bar. I scoffed and rolled my eyes. Luckily, Josh returned at that precise moment and turned the conversation to a debate about whether we should stay for one more round. Knowing I needed to get home and start winding down if I was going to be any good for work the next day, I voted to call it a night and didn't get much resistance.

I stood and snatched my purse from the hook under the table. "You two go ahead," I said, giving Shelby a hug. "I'm going to visit the restroom before I head out."

Josh shook his head. "We'll wait."

"Don't be silly. I'll be right behind you." I rose to my toes and threw my arms around Josh, effectively cutting off any opportunity for him to argue. He still looked hesitant when I released him and stepped back, so I laughed and said, "Really. I'll call you guys tomorrow."

When I exited the bathroom three minutes later, I instantly regretted sending them on without me.

CHAPTER 5

I WAS DISTRACTED COMING out of the bathroom at Rustlers. There had been no paper towels, so I was busy drying my hands on my jeans as I dodged various couples swallowing each other's tongues and grinding against each other in the dark, narrow hallway where the restrooms were located.

So when I practically pirouetted into the open expanse of the main room to avoid one such couple, I nearly collided with a wall of muscle perched at the jukebox.

"Oh, excuse me," I muttered to the man, barely raising my eyes to meet his face. But in the millisecond that I *did* look at him, recognition hit, and I did a double take before quickly stepping around him.

Trevor didn't miss a beat. He spun and fell into step beside me, his long strides easily matching my near jog to get away from him.

"Whoa there, Quinny-baby. Where you going in such a hurry?" Trevor's hands were shoved into his pockets, his posture and gait smooth and easy, as if he didn't have a care in the world.

Heat blanketed my cheeks and chest. I whipped my head toward him, but my pace never slowed. "Don't call me that!" I growled.

My anger only intensified into a small inferno when he chuckled.

When we reached the entryway, I hesitated, trying to figure out how best to pick my way through the throng of men standing around chatting with pint glasses in their hands. I turned sideways, sucked in my stomach, and tried to slip through without brushing against anyone. Several of the men smiled down at me, and a few were brazen enough to let their eyes roam over my body. I seriously regretted wearing the tank top. Though the summer heat had come with a vengeance, I should have opted for a burka.

One lumberjack-looking fellow leaned down as I passed in front of him, his long beard wagging as he attempted to speak, though I couldn't understand a word he was saying. The glassy look in his eyes told me all I needed to know. I opened my mouth to mutter some polite excuse for not stopping but didn't even get the chance. Trevor wrapped a strong arm around my waist, pulled me against him, and barreled us through the crowd. The remaining bodies parted like the Red Sea, and a cool breeze smacked me in the face as he propelled me outside.

My brain finally caught up, and when I registered that Trevor's arm was still firmly around my waist, I shoved an elbow into his side and was rewarded with a satisfying grunt.

He immediately dropped his arm and glanced down at me. "You're welcome." His tone was indignant, but I really didn't care.

Dust swirled around our feet as we walked and settled in a thin coat on his black boots while turning my white Keds a dingy shade of ochre. Rustlers was old school. The owner didn't believe in paved parking lots. He liked having the surrounding environment as rugged as his decor, something I had failed to consider when I'd chosen my footwear that evening. So I forged on through the dirt and rolling gravel toward the dense tree line at the back of the lot. And so did Trevor.

"What are you doing?" I huffed and glared up at him.

He kept his gaze focused ahead, scanning from left to right and back again. "Walking you to your car."

"I don't need an escort. My car is just over there." I pointed at my silver Xterra parked at the end of a row about halfway to the tree line. Though it was nearly ten o'clock, the parking lot was still packed with mostly pickups and rugged SUVs.

Trevor snorted, his swagger prominent. "Let me guess—you're the kind of woman who hates when a man opens doors for her and gives the poor sap a verbal browbeating for being a sexist pig."

I pressed my lips together, puffing my cheeks out with the effort of restraining the string of profanity and insults clawing to escape. My gaze wandered to the right and focused on the light trails made by the headlights of passing cars on the adjacent road. Refusing to let him get a rise out of me—as he often did and thoroughly enjoyed—I swallowed what I wanted to say and regained my composure. I would *not* let him win this round.

With a sweet smile, I turned back to him. "I'd be interested to know how you conduct your investigations, considering how you seem keen on forming conclusions with little to no evidence." I pretended to brush a stray lock of hair behind my ear to give the appearance of being at ease. "For your information, I love when a man opens doors for me. Every time it happens, I regain some small shred of hope for humanity."

He smirked and glanced down at me before resuming his scan of our surroundings. "You just won't let him walk you to your car."

"I won't let someone who collects women's panties like germs in a preschool walk me to my car."

Speaking of which, I quickly did my own scan to see if I recognized any faces in the parking lot. The last thing I needed was for someone from the department to see the two of us walking to my car. Given his reputation, I had no doubt the logical conclusion would be that he and I were headed somewhere to hook up.

I picked up my pace, but Trevor stuck with me. So I picked up my pace some more. Again, he remained at my side.

The sound of gravel crunching beneath our hasty footfalls was punctuated by a cackle from some woman on the other side of the lot. Though it was late in the evening, we were in the midst of twilight, and the navy-gray light cast an ethereal glow on everything not swallowed by the deep shadows. A slight breeze kicked up again, and as it did, the creak of the swaying branches in the thicket of trees just ahead began a mournful song.

When we finally reached my car, I breathed a sigh of relief, and it was only then that I realized I hadn't yet fished my keys out of my purse. Normally, I would have done that before leaving the relative safety of the bar, but Trevor, as per usual, had thrown me off my game.

As I combed through the myriad items in my midsize bag, I could hear the damn keys jingling, but somehow, they managed to keep evading me.

Trevor snickered. "If you want to spend time in a dark parking lot with me, you don't need to pretend you lost your keys to make that happen."

I pressed my lips together again and removed my purse from my shoulder to shove it into his chest. He instinctively caught the bag and held it in place, giving me the opportunity to dig into the contents with both hands, my head bent to the task until it was practically in the purse as well. I burrowed through that sucker like a starving racoon digging through the trash.

Finally, my fingers brushed against the cool metal of my keys, and I pulled them out, raising them high in victory. Trevor laughed at my triumph, making me realize how juvenile I must have looked. So I snatched my purse back from him with my free hand and repeatedly punched the unlock button on my key fob until I heard the locks disengage.

Just as I reached for the door handle, Trevor placed a hand on my forearm. I froze, my eyes glued to his strong fingers, and noticed how his tan skin contrasted with my paler complexion.

He didn't say anything, just waited for me to look at him. And when I did, my stomach did a little flip. The intensity of his azure eyes framed by long black lashes was jolting.

I was suddenly aware of the heat beneath his fingertips and little zaps of electricity emanating from his touch. The sound of cars whizzing past us became a quiet hush mingling with the night wind and the low croons coming from the jukebox inside.

Trevor leaned down, the movement small but meaningful. He wasn't close enough to kiss me, but he was close enough to let me know he was thinking about it, a fact driven home as his eyes dipped to my mouth. I didn't know how long I stood there watching him watching me, but when he said my name, it was more like a faint memory than a present moment.

"Quinn?"

"Hmm?"

He leaned even closer, his eyes rising to mine.

"Since I walked you to your car, does that mean I get to add your panties to my collection?" A huge jackass of a smile broke across his face.

My eyes widened, and all I could see was red. I yanked my arm away from him and launched myself at my car, snatching the door open and vaulting inside in one motion. The sound of Trevor's belly laugh filled my ears and drove my rage to new heights.

"Trevor Ryan, you are *the* most asinine, vexatious, narcissistic troglodyte I have ever had the displeasure of knowing!" I jammed my key into the ignition and started the engine.

Trevor was bent over, holding his stomach as he howled with laughter, his face turning redder by the second. "Aw, come on, Quinny-baby. It was a joke!"

I growled and leaned out to grab my door handle. "Don't. Call. Me. That!"

Slamming my door shut, I threw my car in reverse and left Trevor in a cloud of dust as he wiped tears from his eyes and watched me drive away.

Damn that man and the sperm that created him.

CHAPTER 6
Trevor

THE MORNING after we'd found Rebecca's body, I pulled up to the medical examiner's office bright and early. Gabe was waiting for me, leaning against his patrol unit with his phone pressed to his ear. Like me, he wore short sleeves. Though the sky was a brilliant shade of jaybird blue, and the sun shone without a cloud to challenge it, the air was crisp and raised the flesh on my arms as I climbed out of my black-and-white, a coffee in one hand and a notepad in the other.

"I love you, too, babe. Good luck with the writing today." Gabe ended his call and slipped his phone into his chest pocket, still leaning against his cruiser with his ankles crossed and a smirk on his face. "Mornin', sunshine."

I mimicked his stance and gave him a middle-finger salute.

He laughed. "All these late nights and early mornings ruining your cheery disposition?"

I flashed a shit-eating grin. "I haven't had any complaints where it matters."

"Speaking of which..." Gabe pushed off his car and started walking toward the entrance of the building. I fell into step beside him. "Which one did you go home with? The redhead or the blonde?"

I lifted my sunglasses and propped them on top of my head, giving my partner a confused look. "What do you mean, 'which one'?"

Gabe reached the door and yanked it open, stepping back so that I could enter first. "Tell me you didn't take them both to bed."

"Why not? It was the only diplomatic thing to do. They both got what they wanted." I flashed a grin as I walked through the door.

Gabe shook his head as though he was actually surprised by the news. It wasn't like it was the first time I'd engaged in a ménage à trois. Though I had to admit it wasn't as fun as it used to be.

With Gabe behind me, I allowed my smile to slip and thought back to the previous night. I hadn't really intended to go home with both women. When I walked them to the bar to buy them a round, it was just to put an end to the catfight and all the attention they were drawing, including Quinn's. I'd caught the look on her face when I was trying to break up the scuffle. It was the same look she gave me whenever we were in close proximity to each other—the one that said I was so far beneath her that I was practically back on top.

That look was the same reason I'd hesitated when I saw Quinn's friends leave while she went to the john. With the way she was turning heads, there was no way in hell I wanted her walking through that dark parking lot alone, but I also knew she was more likely to swing her purse at me than let me walk her to her car. I had contemplated just minding my own business and remaining in the company of women who *actually* wanted me around rather than risking being eviscerated by Quinn's tongue. But in the end, I would rather accept her disdain than risk something bad happening to her. So I had left the new besties knocking back shots of Jager like it was going out of style and propped myself up at the jukebox to wait for Quinn.

True to form, she didn't waste an opportunity to remind me

just how little she thought of me. I must have been even more fucked up than I realized to keep lusting after a woman who couldn't stand the sight of me, but no matter how many women I lost myself in, Quinn was the only woman who had managed to burrow herself deep enough under my skin to still hold my attention—even if it *was* only because she had created a festering boil. As for the blonde and the redhead, they were just the aftereffects of Quinn's claw marks.

Coming to the end of a long hallway shrouded in fluorescent light and blue carpet, I shook my mind free of the drama from the night before and walked through the doors that led to the examination room. An unfamiliar John Doe was laid out on the metal table where autopsies were performed. It didn't look like the doc had gotten started on him yet.

At the sound of our approach, Dr. Vic turned around from the long counter on the opposite side of the room where he had several stacks of file folders, a few of which were lying open. His gray eyes, exaggerated by his Coke-bottle glasses, appeared larger than the rest of his features, and though he was also tall and lanky, there was nothing nerdy about him. Instead, there was something in the sharpness of his eyes and the way that he conducted himself that commanded respect. He was only forty, but I'd witnessed colleagues of his who were twenty years his senior bow in deference to his professional opinions and expertise.

"Hello, gentlemen." Dr. Vic's smile reached his eyes. "Right on time, as usual. I expect you're eager to learn the manner in which Mrs. Tate was killed." He said it more as a statement than looking for confirmation.

I tapped the notepad I was holding against the palm of my opposite hand, ready to get to the dirty details so that we could nail the bastard who had brought us there. "Tell me you have good news for us, Doc."

The good doctor adjusted his glasses, pushing them higher on the bridge of his nose, then turned back to the counter and started shuffling through one of the stacks of folders.

While we waited, I glanced around the room, more for something to do than to memorize details. I'd spent more time in that place than I cared to think about, and I never grew any fonder of it. The room was devoid of windows and relied solely on the fluorescent tube lighting that ran along the ceiling. The combination of cold light, the gleaming lime-green tile floor, and the sterile surfaces that reeked of chemical cleaners was enough to depress even the cheeriest of Pollyannas after a while. I would never understand how the doc could spend so much time in that room and not blow his brains out.

When Dr. Vic turned back around, he ran a hand through his dark hair and offered a tight smile that made me antsy. I had a feeling we weren't going to like what he had to say.

"The official cause of death is asphyxiation by strangulation," he said, passing me an open folder that contained photos of Rebecca's battered body.

Gabe stood next to me, eyeing the photos as I slowly flipped through them.

Dr. Vic cleared his throat and continued, "Due to the extensive bruising and swelling around her throat, I believe he strangled her multiple times, bringing her near death then allowing her to recover before strangling her again, doing so repeatedly until finally strangling her to death."

I came to a photo that was a close-up of Rebecca's slender throat. Now that it had been wiped clean of the mud and leaves that had clung to it when we photographed the body at the dump site, I could see exactly what the doctor was indicating. It would have been easy for a large man to wrap his hands around her neck and squeeze the life from her.

Gabe and I remained silent, so the doctor continued. "All of her wounds, with the exception of the fractured hyoid bone, occurred premortem. She sustained severe lashing from an unknown object that caused the skin to peel away from her body in several areas. I also found a substantial amount of salt in her wounds."

My mouth tightened. "He tortured her," I said. "He rubbed salt in her wounds to maximize her pain."

Gabe nodded but added nothing.

I looked up from the photos and found Dr. Vic watching us closely. "What else?"

He adjusted his glasses again. "As you can see from the photos, her wrists and ankles bear signs of restraints. I found what appear to be rope fibers embedded in the lacerations at both sites."

"Did you find any defensive wounds?" I hadn't seen any upon examination at the dump site, but with the elements and animals having already gotten to her, I hadn't been able to make a conclusive determination.

He shook his head. "No. No defensive wounds."

I glanced at Gabe. He met my eyes, saying a lot without saying a word.

"Time of death was around midnight," Dr. Vic continued, "approximately fifteen hours before her body was found."

Resuming my examination of the photos, I flipped through the remaining stack. "Did you find any obvious DNA? Hair strands? Skin under her nails?"

He shook his head. "No, but I swabbed several locations on her body, so there is still the hope that we'll find something latent."

I nodded and, having come to the last photo, flipped the file shut. "Anything else?"

"Yes. I did find traces of an oily substance on various parts of her body, especially on the front, where it was protected from most of the elements after she was discarded." He shoved the flaps of his lab coat out of the way and stuck his hands in his pockets. "I think it is also important to note that there were no signs of sexual assault."

My eyebrows rose. Now, that, I wasn't expecting. She was found practically naked except for tattered lingerie and tortured by someone who clearly got off on hurting her, yet there was no sexual component. *What the fuck are we dealing with?*

As if Dr. Vic had read my thoughts, he said, "Normally, I wouldn't offer speculation, just the facts. But I feel in this instance, I can confidently say that whoever killed her and whatever their motive, they enjoy the torture almost as much as the kill."

I allowed that comment a moment to percolate. *Someone who enjoys the kill. Fan-fucking-tastic.*

Gabe and I asked a few more questions that didn't yield much and scribbled down some notes before thanking the doctor for his time and leaving him to his next cadaver.

When we regrouped at our patrol cars, I put my shades back on and took a moment to notice how much hotter it already was since we'd walked inside.

Gabe puffed out his cheeks as he slowly released a breath. "No defensive wounds."

I nodded.

"So we're back on the question of whether she knew her killer. Maybe there are no signs of her putting up a fight because she felt safe until she suddenly wasn't. By then, he already had her subdued."

"Yeah, could be. Or..." I sat on the hood of my cruiser and crossed my arms. "Maybe he had a weapon and convinced her that if she cooperated, she'd live."

Gabe watched cars passing by on the road behind me for a beat before responding. "On a separate note, I swung by the department before heading here to see if any of the information I'd requested had come in yet."

"And?"

"Rebecca's phone records were waiting for me. I haven't had a chance to look them over in detail yet, but a couple of things stood out."

"Such as?"

He brushed a hand over his buzz cut and dipped his chin. "Well, first off, the last location where her phone pinged was BFE. Out in the middle of the woods with nothing around for miles.

We still haven't been able to locate her purse, her car, or her cell phone, so the question is whether she drove herself out there or not. But her cell phone was clearly made untraceable long before we found her body, so if someone took her out there, why was her cell phone still with her and traceable at that point?"

I ran my hand over my jaw and focused on the brick wall behind Gabe, trying to imagine a scenario in which those facts would add up. But I drew a blank and shook my head. "Was there anything else that seemed off?"

"Yeah, one other thing. She and her husband texted late in the afternoon on the day she went missing." He shrugged. "It was a pleasant exchange. Shortly after that, she received a call from her mother. They spoke for about fifteen minutes, then she received one more call a half hour later." Gabe waited until a young woman in a business suit who had just exited the building was out of earshot before continuing. "That call was from an unavailable number, and it lasted five minutes."

I stared at him but didn't offer any thoughts, so he continued, "If she was talking to someone for five minutes, you'd think it would be from a number listed in her contacts or would show up as a business or something."

I tilted my head. "This *was* Rebecca Tate, though. She and those who retained her services had good reason to be discreet. Maybe she didn't keep any client information on her phone."

"Yeah, that's a fair point." Gabe sighed and stepped off the curb, took up a position next to me on the cruiser, and crossed his arms. "All right, so what do we have, and what do we want to focus on next?"

I barked out a cynical laugh. "Well, DNA evidence isn't looking great so far. We have a mysterious last phone call and a ping on her cell that places her in the middle of nowhere with no explanation as to what she was doing there. Our victim's car is missing along with several of her personal items, her husband was out of town, and we have no eyewitnesses. I'd say the asshole up Shit Creek has better odds."

Gabe chuckled and looked away. "You really *are* in a fine mood this morning."

He was right. I wasn't usually the pessimistic type, and I wasn't sure what the hell had crawled up my ass since the previous day. I pushed off the car then went around to the driver's side, opened the door, and tossed my paperwork and the ME's photos of Rebecca onto the passenger seat. Gabe was still perched on my hood, his head turned in my general direction, but his eyes were taking in the details of the who and what around us.

I placed an arm on the hot roof of my cruiser and slung the other over the open door. "Let's get started with the rest of the interviews. See if anyone has any information about grudges against Rebecca or William or any secrets either of them was keeping."

Gabe stood and faced me.

"Let me know when those financial records come through too," I added. "Maybe we'll get lucky, and this will turn out to be an isolated incident of bad debts with the wrong people."

Gabe started to make his way to the driver's side of his own cruiser. "Copy that. And while I'm taking care of all that"—he put his sunglasses on and pulled them down the bridge of his nose so that he could look over the top of the frames at me—"why don't you reach out to Dispatch and request a copy of the call reporting the body." Gabe flashed a rare grin. "I'm pretty sure Blair is on today, and I'm sure she'd be more than happy to expedite any of your requests."

I gritted my teeth, and even though my shades shielded my eyes, I was pretty sure he could still feel the impact of my glare because his laughter didn't stop until he climbed into his cruiser and shut the door. Gabe took off a moment later and left me standing in the open door of my black-and-white, watching the growing traffic whip by behind me. A trickle of sweat made its way down my back, the heat from the sun and from the blacktop beginning to feel like an oven.

It was still early in the investigation, and the case could easily turn out to be an act of vengeance or even a random kill. But the sensation of fingernails clawing at the underside of my skin said there was more to the story. Whatever the circumstances, part of me believed that Rebecca had a secret and that secret had gotten her killed.

CHAPTER 7
Trevor

T HE WEIGHT PLATES on the ends of my barbell clanked as I set the bar back on the ground, my sweat-soaked gray tank top showing the extent of my frustration. It had been four days since we'd recovered Rebecca's body, and we still didn't have a solid lead.

"You're a hundred percent sure there was nothing hinky in their financials?" I asked Gabe as I stepped aside for him to take his turn with the barbell.

Hinging at the hips and setting up for a deadlift, Gabe gripped the bar and pressed his lips into a firm line as he straightened, his effort outlined in the cords of muscle straining in his neck. "I'm sure," he grunted.

I propped my hands on my hips and kept my eyes on his form and the weight. Gabe and I hit the gym together on the regular. We were pretty evenly matched, which made us good spotters for each other. But even more importantly, the gym was where we tended to do our best thinking. And God knew we needed some inspiration right about then.

We had gone through our entire list of people to interview. The only thing that had resulted from all that work was that I was more confident than ever that Rebecca's husband was innocent of any involvement in her murder. Which, I supposed, was something, at least.

Gabe finished his set, grabbed his towel from where it was hanging on the squat rack, and wiped the sweat from his face and neck. He was a quiet man by nature, but he had taken it to a new level the past couple of days. I knew it was because the case was getting to him as much as it was getting to me.

He tossed his towel back over one of the spotter arms and turned his head to gaze out the large windows to our right. The gym was basically a big square. A wall of windows lined the front of the building and showed off a good portion of the parking lot. When you entered, the front desk was to the right, and the free weights, where we spent most of our time, were to the left. There was also a group fitness room that took up most of the back right corner.

I waited for Gabe to work through whatever was going through his head by knocking out another set of deadlifts. When I finished, he turned his attention back to me.

"I want to talk to Quinn," he said.

"About what?"

"About the call."

I nodded and chewed on the idea for a moment. Per Gabe's demand, I had called over to Dispatch after leaving the ME's office and requested a copy of the call reporting Rebecca's body. Blair had it in my hands within the hour, though it hadn't come free of charge. For nearly half an hour, I'd had to endure that woman's not-so-subtle hints about her desire to hook up with me. It was only when the dispatch center blew up with calls about a traffic accident that I was finally able to slip out while she was busy.

"We've listened to the call a dozen times," I said. "The guy sounded like a freak, but without any identifying information, I don't know how Quinn's gonna be able to help."

Gabe unscrewed the lid on his water bottle and took a long swig before responding. "We won't know until we ask."

Fair enough. I made a show of looking at my watch. "Well,

considering that woman is about as routine as the sun rising and setting, she should be here any minute."

Quinn frequented the gym as often as we did. And I knew that because her squad rotated with ours, which meant we kept the same schedule. Just like Gabe and me, she liked to hit the gym after work, which meant I always enjoyed the view in there.

As if conjured by my thoughts, Quinn sailed through the front door and headed toward the locker rooms at the back. I shot Gabe a devilish grin. "Well, how 'bout that? Just like clockwork."

I angled toward Quinn, but I'd barely taken two steps before Gabe locked onto my arm and yanked me back. I looked down at his hand then gave him a what-the-fuck look. "What? You said you wanted to talk to her. So let's go talk." I started toward Quinn again, but Gabe wouldn't let go.

"I didn't mean *here*," he said through gritted teeth.

Pulling my arm free of his grip, I shrugged. "Why not? She's here. We're here. What's the problem?"

"The problem is that she's off duty and probably likes to use this time to forget about work. I'm not bothering her with this on her time off. That woman works too many hours as it is."

I snorted. "You're one to talk." I pivoted and jogged after Quinn before Gabe could stop me again. She was almost to the locker rooms, eating up the ground with her eyes forward. I smiled, loving the way she contrasted every other woman in the place. Whereas the other women sported tight clothes, bright colors, and gobs of makeup and spent more time looking around to see who was checking them out than they did actually exercising, Quinn was the complete opposite. She was dressed in an old pair of sweats with UNLV written vertically down one leg. Her baggy T-shirt showed none of her delicious curves, and she had her curls thrown up in a messy bun on top of her head. As usual, her body language gave off a strong "don't even fucking think about hitting on me" vibe.

Gabe was grumbling behind me as I closed in on my target, but he followed nonetheless.

Coming alongside Quinn, I slung my arm around her neck, letting my hand dangle over her opposite shoulder. "Hey, Quinny-baby. What's shaking?"

When she turned to look at me, I flashed my most charming smile. She scowled and threw my arm off of her shoulder.

"What do *you* want?"

I pretended to grimace. "Still mad about the other night, huh? I let you keep your panties!" I said, as if that should have earned me her undying gratitude.

Instead, her face turned bright red, and she spun on me faster than I could track the movement.

I slammed on the brakes to keep from running into her and loved every bit of the hellfire raging in her eyes.

"Quit talking about my panties!"

A couple of young women nearby snickered and looked between us, clearly hoping we would continue the discussion so that they could get the rest of the details. Quinn spared them a glance, and I could practically see her kicking herself.

I chuckled. "You can stop pretending you come here for any other reason than to watch me flex."

She raised her eyes to the ceiling and placed the back of her hand on her forehead, feigning a theatrical southern belle. "Oh yes. I just *cannot* begin to express how much I enjoy the pit stains and the sound of your caveman grunts." Then she leveled her eyes at mine and offered a saccharine smile. "Tell me, Ryan, how is it that you always just happen to be here when I'm here? Tracking the LoJack in my car?"

I leaned down bringing my nose within an inch of hers. To her credit, she didn't back down. "No need for such high-tech devices when I can set my watch by your unadventurous routine."

Quinn's nostrils flared, and her lips pressed into the sexiest little pucker.

Before our banter could go any further, Gabe stepped forward and cleared his throat. The surprise on Quinn's face indicated she'd been so preoccupied with our duel that she hadn't even noticed him standing behind me.

Gabe offered an apologetic smile. "I'm sorry we disturbed you, Quinn. We had a few questions about the call you handled regarding Rebecca Tate, but it can wait until tomorrow, when you're back on duty."

Quinn's affect completely changed as she focused on Gabe. Her shoulders relaxed, and a sweet smile curled the corners of her plush lips. "Hey, Gabe. That's all right. If it will help find Mrs. Tate's killer, I'm happy to tell you anything you want to know."

I grinned and raised my eyebrows. "Anything?"

Quinn's scowl returned. "About the case," she snarled.

I snapped my fingers as though I'd missed a great opportunity.

Gabe nodded toward a nearby corner far enough removed that we wouldn't be overheard. I let him start the conversation.

"We're hitting a dead end on this case. I just want to get your impressions about the call. Is there anything you can think of that seemed odd or maybe didn't seem important at the time but could be worth mentioning now?"

Quinn dropped her eyes to the floor, her brow creasing. After a few seconds, she looked up again. "The call wouldn't geo-verify."

She said it as though we should know what that meant. When Gabe and I exchanged glances then settled vacant stares on her, she elaborated. "When a call comes into the center, typically, I can see the latitude and longitude of the caller, and either a specific or a fairly precise location will populate. The caller's phone number will also appear on my screen. None of that happened with this call."

"How often does that happen?" Gabe asked.

Quinn tilted her head from side to side and pursed her lips. "We get calls a few times a week where we don't get a lot of information off them, and that can be for various reasons, but I have never had a call where there was just *nothing*."

The gnawing feeling in my gut that I'd been trying to ignore for the past few days was growing by the second.

Clearly, Gabe didn't like where the conversation was headed either. His body practically vibrated with tension. "What else?" he asked.

Quinn licked her lips and hesitated before answering. "Well, I'm sure you've listened to the call and noticed that the caller seemed a bit... *evasive.*"

We both nodded.

She continued, "I'm accustomed to having to drag information out of callers. A lot of people just want to alert us to something, but they don't want to get involved beyond that. We try to get their contact information, and they don't want to provide it. Often, they just don't want to get in the middle of anything. They're afraid of retaliation. Or sometimes, it's because they've had their own trouble with the law and they don't want any more contact with the cops than necessary." Quinn wrapped her arms around herself. "This felt different, though. It almost felt like..." She looked down again.

The creases in my forehead deepened as I gently tapped her elbow. "Like what?"

Her eyes met mine, and I could see the war going on inside of her. She was questioning whether she should say what was on the tip of her tongue.

She took a deep breath and let it go. "It felt like he was *playing* with me."

That sentence hung between the three of us, the weight of it adding to the burden we already felt to bring justice to Rebecca and her family.

Gabe was the first to break the spell. He squeezed Quinn's shoulder. "Thanks, Quinn. We appreciate everything you do."

She smiled in return. Maybe I was reading too much into a look, but I could swear Gabe's gratitude had hit a tender spot. And tender spots were not something I was accustomed to seeing when it came to Quinn. When her gaze turned to me, I searched her eyes for something. What, I wasn't sure. Confirmation that she was okay, maybe or that she was still my tough-as-nails Quinny-baby, and that fire that I loved to stoke wasn't dying.

But her eyes were unreadable when she turned and resumed her trek to the locker room. I watched her go until she was out of sight, but her words continued to echo in my ears. Quinn's answers to our questions hadn't brought us any closer to cracking the case, but they had accomplished one thing. She had just confirmed what my gut had been telling me all along. The case wasn't a simple homicide, and whoever was responsible for Rebecca's murder might just be getting started.

CHAPTER 8

Quinn

AFTER SECURING my gym bag in a locker, I joined Shelby in the group fitness room. She was already stretching in preparation for our kickboxing class. I rolled my head and shoulders in circles, trying to release the tension that had built up throughout the day. I was so ready to get my sweat on and leave the stress of work in a puddle on the floor.

The gym was my sanctuary, the endorphins my drug. Working up a sweat and feeling the burn in my muscles and the strain in my lungs was what kept me sane and free from the booze and sleep-med cocktails many of my partners relied on to unwind at the end of the day.

I faced Shelby. She stood with her back to the large window that allowed us to see everything on the main floor of the gym. Unfortunately, that also meant that all the muscle-bound jocks pushing iron had an unobstructed view of us as well. Most of the time, once class got started, I didn't think about it too much, since the instructor's stage was on the opposite wall. But at the moment, Shelby suddenly hinged forward, reaching for her toes, which left me staring directly at Trevor Ryan, who was also staring back at *me*.

He flashed the cocky Casanova grin that had made many legs

spread. I narrowed my eyes into slits in challenge. He was trying to get a rise out of me, as was always his goal, so I made an exaggerated show of turning my nose up and looking away.

Shelby straightened and balanced on one leg as she pulled the opposite heel into her butt. She was gazing at the floor, and only then did I notice how quiet she had been. I studied her for a moment. Her dark-blond hair with beautiful golden highlights was pulled into a high ponytail and shimmered beneath the can lighting. Her attire was simple, a sleeveless white shirt paired with black leggings, but with her athletic curves, simple looked exquisite. Her hazel eyes, however, belied the mask she was trying to hold in place. Usually full of sparkle, they were flat and even a little sad.

"Hey." I waited for her to look up. "What's going on with you?"

She frowned and shrugged. "Nothing's going on."

"Mm-hmm."

She didn't respond.

I straightened my arm and pulled it across my chest to stretch my shoulder. "Shelby, we've known each other practically our entire lives. Do you really think I'm going to buy that?"

When she met my stare, I raised my eyebrows and waited.

Rolling her eyes, she shifted her weight to one hip and put her hands on her waist. "I think Josh is having an affair," she blurted.

My eyebrows reached new heights. It felt like the wind had just been knocked out of me. "What?"

Shelby's eyes shimmered, and a small sniffle escaped. She avoided looking at me, choosing to focus on the pale hardwood floors instead.

I moved closer, dipping my chin in an effort to get her to look at me. Softening my tone, I asked, "Why do you think he's cheating?"

She shrugged again, and in a voice that sounded far too fragile to belong to Shelby, she said, "We've been having a lot of problems. He doesn't look at me the way he used to." She sniffled again and swiped at her nose with the back of her hand. "It's like I'm more of a burden he has to deal with than a lover he wants around."

I couldn't believe what I was hearing. *How was I oblivious to this?*

"How long have you two been having these problems?"

Again, her eyes dipped. "A few months."

A few months. And she hadn't said a word. That didn't make any sense. Ever since we were kids, we'd told each other everything.

I took her hand and gently squeezed. "Why didn't you tell me?"

She took a quivering breath and looked around the room before answering. "You've been so stressed about work and the supervisor position and those awful women you have to endure. I just didn't want to add to your worries."

My stomach sank in a hard and furious drop that left me feeling like I might need a trash can to vomit in. I had been so wrapped up in work and commiserating over my misery that not only had I failed to notice my best friend's world was falling apart, but I'd also caused her to feel that she had to face it alone in order to protect *me.*

Shelby let go of my hand and plucked her shirt away from her chest to use it to dab at her eyes. "And I was embarrassed."

"About what?"

She let out a harsh laugh. "I don't have much to show for my life, Quinn. I have no career to speak of. We're buried in debt, and that's also thanks to me and the fact that I just *had* to leave steady employment to start my own business. Which, by the way, has been a monumental flop." Shelby shook her head, disgust painted across her face. "My marriage was the only thing I could point to that I hadn't failed at."

My mouth tightened. *This doesn't sound like Shelby.* She had always been the easygoing one between us, trusting fate to have our backs. Growing up, I'd always been convinced the sky was falling. Shelby, on the other hand, was the kind of girl who had danced in the rain.

I took a moment to wrap my brain around everything she was telling me, wanting to ensure I chose my words carefully. Then I exhaled sharply and tucked a stray hair behind her ear. "You listen to me, Shelby Johnson."

When she didn't look at me, I gave her shoulder a little shake. Slowly, her gaze circled back to mine, but it was guarded, as though she was already choosing not to believe whatever I was about to say.

"Shelby, do you have any solid proof that Josh has been unfaithful?"

She crossed her arms, the muscles in her jaw tightening. "No."

I nodded firmly. "Since day one, Josh has only had eyes for you. And the money troubles are not yours alone. Josh supported you in leaving that dead-end job that had you contemplating jumping off a cliff daily."

Shelby's expression softened, so I pressed on before I lost any of the ground I'd gained. "You are an extremely talented interior designer, and you love what you do. It is only a matter of time before the right people catch sight of your work and you have more business than you can manage on your own. Josh believes that, too, and that's why he's been picking up the extra hours at work. He wants you to pursue your dream."

She sniffled again, but that time, when she wiped away a stray tear, another didn't replace it.

A group of women filed into the room, drawing our attention to the fact that class would be starting shortly.

I lowered my voice. "Talk to Josh, Shelby. Find out what's really going on before it's too late and you two really do have a problem that you may not be able to come back from."

She searched my eyes, and after several moments, the tension left her body, and she nodded, offering a small smile.

I beamed and gripped both of her shoulders, giving her a little shake to lighten the mood. "And whatever happens, we're in it together. No more secrets. Promise?"

Her smile grew, the corners of her eyes crinkling. "Promise."

* * *

TWO DAYS LATER, I sat in Dispatch, still preoccupied by what Shelby had shared with me. My fingers flew across my keyboard as I responded to radio traffic, but my mind was with my friend. I still felt awful for failing to be there when she needed me, for failing to even notice that she had been quieter than usual and that the light in her eyes had dimmed. But that was going to change. I had resolved that same night to no longer share the stresses of my job with her.

I didn't want her worrying about me, especially with something as big as her marriage hanging in the balance. Instead, I would keep my mouth shut about work and just be there, however and whenever she needed me.

A break in the radio traffic had my senses tuning in to the activity in the rest of the room. Julia sat beside me, working our secondary law channel. She had the speaker on her radio turned up, and one of our officers was providing a name and date of birth for someone he was contacting.

The phone rang, as it had ceaselessly all morning. I glanced at the monitor that showed incoming calls. It was our non-emergency line. Blair answered on the second ring. She was strictly call-taking, since Meredith was working the fire radio.

Taking a deep breath, I leaned back then exhaled slowly, making a conscious effort to release the tension. The day had been pretty busy by Eden Falls standards. It still wasn't anything compared to my Las Vegas Metro days, but it was enough to keep us all busy and focused on work rather than the office politics and cliques, something for which I was extremely grateful.

I interlocked my fingers and wiggled my wrists back and forth then stretched my fingers and forearms while keeping an eye on my screen for whatever call Blair was going to send through. My ears perked up when her tone turned sharp.

"No, you can give me your name and phone number first," she said.

My back was to her, but I still had no call on my screen, and I couldn't hear her typing. I groaned inwardly. *Here we go again.*

Blair had a bad habit of being abrasive with callers. It set them on edge and made it difficult to get all the information we ideally wanted to provide to the field units. It also meant that her call times were horrendous, yet another reason I didn't understand how or why she had been promoted to supervisor or how she managed to hold the position.

I took another deep breath in an attempt to quell my growing frustration. She should have at least had enough information by that point to send the call to my screen so that I could determine who I was going to assign it to.

Blair's voice grew louder and sliced through the dulcet communications Julia and Meredith were engaged in with their respective field units. Julia glanced sideways at me, her shoulders starting to creep toward her ears.

When Blair got into those moods, everyone began walking on eggshells. I gave Julia a tight smile and a nod of encouragement to just keep focusing on her radio traffic.

Heat pooled in my cheeks and began to creep down to my chest. With another calming breath, I closed my eyes and soothed myself with thoughts of how I was going to whip that dispatch center into shape if I could just get the damn promotion.

"Yes, she is here, but you are not going to talk to her. You are going to talk to *me*."

My eyes flew open, my ears instantly tuned to only Blair. I swiveled in my seat to look at her, wondering what the hell was going on with that call.

"Sir, I want your name and phone number before we go any further." Blair's eyes were narrowed at her monitor, her fingers in a death grip around her phone. She was definitely pissed. Blair got off on the power of her position, of being able to make demands of people and hold, at least in part, the fate of their call in her hands, and if any of our callers challenged that power, she became downright hostile.

But there was more than just her poor phone etiquette that had my attention.

I glanced again at the monitor that showed our open lines. With my mouse, I double-clicked on Blair's call to pull up the caller's information. *Nothing*, just like when Rebecca's body had been reported.

A chill raced through my body. *Could this be the same man?*

"You don't get to decide who you talk to," Blair snapped.

I turned to face her again. "Blair!" I hissed, trying to avoid the caller's hearing me.

She ignored me.

"Blair!" I tried again. "Who does he want to speak to?"

She didn't even spare me a glance. Instead, she swiped her hand at me like she was shooing a fly.

I pressed my lips together as she continued to argue with the caller. She was going to lose him. I couldn't let that happen. Gabe and Trevor had already admitted they'd hit a dead end on the case. The call could provide some clue that would enable them to pick up the trail again.

"Blair!" I said more loudly and insistently, so much so that Meredith and Julia both whipped their heads around, their eyes wide and dancing back and forth between Blair and me.

"Who does he want to speak to?" I asked.

Blair turned her head in true *Exorcist* fashion, her pale skin cherry red. "*You,*" she mouthed with more emphasis than necessary.

I paused for a moment, knowing that I was about to supersede my direct supervisor and would pay dearly for it.

CHAPTER 9

"Take the radio," I ordered Blair then spun around and snatched up my phone and joined the line.

"Hello?" I waited for him to respond.

Silence.

"Is this the man I spoke with the other day? The one who reported a body in the woods?"

A heavy breath followed. Then a deep timbre, undulating with rage, filled the empty space. "Tell that cunt to watch her back! I'll teach her who's in control when I cut her heart from her chest!"

My heart started to gallop. The venom dripping from his words was ice in my bones. I fought to bring my breathing and pulse back under control. First rule of dispatch: never let them see you sweat.

"You wanted to speak to me. You've got my full attention."

He went silent except for his ragged breaths.

I waited, sensing that more prompting was just going to piss him off further.

After several moments, his breathing shifted, becoming slower and much quieter. I continued to wait, allowing his executive thought processes to override his primal physiology.

And it worked. When he spoke next, he sounded as he had the first time—cool, calm, fully in control, and with a touch of amusement.

"I called to report another body, but that bitch didn't seem too interested, so perhaps I should just let it rot where it lies."

My mouth went dry. *Another body.*

I didn't know yet how much I should challenge the man. Control was clearly important to him, so maybe I could put him at ease by playing dumb—give him the sense that I was no real threat so that he would let down his guard and reveal something useful.

"How is it that you managed to find another body?" I bit my lip, waiting to see which way it was going to go, and could feel the eyes of my partners on me. The room had gone silent. Even the phones had stopped ringing, as though the cosmos waited with bated breath as well.

His tone held a sneer. "I didn't take you for the type to lie down and play dumb. Perhaps I overestimated your value."

Asshole. Fine. If that was how he wanted to play, then that was how we would play. "All right. Then why don't you just tell me why you're killing these people?"

He snickered. "Oh, I'm doing a lot more than that."

Another chill crept over me. I'd heard the details of what Rebecca had been subjected to. He was right. He was doing *a lot* more than just killing.

My voice deepened as unadulterated hate seeped into my blood. "Where is the body?"

"Do you really think I'm going to tell you just because you asked?"

"No. You're going to tell me because that's why you called."

He chuckled darkly. "Mmm. Very good. I'm sorry—I didn't catch your name."

My spine stiffened. I knew without a shadow of doubt that I was engaged in a careful dance with a man who bore no conscience, which meant a man who had no limits to his depravity. *Do I really want him to have my name?* The department was small, and I was the only Quinn in town. It wouldn't be difficult for him to find me if he decided that was how he wanted it to go. But for those same reasons, it wouldn't be difficult for him to uncover my identity even if I did provide him with an alias. So I might as well show a little cooperation in hopes he would do the same.

"Quinn," I said finally.

"Very good, Quinn." The pleasure in his voice had me second-guessing my decision.

"Now that we're in this together, Quinn, I will explain the rules of the game. I dump a body. Then within twenty-four hours, I'll call in to report its location."

My brow creased. "Why would you offer up that kind of information?"

"It's part of the game."

"Have you played this game before?" I was sure I already knew the answer, but I wanted him to confirm it.

"There is, however, one catch, Quinn."

I waited for him to elaborate, but he wanted me to ask.

My pride shouted at me to tell the asshole to go to hell and enjoy the trip, but the dispatcher in me would grovel in any way necessary to prevent another murder. So I would play his game and use every interaction as an opportunity to mine for something, *anything*, that would tip his hand.

"What's the catch?"

I could hear his smile. "I will not endure another unfortunate interaction with a lowbrow like the one who *attempted* to handle this call. If I am forced to speak to anyone other than you, I will not divulge the location of the next corpse or any of those that follow. This town will be left wondering what happened to those who simply... vanished."

Blood drained from my face. He had a lineup of victims, people whose days were already marked with the dates of their death. And he wanted me to be a part of the show. I was speaking to the devil incarnate, staring down the barrel of a Faustian deal.

"Tick-tock, Quinn. I haven't got all day."

My grip tightened on my phone, my thoughts whizzing by faster than I could track. He wanted me to be his sole contact, the conduit for his confessions. That wasn't the kind of thing I could just agree to without running it past a supervisor.

I thought of Blair sitting behind me. If I asked her, she would shoot me down in a heartbeat, not only because it was *me* asking but because Blair liked to be the one in the spotlight. If I were to agree to it, I would have to become a central character in this madman's plot. Blair wouldn't like me getting that kind of attention.

I could take it to the dispatch manager, but she wasn't around for me to ask. Besides, she would tell me to defer to my direct supervisor, which brought me back to Blair.

My heart began to race again as I sensed his growing agitation. I needed to buy some time until I could figure out how to proceed. "I'll have to run it past my supervisor."

"No dice, Quinn. This is a one-time offer, and it expires in ten seconds."

Son of a bitch! I couldn't lose this guy. If he went silent, the bodies would pile up. Sure, maybe he would slip up at some point and leave behind some evidence that would eventually lead us to him. *But how many people would die in the meantime?* We had a much better chance of apprehending him sooner rather than later if I was able to keep the line of communication open.

I knew then that I already had my answer, even if it meant I was going to be in hot water. In my mind, there was no other option.

"Quinn—"

"Yes. Okay."

"Excellent."

I could tell from the way he said it that he'd known all along I would agree but was pleased by how easily he'd forced my hand.

"Are you ready to learn where I disposed of the second body?"

I clicked into the location field of my call-taking screen then hovered my fingers over my keyboard, ready to enter the information so that Blair could get units heading that way. "Yes."

"Walea Falls Campground."

I typed in the location and added the pertinent details of our conversation to the call notes in a matter of seconds. I also placed Trevor's and Gabe's call signs on it so that Blair would give it to them specifically. "Where in the campground?"

"If your officers have two brain cells to rub together, they'll be able to piece it together relatively quickly. If not, I guess this isn't going to be much of a game."

I ground my molars in response to the boredom in his voice. Since I still had my earpiece in, I could hear Blair dispatching the call. Trevor answered and advised he and Gabe were en route and requested we notify the sheriff's office, since the location was in their jurisdiction.

Turning my attention back to the call, I listened for a moment to determine whether I could hear any background sounds that could indicate the guy's location, but it was completely silent.

So I tried a different approach. "Considering we're going to be working together, and you now have my name, how about you give me your first name as well? A sign of good faith."

I knew it was a long shot, but even if he gave me a false name, it could still hold a clue to his real identity.

His tone seductive, he said, "I'm just an old fiend, Quinn. I don't provide faith."

Though I opened my mouth to question him further, he hung up before I could get the words out.

I leaned forward and propped my elbows on the desk, planting my face in my palms. *This is a disaster.*

No. Disaster didn't even begin to describe it.

This is a clusterfuck.

Eden Falls had a serial killer on its hands, and judging by that call, I knew the body count wouldn't be slight. I had just made a deal with said serial killer that I had no business making, and I had no idea how I was going to pull enough strings to actually follow through on that commitment. The guys were on their way to a second body in another agency's jurisdiction. And to top it all off, I had to submit myself to Blair's wrath for what would be a valid accusation of insubordination and would be rubbing her teeth marks out of my ass for weeks. I was having difficulty recalling why I had thought it was a good idea to get out of bed that morning.

Sighing deeply, I raised my head. Julia cast a furtive glance in my direction, but my partners remained silent—too silent. The tension in the room was thicker than Sofia Vergara's accent.

Okay, Quinn. Time to pull yourself together. I sat up straighter and squared my shoulders. The second rule of dispatch was to prioritize and clear. So that was what I was going to do. The situation with Blair was what it was. She was going to choose the place and time for my ass chewing, so there was no point in worrying about it at the moment. The second victim was already dead, and we knew the location of the body. There was nothing more I could do there.

The deal I had made with the killer, though, and how far I was willing to go—that was something I needed to figure out fast. As the situation stood, I was going to get written up, and my chances of securing the supervisor position were significantly less. But if I chose to force the issue on the deal I had made, it might cost me my career, the thing that had been the sole focus of my adult life.

As much as I hated work at the moment, I lived and breathed for the job. I loved being the lifeline for someone when their whole world was turning to ashes around them. And I loved supporting our first responders, being the calm voice in the midst of chaos. I loved that after every shift, I went home knowing that I had done something that mattered. Dispatch wasn't a job. It was my *identity*, and I would be lost without it.

The crux of the situation was that I would need to put my

career in jeopardy to stand a chance of getting the necessary approval to see this thing through. It would require that I commit a cardinal sin in the world of law enforcement. I would have to jump the chain of command.

I tapped my index finger on my desk and turned my bottom lip into raw meat as I weighed my options. A call pierced the silence, and Meredith's radio crackled, bringing the sights and sounds of the room back into sharp focus. Within seconds, the dispatch center was a flurry of activity. Calls poured in, radios squawked ceaselessly, and the tapping of keyboards reverberated throughout the small space.

It didn't matter that I had been pulled from my contemplation to focus on the new calls popping onto my screen. I had made my decision. And as soon as work was over, I would march straight to the one person none of my supervisors would challenge, and I would do whatever it took to get him to sign off on my direct and ongoing involvement in the case.

The chief of police wouldn't know what hit him.

CHAPTER 10

Trevor

I WATCHED from ten feet away as a couple of sheriff's crime scene techs pulled a petite figure from a line of dumpsters at the rear of the campground. A large radius had been blocked off with yellow police tape. Dozens of onlookers pressed against the boundary, trying to get a better view.

The day was hot, with the sun directly overhead, but the dumpsters were covered by shade provided by the line of timber standing at their back. The dumpsters at that particular campground were set apart from the actual campsites, providing campers with relief from the rancid smell of waste. Unfortunately for us, that also meant the glade enjoyed a certain amount of privacy.

Gabe shifted beside me, his arms crossed and his expression blank. The news crews were snapping pictures with their telephoto lenses, the journalists thrusting microphones in the faces of the deputies charged with holding the public at bay.

Six days. That was how long it had been since we'd last done this song and dance. Technically, Gabe and I didn't need to be there. It wasn't our crime scene. We could just let the sheriff's office handle it and wipe our hands clean of it. But there was no way in hell we were going to step off the line on this. Whoever the killer was, he clearly wanted Eden Falls PD involved—something he was going to regret.

The crime scene techs, one at the victim's head and one at her feet, gently laid the body on a large piece of plastic that was sprawled on top of the mud. The entire area around the dumpsters was one giant mud pit, the damp earth constantly churned from both foot and vehicle traffic. A number of deputies surrounded the body and the dumpster she had been pulled from, so we hadn't yet been able to get a good look. We were simply waiting for the invitation to someone else's party.

I shifted my weight between my feet. I was good at a lot of things, but standing still wasn't one of them, especially when I was confident I was about to process a murder scene with a victim I knew.

A sultry voice filled my ear, and I felt some of the restlessness slip away. I allowed my eyes, hidden by my shades, to close for a moment, and I focused on the tantalizing tones. Quinn's voice had a quality to it that brought peace to even the most chaotic and stressful of situations. That was why she was a favorite among the officers. Regardless of the dangers and trials we faced, if Quinn was in our ears, we felt grounded. Her voice never rose or filled with panic. She was just calm and self-assured. And we knew she had our backs. Quinn would stop at nothing to send the whole damn world to help us if need be.

A small smile played at my lips, despite my effort to keep my expression neutral for the cameras and onlookers. I was glad Quinn was back on the radio while we dealt with the call. It had me questioning, though, why she had stepped off earlier. It wasn't unusual for one dispatcher to cover for another for a few minutes for bathroom breaks, but when Blair dispatched Gabe and me to the crime scene, I'd been in my cruiser and glanced at my computer for the details. I noticed Quinn's initials appearing beside each of the call notes. And after the call had been updated for the last time, Quinn was back in my ear. It was odd, and I had every intention of following up with her after we were done.

"Ah, shit."

I opened my eyes and turned my head to Gabe. When I followed his gaze, understanding dawned.

A gap had appeared between the deputies and crime scene techs, enough that I could make out short platinum-blond hair and violet bangs.

Eloise.

"This motherfucker is going down," I growled quietly.

A man wearing a brown polo shirt and slacks with a badge and sidearm clipped to his belt raised a hand and curled his fingers toward himself, signaling for us to approach. Once we joined the circle of figures, we had an unobstructed view of the body.

"I'm Detective Braden Kincaid," the man in the polo shirt informed us.

Gabe and I both nodded in acknowledgement.

"I'm Officer Gabe McNeil, and this"—Gabe tilted his head toward me—"is my partner, Officer Trevor Ryan. Eden Falls PD."

"Do either of you happen to know who the victim is?" Kincaid asked.

We both nodded.

"Eloise Jackson," I said, keeping my eyes trained on the body. "Twenty-three years old, married, a hairstylist at a hole-in-the-wall salon in Eden Falls."

"Was there a missing persons report for her?"

I shook my head. "No."

Scanning the body, I noted the shocking similarities to the last one. My fear had been confirmed, and there was no longer a question about what we were dealing with.

I looped my thumbs over my duty belt and nodded toward Eloise's body. "We had a homicide last week that matches this MO," I said to Kincaid. "The lingerie. The gouges all over her body. The marks around her wrists and ankles and signs of strangulation—it's all consistent."

The only thing that was different was that the flimsy fabric that clung to Eloise's lifeless form was candy-apple red, whereas Rebecca's had been black.

Kincaid grunted. "Do you have any suspects?"

I studied the dumpsters and our surroundings, looking for anything out of place as I tried to piece together what had happened. "No, but our dispatcher advised that the man who called this body in was the same man who called in the last, and he's taking credit for both homicides."

Kincaid dropped his eyes to Eloise and nodded. "I'll make sure you get copies of everything pertaining to this case." He lifted his sharp gaze to us. "I'd appreciate it if you would do the same."

We nodded. The crime scene had been pretty badly contaminated because it was a public campground and it was the start of summer. People were itching to get outside after a long winter, so the campground was nearly at capacity. We figured the body had likely been dumped in the night, so it had gone undetected for at least ten to twelve hours. All the fresh tire tracks and footprints indicated numerous people had come and gone during that time, discarding their waste on Eloise and going about their business.

Needless to say, I wasn't too hopeful that Kincaid and his men would have much luck collecting any solid evidence from the scene itself. And I knew from overhearing several of the deputies report to Kincaid that they had questioned the campers nearest to the dumpsters, but they didn't have a single eyewitness. No one had heard or seen anything unusual between the previous night and the time when deputies arrived on scene.

But maybe we would get lucky, and the body would hold additional clues. Since Dr. Vic was the ME for the entire county, he would be handling the autopsy, which meant we would have direct access to the details and anything he found.

After sharing the last of our notes with Kincaid, Gabe and I made our way back to the cruisers. Instead of climbing inside and heading back to Eden Falls, we took a moment to scan the landscape. Since we were no longer protected by the shade of the trees, the heat quickly scorched my skin, and sweat trickled down my back.

I focused on the whirl of activity straight ahead once more, my mind automatically throwing up images of Rebecca's crime scene for comparison. "He could have left her anywhere. The woods would have provided a lot more cover, and this place gets a high volume of traffic. Especially this time of year. So why dump her here?"

Gabe grunted. His own gaze was aimed at the nearest campsite about a quarter mile to our left.

I eyed the dumpsters, a thought niggling its way into my consciousness. "You think it's a coincidence that both bodies were left lying in trash?"

Gabe swung his head around as he zeroed in on the scene again. "I don't think anything with this guy is a coincidence."

Neither did I.

Releasing a heavy breath, I spread my feet wide to take some of the pressure from my duty belt off my lower back. "Okay..." My tone was all business. "What do the victims have in common?"

Gabe shrugged and shifted his weight from one hip to the other. "They're both female and Caucasian."

"Both married," I added.

We fell silent. That was where the similarities ended. Rebecca was in her forties. She was wealthy and had enjoyed great success in her law career. She had no biological children, but she had an adult stepkid from William's first marriage, and they lived in an expensive housing complex on the outskirts of town.

Eloise was basically Rebecca's opposite. Young, no kids, and the salon where she worked wasn't exactly catering to the Rebeccas of the world. Her clothes were secondhand, and she lived in a run-down trailer in Eden Falls's only trailer park with her shithead husband.

"That girl never had a chance," Gabe said almost to himself.

A lump lodged in my throat as I recalled our history with her. Eloise was sweet and kind of shy in a way that had given the impression she didn't think she deserved to take up space. Her jade eyes were always heavily lined with black, and she liked leather-studded jewelry.

Growing up, we'd see her around town, but she was eight years younger than us, so we didn't pay her much attention. Not until her senior year of high school when Gabe and I were rookies on the force did we get to know her better. She lived in the same trailer park back then, and we responded almost weekly to domestic disputes between her meth-addicted parents. Their place was always a pigsty, dirty dishes and rotten food everywhere.

We had tried to have Eloise pulled from the home, but it had been determined that there wasn't enough to justify such drastic action. So Gabe and I made it our mission to check on her regularly. Then as soon as she turned eighteen, she ran off and got married to her piece-of-shit boyfriend, who had continued the cycle of abuse in her life.

That girl had left the world the same way she entered it—in violence and misery.

I sighed and turned away from the crime scene. "Let's head back to the station and start figuring out which of Eloise's friends and family we want to talk to first." Maybe this time, when we traced our victim's last hours, we would get lucky and find something that would jumpstart the case again.

Gabe nodded. "I also want to issue a public notice. Get everyone on high alert to keep their eyes peeled for anything suspicious and to be wary of people they don't know."

As I was climbing into my car, Quinn raised my call sign and requested my status. I smirked, thinking of a smartass remark that would really get her knickers in a knot, but in rare form, I decided to keep it professional and simply said, "I'm clear with Twenty-Five Adam Two. We're en route to the station."

I glanced at my watch. Realizing the time, I threw my car into drive and stepped on the gas. Quinn would be going off duty soon, and I still wanted to talk to her about why she had jumped off the radio to handle the call.

And there was no way in hell I was going to miss an opportunity to interrogate my sexy little siren.

CHAPTER 11

I STARED at a gray-blue door and took a deep breath then slowly released it as I adjusted my polo shirt and slacks. Before I could change my mind, I rapped the door with my knuckles beneath a name plate that read Chief Kelly. A deep voice, muffled by the barrier between us, called for me to enter.

Steeling my spine, I turned the doorknob and walked into the small office with as much feigned confidence as I could summon. Chief Kelly was a nice man, but he was military through and through. I wasn't expecting him to overlook that I was superseding every person between my rank and his.

"Hello, Ms. Martin." The chief's smile reached his blue eyes, his white mustache twitching with the upturn of his lips.

I matched his friendly expression. "Hello, Chief." Behind my back, I wrung my hands. "I was hoping I could have a word with you before you leave for the evening."

He raised his bushy eyebrows and extended his hand toward the empty visitor's chair in front of his desk. I quickly took a seat, running my sweaty palms down the thighs of my black slacks.

The chief patiently waited, folding his hands on top of his desk. Behind him, a large picture window framed one of the many impressive mountain ranges that surrounded our small town.

Most of the snow had melted from their caps, and sunbeams stretched down from a bluebird sky to highlight what remained.

Licking my lips, I squirmed in my seat as I tried to decide how I wanted to start the conversation. When the chief's eyebrows started to migrate north again, I realized that if I was going to do it, it was now or never.

Offering another small smile, I managed to locate my backbone and jumped into the conversation with both feet. "Chief Kelly, I have a unique situation I would like to discuss with you. I'm sure by now you're aware that we have been receiving calls from an individual claiming to be responsible for the murders of two women."

The chief offered a pensive nod.

"I spoke to this man for the second time today." Butterflies began to beat the insides of my stomach as I contemplated how to phrase the next bit of information. After vacillating about how much effort I should put into refraining from throwing Blair under the bus, I finally decided the hell with it and just told the chief like it was. "I wasn't the one who originally answered his call this afternoon, but after he and the call-taker got into an argument due to his insistence on speaking with me, I picked up the line. He then confessed to the murders and his plans for additional victims."

Chief Kelly sat back, leaning on one hip. I couldn't begin to guess what he was thinking as his crystal eyes studied me.

I pressed on. "He also made a request. Something I didn't include in the call, and that's what I would like to discuss with you."

"Go ahead."

I could understand how the chief had been so effective as a law enforcement officer all those years. The man had a hell of a poker face.

I sat up straighter and squared my shoulders. "He is only willing to speak to me."

Chief Kelly went absolutely still, his eyes locked on mine and unblinking.

"He advised that if he is forced to speak to anyone else, he will stop calling, and we'll just have to hope the bodies turn up at some point."

"What's your take on him?"

"Excuse me?"

"Do you really think he'll stop calling, or is he just trying to see how easily he can manipulate us?"

I dipped my eyes to the dingy carpet, considering his question for a moment before answering. "He requires control. I absolutely believe he will stop calling if we disregard this demand. It might even cause his behavior to escalate."

Chief Kelly's eyes shifted over my right shoulder. The door to his office was still open behind me, allowing him to see the bullpen, where all the officers' desks were located in a large, open layout.

Without warning, the chief shouted, causing me to jump. "Ryan! McNeil! Get in here."

My eyes widened. *Why the hell is he calling* them *in here when we're right in the middle of a very serious discussion?*

At the sound of them entering the office, I stood and stepped to the side to make room for all of us. Gabe entered first and offered me a smile and a polite nod. I smiled in return, then my eyes instinctively moved to Trevor as he cleared the doorway. When he saw me standing there, a flirtatious smirk slowly curled the corners of his lips. His blue eyes flicked briefly down my body then returned to my face.

I quickly dropped the smile I'd worn for Gabe and replaced it with a glower. Trevor chuckled in response, his eyes crinkling at the corners.

He then turned his attention to the chief. "Hey, Chief. How's it shakin'?"

I rolled my eyes. He really was incorrigible.

The chief ignored Trevor's flippant greeting and got down to business. "Fill me in on the body dump."

Gabe leaned against the back wall and crossed his ankles while looping his thumbs over his duty belt. "It was Eloise Jackson."

I knew the woman only by name, having handled several calls for domestic disputes at her residence, but the chief seemed more familiar with her, because a shadow of sadness floated across his features.

Trevor spoke next. "Her body was tossed into one of the dumpsters at Walea. Same MO as Rebecca."

I watched Trevor out of the corner of my eye, noting that the humor had left his face. He was suddenly all business. I hadn't had too many opportunities to see him in the field. Most of my interactions with him occurred when he stopped by Dispatch or when I encountered him at the gym. In those instances, he was always so flirty and jocular. But at the moment, authority radiated from his imposing frame.

Intrigued by the change, I ran my gaze down his body, taking in the way his black uniform hugged every dip and curve of his muscles, from his broad back and python arms to his well-rounded glutes. As usual, his golden hair was gelled, and he'd spiked it along the top, giving him a polished yet roguish appearance.

My name reached my ears from some distant place. When it came again, I realized that everyone's eyes were on me as though waiting for something. My cheeks flamed, and I turned to the chief. "I'm sorry. What?"

The five-alarm fire in my cheeks was making its way down my chest. *Please tell me no one* actually *caught me checking out Trevor Ryan.* I wanted to face-palm myself.

Chief Kelly spoke slowly. "I asked you to tell Ryan and McNeil about the suspect's request."

"Oh. Right." I cleared my throat and cast a furtive glance between the two officers. "He's only willing to speak to me from here on out."

Trevor snorted. "What did he say when you told him to go to hell?"

I turned my body toward him and crossed my arms. "Actually, I agreed."

"What?" The word came in unison from all three men. I'd forgotten that I had left that part out for the chief.

To salvage any damage from the proclamation, I turned my attention back to him. "Chief, it's really no different from what I already do. I answer and dispatch calls that come into the center and do my best to collect all pertinent information. I don't think this needs to be an issue."

The chief worked his mouth while keeping his eyes trained on me.

Trevor closed the small distance between us until the heat from his body felt like it was consuming all of the oxygen in the room. He stood so close to me that to maintain eye contact, his chin was practically tucked to his chest, and my head couldn't crank back any farther. "The difference," he hissed, "is that he zeroed in on you."

I pressed my lips together, trying very hard to maintain a degree of professionalism in front of Chief Kelly. Using my shoulder, I pushed against Trevor, hoping to get him to take a step back. He didn't. So I ignored him and focused on the chief. "I really think this is a small concession for the greater good."

Trevor scoffed, but I didn't let it deter me. "We all know that the more interactions we have with this guy, the greater the likelihood he slips up. Besides, it's not like I'm going to be out on the streets, hunting him down. It's just a phone call."

Trevor put his hands on his hips and turned away, pacing to the other side of the room. Kelly's eyes followed him then returned to me. "All right, Ms. Martin. We'll give him what he wants for now."

Trevor spun to face the chief, his eyes wide. "No fucking way!"

My jaw dropped. *Did he really just say that to the freaking chief of police?*

The chief remained unruffled and simply held up a hand to silence Trevor, who, at the moment, looked as though his head was about to pop off his neck.

Trevor wasn't deterred. "Chief, this is a really bad idea." He threw his hand up in my direction. "She's not equipped to handle this sort of thing!"

My blood went from ninety-eight degrees to boiling in an instant. *Not* equipped? So that was what it was really about. He didn't think I had the chops to hack the situation.

My hands fisted at my sides as I spun on Trevor. "If I can wrangle a bunch of arrogant, narcissistic cops and soothe a nonstop stream of irate, screaming callers on a daily basis, I am more than capable of handling a few phone calls from this maniac!"

"This guy is out of your league, Quinn!"

"Well, obviously, I'm doing something right, because he insisted on talking to *me* today and almost hung up on Blair when she refused."

Trevor blanched for just a moment before his eyes narrowed and his face turned scarlet again. "You are not going through with this!"

"The hell I'm not."

Trevor started to march toward me but came up short when the chief cleared his throat—loudly. Our bodies remained facing each other, but our heads spun to face Chief Kelly.

"As I was saying," the chief continued calmly, "we will go along with it for now, but if at any point I feel that the benefit no longer outweighs the risks, we will decide on another course of action."

Trevor opened his mouth to argue, but Chief Kelly silenced him with a look of warning. "Ms. Martin, you may go. Ryan and McNeil, I want you to stay."

I glared at Trevor and turned to leave, lifting my chin just enough to make it clear that I had won, and upon my exit, I uttered a silent vow. Before the case was over, Trevor Ryan was going to eat his words.

CHAPTER 12

Trevor

I WATCHED Quinn as she left the office, her victorious strut giving me the itch to smack her ass. *Am I the only one who has any brain cells around here?* I couldn't *believe* the chief was actually on board with that plan.

Swinging my gaze back to my boss, I said, "You realize that by giving her the go-ahead, you just basically served one of our own on a silver platter to a homicidal freak, right?"

Chief Kelly's face softened ever so slightly as he straightened in his chair. "I understand your concern, Trevor."

My eyebrows shot up. "Do you?" I turned to Gabe. "Are you gonna back me up on this or what?"

Gabe was still leaning against the wall and threw his hands up in a way that said, "Leave me out of this."

I growled and started pacing in front of Chief Kelly's desk.

"Look," the chief began, "considering this man only calls in when he wants to report a kill, Quinn's interactions with him will be limited."

I snorted. "Yeah, until he decides jacking off to the sound of her voice doesn't do it for him anymore. Then what? What if he decides she'd make a nice little addition to his kill count?"

Chief Kelly stood and placed his fingertips on his desk. "I

don't intend to let anything happen to Quinn, and that is why I want you to stay close to her."

My feet halted. "Come again?"

"I want you to coach Quinn. Instruct her on what to say and what not to say."

I rolled my eyes until they were halfway to the back of my skull. "Yeah, 'cause she's always so inclined to listen to me."

The corner of Chief Kelly's mouth quirked. "She's not going to have much choice, since you're the lead on this investigation, and you're going to be working alongside her in Dispatch."

Gabe coughed. It sounded suspiciously like a laugh.

My voice rose to a pitch it hadn't attained since puberty. "Dispatch? You're fucking with me."

"Not in the least. You'll be able to work on the investigation while simultaneously being available to Quinn, should she need your assistance when the suspect calls." He straightened and placed his hands in his pockets. "Obviously, the goal is still to catch this asshole before he kills again, but should we fail to do that, I want you to coach Quinn through the next call."

"And how the hell am I supposed to conduct this investigation if I'm sitting on my ass in Dispatch?"

The chief was unfazed. "You and I both know how much of an investigation is done from a desk. You can still respond to the crime scenes, but any interviews or other legwork can be handled by McNeil."

Putting my hands on my hips, I turned away, trying not to say something that was going to get my ass fired. The chief had already allowed my insubordination to slide more than he normally would have.

"Look at it this way..." he said.

I turned to face him, my shoulders bowing with resignation.

Chief Kelly removed his jacket from a coat rack that sat in the corner behind his desk and began pulling it on. "The closer you work with Quinn on this, the better chance we have of getting the guy to slip up, which means the sooner we catch him and the sooner you get out of Dispatch and back on the street." He raised his eyebrows, as if that reasoning just made everything so much better.

With a few parting orders from the chief, Gabe and I left his office. Stalking to my desk, I curled and flexed my fingers in an effort to dissipate some of the frustration pooling in my veins. I picked up a file, flicked the cover open, then promptly shut it again before slapping the file back down on my desk. Turning to Gabe, I asked, "Can you believe this horseshit?"

He smirked.

"What?" I demanded.

Gabe casually pulled his chair out from his desk, which sat to the right of mine, and took a seat, spinning so that his body faced me. "It wasn't too long ago that *I* was pissed off by the chief's insistence on putting us on Alex's case, and *you* found that whole situation pretty damn funny despite the fact that I did not."

Scowling, I took a seat in my own chair. "That's not even close to the same thing."

Gabe didn't respond. He just sat there, propping his elbow on his armrest as he covered his mouth to hide his smirk.

I swiveled my chair to face him as well and leaned forward, thrusting my pointer finger down on the desktop. "If she is going to insist on going through with this suicidal plan, then I am going to make her life a living hell until she decides it's not worth it."

Gabe turned back to his desk and muttered something.

"I'll meet up with Quinn in Dispatch at the start of shift tomorrow and lay down the law about how this is going to go down."

My partner glanced sideways at me then went back to fiddling with some paperwork.

"Why don't you start with the interviews for Eloise's case," I continued, "and since I'm going to be chained to a desk, I'll start combing through ViCAP to see if this guy's MO pops up on any other cases."

ViCAP was a federal database to which law enforcement from

around the country could contribute case files related to violent crimes and missing persons. If our guy had killed elsewhere, and I was willing to bet he had, there might be information from another agency that could help us to solve the case.

Gabe grunted. "Sounds like a plan. Why don't you get to work on getting Eloise's phone and financial records, too, and I'll hit the ME's office in the morning."

I nodded, my mind already returning to Quinn. If I took her out of the equation, I could acknowledge that having a direct line of contact with our key suspect was a valuable opportunity. And as much as I loathed the idea of being stuck in Dispatch all day, it was good foresight on the chief's part to ensure that someone with more experience dealing with the criminal element was there to intervene if need be.

Still... it was *Quinn*. When I'd heard that the asshole had demanded to speak to her personally, I could have torn the chief's office to shreds.

I might have lost the first round, but the battle wasn't over. If Quinn thought it was going to be a walk in the park, she had another think coming. I would be in Dispatch in the morning, all right—glued to her side and making her life miserable until she came to her senses.

CHAPTER 13

Trevor

AFTER BRIEFING THE FOLLOWING MORNING, I collected my laptop, the case file, and my notes and headed to Dispatch, which was a short walk from the station. The two buildings sat adjacent to each other and shared the back parking lot, where the black-and-whites and personnel vehicles were parked.

A cool breeze brushed past me, carrying with it the sound of birdsong. Looking at the mountains in the distance, I noticed how sharp their contours were beneath the deep-blue sky, which was speckled by only a few fluffy white clouds. I took a moment to drink it all in, loathing that I was going to be stuck in what was basically a box for the rest of the day.

When I entered Dispatch, the heavy metal door slammed shut behind me. My eyes took a moment to adjust to the dim atmosphere. The sounds of garbled radio traffic and the pinging and dinging of various notifications guided me down a long hall that eventually dumped me into the heart of our communications center.

Four sets of eyes turned on me at once, each of them filled with a different emotion. Blair wore a faint smirk, her gaze running down my body and conveying every lustful thought. Meredith sat beside her, her shoulder-length bleached hair pulled into a high ponytail that swung back and forth as she looked between Blair and me, practically drooling in anticipation of some good gossip. Then there was the young girl working the fire radio. Julia, I thought her name was. Her eyes were big and round, her lips slightly parted. As soon as my eyes met hers, a blush bloomed over her entire face, and she abruptly turned back to her screens.

And last but far from least was Quinn. Ever the overachiever, she managed an impressive display of about ten different emotions in a span of as many seconds before finally landing on lethal hostility. With a smirk, I strutted over to her and promptly dumped my work on her desk. She made a small sound of protest but said nothing as her eyes followed me to the edge of the room, where I snatched a spare chair and dragged it back to her workstation.

After dropping into my seat, I scooted so close to her that our elbows touched. She yanked her arm away but continued to look at me as though I had lost my damn mind. Ignoring her, I proceeded to unpack my laptop and paperwork and slapped them down on the empty bit of desk beside her keyboard.

When I opened the laptop and began entering my login credentials, she finally spoke. "What do you think you're doing?"

I spared her only a moment's glance before returning my attention to my computer. "Well, thanks to your insistence on being intimately involved in this case, Chief Kelly has ordered me to remain close to you and to instruct you on how to proceed with any further calls from our suspect."

Her eyes were wide and locked on me, but I pretended not to notice. I flipped open the case file and thumbed through a few pages then made a show of intending to place it back on the desk and realizing I didn't have enough work space.

"Here," I said, "I'm just going to..." I nudged Quinn's main keyboard several inches to the left before proceeding to spread out the file.

That did it. Quinn immediately shoved my paperwork away until it was in danger of toppling from the desk. "Since you seem to be visually impaired, among other things, let me point out that there is more than one spare workstation in here," she said as she jerked her keyboard to its original position and simultaneously indicated a few of the vacant areas in the room.

I gave her a shit-eating grin as I reorganized my paperwork in a way that conveyed I wasn't going anywhere. "Like I said, the chief ordered me to stay close."

Her lips puckered, and her nostrils flared. "I hardly doubt he meant for you to sit in my lap," she snapped.

"Would you prefer to sit in mine?" I waggled my eyebrows.

A growl emanated from her, but before she could say whatever was brewing in that pretty head of hers, the phone rang.

"Eden Falls Police Department," she answered, just as sweet as could be. One day, I *would* get her to speak to me like that.

As she proceeded to handle the call, I let my body take up more than its fair share of space. I leaned into her slightly, bringing our arms back into contact. She was trying to type, and my movements kept causing her to miss her strokes. Finally, she elbowed my arm out of her way.

I grabbed my notepad and flipped to a new page as I glanced around the room only to find Meredith and Blair watching us from over their shoulders. Meredith's expression was one of rabid interest, but Blair's, with her eyes narrowed and her mouth set, seemed calculating.

Having wrapped up the call, Quinn set her phone down and cast a cautious glance toward the two women before returning her attention to me. "Look, Ryan, I don't know what your motive is for this act you're pulling, but I have a job to do, and you will not interfere with it."

My gaze fell to her sassy pink lips before making its way back up to those golden eyes. "If you want me gone, all you have to do is say the word."

"I want you gone."

"Not that word."

She had left the top couple of buttons on her blue polo

undone, and through the small opening, I could see the skin on her chest beginning to mottle.

"What word, then?" she ground out.

I moved my face closer to hers so that she could hear me as I dropped my voice to nearly a whisper. "Tell me you've decided not to follow through on this idiotic endeavor to woo a serial killer, and I'll be off like a prom dress."

She scoffed and rolled her eyes as she looked away. I waited her out, remaining in her personal space, my only movement the rise and fall of my chest with each breath. When she turned back to me a moment later, her eyes were granite.

"In that case, welcome to Dispatch. You're here to stay." Her tone was eerily calm, and I knew that the only thing I had accomplished was getting her to dig her heels in so deep that not even a hurricane could knock her over.

I should have coerced Gabe into talking some sense into her. She at least tended to listen to him. I wasn't sure whether her stubbornness was because she was that committed to the case or just committed to doing the opposite of what I wanted. I should have wholeheartedly encouraged her to play patty-cake with this psycho. Then she no doubt would have adamantly refused.

My molars grated against one another as I attempted to keep from showing how much she was getting under my skin. The woman was like one of those damn mosquito bites that wouldn't stop itching.

I had no idea how long we sat there squaring off, unblinking, but I finally recognized that nothing I said or did was going to get her to back down, because she was not only fighting to be involved in the case, for whatever reason, but she was also fighting for her pride.

If I couldn't keep her safe by keeping her away from the killer, then I would keep her safe by staying close and making sure she knew exactly what lines she couldn't cross.

With a sigh of resignation, I nodded once and eased away from her just a bit. "All right, then we're going to lay down some ground rules." I meant business, and she had better recognize it, because if she stepped one toe out of line, I was yanking her off this case for insubordination, and it would be within my purview to do so.

"You will not provide *any* personal information other than your first name," I started.

She balked. "Of course I wouldn't do that. I'm not stupid."

I ignored her and kept going. "I am going to listen in on the calls. If I give you the signal not to respond to something or to terminate the call, you will do so without hesitation."

She sat back and folded her arms but continued to listen, albeit with a scowl.

"We need you to try to get information about how he chooses his victims and why he's doing this. If you can, get him to talk about past crimes. I'm confident this asshole has killed before. The question is: 'how many times and where'?"

Quinn's body language softened a bit. She swallowed, her eyes dipping for a moment. Then she offered a firm nod. I offered the same in return.

Sensing we had reached an understanding, I turned back to my paperwork, and though I remained at Quinn's desk, I gave her plenty of room to go about her business, so she left it alone.

I had no idea what the next several days or even weeks were going to look like, but I couldn't shake the feeling that we were leading the lamb to the wolf. But with the chief and Quinn dead set on the course of action, my only option was to work smarter and faster than the guy who was torturing and murdering the women of the town so that I could get him off the street before he set his sights on the woman I secretly couldn't bear to lose.

CHAPTER 14

Trevor

My chair squeaked as I leaned it back as far as it would go and rubbed my burning eyes. It had been two days since I'd taken up my post in Dispatch, and I was fucking over it. I was tired of looking at a computer screen for hours on end while being deprived of sunshine and fresh air. All day, I was forced to listen to the calls my partners were getting to respond to, while I was stuck in a windowless room, my ears constantly assaulted by the gossip and griping among the women. Quinn was the exception, and it made me respect her even more to know she put up with that shit day after day.

In fact, she had it even worse than I did. As much as I hated the constant come-ons from Blair and the way she and Meredith tried to get my attention throughout the day, I didn't have to deal with them perpetually taking cheap shots at me the way Quinn did. It was pretty obvious there was a battle raging in Dispatch, with Quinn on one side and everyone else on the other. Though Julia seemed to make an effort where Quinn was concerned, I hadn't failed to notice that every time she did, Blair shot her a glare that shut the girl right up.

I sat forward, bringing my chair level, and peered over Quinn's screens to take stock of how she was doing. After sharing her desk that first day, I had since moved to the empty space across from her. As much as I enjoyed antagonizing her, it had pretty quickly become clear that she was miserable in this environment, and I didn't want to add to what she was already enduring. Though truth be told, I missed having her next to me.

My gaze roamed her face and posture as I tried to read her emotional state. Her head was bent. She was probably looking down at her phone. Her curls had been down when she'd started her shift that morning, but she had since tied them on top of her head in a loose knot that allowed the shorter pieces to fall free. The blue light from the monitors reflected off her creamy skin, which, at the moment, was flushed and held an attractive glow. That was another thing I had discovered about the comms center —it got as stuffy as hell and grew even more suffocating as the day went on.

I had no idea how long I sat there watching Quinn, lost in contemplation about all the little things I was learning about her and all the questions I still wanted answers to. One of those questions was why she didn't stand up for herself when it came to Blair and Meredith. I had been tempted to step in on more than one occasion but held back each time, knowing that Quinn wouldn't appreciate my fighting her battles for her. But it piqued my curiosity as to why she was such a hellcat when it came to putting *me* in my place but just sat there and accepted all the cheap shots from those spiteful biddies.

"You sure look like a man with a lot on your mind." Blair's coquettish tone ripped me from my thoughts and brought my attention around to where I found her leaning back in her chair, eyeing me. Then her gaze slid to Quinn.

Sitting up a little straighter, I refocused on my computer, once again trying to make it clear that I wasn't interested. I didn't play where I worked—too messy. But even if I did, I wouldn't go near Blair, even if she were the last woman on earth and the survival of the human race depended on us procreating. The woman was equal parts venom and drama. Not to mention that every time she came on to me, I seemed to fall even further in Quinn's estimation.

Without taking my eyes off my screen, I grunted in response, hoping it would discourage further comment. It was nearly end of watch anyway, and I needed to get back to work, sifting through the ViCAP database. Over the past couple of days, I had received several returns on my queries that held possible connections to our case. So I had made it my mission to weed out the ones that were an obvious no.

The lack of movement in the investigation had been beyond frustrating. We hadn't learned anything new from Eloise's crime scene or her autopsy report. And knowing that the killer could call at any moment to tell us we had failed to prevent another death was weighing on us all. But I think it weighed most on Quinn. I hadn't been able to get her to go home for more than a shower and a change of clothes since she agreed to be the point of contact for the killer.

The dispatch center had a couple of rooms with a cot in each, meant for those rare times when personnel needed to pull unusually long hours because of emergency situations. Quinn had taken to sleeping in one of the rooms to be available when the killer called, and I hadn't been able to persuade her otherwise.

A *ding* from my computer informed me that a new email was waiting. Hoping that some of the information I had been waiting for had finally arrived, I clicked out of my current screen to check the message. It turned out to be an encrypted email from Eloise's cell phone provider.

Once I had the document open, I did a preliminary scan, and one entry snagged my attention almost immediately. I frowned at the screen.

"What's wrong?" Quinn asked softly. When I glanced up, I found her studying me with concern.

I shook my head and continued staring at the document. "Nothing, per se. Just something interesting."

"About the case?" She didn't even need to clarify which case she was referring to. At the moment, there was only one case anyone was talking about.

I nodded.

"Anything I can help with?"

When I looked at her again, the desire to be useful shone from her eyes with such clarity that there was no way in hell I would say no. Besides, Quinn had a sharp mind. It couldn't hurt to get her thoughts on the matter.

I leaned back again and laced my fingers behind my head. "I just got an email from the second victim's cell phone provider. I'm looking over her call log, and the last call she received was from an unavailable number, and it lasted a little over three minutes."

Quinn nodded. "Okay."

"The first victim's phone log showed the same. A call from an unavailable number, and it lasted five minutes. It was also the last call she had received." I shrugged. "Could be something. Could be nothing. But we can't trace it."

Quinn's brow creased as she looked down at her desk. I could almost hear the wheels turning. A moment later, her eyes rose.

"He referred to this as *his* game," she said. "And both times he's called in here, I haven't been able to get *any* information from his phone." She chewed her lower lip. "Do you think he could be calling the victims to taunt them before killing them?"

Pursing my lips, I mulled over the idea. "It's possible. The ME did say that we're dealing with someone who enjoys the torture almost as much as the kill. Maybe scaring them first is part of how he tortures them."

Pain filled Quinn's eyes, and I considered whether I should have kept my mouth shut. Before I could decide, the phone rang. Quinn answered it, so I went back to looking over the call logs. A heartbeat later, something in her tone got my attention. One look at her, and I knew she had our guy on the line.

Quinn had set me up with a spare handset that was connected to her line. I snatched it up and listened in.

"Are you calling to report another body?" Quinn asked.

A callous snicker followed. "Not yet."

The promise in those two words did not go unnoticed. My eyes were on Quinn as I took in every detail—the way her fingers were tinged white as they gripped her phone, yet her breathing remained even, and her shoulders were relaxed. She was utilizing her training to disengage her body's fight-or-flight response.

"Then why are you calling?" she asked.

"Because you intrigue me, Quinn."

Motherfucker. I knew *this was going to happen.*

My grip also tightened but not because my brain sensed a threat. A different primal instinct was taking hold, and it was all I could do to stay seated and silent.

When the deep voice came again, it was breathy with ecstasy. "I want to give you an opportunity, Quinn. One that I've never given before."

Her eyes shot to mine. I could feel that the tension radiating through my body was also showing on my face. The muscles in my jaw quivered, and my brow furrowed, but I held her gaze, letting her know I was right there with her even though my instincts were spinning like a weather vane in a cyclone. I didn't like where the conversation was headed.

The killer remained silent for a long spell, so Quinn prompted him to continue. "I'm listening."

He made her wait for it, and with each second that passed, Quinn's tension became more palpable. But the stress didn't show on her face until she heard the words he spoke next.

"I'm going to give you the chance to save *lives*. That is, if you're willing to pay my price."

CHAPTER 15

Quinn

ALL RATIONAL THOUGHT vacated my head. I searched Trevor's face, his expression indicating he sensed a trap.

"Well?" the killer prompted.

"You have my attention." I focused on keeping my breaths deep and even, knowing it was crucial not to let on that I was rattled. It wasn't so much that I was engaged in conversation with a sadistic killer but rather that I didn't want to do anything to screw it up. I felt as though fragile lives were nestled in my palm, and one wrong move would douse their flame.

"Here is how we'll proceed," he began. "I'm going to ask you some questions of a personal nature, and you're going to answer them."

My stomach plummeted. *Of a personal nature?*

"In exchange for those answers, I will provide clues to the next woman. If you're clever, you will be able to piece together that information and intercept her before I do."

My hands grew damp, my grip slipping on the hard plastic of the phone in my hand. *How far down this rabbit hole am I willing to go? How personal are these questions going to get?* For years, I had carefully guarded the private details of my life, maintaining a firm boundary between work and everything else. But that lunatic was essentially bribing me to tear down that wall and expose my most vulnerable parts.

Still, without knowing exactly what to ask, how likely is he to uncover what I want to keep hidden?

Trevor, probably sensing my hesitation and knowing what it meant, firmly shook his head at me.

I swallowed hard and looked away. "Why would you have any interest in my personal life?"

"You've got to pay the piper, Quinn. That's how this game works."

It didn't take a genius to know that saying yes to his proposition was stupid. He had a reason for wanting details about me. Still, if I said no, I would always wonder if I could have saved a life —or several—if I had just been willing to sacrifice myself.

I glanced at Trevor again. His eyes were hard, and his mouth was a thin line, a warning that spoke volumes. But did I listen?

"All right. You have a deal."

I didn't know what terrified me more, that I had just promised to give a serial killer whatever information about me he wanted, or that Trevor's face was turning ten shades of red.

A purr from the other end of the line tickled the fine hairs in my ear, causing a shiver to cascade down my spine. "I'm pleased to hear it, Quinn. There is just one more thing you need to know."

I stopped breathing.

"Once I provide the clues, you will have until midnight the following day to solve them. When the clock strikes twelve, another life will end, and our next conversation will be me telling you where to locate the corpse." He let the words hang between us as both a promise and a threat. "I'll be in touch."

Only after he disconnected did I realize all the air had left the room.

Trevor was the only one who had actually heard the call, but my partners clearly knew that something grave had transpired by the way their bodies remained immobile and their eyes darted between me and the man slowly rising from his desk.

Trevor's gaze was fixed on me as he pulled himself to his full and intimidating height. He reached across the short distance that separated our workstations and gripped the phone that I still held to my ear. Slowly, he placed it on the desk.

My eyes were wide as I took in every detail of the rage that he was barely managing to keep a lid on.

"Outside." The word slid through clenched teeth, his tone icy enough to freeze the summer heat.

I nodded and dipped my chin as I rose from my chair. After muttering to my partners that I would be right back, I followed Trevor as he led me down the dark hall toward the entrance of the building. The memory of Blair smirking, knowing what kind of ass chewing I had coming my way, made the march to my fate ten times worse.

Once outside, Trevor waited for the heavy door to shut behind us. As soon as it did, he unleashed every ounce of fury. "What the *fuck* were you thinking?" It seemed like he expected an answer, but as soon as I opened my mouth, he launched another assault. "You're supposed to be smart, Quinn! You're supposed to be a professional! What part of disregarding a direct order fits with either of those?"

He turned away and faced the distant mountains. Other than the grassy knoll on which we stood, a picnic table shaded by a hickory tree was our only witness. I often ate my lunch at that table when the weather was nice.

Suddenly, Trevor turned back around and brought his body within inches of mine, the waves of heat pouring off him impossible to miss. I cranked my head back to look him in the eye as he towered over me.

"I should pull your ass off this case! After that stunt, there's no way the chief is going to continue to have your back on this."

Lava pooled beneath my flesh. I should show some humility. After all, everything he was saying was true, and he *was* the lead on the case. But I just couldn't bring myself to be meek where he was concerned. So after turning my tongue into ground meat with the effort not to make the situation worse, I lost the battle with my self-control. "I did what I do every damn day!"

Trevor pulled back a bit, clearly shocked by my sudden outburst.

"I made a split-second decision, and I'd make the same one all over again, given the chance!" I poked a finger into his chest, punctuating each word that followed. "And I dare you to look me in the eye and say you wouldn't have done the same!"

"That's not the point!" he countered. "What you just agreed to isn't just stupid. It's dangerous. You are a single woman living alone, Quinn. And now you're just going to hand over the details of your life for him to decide how he wants to use that information." He put a finger to his head. "Think about it! This is a small town. It won't take much for him to be able to track you down and—"

"Contrary to what you obviously think, I am *not* an idiot! I know full well the risks involved, but I don't care how much danger I'm in if it means that we might actually be able to save someone!" I crossed my arms and waited for his counterattack. It didn't come.

Instead, his eyes simply darted back and forth between mine. Then he snarled and turned away again, putting several feet of distance between us. I tracked his movements, leaving the ball in his court. When he halted, he dropped his head and put a hand on the back of his neck.

A slight breeze stirred, rustling the leaves of the tree and cooling my skin. As it swirled around me, it took some of my tension with it.

Maybe it had done the same for Trevor, because when he drew near again, there was only worry in his eyes. "Every bone in my body is screaming for me to take you off this case."

It wasn't a threat, more like a confession of torment.

When I didn't respond, he came a few steps closer, placing his hands on his hips and relaxing his posture. "His price is going to be steep, Quinn. He's going to make it hurt."

I nodded, the knot in my stomach returning at the thought of it. "I know. But to me, there really was no choice."

Sighing, he half-heartedly threw up his hands. "I guess that's it, then." He shook his head like he couldn't believe what he was agreeing to.

I offered a small smile. "At least one good thing came from that call."

He raised an eyebrow.

"We're not dealing with victims of opportunity. He picks them ahead of time, and he must stalk them to some degree, if he's able to provide clues to their identities."

Trevor worked his jaw back and forth then inclined his head. "True." He studied me for a moment, his crystalline gaze softening. Then he gently squeezed my arm. "By the book from now on. Yeah?"

I nodded and dropped all obstinacy from my stance. "Yeah."

Since we'd reached an understanding, Trevor returned to Dispatch while I took a moment for myself, allowing the sunshine to soak into my skin. *This is it. The most profound moment of my career, and the stakes couldn't be higher.* But there was no turning back. All I could do was wait for the killer to call again. Then his macabre game of "You Go, I Go" would commence.

CHAPTER 16

Quinn

I DRUMMED my fingers on the desk, staring at my monitor without actually seeing it. It had been nothing but a waiting game since I last spoke to the killer more than forty-eight hours ago, and every minute that passed without a call from him added another knot in my already-twisted intestines.

Movement from the other side of my monitor brought my gaze back into focus. Trevor was shifting in his seat again. He'd been doing that a lot. And he'd been flicking his eyes to me every few seconds, as though I might combust at any moment and take out the entire dispatch center with me.

I *did* feel a bit like a live wire, so perhaps his concern wasn't too far misplaced. The comms center had been fairly active, which was both a blessing and a curse. Staying busy helped to distract me to a certain extent, but at the same time, whenever one of our nonemergency lines rang, my stomach was in my throat again.

The sleepless nights weren't exactly helping either. Ever since I had agreed to the new rules of the game, my mind turned over and over as I thought about what I might be forced to reveal and whether I was even smart enough to figure out his clues. *Will this be worth it? Or will I expose my dark secrets to the light, only to still lose in the end?*

Riiing. My body jerked as my eyes landed on the phone sitting at the edge of my desk. It took a second ring to bring my brain back online. As the third started, I snatched up the receiver and stabbed the answer button on the keypad.

"Eden Falls Police Department."

A gust of breath escaped my lungs when the shrill tone of an irate soccer mom, with whom I was familiar, hit my ears.

"How many times do I need to call about people parking in front of the soccer field when they *don't* have kids playing soccer?"

For once, I was glad to hear the woman's voice. She knew the drill as well as I did, so it took only a few minutes to handle the call, in which I assured her that I would send someone to the soccer fields. When I disconnected, the dizzying wave of relief that displaced the overdose of adrenaline made me realize how desperately I needed to get a grip on myself, or I would never be able to hold it together for the real thing.

Relax, Quinn. This is what you're trained to do.

I had handled a lot of crazy situations in the course of my dispatch career, especially during my time at Las Vegas Metro. Not since the days when I was brand-new to the job had I felt so unnerved. Usually, nothing rattled me. But everything about this situation felt different.

Sensing that I was being watched, I looked up from my workstation and found Trevor staring at me. The corners of his mouth turned up slightly as he offered an encouraging nod. I returned the gesture, appreciating the show of support. When he dipped his head back to his paperwork, I took the opportunity to study him for a moment.

During those first couple of days when he'd taken up post in the comms center, I'd had serious doubts as to whether the place would still be standing after a few days with the two of us trapped together in such a confined space. Between his God's-gift-to-women complex and the way Blair and Meredith threw themselves at him, I had nearly been ready to offer myself up to the killer.

But things had been different between us ever since our blowup outside the dispatch center. He was treating me more like a partner and less like a subordinate, finding little ways to show he had my back. And, though my partners were still acting like a couple of sex-crazed buffoons, Trevor had, surprisingly, been rather aloof toward their advances.

Riiing. Another call on the non-emergency line.

"Eden Falls Police Department."

"Hello, Quinn. Are you ready to pay the piper?"

His voice scraped over me like sandpaper. Suddenly, my senses were on high alert. Trevor must have noticed, because his body had gone taut, and he was reaching for the phone that was connected to mine.

"Yes, I'm ready."

"Good." His voice held a smile. "Let's start with some easy questions. Get to know each other a little better."

"Oh?" I kept my voice light. "Do I get to learn some things about you too?"

He chuckled as though he found my sarcasm rather amusing. "Come now, Quinn. I took you for the type to enjoy a challenge. You wouldn't want to make this too easy, would you?"

"I'm just curious what would lead someone to kill people for sport." I hoped that by carrying on a conversation and showing interest in him, I could build enough rapport that he might be tempted to share a few things. At the very least, it gave me an opportunity to listen for background noise that could provide clues to his location.

"Perhaps someday, I'll tell you. For now, this conversation is going to be about you. And if you follow through on your end of the deal, it will also be about the lovely young lady I am itching to get my hands on."

Bile rose in my throat. I clenched my teeth to force it back down. A woman out there was marked for death, and she had no idea. She was someone's daughter, perhaps a sister or a mother, and her fate would be determined by whether I was smart enough to beat this sadist at his own game. The weight of it all pressed down on me until it was difficult to breathe.

"Let's get on with it, then," I said.

He didn't waste a second. "What is your full name?"

"Quinn Elizabeth Martin."

"Mm-hmm. And where were you born and raised?"

"Henderson, Nevada."

"Ah, from the desert to the mountains. Interesting."

I shifted in my seat, hoping he wouldn't ask why I had made such a drastic move.

After asking for my birthdate and school history, he started to lob some hard-hitting questions.

"Tell me about your home life growing up."

I pictured my mother and savored the warmth that spread through my chest. "It was just my mother and me."

He seemed intrigued by that. "Hmm. Where was your father?"

And just like that, the warmth was gone. "I don't know. He took off one day when I was little, and I haven't heard from him since."

"You never tried to find him?"

"No."

A long pause followed. I was sure he was contemplating all the ways he could use my daddy issues against me—all the ways they made me vulnerable. Well, he could certainly try. It wouldn't be the first time they had gotten me into trouble.

Trevor shifted on the other side of the desk, and my eyes instinctively found him. His face was a mask of disdain that undoubtedly mirrored mine.

In a tone that sizzled with delight, the killer asked, "How old were you when you gave yourself to a man?"

I was all too aware of the way Blair and Meredith, who had swiveled their chairs around to face me, leaned in. What I hadn't realized until just then was that Blair had joined my phone line so that she could hear everything and relay it to the others.

"Twenty." Heat bloomed under my collar. I focused on the screen directly in front of me, trying to make the rest of the room disappear.

"And how many men have you had?" He asked it the way someone would if they were expressing polite interest in a new acquaintance. He was trying to humiliate me, and it was working. I punched the mute button on my keypad, took a deep breath, then unmuted the call.

"Two."

Movement from my left drew my attention back to Blair and Meredith. The two of them were snickering and whispering to each other. Julia, who sat adjacent to them at the fire radio, just looked as though she couldn't bear to witness the situation any longer.

The killer made some trivial comments of interest, but I only half listened, since I was temporarily distracted by Trevor. He still had his receiver pressed to his ear, but he had turned toward Blair and Meredith and said something I couldn't quite hear. Whatever it was, the smirks slid from their faces like dresses falling to the floor.

Trevor turned back to face me and held my gaze. He was steady and calm with a touch of something I couldn't quite decipher.

"I'm curious, Quinn," the killer continued. "With only two lovers, when was the last?"

You son of a bitch. I considered lying. Outside of the things that could easily be fact-checked, like where I'd attended college, how would he know whether I was telling the truth? Still, he had already proven rather cunning and resourceful. *Am I really willing to risk someone's life just to save my pride?*

"Quinn?"

"Five years."

More excited movement came from my left. I refused to look at my partners. I wouldn't give them the satisfaction. Instead, I focused on Trevor. He was the only one who hadn't shown even the slightest reaction to anything I had shared. Everything from his body language to the way he held my gaze told me that he was right there with me, and we were in it together.

The killer gave a long, slow whistle. "Why the dry spell, Quinn?"

Knowing that both the killer and my partners were preying on me, trying to spot vulnerabilities—weaknesses that could bring me to my knees—I squared my shoulders and put iron into my words. I may have felt like crawling into a hole, but I wouldn't give any of those people the satisfaction of knowing that. "I didn't care for the last experience. I haven't been eager to jump into another."

Please don't ask why. Don't ask.

To prevent him from following that line of questioning any further, I grabbed for the reins on the conversation. "I thought this was supposed to be quid pro quo. When do I get details about your next victim?" My tone was demanding.

A laugh devoid of humor followed. "You're correct, Quinn. A deal is a deal." I heard a slight rustling, perhaps a shifting of his phone to the other ear. Other than that, the line had been absolutely silent, save the sound of his voice.

He gave a wistful sigh. "She is quite lovely. I've never had one like her before."

I opened a call-taking screen and began entering notes. *Never had one like her before.* Maybe he was referring to her age or race. Considering the first two victims had had more than twenty years' difference between them, I went with the latter.

"Are you referring to her race?" I bit my lip, half expecting him not to answer.

A pause followed.

"Yes."

Air filled my lungs. A spike of euphoria shot through me. It was a small victory, but it was something.

I typed feverishly. "What else?"

"She spends her time with evil men, all of whom are dead."

My fingers halted, hovering over my keys. *Dead evil men.* She spends her time with them. *A profession?*

"Does she work at the morgue?"

"She has a certain..." He paused, as though considering his words. "*Affinity* for the Peach State."

Georgia.

I added that information to the call. "Is she from Georgia?" I asked, waiting to see if he would answer me that time.

"And let's see... I think one more will suffice."

I glanced at Trevor as I waited for the final clue. His pen hovered over a notepad he'd been scribbling notes on, and his face might as well have been carved from stone, because I couldn't even begin to get a read on how he thought the call was going.

"She has been plagued by falls," the killer said. "The first she had no control over. The second was after she took what some would call the biggest fall of all."

My mind immediately went to work on the clue, but I came up empty. I had to try to get something else from him.

"How old is she?" I hoped something as benign as that would make him feel comfortable throwing me a bone.

He hummed, the sound rich and deep. "Remember, Quinn. You have until midnight tomorrow. Her fate is now in your hands."

Click.

I sat immobilized. My fingers remained over my keyboard, my phone perched on my shoulder with my ear pressed to it, my eyes staring at the flashing cursor on my screen.

Glancing at the clock in the bottom right corner of my monitor, I noted the time. *Thirty hours.* That was all the time I had to save a woman's life. *How the hell am I supposed to do that with the bunch of horseshit he gave me as clues?*

I swallowed the lump in my throat and returned my phone to the desk. After typing the last of the notes in the call log, I slumped back and took a moment to allow the past ten minutes to sink in. It was time for shift change, but I was hardly aware of what was going on as my partners swapped positions with the next squad. All I could think about was the life sitting in my hands and that all those personal details I had shared were going to live in perpetuity on that recording—a recording that was going to be shared with every officer working the case and could very well be played in a court of law if we actually managed to catch the guy.

Not until a strong hand landed on my shoulder and gave it a little squeeze, was I finally pulled from my trance. I looked up and found Trevor standing over me. He squatted so that we were closer to eye level.

"You did great, Quinn."

I shook my head, unable to meet his eyes. I hadn't done great. That asshole had control of the call the entire time. There wasn't one thing he had said that hadn't been entirely intentional. All the wins were his.

Trevor gently shook me. "Come on. We've got work to do." He stood, and only then did I realize he had already packed up all of his stuff.

"Where are we going?" I asked.

"To the station. I'll have some food delivered. We've got a long night ahead of us."

A killer on the loose, a life in the balance, and nothing but thirty hours and *me* standing between the two. *A long night?* That was an understatement.

CHAPTER 17

Trevor

I STARED at the words written in blue ink on the whiteboard, just as I had for several hours. My eyes were bleary, and my brain demanded sleep. But sleep would have to wait. The tiny room Quinn and I had commandeered within the station to use as a sort of command post had long ago grown stuffy and stale. It barely afforded enough room to move about and stretch my legs as it was, but with the small metal table and two matching chairs that normally occupied the center of the room pushed to one side, the only way I could pace was if I wanted to do circles around Quinn. I wasn't good at being caged, and the past week had been nothing but one long incarceration.

Out of the corner of my eye, I caught Quinn stifling a yawn and immediately cussed myself out for my whining. She had to be in even worse shape than I was, considering she'd been sleeping on that damn cot in Dispatch for nearly a week. Not to mention that she had spent half a decade in that windowless viper pit she called work.

Quinn shifted her weight to her right hip, her eyes moving across the string of text over and over. Between the fingers of her left hand, she held an Expo pen, the tip brushing the ends of the curls sticking out of her bun as she rubbed the back of her neck.

A smile tugged at my lips as I watched her, entranced by her every movement. I had always found Quinn impressive, but my respect for her had reached a whole new level in the days we had been working the case together. Thinking back on the argument we'd had outside of Dispatch, I recalled the fire in her eyes and the steel in her backbone as she went toe to toe with me when I threatened to pull her from the case.

It had been a long time since I'd been that angry. But when she squared off with me on that lawn, her creamy skin glowing gold in the light of the setting sun, and vowed that she would gladly sacrifice herself if it meant having the chance to save a stranger, all the fight had gone out of me. It was clear she meant every word. And while I might have felt that she was being reckless, she was also being selfless. I couldn't stay angry with her for being motivated by a heart of gold.

And nine hours ago, she had proven her resolve once again during that damn phone call. Quinn was fiercely private. I had worked with her for five years and hardly knew anything about her personal life. For her to share such intimate details about herself, knowing the whole department would be privy to it and while having to endure the snickers and comments from her partners, showed how far she was willing to go in service to those who got caught in this man's web.

Though I had to admit I'd been squirming worse than Quinn as I listened to her answer one question after another. Part of me had been so drawn in by the desire to learn everything I could about her that I'd had to keep reminding myself to focus on the killer, trying to pick up on anything that could be of use. The other part of me wanted to rip the phone from Quinn's hand and end the call. With the questions he had asked, he had everything he needed to infiltrate her life. And that made me nervous, which was all the more reason we *had* to get a break in the case sooner rather than later.

Quinn sighed and capped the pen then began jabbing it into her thigh over and over. My attention was drawn to the short curls at the nape of her neck. I fought the desire to wrap one around my finger. Then I began tracing her profile with my eyes, from her forehead, down her cute nose, which rose slightly at the end, then to the plush curves of her lips. She had some great lips. I'd always had a hard time keeping my eyes off them. They were full, pouty, and just the right shade of pink.

In my mind, I replayed some of the more intimate details of her call with the killer. *How many men have you had? Two. Two. How is that possible?* Quinn had to have had men beating down her door and lined up around the block. I knew she didn't have a shortage of prospects, given the *many* conversations I'd heard about her in the department locker room. A lot of our single officers and a few of the not-so-single ones had expressed plenty of interest in her. I never contributed to those conversations, but knowing that Quinn would have been mortified to find out she was the subject of them, I'd become a pro at successfully changing the topic. So it left me wondering what had been so bad about her last relationship that she'd chosen celibacy for the past five years.

A small growl from Quinn brought me out of my contemplation. When I looked at her and raised my eyebrows, she asked, "What's the status of the evidence? Have you learned anything new?"

I pressed my lips together and shook my head, returning my eyes to the whiteboard. "Hopefully the lab results will give us something, but it's going to be a while before we get them back."

Quinn's shoulders crumpled a little further. I wished I could tell her I was hot on the killer's trail, and it wouldn't matter whether or not she could solve those clues.

"I did manage to find several cases in other jurisdictions that are a strong match for our guy," I continued. "I've only spoken to a few of those agencies so far. It hasn't yielded much, but if he really was responsible for the homicides in those other places, he's had plenty of time and practice to perfect his methods."

Quinn turned her face to me, fatigue and worry heavy in her eyes.

I squeezed her shoulder. "It's okay, Quinn. We're just going to keep taking this bit by bit. That's all we can do."

She nodded solemnly. The strain didn't vanish from her face, but she straightened her spine and squinted once again at the clues we'd written on the board.

"Okay," she said. "Let's start at the top." She pointed at the first clue. "He hasn't had one like her before, and he confirmed that he was referring to her race."

I nodded but didn't interrupt her thought process.

"Considering the first two victims, we know she's not Caucasian, then." Quinn pinched her bottom lip. "It's unusual for a serial killer to kill across races, though."

"I agree. But if I'm right about those other cases, and he really is responsible for all those murders, he really isn't particular about race."

Quinn pivoted toward me. "So let's assume for now you *are* correct. What races have been represented?"

I flipped through the catalog of images in my head, which were seared in my memory from studying the various case files. "White. Black. Hispanic." I ticked them off on my fingers. "Some were of mixed descent."

Quinn scrunched her mouth to the side, her gaze still focused on the first clue scrawled in her elegant handwriting. "Okay. Well, that's something, I suppose, but it still leaves a lot of options."

I shook my head. "Not really."

Her brow creased. "What do you mean?'

"Eden Falls doesn't exactly have a huge amount of diversity."

"True. So where do we focus our attention?"

"Asian or Native American. I'd put my money on Native American. Their numbers are a lot bigger here. It gives him more women to choose from."

Quinn gave a decisive nod. "Okay, let's write both possibilities down, but we'll keep our focus on Native American for now."

She started to walk in front of me, headed toward the whiteboard with her marker in hand to add that note to the multitude we'd already scribbled over nearly every inch. As she drew even with me, she was so busy looking at the board that she failed to notice where my feet were planted. Her toe caught the edge of my boot, her upper body flying forward as her lower body stopped at the point of contact. Instinctively, I reached out to catch her, wrapping my hands around her waist as I pulled her against me. Quinn's back was now pressed to my chest, my arms locked around her torso like a vise.

She turned her face up to mine in surprise, and I found myself drowning in pools of honey. Her amber eyes were so transfixing that I couldn't look away. Under my hands, her breaths came fast and shallow, her body not yet realizing there was no longer danger. I knew I should put her upright and step away. She wouldn't appreciate having my hands on her. She'd made it clear on several occasions that I was nothing but a man whore in her mind and that hands that had touched so many other women would never touch *her*.

Still, when she didn't pull away or struggle to release herself from my grip, some small part of my brain dared to ask, "What if?" My body responded to the feel of her against me, urging me to move even closer. Quinn's lips parted, and my eyes immediately tracked the movement. I noted her soft breaths still escaping in little puffs. I wanted to know what it would be like to slide my tongue between her teeth—to taste and explore every corner of her mouth, her pillow-soft lips pressed so fiercely to mine that not even a wisp of a breath could travel between us. My hand was still splayed across her abdomen, and I tightened my grip as the fantasy played out.

Quinn stirred against me, gripping my arms, which she had instinctively latched on to during her fall. Her eyes, open just a little wider than normal, searched mine for a moment, too fast to be able to read whatever had flashed behind them. Then she looked away, a sheepish smile touching her lips.

"I'm sorry," she said, tightening her grip on my arms as she attempted to right herself.

Reluctantly, I released my hold on her, moving one hand to her left shoulder and the other to her right side, lending support until she had her balance.

I cleared my throat. "You good?"

She pressed her lips together and offered a firm nod. The red in her cheeks was too adorable to try to ignore. "Thanks for catching me," she mumbled before ducking her head and resuming her mission.

When she was done jotting down her notes, she stepped back, took a big breath, then pointed at the next clue. "She spends her time with evil men, all of whom are dead."

I ran a hand along the back of my head, trying to get my mind back on track and off the feel of Quinn. Puffing my cheeks, I thought for a moment, then I blew out a breath and ran down the list of possibilities that sprang to mind. "Who deals with dead men? Morticians. Coroners." I held my hand out, palm up, like I was serving her the idea on a platter. "Coroners deal with dead suspects and criminals on a regular basis. Maybe that's what he means by evil dead men."

She nodded, still staring at the clue. "And since every deputy at the sheriff's department is also a coroner, there's a possibility that it could be one of their female officers." She scrunched up her face and tipped her head to the side as though the change of angle would make the meaning of the clue clearer. "Do you think he would go after a cop, though?" Her tone indicated that she didn't think so.

I shrugged. "Who knows. This guy is an arrogant asshole. He thinks he's untouchable, and he clearly *hates* law enforcement. He believes we're all beneath him. What better way to degrade a female cop than what he does to these women?"

Quinn nodded again and wrote down the two possibilities I'd offered. "Who else could he be talking about?"

We were both silent for a moment.

Then she added, "Our medical examiner is a man, so it can't be that." After another pause, she whispered the words "dead men" several times. "What about the people who work in grave-yards and cemeteries?" She looked to me for input. "You know, maintenance crews, the people who sell plots... that sort of thing."

I tipped my head from side to side before answering. "It's possible. But he said *evil men*." Some of the people in a cemetery were evil, but a lot of them weren't.

Quinn snorted. "Man *is* evil. I guess it depends on what *he* considers evil."

She had a point.

"He didn't answer me when I mentioned the morgue," she added.

"True, but the same argument about the cemetery applies."

She pursed her lips and exhaled through her nose.

We fell into a long silence. Though we had the door to the room closed, its small glass window showed no signs of activity in the bullpen. All the night-shift officers were probably in the break room, eating and drinking coffee while watching television in an attempt to stay awake and keep from losing their minds to boredom.

I cast my eyes to the large clock on the wall. The movement of the second hand was like a drumbeat in the otherwise silent space. We were only a couple of hours from the zero six hundred shift change, and Quinn and I had already eaten up a chunk of our allotted time to figure out these fucking meaningless clues.

A prickle caressed the nape of my neck. Maybe that was the point. Maybe the clues weren't actually solvable, and they didn't actually contain the identity of the prick's next victim. Maybe it was all a bunch of smoke and mirrors for the benefit of gleaning information about Quinn that would make her wholly vulnerable to whatever plan was housed in that sick and twisted mind of his.

Quinn gasped and turned her head toward me so fast that another spiral fell free from her bun. "What if he's using 'dead' in the metaphorical sense?" Her eyes bounced back and forth between mine.

My brows crested. "Huh?"

"What if the men she spends her time with aren't *actually* dead but are considered 'dead men'"—she put air quotes around those last two words—"because they're living on borrowed time?" Her eyes sparked, and her breaths became shallow again, this time from excitement.

"Where are you going with this, Quinny?"

She let the nickname slide, so she must have really thought she was onto something.

"Inmates," she said simply then started churning her hand in small circles like she was encouraging me to put the pieces of the puzzle together. "Inmates who are condemned to death. A death row corrections officer spends their time with evil men who are, for all intents and purposes, dead men walking."

I contemplated the idea. It was clever. I would never have thought of it. But I wasn't sure it was the right answer. "It's smart, Quinn. But we don't have any prisons nearby that house death row inmates. The nearest one is more than five hours away."

Watching her deflate in response to my words felt like a punch in the gut. I knew Quinn well enough to know that she had put the full weight of the victims' lives on her shoulders the moment she agreed to the exchange with the killer. If we didn't manage to save this woman, Quinn would consider it a personal failure and blame herself. I couldn't let her endure that kind of guilt.

I jerked my chin at the whiteboard. "Let's spend some time on the third clue."

"She has a certain affinity for the Peach State," she read. "I'm thinking she's either from Georgia or maybe went to school there."

I crossed an arm in front of my chest and propped my other elbow on top, using my hand to scrape the whiskers of my beard. "So we have a Native American woman who is a resident of Eden Falls. She has connections to Georgia, and she works in a setting that involves dead men. That's not a bad start, Quinn. Especially considering how small Eden Falls is." I nudged her with my elbow. "We're still in the game here."

She squeezed the back of her neck again before nodding to the board. "What about that last clue?"

This time, I read it. "She has been plagued by falls. The first she had no control over. The second was after she took what some would call the biggest fall of all."

"My first thought," Quinn said, "was that she suffers from a medical condition that makes her fall. Epilepsy or something like that. But only two falls are mentioned, and the second—it sounds like she had some control over that one."

"He could be referring to some kind of risk," I said.

"Such as?"

I shrugged. "I don't know. But the way he uses 'fall,' it could be a synonym for a failure."

Quinn's eyebrows shot up, and she slowly twisted to look at me.

One corner of my mouth tugged upward. "What? You didn't really think I was just a dumb jock, did you?"

Her rueful smile spread slowly as she turned back to the board. "I don't spend my time thinking about you. Period."

The sass in her tone made my blood pulse faster. The only thing I liked better than sparring with Quinn was when she sparred back. And I was glad that, despite the crushing pressure she was under, she wasn't letting it extinguish her fire.

"I think you're right, though," she said.

"'Bout damn time those words came out of your mouth."

"Never had a reason to say them until now."

I chuckled, loving the way her pert nose tipped a little farther north as she said it.

"So what are we thinking?" she asked. "A job loss, maybe? Or..."

After several heartbeats had passed, I slanted my eyes toward her. "Or what?"

"Love?"

I wrinkled my nose. "Love?"

She snickered. "Yes. Some would call falling in love the biggest fall of all."

I read the clue again. *She has been plagued by falls...* "So she falls in love a lot?"

Quinn shook her head, her loose curls bouncing. "I don't know," she said quietly. Then she growled again, her frustration echoing off the walls of our tiny space.

Without thinking, I placed my hand on the small of her back and felt the heat from her body transferring to my palm. "We have a pretty good start with the first three clues. Let's get to work on those and see how far it gets us."

She looked up at me over her shoulder. "How do you propose we do that?"

I glanced at the clock on the wall again. "We have a few hours before business hours start. We can make some calls before then, but we're only going to be talking to skeleton crews. So let's get to work combing through our databases and social media. We try to find a woman at the intersection of where the answers to our first three clues meet. Then once eight o'clock rolls around, we'll start calling all businesses within a hundred-mile radius that deal with dead men. Hospitals. Morgues. Cemeteries. All of it. We just keep going until we find someone who matches the clues."

Quinn's golden eyes held mine. "Or until the clock runs out."

I nodded. One way or another, it would be over by midnight. The clues might very well have been a wild goose chase—something meant to distract us. But until we had evidence of that, for both our sakes, we had to do everything in our power to get to his next victim before he did.

CHAPTER 18

Trevor

Hours later, we still didn't have an identity for our victim, and midnight was fast approaching. Knowing we wouldn't hear from the killer, Quinn spent the entire day cooped up in our tiny command post, combing through every major social media platform while simultaneously making call after call in search of our woman.

I'd popped in and out to check on her and help make calls in between working with Gabe to coordinate and mobilize the field units for the hunt, which included tying in with the police at a nearby reservation in hopes that they would know who the clues pointed to. So far, it had been one fucking dead end after another.

"She's gonna take this hard," Gabe said quietly.

Sitting on the edge of my desk, I faced the room where Quinn was bent over the small metal table, flipping through her endless pages of notes. At Gabe's words, I glanced to where he was perched on the short end of his desk, facing me. His arms and ankles were crossed in a way that indicated ease, but I knew from years of being a friend, a brother, and a partner that he was anything but relaxed at the moment.

I followed the direction of his gaze, and it led me back to Quinn. I clamped my hand on the back of my neck and squeezed as I tried to ease some of the tension that had given me one hell of a fucking headache for the past six hours. "Yeah, I know." I didn't like the resignation in my voice. Glancing at my watch, I exhaled slowly at the numbers staring back at me. It was a quarter to midnight.

Gabe unfurled himself from the desk and arched his back as he reached his arms above his head. His voice tight from the stretch, he asked, "You want me to stick around for a bit longer?"

What he was really asking was "Do you want me to stay until you break the news to Quinn?"

My eyes found her again. Her movements were frantic as she bounced between her laptop and her notes. We'd finished calling everyone we could think to call long ago, at which point she had attacked and exhausted every database and online resource she could think of, desperately trying to find that needle in a haystack.

I shook my head. "No. You go on home to Alex."

"You sure?"

"Yeah. We need you sharp tomorrow. You're going to have a body to process."

Gabe glanced at Quinn one more time then pressed his mouth into a hard line and slapped me on the shoulder before heading out.

I took a deep breath and pushed off from the desk, making the long walk to the small room. Quinn didn't even look up when I entered. After pulling out the only remaining chair, I took a seat beside her.

"Quinn."

"Hmm." Her eyes remained on her screen.

"Quinn, it's over."

She shook her head with the defiance of a small child. "No, it's not. We still have a few minutes."

With my thumb and forefinger, I rubbed my eyes. I really hated having to constantly be the one to disappoint her. "Quinn, it's too late. He already has her."

She started to protest, but I cut her off, needing her to stop tormenting herself and understand what I was saying. "He takes his time with them. That means he has already had her for a while now. He's just waiting for the clock to strike twelve to put her out of her misery."

Quinn froze. Her fingers were light on her keyboard, her eyes still focused on the screen. But her shoulders no longer moved with her breath. Her eyelashes no longer fluttered.

I waited.

Seconds felt like minutes. Then her hands went to her face. They barely made it in time to cover the first of her tears. Gentle sobs broke through the barrier meant to hide what she considered weakness.

I could have sworn I heard my heart crack, and it reverberated in that hole of a room, drowning out the sound of that damned clock and ricocheting off every bone in my body with no place to escape. It was only the second time in my life a crack like that had ripped through me.

Leaning forward, I brought myself closer to her and put a hand on her arm. She shook me off, her sobs growing stronger. I hesitated for a moment before wrapping my arms around her. Her body stiffened for a heartbeat, then she melted into me. Though her hands still covered her face, she leaned her shoulder into my chest and shook with the force of her pain. And I simply held her, whispering words that I was sure she couldn't even hear and frankly didn't need to. I just wanted her to know I was there.

After a long while, her tears stopped flowing, and her breathing became normal. She slowly eased herself away from me, straightening in her chair and wiping away the last of the evidence that her implacable mask of control had fallen.

There wasn't much left to say. She wouldn't want me acknowledging that she had shown emotion, so I did what men were good at and focused on the practicalities. I brushed her elbow with the tips of my fingers. "Come on, Quinn. I'll take you home."

She sniffled. "My car—"

"Leave it here. You haven't slept for almost two days, and you've been through hell. I don't want you driving. I'll pick you up at eight o'clock and bring you back to work."

She nodded then climbed to her feet and walked past me toward the exit, keeping her eyes to the floor. I was grateful the station was dark and empty as we walked through it. She would have been humiliated if anyone had witnessed her tear-stained face.

And I was glad she had let the stress, anger, and hurt flow out of her with every saline drop that had rolled down her precious cheeks, but it worried me too. In all the years I had known Quinn, I'd only ever witnessed two emotions—totally calm and completely pissed off. And the latter was usually directed at me.

As I noted her sluggish steps and sagging shoulders, I prayed that the case—the killer—wouldn't create a fracture in her that not even time could heal.

* * *

WITH MY ELBOWS braced on the workstation, one hand pressing my cell phone to my ear, I used the other to flick the end of my pen against the desk at a tempo that Dave Grohl couldn't have matched.

"Detective Alvarez."

I stopped tapping and sat up straight. "Detective Alvarez, this is Officer Trevor Ryan. I'm with the Eden Falls Police Department. I have some questions regarding a case I'm working on."

Alvarez sounded like he was in his late thirties to early forties. Despite his last name, I could only detect a hint of an accent.

"Eden Falls, huh? Where might that be?"

"Northwestern Montana."

He hummed. "Never been up to Montana. Too cold."

I grinned. Since his number had a San Diego area code, I wasn't surprised to hear that he didn't particularly care for a colder climate.

"Maybe, but I'd argue we have better fishing."

He laughed. "All right. I'll give you that one. So what can I do for you, Officer?"

I leaned back, spreading my legs wide. "We've got a situation on our hands, and I'm hoping you can offer some insight." I glanced at Quinn. She was mostly concealed by her monitors because I was sitting so low in my chair, but I could see her eyes. She wasn't paying any attention to me, but I lowered my voice anyway. "I came across a case you worked on about fourteen years ago involving a series of women who were tortured and murdered."

Alvarez listened quietly as I relayed the similarities between our two cases. When I finished, I waited for him to chime in and confirm that I was right. But the silence stretched on for several seconds. Finally, he whispered, "Son of a whore."

My eyebrows popped up. "Does that mean you remember the case?"

"Yeah, I sure as fuck remember the case. It was my first one as a detective, and it's been a stick up my ass ever since."

Who the hell would put a rookie detective on a case like that?

He answered my silent question with his next breath. "Since I was new, they partnered me with a salty old dog who had a repu-tation for almost always getting his man." Alvarez must have been sitting at his desk. Phones ringing and a multitude of radios squawking filled the background. "We worked that case like dogs, night and day, for a month. Then"—he snapped his fingers—"the guy vanished. No more bodies. No more calls."

The way he told the story was matter-of-fact, but it didn't take a trained ear to hear the contempt beneath his words. "Every time I had to go to another family and tell them what had happened to their daughter or mother or wife, all I could think of was getting my hands on that guy and making sure he got as good as he gave."

Something stirred beneath my skin in response to his words.

"Every year," he continued, "I pull out that case file and comb through it again, hoping I'll find something I missed the first few hundred times."

I had a feeling I would find myself buried under the same crippling weight of regret if I failed to stop the killer—to get Quinn clear of all of it and bring justice and closure to the victims and their families.

A call rang into the dispatch center. My eyes cut to Quinn again. Once she was busy focusing on the call, and I knew it wasn't our killer, I returned my attention to Alvarez. "We have three victims so far. Well..." I spun my chair until I faced the open part of the room then got up and walked into a corner to get as far away from the ladies as I could while still keeping an eye on Quinn. "Technically, we have two bodies, but we know a third is coming."

"How do you mean?"

I explained the situation with Quinn. "Did he play any games like that with any of your dispatchers or officers?"

"No. He just called in to tell us where we could locate the bodies... after making it clear that we were too stupid to catch him, that is."

That definitely sounded like our guy.

"Could be that his MO has changed a bit over time, though. Maybe the thrill of it all was wearing off, and he needed to do something to make it more exciting again."

I nodded and gripped the back of my neck. "Yeah, I've considered that, but I tracked down six other departments that I'm confident have dealt with this shithead, and I've talked to them all. He's never interacted like this before."

The killer *had* told Quinn that the offer was a first of its kind, but I'd been hoping that was bullshit and he had told others the same just to get them to agree to his terms.

"Hmm." Alvarez was silent for a long beat. Then he asked, "When you talked to these other departments, did you learn anything useful?"

I expelled a deep sigh. "Not really. But I did notice a pattern."

I glanced at Quinn again. She had finished with her call and once again had her eyes down. I was accustomed to her keeping to herself when she was in Dispatch, but all day, it had felt as though a shadow had swallowed every bit of her. She was dreading the call we all knew was coming.

"What pattern?" Alvarez prompted.

"Seven victims." I started to pace in a small circle, needing to burn off some of my pent-up energy. "He kills seven women, then he disappears. And it's entirely possible I haven't tracked down every case related to him, but of the ones I've found, it appears he has a decent cooling-off period."

"How long?"

"Roughly two years, give or take."

Alvarez let out a long, high-pitched whistle. "That's a long cooling-off period."

"Yeah, and likely part of the reason he hasn't been caught yet."

Alvarez agreed then said, "If there's anything else I can do to help, just say the word." He took a heavy breath. "Out of all of the cases I've handled at this point, this one bothers me the most. I'll go to my grave satisfied if I can finally give those families some closure and be a part of nailing his ass to the wall."

"Will do. Your case was the oldest I've found so far. I was hoping you were going to tell me he made some pretty big rookie mistakes."

His tone once again laced with regret, he replied, "I wish I could, man. It was scary how clean this guy was. Never a print. Never any DNA other than what belonged to the victim. It was like the fucker was the devil incarnate. Just vanished into smoke, never leaving a trace."

I nodded, pressing my lips together so hard that they tingled. "Yeah, that's pretty much been the story with every other department."

The dispatch line rang again. Out of habit, my eyes went to Quinn. I looked away then did a double take. Her body had gone completely rigid, her knuckles white where they hugged the phone.

Moving quickly back to my desk, I said, "I've got to go. Thanks for your help. I'll let you know if we get a break in the case."

Being a cop, he understood the need to disconnect quickly and didn't waste any time. As soon as I was back at the desk, I threw my cell down and snatched up the receiver connected to Quinn's line.

A familiar voice, deep and breathy, snaked through the phone. "I have to say, Quinn, I am really enjoying playing this game with you."

Quinn didn't respond.

"If you were honest with yourself, you would admit you've never felt more alive."

A muscle twitched in Quinn's jaw. When she spoke, her voice was achingly quiet. "What did you do with her?"

The killer sighed as though he needed a moment to recall the answer to her question. "Pre- or postmortem?"

Quinn's eyes narrowed to slits.

"So quiet today, Quinn. That's not much fun."

"You said that if I failed"—her throat bobbed—"you would tell me where you left the body." Quinn's face was aglow from the light of her screen, but her eyes were flat, as if her pupils were swallowing the light, refusing to let those honey orbs shine.

All jest left the killer's voice, supplanted by the hatred and revulsion that undoubtedly drove him. "Her carcass is in a receptacle behind that redneck tavern that barely passes for a legitimate establishment. Your officers are no doubt familiar with it."

Rustlers.

Quinn began typing. A moment later, a chime alerted Julia, who was working the main law channel, that Quinn had sent the call notes through. Julia's voice echoed in my head as I heard her dispatch it, both in person and through my earpiece. I registered

Gabe advising he was en route, then my full attention returned to Quinn.

The killer's diatribe continued, his tone taunting. "I do hope you'll be more talkative the next time we speak, Quinn. You'll have to if you really want the chance to save the next one."

"Why are you doing this?" Quinn asked.

"Have you ever heard the story of the scorpion and the frog?"

A pause followed. "Yes."

"Then you know why I'm doing this."

The line went dead. Quinn lowered her phone to the desk then put her fingers to her temples and made small circles.

I set my phone down as well and pulled my heavy uniform jacket from the back of my chair. It was late in the day, and it had been raining nonstop with gusting winds—perfect conditions for our killer and hell for our crime scene. I needed to get to Rustlers fast to help Gabe preserve the scene before the elements and untrained officers destroyed our evidence.

But one look at Quinn and the defeat carved into her body, and I hesitated. "What was the scorpion thing all about?" I asked her.

She dropped her arms to her desk and looked up at me with weary eyes. "It means that torturing and killing these women is just who he is." She slumped back, scanning each of her monitors.

I walked around the desks and squatted next to her. She didn't look at me.

"You did everything you could for this woman, Quinn. *Everything.*"

Refusing to meet my eyes, she shook her head. The movement caused her ponytail to swish back and forth.

"None of this is your fault." I put my hand on the back of her neck and gave it a little squeeze, her gathered curls tickling the back of my hand. "If you let yourself believe you failed her, he wins."

Finally, she turned her face to me, her eyes searching mine as though she was trying to decide if I was telling her the truth.

"I have to get to the crime scene before it gets trampled. Go straight home after work, and I'll check on you once I wrap things up. Okay?"

She nodded, the movement completely devoid of energy.

I gave her neck one more reassuring squeeze before I stood and stalked out of Dispatch. The heavy door slammed against the brick wall as I threw it open. Wind and rain slashed at my face as I jogged to my cruiser with one thing on my mind.

The killer was right in that I was very familiar with our redneck tavern, enough to know exactly where every surveillance camera was located. Adrenaline surged through me as I catapulted into my car and peeled out of the parking lot.

We might have finally gotten the break we'd been waiting for.

CHAPTER 19

Trevor

MY EYES TRACKED the vehicle for the dozenth time. A dark-colored sedan with tinted windows. I glanced at the time stamp as the car entered the parking lot, then my eyes shot to the license plate, which was a blur of white and black, but the edges had enough sharpness that I was hopeful we could get something from it after the tech guys had a chance to work their magic.

The vehicle disappeared from the footage. I clocked the time stamp again, watching the seconds slip by in utter silence. There was no other movement during the sixty seconds the car was out of the frame, with the exception of trash blowing across the parking lot and the swaying and thrashing of the trees that bordered the property.

Then the suspect's vehicle reemerged, accelerated out of the lot, and turned west on Fir.

"Eighty-three seconds," I said to Gabe, "from the time the vehicle entered the lot to the time it exited."

"He knew exactly where he was going." Gabe stood with his feet apart and his arms crossed, his brow furrowed as he continued to watch the surveillance loop.

Scott, the bar manager-slash-bartender at Rustlers, sat at the computer, silent and working the controls to the surveillance system per our instructions.

"Let's get it over to the geek squad and see what they can do with that plate," I said. "I also want to send the footage to the FBI field office in Billings. See if they can tell us the make, model, and year. Once we have that, we can get a BOLO out on the vehicle and get every law enforcement officer in the state looking for this guy."

I watched the replay one more time. The car windows were too dark to make out any details of the driver, and I would bet everything I had that he'd known there weren't cameras out back, where he tossed the body into the dumpster. But the surveillance footage was at least *something*.

After thanking Scott for his cooperation, Gabe and I headed outside, where the storm was still raging. Our uniforms were soaked through, and beads of water gathered on Gabe's buzz cut. Our team had worked feverishly to preserve as much evidence as possible, and to that end, we had managed to wrap the body quickly to transport it to the ME's office, where we could process it without fear of the elements ripping something of value away.

With the exception of a few stragglers, Gabe and I were the last on scene. I scanned the area surrounding our favorite hang-out. "This was a smart choice. Outskirts of town. No other buildings near enough to create a risk of any other surveillance cameras picking him up, especially with his direction of travel."

Gabe grunted, his eyes painting broad strokes across the parking lot and nearby woods. The killer had chosen a route to and from Rustlers that allowed him to skirt the edges of town. He clearly knew his way around.

Water streaming down his face, Gabe jerked his chin toward our cruisers. "Let's get out of here."

We walked shoulder to shoulder, the wind whistling in my ears loudly enough that Gabe had to shout for me to hear him.

"We still on for tonight?"

We had plans to meet up with Alex and Gabe's sister, Liz, at Rustlers, something we did on the regular that allowed the girls to sit and enjoy drinks and conversation while Gabe and I got in a few rounds of pool.

I nodded. "Yeah, I could use the distraction. But I wouldn't mention any of this"—I hooked my thumb toward the bar behind us—"to Liz and Alex."

Gabe snorted. "No fucking way. Though they might be pissed we didn't say anything when the gossip mill reaches them tomorrow."

I grinned and shrugged. "That's tomorrow's problem."

He barked out a laugh. "You mean that's *my* problem, because you're not going to be anywhere near them tomorrow."

"Hey, don't hate the player. Hate the game."

A lopsided grin curved up his face as he shook his head and looked away.

We made it to our cars, and I called out to him over the roof of mine. "I'm going to be a little late. I have something I need to take care of first."

He gave me a two-fingered salute then dipped into his vehicle.

An hour later, I had traded my uniform for a pair of jeans and a black T-shirt and my cruiser for my truck and was pulling into Quinn's driveway.

Her house was built in an L-shape, with the garage facing the driveway and the main body of the house curving around to the right. The place was cute, perfect for a young, single woman. The front porch was small but welcoming, with flower baskets hanging on either side of the steps leading to the front door, where large windows, glowing yellow, stretched out on either side. The light-gray paint with white trim made the house look bright despite the dismal weather.

I took the shallow porch steps two at a time and rapped on her door, frowning as I noted the narrow glass panes side by side, which provided a decent view of the entryway beyond. Movement through the glass informed me that Quinn would be answering the door in three, two, one...

"You should get a door that doesn't allow people to see inside your house" was my way of greeting her.

She frowned and rolled her eyes before turning away, leaving the door open for me to let myself in. Once inside, I did a quick scan, taking in the decor and inhaling the scent of Quinn—honeysuckle and sunshine.

I'd never actually been in her house. It was everything I expected—clean and organized, with enough small touches to make it feel homey, but no one could ever accuse her of having clutter.

She walked into the living room then folded her arms as she spun to face me. "I figured it out." Her expression was flat.

I let my gaze slip down her body, taking in her bare feet, black leggings, and oversize blue sweater. "You figured what out?"

"The clues."

Understanding dawned. Gabe and I along with the rest of the officers on scene had been able to ID the victim as Cheyenne Dennington right away, and we had added her information to the call notes. Quinn must have put her research skills to work to figure out where we had gone wrong.

She held up her hands and shook her long sleeves out of the way as she ticked the clues off on her fingers. "Obviously, we were right about her race. But that clue about her spending time with evil men who are dead?"

I lifted my eyebrows, not wanting to steal her thunder and need to confess how we'd failed—or in her mind, how *she* had failed.

"She was a bank teller! Dead men. Dead presidents!" Quinn threw her arms wide. "Money is the root of all evil."

I nodded to show that I understood but remained silent, sensing she needed to blow off steam by running down the details with me.

Quinn resumed the count on her fingers. "That whole thing about having an affinity for the Peach State? She lived on Georgia Lane!"

She began to pace between her coffee table and the fireplace. "And that whole thing about being plagued by falls and the first one being out of her control, but the second one was after she took the biggest fall of all?" Quinn stopped pacing and faced me, throwing her hands up in the air again. "She grew up in Great *Falls*! As in she didn't have any control over where she was born. But then she moved to Eden *Falls* after she *fell* in love."

I took a few steps toward her. My tone encouraging, I said, "So you were close on that one. It *did* refer to falling in love."

Quinn growled and waved me off. "I wasn't close. Not even remotely. I was never going to find her with the information I was chasing."

"Quinn—"

"Don't." She started pacing again.

Sighing, I rubbed the back of my neck, keeping my eyes on the trail she was carving into her plush white carpet.

I needed to get her out of there. If I didn't, she was going to drive herself crazy, ruminating all night. I tipped my head in the direction I assumed her bedroom was located. "Go get changed. I'm taking you out."

Her steps halted, and she looked at me like I had lost my mind. "I'm not going anywhere with you."

My headache was returning. I sighed and closed the distance between us until all six feet, three inches of me was towering over her five-seven frame. "You *are* going somewhere with me, and that's a direct order."

Quinn scrunched up her face, her brows drawing together. "I'm off duty, and this has nothing to do with the case, so I'll let you guess what you can do with your orders."

I fought the smile that was trying to work its way onto my face.

"Besides," she added, "I'm going back to the station."

My eyebrows jumped to my hairline. "Excuse me?'

Quinn threw me a look that silently asked if she really had to explain it to me. "He might call with the clues to the next victim. I have to be there."

Widening my stance, I folded my arms and squared off with her. "First of all, he's not going to call tonight."

"How do *you* know?"

"I know. This asshole wants to savor the experience. He's not going to rush things along. Second, my taking you out tonight is a requirement of you remaining on this case."

She parked her fists on her hips. "You can't do that."

"Yes, I can. You're unraveling, Quinn. This guy is getting into your head, and I'm going to help you learn how to keep him out. If you can't demonstrate to me that you can take care of yourself while you're on this case, then you won't be on it much longer."

My tone left no room for argument. Quinn pressed her lips together and lifted her chin as she tried to decide whether I was bluffing. When nothing in my stone-cold expression changed even slightly, she growled and stomped off down the hall, mumbling. I decided I was glad I didn't know what she was saying.

In less than five minutes, she reappeared in the entryway, her weight shifted to one hip and arms crossed as she tapped her foot. When I reached her, I extended my arm toward the door and offered a slight bow. "After you."

Her response was a snarl. I let loose a grin only once her back was to me.

"Where are we going?" Quinn asked in a sullen tone as I opened the door to my Chevy Silverado for her.

"Rustlers."

She paused with one foot on the sideboard and one still on the driveway then turned her wide eyes to me. "You can't be serious."

"I am. And we're meeting Gabe, Alex, and his sister, Liz,

there, so—" My hand made circles to indicate that I wanted to hurry things along.

Apparently realizing that arguing was pointless, she finally climbed into the truck. I had no idea how the night was going to go, but with the mood Quinn was in, it sure as hell wouldn't be dull.

CHAPTER 20

TREVOR DEFTLY MANEUVERED his truck through my neighborhood, driving with the ease and precision of someone who had been well trained to operate a vehicle at breakneck speeds without killing civilians and creating a lawsuit for his department. And if the driving didn't tag him as a cop, the way his sharp eyes were always moving, always scanning definitely gave him away.

As he pulled out of my neighborhood and onto Aspen, I slid down in my seat and did my own reconnaissance to see who was around. The streets were empty, most likely due to the inclement weather. Still, going out wasn't worth the risk. "You know, I really don't think it's a good idea that we're seen together outside of work."

When Trevor didn't respond, I turned to look at him. The son of a bitch was *smirking*.

I gave him the scowl that was never far from the surface of my face when he was around. "What?"

"You don't need to worry about people thinking we're on a date. Like I said, it's a group thing."

I sighed through my nose, still irritated that he had dragged me from my house and forbade my return to Dispatch. "How can you simply go to the bar and have a good time after you literally just examined the brutalized body of someone you know there?"

At least, I assumed he knew her, because there were only two banks in Eden Falls, and everyone at the department used the same one—the one where Cheyenne Dennington had worked. A dark, heavy feeling descended on me when I allowed myself to realize I would never see her in that bank again. Every time I walked in there, I would see her face in my mind—always smiling and friendly. The finality of a life snuffed out like a candle's flame was too much to think about. It was easier to pick a fight with Trevor than to face the ugly battle raging inside me.

Trevor shifted in his seat so that his body angled toward me just a bit, his left hand guiding the steering wheel while his opposite elbow took up residence on the console between us. "Our town may be small, but you know as well as I do that a lot of messed-up shit happens here. I've seen a lot that I wish I hadn't, and *because* the town is so small, I almost always know the people involved, at least to some degree."

He shrugged as he zeroed in on a lone figure strolling down the sidewalk in the opposite direction with a hood covering their face. Apparently, the person passed whatever cop test Trevor had just used to size them up, because he dismissed them and turned that assessing gaze on me. "I learned a long time ago that it's important to have a way to wind down and put the details of the day in the rearview mirror."

My house wasn't far from Rustlers, so though we had left only minutes ago, we were already pulling into the gravel parking lot of the bar. Trevor kept his monologue of sage advice rolling while he looked for a spot he liked. "Gabe actually taught me that."

"Why? Were you having issues dealing with the job?" I was being snarky. Trevor never seemed to take anything seriously enough to have any sleepless nights. But his expression turned grave in a blink, and I felt a little pang of guilt for my attitude.

"No, not me," he said. "Gabe."

I whipped my head around, raising my eyebrows.

Trevor pulled his lips in and nodded. "Yeah, it was after he left the Marines and came home. He was having a hard time dealing with all the shit he'd seen and done when he was deployed. He had to figure out a way to live with it. So..." Trevor shrugged. "Once we finished the academy and started working the street, we met up after our shifts to hit the gym, then we came here." He nodded toward the bar. "We shot some pool. Had a few laughs. Anything to forget the shittiness of the world for a bit and just have some fun and distraction."

Having settled on a parking space, Trevor backed into it, but he didn't kill the engine right away. Instead, he took off his seat belt and sat back like he was inclined to stay there for a while. "Of course," he continued, "now that Gabe has Alex, we don't shoot pool together as often as we used to, but I still keep up the ritual of unwinding after work. Even if I don't have my wingman." He flashed a mischievous grin.

I rolled my eyes. "So that's the reason for all the women?" I shimmied my shoulders from side to side. "Come to Rustlers. Shoot a few rounds of pool. Take someone home who can help you forget the day?" My judgment slithered from every word, but I really didn't care. It wasn't like Trevor Ryan was going to give a damn what I thought of his nocturnal activities.

Although when I turned to him for confirmation, a shadow passed over his eyes, but it was gone so fast that I questioned whether I had really seen it.

Before I could think about it too much, that charming smile was back in place, and he said, "Hey, a man's got needs." Then he jerked his head toward the bar. "Come on. Time to teach you how to put the day in the rearview."

When we walked into Rustlers, I was shocked to find that it was packed. I guess the parking lot should have been an indication, but I was so busy being annoyed at Trevor that I hadn't really registered all the vehicles. Trevor waved to someone I couldn't see over the crowd, and as if it was the most natural thing in the world, he reached back, took my hand, and guided me through the throng of bodies that pressed in on us. People parted like the Red Sea as his towering frame approached.

When we reached a high-top table that sat alongside the raised platform where the pool tables were sectioned off, Trevor pulled me forward and ushered me into a tall chair. On the other side of the table, two women, equally beautiful in completely different ways, beamed at me.

Trevor placed his hand on the back of my chair, a bolt of electricity zinging through me when my shoulder brushed against his fingers.

"Quinn," he said, extending a hand toward the first woman, who sat to the left. "This is Alex, Gabe's fiancée and handler."

I knew who Alex was from my involvement with her case nearly a year ago. There had been no shortage of photos and camera footage capturing the mahogany-haired beauty during what I now knew to be one of the worst periods of her life. But I had never actually met her in person, and the warmth radiating from her dazzling smile and jade-green eyes was unexpected for someone who came from fame and fortune.

Alex extended a hand across the small round table. "Hi, Quinn. It is such a pleasure to meet you."

I shook her hand and offered a polite nod in return.

"And this," Trevor said with a challenge in his voice, "is Liz. The ballbuster and all-around pain in the ass of the McNeil clan."

Liz shot daggers at Trevor with her violet eyes, a smirk playing at the corners of her lips. Then she tilted her nose up and completely dismissed him as she turned to me. "Not to worry, Quinn. You're in far better company now."

Trevor chuckled and shook his head as he did a visual sweep of the room.

Liz only allowed him a moment to do so before she started shooing him away. "All right, all right. We've got her. You can go join the other Neanderthals now."

Trevor threw his hands up in a gesture of surrender before

turning to me and saying under his breath, "She's tiny but mighty."

The complete affection and adoration in his voice for the two women was unexpected, to say the least. As Liz flagged down a waitress to come take my order, Trevor leaned in a little closer until his breath tickled my ear. "I'm going to play a few rounds of pool. If you need anything, holler. And remember"—he nudged me with his shoulder—"rearview mirror." And with a cocky grin, he was gone.

Once Alex and Liz were convinced I had everything I needed, we fell into what I was surprised to find was easy conversation. Our heads were bowed toward the center of the table so that we could hear one another over the excited chatter of the room and the jukebox blaring on the far wall. The two women, who already seemed like sisters even though it wasn't official yet, discussed the masquerade ball that Liz was planning as part of her duties as the event coordinator for the city council.

"Gabe already threatened to tie me to the farthest fence post on the property and leave me for the bears if I added any more duties to that list I gave you." Liz flung her hand nonchalantly in the direction of her brother and the pool tables.

Alex laughed, the sound a rich melody. "I *am* under a tight deadline at the moment, but I can handle one or two more things. Just don't tell him."

The look of both glee and mischief dancing in Liz's eyes caused a laugh to bubble up from my chest. I really hadn't expected to have a good time, but I had to admit the two ladies made it difficult to maintain a sour mood, and the differences in their personalities created the perfect balance.

Alex exuded grace and poise. Her tall, slender frame was the envy of all women, but she wore her beauty casually, as though she was completely unaware of it. She was the quieter of the two, obviously preferring to do more of the listening than the talking, but when she did speak, her words were thoughtful and filled with compassion.

Liz, on the other hand, was a live wire. Every bit of her five-foot-four-inch frame was packed with sass and gasoline, and her mouth was the flame. She was direct, delivering the cold, hard truth without pulling any punches, but she somehow managed to do it while making you smile and love her even more. And her violet eyes, set against the dark brown of her pixie cut, held a wildness that a herd of stampeding horses couldn't rival.

"So, Quinn"—Liz pinned me with her gaze—"Trevor tells us some wacko is making your life hell."

Alex's eyes rounded, her mouth parting with surprise. Under her breath, she admonished Liz, who waved it off and kept her expectant eyes on me.

I squirmed in my chair, trying to decide how to respond. "Uh, yes. You could say that."

Liz nodded knowingly. "Unfortunately, the majority of the Y chromosomes seem to have that effect."

I was taking a sip of my drink when she made the remark, and the combination of her words and dry tone made the liquid shoot into my nose. My eyes instantly filled with water as a choking fit took hold.

Liz promptly jumped down from her chair and gave me several good whacks on the back until the coughing fit subsided.

"Better?" she asked, raising her eyebrows.

"Better. Thank you," I said, my voice hoarse.

She nodded and reclaimed her seat.

Alex, apparently picking up on something in Liz's words, cast sorrowful eyes toward her friend. "I take it things are still rough with Mark?"

Liz swallowed and nodded, letting her gaze dance over the crowd. "He's just gone a lot. And when he *is* here, he's always snapping at the kids and me. If it were just me, I could tolerate that better, but I see the damage in Connor's and Lily's eyes each time he does it with them." She lifted a shoulder and shook her head. "That, and I feel like I don't even know him anymore."

Alex furrowed her brow. "What do you mean?"

"I don't know." Liz waved a hand to indicate it was probably nothing. "I just feel like he's keeping secrets. I don't have any proof, though."

I dropped my eyes to my drink, feeling like an intruder in their private moment.

Alex, recognizing my discomfort, wrapped an arm around Liz's shoulders and gave her a squeeze as she changed the subject. "Well, I'm glad you have the masquerade ball to focus on right now, because if anyone is going to throw the party of the year, it's you."

A twinkle filled Liz's eyes as she beamed at her soon-to-be sister-in-law. "It *is* going to be one hell of a shindig."

I was about to ask Liz how she had acquired the role of event coordinator for the town, but a pair of arms suddenly appeared from behind me and wrapped around my neck and squeezed until I almost couldn't breathe.

"What are you doing here?" Shelby's peppy voice sang in my ear.

I laughed, then my hands went to her arms, and I squeezed her back. "I am under strict orders to unwind. What are you doing here?" When she released my neck, I twisted to look at her, expecting to find her other half nearby. "Where's Josh?'

Shelby's smile faltered for a moment before she snapped it back into place. "I don't know. At home, probably. I just wanted to pop in for a quick drink."

I nodded as though I understood but narrowed my eyes, trying to read the script below the words. Deciding she would tell me whatever was going on when she wanted to and perhaps didn't relish the thought of spilling her troubles in front of strangers, I let it go. "Shelby, this is Alex and Liz." I nodded to each of the women respectively. "Ladies, this is my ride or die, Shelby."

Shelby chuckled and waved to the other women. "Raising hell since there was hell to raise."

I laughed and shook my head then drained the last of my

drink. Shelby was trouble with a capital *T*, and I had always admired that about her. The girl didn't know the meaning of fear.

Liz spoke next. "Would you like to join us, Shelby? We're having a girls' night. Well..." She rolled her eyes and tossed her head toward Trevor and Gabe. "Mostly."

"I'd love to!" Shelby stepped onto the rungs of the chair to my left and dropped herself in the seat. She also knew no strangers. That was another thing I envied.

Shelby jumped right into the conversation, during which she and Liz did most of the talking, while Alex and I were content to simply chime in here and there. Then a waitress appeared at my side and placed a drink in front of me. It looked identical to the one I had just finished, but I hadn't ordered another.

"Excuse me, miss."

She turned to me, raising her eyebrows.

"I think this belongs to another table. I didn't order a drink."

She flicked her eyes behind me, jerking her chin toward the pool tables. "Trevor sent it over." Without waiting for a response, she spun and walked away.

I turned around, searching for Trevor. He was bent over a table, lining up his next shot. When I looked down at my drink again, my brain still not fully registering how it had gotten there, Shelby knocked her elbow against mine.

"What?" I asked when I found her smiling at me like the Cheshire Cat.

She glanced over her shoulder at Trevor before turning back to me, gyrating her eyebrows.

I scoffed. "Oh please. It's not like that. *He's* the one who ordered me to come out tonight. He's just trying to get me tipsy enough that I'll stop thinking about work."

"Good. I like him even more, then."

Shelby mercifully let it go and returned her attention to the conversation Liz and Alex were having. Half-hidden by my lowered eyelashes, my gaze darted to Trevor again. He was leaning against a pool table that wasn't in use, twirling his cue stick while he talked to Bryan, one of our firefighters. I was surprised to find that Trevor wasn't even looking my way to make sure he got credit for his gesture with the drink, and I didn't know what to make of that. Most of the men I knew would have expected a medal or something.

I was slowly coming to the conclusion that Trevor was more of an enigma than I'd thought possible. I had always pegged him as a shallow, conceited sex fiend with an inability to take anything seriously. Though I wouldn't concede that I had any of that wrong, I *was* willing to consider that maybe there was room for a bit more behind that pretty-boy facade.

I turned my attention back to the table in time to notice a tall, handsome man approaching, his eyes on Liz. When he reached our table, he rested his arms on its small surface, taking up a position between Liz and me, though all of his attention was on *her*.

Shelby leaned over to whisper in my ear without taking her eyes off the man, "*Yum.*"

I rolled my eyes in response, but I was captivated by what was unfolding.

"Allow me the pleasure of buying an exquisitely beautiful woman a drink." His smile and charm were so captivating that even Liz, who struck me as utterly unflappable, blushed and began toying with the short hair at the nape of her neck.

"Um, thank you for the offer, but I am, uh—" Her eyes traveled over the contours of his face, her breath becoming shallower. "I'm married, actually," she finished finally.

He nodded slowly, still transfixed by her. "Does being married mean you're no longer allowed to meet new people?" His tone was easy enough, but the real question was clear and hung between them. *How committed to your marriage are you?*

Liz flushed a deeper shade of red, her eyes growing a little wider. Her next words tumbled out of her mouth in a rush. "Quinn is single!" She pointed at me with a finger that felt like an accusation.

My eyebrows shot to my hairline as my spine stiffened. The

man slowly turned toward me. Seeing him up close and straight on, I understood why Liz had become a bumbling mess. He was *gorgeous*, with dark hair that was short on the sides and wavy on top. His eyes were chocolate, and a perfectly manicured goatee rested on his square jaw. Thin, wire-rimmed glasses gave him an air of sophistication. His only blemish was a thin white scar that cut through his mustache on the right side of his Cupid's bow. Even that only added a roguish element to his appeal.

As his eyes slid over my features, the way mine had just done to him, a flush worked its way up my neck and into my cheeks. Both from the way he was looking at me, taking in every detail, and because I knew I was just the consolation prize—the only single woman at a table of beautiful brides.

The stranger's sensuous lips curved into a feline smile. "Quinn, is it?"

I nodded but found that my voice had gone missing somewhere between his joining our table and the way he was eyeing *my* lips.

"Would you like to find someplace a little quieter where we can talk, Quinn?"

I was *so* not good at this kind of thing. My stomach was doing somersaults and backflips at the same time. It wasn't that I was tempted to take him up on his offer. It had more to do with the pure sexual energy that poured off him and was being directed at me.

My brain was short-circuiting, and for the love of God, I couldn't think with the way he was tasting me with those eyes.

Before I could think of an appropriate answer, a menacing presence rippled at my back. The stranger's gaze slowly lifted from mine and climbed until it was focused well over my head. A shadow had fallen across our wooden tabletop, and out of instinct, I twisted in my seat to find the source. Trevor had placed himself behind me. The heat pulsing off him scorched me as his body brushed mine. But what was truly captivating was the raw power in his glacial eyes.

Trevor and the stranger stared at each other, engaged in some unspoken struggle, with me trapped between the two.

After several uncomfortable moments, the man finally ended the conflict when his face broke into a smile. He dropped his gaze to me and said, "It appears you're not as available as your friend thinks." With a small wink, he turned and disappeared into the dense crowd.

Shelby, obviously sensing the need to break the thick tension still hanging in the air, climbed from her seat. "Well, I should probably head out." She flicked her eyes up to Trevor, who was still standing behind me. Then she leaned in to whisper into my ear again. "Since it doesn't seem that you need a wingman tonight." She giggled and grabbed her purse from the table. Before leaving, she took my head in her hands and forced me to give her my undivided attention. "Take care of yourself, sweetie. The job is getting to you. I can see it." She pulled my head down just enough to plant a kiss on top. Then she was gone.

Acting as though nothing at all peculiar or uncomfortable had just transpired, Trevor slipped into Shelby's vacant seat and started a random conversation with Gabe, who had parked himself next to Alex. I didn't know what to make of Trevor's behavior with that man—or of the arm he had resting on the back of my chair. Even more confusing were the tingles skipping down my spine from where my back kept brushing that arm.

Maybe after five years of no intimacy, my body was just reacting to the nearest testosterone source.

"Well, that was exciting." Liz smirked, her gaze boring into Trevor.

Trevor met her stare, but a hint of a smile was all he offered in return. Liz rolled her eyes and dismissed him, turning her attention to me. "That was a *taste* of what it was like for me growing up with three brothers."

Gabe and Trevor exchanged bemused looks.

"You have three brothers?" I asked. I had heard Gabe talk

about Liz on occasion, but I had never heard him mention brothers.

Liz flattened her eyes and pressed her lips together in a show of annoyance. "Yeah. Tweedledee here." She hooked a thumb toward Gabe. "Tweedledum, who is currently deployed somewhere that not even we are allowed to know about."

My eyes shifted to Gabe.

"Our older brother, Mason," he said. "He's in the army."

I nodded and went back to Liz.

"And Tweedle Jackass," she finished, pointing at Trevor.

My brows narrowed as I looked at Trevor.

Noting my confusion, Liz explained. "Trevor is the fourth member of the McNeil brood. He and Gabe latched on to each other in grade school and never let go. Mom always joked that they were twins from separate wombs."

The look passing between Gabe and Trevor was precious. I could practically picture them as two little boys, one fair-haired and one dark, both with dirt stains on their cheeks and clothes and undoubtedly turning their mothers' hair gray. But I could see the brotherly love between them as clear as a blue sky on a cloudless day. And that love apparently extended to Liz.

Trevor nodded toward Liz and provided his two cents. "Gabe and Mason needed reinforcements with that one. She was like a hellcat on acid when we were in school."

That garnered a hearty laugh from everyone at the table, including Liz, who was beaming at Trevor in the way that only a sister with shared memories she would treasure forever would.

"And speaking of brotherly duties..." she said.

"Ah, shit," Trevor and Gabe said simultaneously.

Trevor turned his crooked grin on me, his blue eyes twinkling as he tipped his chin up as if to say, "Wait for it."

Liz didn't let the interruption deter her. "You'd both better make an appearance at the masquerade ball."

The boys immediately began to protest. But one gentle hand from Alex on Gabe's arm, and he settled right down.

He looked deeply into her eyes as he said, "Okay. I'm in," and was rewarded with a huge smile and a lingering kiss.

Something stirred inside me as I watched the two of them interact—the way he was so attentive to her, their smoldering glances at one another, and how they seemed to be able to communicate without words.

Liz turned to Trevor and raised her eyebrows.

He stared her down for several moments, and I nearly jumped out of my chair when his warm hand landed on my back. "Fine. I'll go if she does," he said, tipping his head toward me.

"Of course Quinn is going," Liz said, as though anything else would be preposterous. "And we'll go as a theme!" she added, clasping her fingers together in pure glee.

Nothing but gibberish poured out of my mouth as I tried to figure out what response would get me out of the group activity without offending anybody.

Gabe came to my rescue. "If you two think I'm going to let you get away with forcing Quinn into this, you've got another think coming."

Liz turned her pleading eyes to me. "Please come, Quinn. I promise you'll have a wonderful time."

I didn't know if it was the magic Liz seemed to possess or the comforting and equally confusing brush of Trevor's thumb on my shoulder blade from where his hand once again rested on the back of my chair, but from somewhere far away, I heard myself agree.

Liz practically bobbed right off her chair. "Excellent. I'll take care of everything!"

I could feel Trevor's eyes on me, and when I turned to meet his stare, a rush of something euphoric and heady swept through me. The whole situation felt too intimate—spending time with the people he considered family. The way his thigh innocently brushed mine beneath the table. And most of all, the way his stare was drawing me in with the promise of something that had long lain dormant inside me.

I was seeing another side of Trevor, one that put me in danger of falling prey to his charms. But the case promised enough casualties as it was. No way would I allow my heart and my pride to end up on that list.

Come what may, I was one woman the player wouldn't get to play.

CHAPTER 21

Trevor

THE CHIEF RECLINED in his office chair and ran a hand down his weary face before turning bloodshot eyes to me. "Ryan, what do you want to say about this?" He reached forward to where a newspaper sat on his desk and shoved it a little farther away, as though he couldn't stand the sight of it.

My eyes zeroed in on the bold headline that had greeted me at my front door that morning: *Serial Killer Terrorizes Eden Falls. Local Police in over Their Heads.*

Pricks.

I spread my feet a little wider and kept my thumbs hooked over my duty belt as I looked around the office, noting the sea of police uniforms filling the small space. The chief had called for a mandatory meeting that morning as soon as he'd become aware of the story, requiring all uniforms assigned to the case—plus Quinn —to appear.

"I've already spoken to the editor-in-chief at the paper as well as the journalist who wrote the article," I said, addressing the entire room. "They're refusing to reveal their source, and unfortunately, they're within their right to do so."

Until that point, we had managed to keep the words "serial killer" from the articles detailing the recent murders, mostly by refusing to provide any specifics about the homicides other than victim information and that the investigations were ongoing. But thanks to some unnamed source, every fucking detail had been handed over to the press and consumed by half of Eden Falls over breakfast.

Carlson, with all his bravado and eagerness to be in the mix of the excitement, was the first to speak up. "Everyone in town is freaking the fuck out. What the hell are we supposed to say to them?"

I hit him with a glare that had the cherub-faced pup backing down and remembering his rank. "You tell them the same thing you tell the press. No comment."

Gabe, who was leaning against the wall to my right, spoke next. "We need to do something about all the calls coming into Dispatch. The phones have been ringing off the hook all morning. It's overwhelming the dispatchers, but it also creates a bigger issue as far as the case is concerned. Who knows what this guy will do if he can't get through to Quinn because our lines are tied up with this bullshit."

I nodded and quickly ran through as many solutions as I could think of in a matter of seconds then snagged the best one. "Let's set up an information line." I swung my gaze to the chief, who was slumped down in his chair, taking it all in. "We'll have a dedicated line manned by an officer where people can call in with questions and tips." I then directed my attention to the room again, since everyone, other than Gabe and me, was going to be taking turns on the phone. "The official answer to all questions is still 'No comment,' but at least this way it will keep the dispatch lines open for actual emergencies and our special friend."

Carlson, never knowing when to keep his mouth shut, piped up again. "People are still going to call Dispatch wanting to talk to her"—he jerked his chin toward Quinn, who was standing beside me—"now that they know how she's involved."

Seeing the way Quinn's features pulled even tighter made me want to smack the pink right out of Carlson's cheeks. I had already used up every ounce of willpower earlier at the newspaper office to keep from grabbing that sniveling reporter by his ugly striped tie and dragging him across his desk for writing about how Quinn had had the chance to save the last victim but failed.

I bared my teeth at Carlson and leaned in. "We are *all* going to make sure that anyone who hounds Quinn is given two options. They can call the information line, or we can cite them for obstructing a public servant. Any other questions?" I raised my eyebrows at him with a silent challenge to get smart quick.

Fortunately for him, he pressed his lips together and shook his head, turning his gaze to anything other than me.

"The bigger issue," I continued, "is figuring out where the press is getting their information. Either we've got a leak from inside the department..." I scanned my partners, searching for signs of guilt, but found none. "Or the killer is inviting the press to take part in his game."

Chief Kelly's blue eyes blazed beneath his lowered brow. "You think the killer might be feeding the details of his crimes to the press?"

I shrugged. "It wouldn't be the first time a serial killer contacted the press to ensure he got the attention he wanted."

Gabe straightened a bit and canted his head. "It's a strong possibility, since we've been keeping him out of the press so far. Maybe he got tired of waiting to be credited for his crimes."

The chief swung his gaze back to me. "In those other cases, the ones you think are related, did the killer ever contact the press?"

I shook my head. "No, but he also never singled out a dispatcher, wanting to exchange information. Maybe he's evolving—looking for ways to keep it interesting."

The room fell into a heavy silence as the reality of the situation—of how little control we had—sank in.

Then a sultry voice broke through the bleakness as Quinn angled her body toward mine. "Maybe it's time to play nice with the press. Then at least we might be able to control some of the narrative."

I looked down at her, drinking in the stunning contrast between her honey eyes and dark hair and savoring the way she looked at me as though I were the only other person in the room. Something had shifted between us again in the past couple of days—ever since our night at Rustlers. Though the killer had been silent, and the case had been nearly at a standstill, Quinn had been responding to me differently—almost like a friend or a trusted companion, at the very least. Though there were still times when she pulled away, as if reminding herself to put her walls back up, little by little, she was softening.

I offered a tight smile, not wanting the rest of the room to see what I truly felt for Quinn. "That's a good idea. It'll give us the chance to issue the number to the information line too."

"Good," the chief said, drawing everyone's attention back to him. "Let me know if—"

"Twenty-Five Adam Four," Julia called over the portable radio the chief kept on the edge of his desk.

I keyed the mic at my chest. "Go ahead."

Her next words made the hairs on my neck stand on end. "Quinn's caller is on the line."

QUINN WAS a flash of color as she dashed past me and wiggled her way through the sea of uniforms. She was out the door so fast that I cursed as I shouldered bodies out of the way, trying to catch up to her. By the time I made it out of the chief's office, she had already disappeared through the station's rear entrance toward the parking lot. It wasn't until she reached the door to Dispatch that my longer legs finally made up for her head start.

She yanked the heavy door open, and I reached over her head to hold it for the both of us. Not having the luxury of allowing my eyes to adjust to the dim room, I ran blind down the hallway, using the sound of Quinn's heavy breathing to ensure I didn't get so close to her that I ran the risk of knocking her down.

I was finally beginning to make out details by the time we reached our respective desks. Quinn threw herself into her chair and grabbed her phone. I did the same, but movement from Blair, who was seated at a console to my right, caught my eye. It took me a second to realize what she was doing. Once I did, I snapped my fingers at her.

She turned to me, her phone pressed to her ear. Keeping my voice low to avoid distracting Quinn, I said, "*No one* listens in on this call." I held Blair's gaze until she sulked and dropped her phone to the desk. Then I locked onto Meredith and then Julia, waiting until each of them acknowledged that they understood.

They easily could and likely would listen to the call after the fact, but at least Quinn wouldn't have to deal with their smirks and whispers while she was trying to manipulate the killer into giving something away.

Quinn's voice was suddenly in my ear, drawing all of my focus back to her. I remained standing so that I could see over the top of her monitors and noted the way her shoulders were back and her tone was warm and firm. She sounded like the old Quinn—calm and unshakeable—and the knot in my chest eased a little.

The killer, however, wasn't pleased that he'd had to wait for her, and his savage tone was having a significantly greater impact on my blood pressure than Quinn's.

"I apologize you were forced to wait for me," Quinn said.

"It is *not* a difficult concept, Quinn. Did I not make it painstakingly clear that this game would end the moment I was forced to speak to anyone other than you?"

From the way he bit out each word, I pictured spit flying from his lips. I seriously wanted to rip the asshole's throat out, but I schooled my features to shield my thoughts.

"Yes, you made that clear" was all Quinn said.

There was a pause. The sound of his ragged breathing slowed then vanished.

When the killer spoke again, his voice was cold. Controlled. Completely devoid of the rage that had been there only seconds before. That sudden and extreme shift concerned me more than anything.

"Are you ready to pay the piper, Quinn?"

My eyes were still on Quinn, but hers were on her screen, her shoulders relaxed. Her grip was loose on her phone. Nothing about her indicated she was experiencing any kind of distress.

"Yes, I'm ready," she said.

"You don't go out much, do you?" The question was conversational—playful, even. An image of a serpent smiling at Eve in her garden of paradise flashed through my head.

"No."

"Is that because you would rather stay home alone than have to blow off some poor schmuck who doesn't know you've sworn yourself to celibacy?"

My stomach lurched as I realized what he had just revealed, but Quinn didn't seem to notice. Before I could signal to her not to answer, she said, "Yes, I suppose that's part of it."

"Mm-hmm, and what is the rest?"

Quinn hesitated as though she wasn't even sure of the answer. "I just prefer quiet evenings after a day full of ringing phones and screaming callers."

The killer hummed in a way that indicated he was tasting and digesting her words. "You should try the gym, Quinn." He waited for a response, but Quinn remained silent, so he tried again. "It is a fantastic way to blow off steam. I, myself, enjoy vigorous physical activities. But you already knew that."

If his scornful snicker bothered Quinn, she didn't let on. Her face and body language hadn't shifted even slightly since she'd picked up the phone.

And his next sentence confirmed what I feared from his line of questioning.

"What else do you like to do in your spare time?" he asked.

What else. The bastard already knew Quinn was religious

about hitting the gym, and he was toying with her, waiting to see if she would realize that he had already infiltrated her life. He was subtly conveying that he knew she lived alone and how she spent her time.

"There isn't much else," Quinn replied. "I work a lot."

"That must be why you're so good at what you do," the killer purred.

Something in his tone—in the way he drew out his words—made me suspect he was building toward some climax. Quinn was a mouse in a maze, and he was opening and closing specific doors to direct her movements.

"I'm curious, Quinn—why is a woman of your talent and skill wasting her time in a provincial town like Eden Falls? I can't imagine you enjoy working with a bunch of inept rednecks."

Quinn bristled ever so slightly, her shoulders inching toward her ears, her nostrils flaring as she fought to control her emotions. "I used to work for a bigger agency. I wanted a change of pace."

"Hmm. And why was that?"

Quinn hesitated, her eyes flitting back and forth on her screen as her brain searched for the right answer. "Working in a big city was more stressful. The calls came in like a flood all day long, and there was a lot more violence and ugliness."

A pause followed. Then the killer said, "You're breaking trust, Quinn. If you expect me to give you honest clues to my next victim, then that had better be your last lie."

The color drained from Quinn's face. I became all too aware of the stillness of the room. Though her partners kept their backs to her, it was obvious their full attention was on every word she said. This was exactly what he wanted—Quinn experiencing the agony of her partners hearing every word, witnessing every struggle.

Her mouth began to move, but there was no sound. Then she snapped her jaw shut and dipped her chin until I could no longer see her face. Her long curls fell forward in a curtain meant to hide whatever it was she was fighting to keep secret. In a voice that was quiet and edged with pain, she finally said, "After college, I was hired as a dispatcher for Las Vegas Metro. It was a big dispatch center, and when you're in training, you're an outsider. You haven't proven yourself yet, and most people wash out, so you don't really get to know your coworkers."

I frowned, still training my eyes on Quinn and wondering where this was going.

"Shortly after I completed training, I began dating one of the officers. It was really nice at first. I was young and inexperienced, and he was charming and confident. I felt safe with him."

She paused.

"Keep going," the killer prompted.

Quinn raised her head, and the sheen in her eyes nearly broke me. "Apparently, he liked talking about me—about the intimate details of our relationship—with his partners. It didn't take long for word to spread that we were seeing each other. That was something I'd wanted to keep private. I prefer to keep work separate from my personal life."

"And?"

Something about the way Quinn was dragging out her answer, the way she avoided saying whatever the killer was waiting to hear, caused a wave of uneasiness to wash through me. I glanced to my right, noting that the other dispatchers were utterly still, their spines rigid as they waited for her to continue.

Quinn took a shuddering breath and closed her eyes. "He was married. To one of my partners."

My eyes widened as a cold breath licked down my spine. I couldn't believe it. There was no way that could be true. Quinn was too honorable to ever get involved with a married man.

Whispers filled the silence as Blair and Meredith suddenly came to life, their eyes glazed with the high of salacious gossip they knew would destroy Quinn and the reputation she had built for herself.

I narrowed my eyes at Quinn, knowing that there *had* to be more to the story, but she wouldn't meet my gaze. Her own eyes were downcast, the weight of her guilt and shame evident in the way her shoulders had caved in.

"You didn't know," the killer said.

"No." Quinn's voice was barely more than a whisper.

I breathed deeply through my nose, digesting the bomb that had just been dropped. So that asshole cop had seduced Quinn when she was young and naive then bragged to all his buddies about it, knowing that it would get back to his wife and not giving a shit what it would do to either woman. No wonder she had sworn off men.

My gut lurched when I suddenly realized why all my taunting and flirting had always bothered her so much. She probably thought I was just like that dickhead—a playboy who didn't give a fuck about the women he bedded. Undoubtedly, it was also the reason she maintained a professional distance with everyone she worked with—badges and dispatchers alike.

"What happened when word spread?" the killer asked.

Quinn shifted in her seat, her eyes flashing briefly to where Blair and Meredith sat openly gaping at her. "I became public enemy number one in Dispatch. The environment became even more toxic than it already was. I was sick to my stomach all the time and couldn't eat. The other dispatchers made it their mission to make my life a living hell."

I glanced at Quinn's partners again. Blair wore a feline grin, while Meredith's flytrap was still hanging open. Julia, however, had gone just as pale as Quinn, her soft brown eyes echoing her partner's pain.

The killer spoke again, and I reminded myself to focus. I was supposed to be reading between the lines, listening for background noise, and noting his speech patterns and idiosyncrasies. But *damn*, I couldn't get my attention off Quinn.

"So how did you end up *here*, of all places?" he asked.

Quinn bit her lower lip, her eyes moving across her screen, though I doubted she was actually seeing it. "I knew I couldn't continue to work in that environment, so I decided to leave. I had a friend who liked this area, and I thought a small town with a slower pace would be a good change."

I guessed that friend was Shelby and hoped the killer didn't pick up on the way Quinn had glossed over that part.

She seemed to hold her breath, probably hoping the same.

After a long silence, the killer finally said, "I suppose that is fair payment. Would you like your reward now?"

I turned my teeth to dust at his condescending tone. As though he hadn't already brought Quinn low enough, he had to make it clear how much pleasure he derived from forcing her to publicly declare her scarlet letter.

Quinn straightened a little and placed her hands over her keyboard. "Yes."

The killer sighed nostalgically. "Are you familiar with nightingales, Quinn?"

Quinn began typing, intent on capturing every word related to the next victim. "Yes. It's a bird known for its singing."

A sinister chuckle came over the line. "That's right."

"What does that have to do with the woman you intend to kill?" Her tone had an undercurrent of challenge or rage. I couldn't tell which.

"She is descended from the nightingale once but related twice."

Quinn's brow furrowed, but she entered the clue into her call-taking screen. "What else?"

He laughed again. "In such a hurry, Quinn. If you don't mind, I'd rather savor this time we have together."

Pink tinged the apples of Quinn's cheeks, her eyes flaring. "I gave you everything you demanded. Now I want information about the woman."

His voice was ice when he responded. "Careful, Quinn. Don't forget whose game this is. I can end it anytime I want to."

Quinn pressed her lips together and waited. The killer took his sweet-ass time giving her what she wanted.

"Though she is guilty of stealing life force, she no longer takes, having chosen to give power instead."

The keys of Quinn's keyboard clicked in rapid succession as she kept the phone pinned between her ear and shoulder.

"And let's see," the killer mused and clicked his tongue. "She used to be a real tigress. A queen with a court of her own. Though nothing like her namesake, who chose the Tin Man over the Lion."

As Quinn was still typing the last clue, the killer said, "Clock's ticking, Quinn," then disconnected.

Quinn paused at the abrupt ending to the call. Then she lifted her head, allowing her handset to fall from her shoulder. She caught it and tossed it onto the desk with a loud thud then finished typing the last few words.

An awkward tension filled the room, so thick that it felt wrong to move or even breathe. But Quinn shattered the stillness when she launched from her chair the moment her keyboard went silent, then she stalked from the room, refusing to look at anyone.

CHAPTER 22

Quinn

I BURST through the door of the dispatch center, so numb that I couldn't even register the warm summer day. The heels of my hands flew to my eyes, and I pressed down against the sting that threatened to start an unwelcome cascade. My chest was tight, aching for air, but I couldn't release the lock on my jaw as I clamped down against the emotion that would just add further humiliation to the day.

Get. It. Together. Quinn.

Before I could even attempt to collect myself, the door swung open behind me with such force that it slammed into the building. I didn't need to turn around to know who had just emerged from that viper pit.

He just stood behind me, not saying a word. It only made my rage soar higher as my shallow breaths turned to ragged pants.

Planting my hands on my hips, I hung my head and closed my eyes, clawing for control. A heavy hand landed on my shoulder, and I immediately ripped myself away from it.

Trevor's voice was soft and revealed nothing of what he must have been thinking. "Quinn—"

"Don't."

He took a deep breath and exhaled slowly. "Quinn—"

I turned on him. "I said *don't*." My hands fisted at my sides of their own freewill. The tension in my face and shoulders was conjuring a headache.

Trevor searched my eyes. He opened his mouth to speak then promptly shut it again. Instead, he averted his eyes to the landscape behind me and began rubbing the back of his neck.

I didn't move, just stood there as rigid as a statue, every muscle in my body vibrating.

Trevor turned his gaze on me again and took one step forward. His body was relaxed, but his eyes were wary. "Quinn, I know that was torture—"

I scoffed. "Oh? Do you? Yes, I'm sure you know just how torturous this has been." I threw my arms wide. My words became a vicious snarl. "I mean, I was screwing a married man. I'm a homewrecker, but hey, what the hell, I should just adopt Trevor Ryan's philosophy on living a life of hedonism, right? To hell with those I damage in the process."

Trevor's jaw tightened, his golden skin suddenly tinged with scarlet. He leaned in and poked his index finger toward me. "I am *not* the enemy here, Quinn."

I wasn't so sure. He represented everything that had made me hate myself. Those old wounds, always festering just below the surface, had been ripped open and were pouring out of the gaping hole in my chest. My greatest shame had been laid bare in front of Trevor and my partners, and I knew that by morning, the gossip would have made it department-wide.

"You might as well be," I fired back.

His eyes narrowed, the anger still simmering, waiting for one tiny spark to turn it into a full-blown wildfire. "What the hell is that supposed to mean?"

I took a step closer to him as well, leaving barely any space between us. My hands once again fisted at my sides. "You're just like him."

Trevor's eyes widened and his head reared back as though I had struck him.

"You playboys are all the same! You'll do anything, tell *any* lie, to get between a woman's legs. And once you've had her, you boast to all your buddies about it, telling them how good or awful she was in bed, then you toss her aside like a piece of trash." I shook my head, completely lost in the fog of hate and humiliation. "I've seen you time and again work your magic on one woman after another—an endless parade of pussy to stroke your male ego and feed your own pleasure. And that"—I jabbed a finger into his chest, ignoring that his bulletproof vest kept it from having the impact I desired—"is *exactly* why all your flirting and attempts at charm will *never* work on me. I will never again be fooled by a man like you—like *him*."

Trevor's eyes burned like white-hot flames. His voice was low and lethal when he responded, every word terrifyingly controlled. "I am nothing like that prick you're so determined to compare me to." He leaned in until his face was inches from mine. "And for your information, I have *never* mistreated a woman. All of my dates know up front that I'm not looking for anything more than a good time, and the same is true for them. And I *always* make sure that a woman who gets into bed with me leaves *more* than satisfied."

I gulped, some of my anger cooling as I saw the truth of the offense written across his face.

"As for the other matter"—he took a step toward me, forcing me to step back to avoid having our bodies brush against each other—"you need to rack your brain, because you're clearly forgetting the fact that I have never made a move on you. Sure, I like to give you hell and get under that ice-cold skin of yours, but you tell me *one* time that I've actually made a move."

His eyes held the same challenge as his words. He looked down on me, patiently waiting for me to argue the truth of what he'd just declared. A fresh wave of humiliation washed over me as I realized he was right. He never had tried anything beyond riling me up and flirting a bit. I couldn't decide what felt worse—the embarrassment of having been so wrong about his intentions or the sting of what felt like rejection by a man who wasn't especially particular about his women.

I didn't know what to say or do. The thought of walking away without further comment was appealing, but I really didn't want to go back into Dispatch. I couldn't spend the rest of the day awkwardly pretending I hadn't just admitted my deep, dark secret in front of my partners, knowing that every time they picked up their cell phones and began texting, it was because they were spreading the sordid details throughout the department. But I also didn't want to be anywhere near Trevor. I wanted the conversation to be over. I wanted the day, the week, and the month to be over.

We were still squared off with each other, toe to toe, eyes locked and loaded. Finally, knowing we couldn't stay like that all day and also knowing that the stubborn horse's ass would never break the standoff first, through gritted teeth, I said, "Just stay the hell away from me."

He stared at me for another moment, his eyes flitting back and forth between mine. Then he simply shook his head and turned away, but instead of going back into Dispatch, he marched toward the station.

EIGHT HOURS LATER, my mood still hadn't improved. After my spat with Trevor, I had promptly returned to Dispatch long enough to collect my things and to tell Blair I was leaving. She protested, of course, sputtering at my *telling* her I was leaving rather than asking if I could. But suffice it to say, my give-a-damn was thoroughly destroyed at that point, and I had more important things to worry about, like solving the clues to the next victim. I'd considered shooting a text to Trevor to tell him I was going to work on the case from home but then decided against it. I wasn't ready to speak to him in any form.

I'd spent the first few hours with my notes and laptop spread out on my kitchen table, but the angst of the day and the pressure to save a life made it impossible to sit still and focus. So I finally gave in to my body's demand for physical exertion, and I'd been angry cleaning ever since.

Decked out in my sweatpants, a black tank top, and a pair of bright-yellow dish gloves, and with my hair in an *I Dream of Jeannie* ponytail, I went to town on the grout around the white tile of my kitchen counter. A slight sheen coated my skin, and I savored the feel of the anxiety slowly leaking out of me with my frantic scrubbing. Though every time my brain replayed the call from earlier, despite trying very hard to pretend the whole thing had never happened, the anxiety and anger came rushing back.

I filled my cheeks with air then blew it out forcefully, pausing my scrubbing to glance over at my notepad where I had written the clues to victim four. *She is descended from the nightingale once but related twice.*

Is she a singer? Maybe someone who came from a family of singers. I tried to think of which members of our community were known for their singing. After picking up the pen that sat next to my pad of paper, I jotted down *local bands* and *church choirs*. When nothing else came to me, I tossed the pen down and resumed scrubbing.

Around and around, my thoughts went, a carousel of images. Some of the pictures were from many years ago—a handsome face in a Las Vegas Metro police uniform. Others were of naked, battered bodies left fallen among trash. Then there were the images of Blair and Meredith with their heads bent toward each other as they whispered and smirked. And finally, there was Trevor—towering over me, nothing but hostility in his beautiful features as he essentially informed me that I didn't tempt him in the least.

That last one felt like a punch to the stomach every time it materialized. What bothered me the most was that it bothered me at all. *Why should I care if that's how he feels?* I had zero interest in him, and all I ever wanted where he was concerned was for him to leave me alone.

My gloved fingers suddenly hit tile. The change in sensation halted my movements and drew my attention to the sponge in my hand—the sponge that now had a hole where my first two fingers were poking through. I exhaled sharply again and threw the sponge down on the counter. I was about to grab another from beneath the kitchen sink when a noise outside stopped me in my tracks.

Slowly, I twisted my head toward the front door, my breath trapped in my chest, and strained my ears, listening for sounds that didn't belong. I started to wonder if I was imagining things, but after reminding myself that there was a psycho on the loose who had taken a shine to me, I decided to investigate rather than brush it off. After carefully peeling off my gloves, I tiptoed silently toward the front door, careful to keep out of view of the glass panes in its center.

I still didn't hear anything suspicious, but I paused, glancing back to where I kept a block of knives next to the stove. Then my eyes skipped to the cell phone sitting on the edge of my kitchen table. Before I made up my mind about whether I should go back and fetch either item, the sound of a boot scuffing on cement snapped my attention back to the door just in time for me to see a shadow fall across the entryway as someone crossed in front of the porch light.

My heart hammered in my chest, and my breath was no longer trapped but coming in ragged puffs. A million thoughts raced through my head, and I glanced back at my cell phone. What if I had to call 911? I *took* those calls. I wasn't supposed to *be* one.

Keeping my eyes on the shadow, I backed away from the door, navigating toward the knives. If that sadistic maniac did break in, there was no way I was going down without a fight.

I reached blindly behind me, knowing the knives were close but not daring to take my eyes off the entryway. Images of horror movies in which the young woman being hunted turns away for just a second only to turn back and find the killer standing right in front of her caused my heart rate to accelerate even further until the blood was pounding in my ears. Then, as my hand brushed over the handles of my knife set, the doorbell rang, jolting me right out of my skin.

Wide-eyed, I stared at the door, keeping my hand on the hilt of a butcher knife.

The door rattled as a fist pounded on it. "Quinn!"

I closed my eyes and released a sigh of relief, the hand that had been ready to plunge steel through skin and bone now resting on my decelerating heartbeat.

More pounding. "Quinn! Open up."

My eyelids lowered to half-mast as I grumbled and shuffled reluctantly to the door. When I unlocked it and swung it open, I was none too happy to find Adonis incarnate standing on the other side. "What do you want?" I turned from the door and made my way back to the kitchen in search of another sponge.

Trevor stepped inside and closed the door behind him. "Why the hell did you take off today without telling me where you were going?"

"You just figured that out? Some investigator."

After retrieving a fresh sponge, I tossed the old one and returned my attention to the grout.

"I was giving you space, since you told me to stay the hell away from you, but I didn't think you were just going to up and *leave*."

I shrugged without looking at him. "I needed to start working on the clues, and I wasn't going to be able to focus at work, so I came home."

"You should have told me."

My saccharine tone matched my smile when I replied, "I'm sure you can understand why I didn't feel like talking to you."

Trevor propped his hands on his hips and turned his back to me. The sound of a loud breath slowly being released as he tilted his head back gave me a small sense of satisfaction in an otherwise shitty day. When he faced me again, his expression was unreadable. "Look, it was a rough day. I get that."

I scoffed but kept cleaning.

"Whatever happens, Quinn, you can't just take off like that. I can't protect you if I don't know where you are."

"It's not your job to protect me." I understood where he was coming from, but I couldn't help the defiance in my tone. I was still nursing a bruised ego where he was concerned, not to mention the total loss of my dignity over that stupid phone call.

"The hell it isn't." The force with which he said it made my eyes snap to his. "Take your anger out on me if that helps you to get through this, Quinn. Be angry with me for what that asshole in Vegas did to you. Be angry with me for what this asshole killer is doing to you. Be angry with me for failing to stop the pain and humiliation of what you've had to endure since this started. But do *not* for one second act as though you're unaware that I am fully responsible for keeping you safe."

I set my sponge down and braced my hands on the edge of the counter, allowing my gaze to fall from his face to the gleaming tiles. Finally, I nodded. "You're right. I'm sorry. I should have told you I was leaving."

He was silent, as though he'd expected a lot more fight out of me. But he was right—I was making his already difficult job even harder simply because I was blaming him for things he hadn't done.

I turned so that my back was pressed against the counter and folded my arms. "It won't happen again."

He studied me for a moment then nodded once. I figured that would be the end of it, and he would let himself out, but his next words raised the hatchet from where we'd just buried it.

"You're also not going to be staying alone anymore until this is over. So either I'm staying here, or you're coming to my place."

My eyes rounded, and my jaw dropped. "Over my dead body!"

Trevor's eyes narrowed. His tone full of steel, he said, "If things stay as is, it *will* be."

"I am *not* going to let you stay here! There is enough gossip circulating about me at the department as it is. I'm not going to add to that by giving people a reason to think I'm your latest conquest!"

Trevor sucked his lip between his teeth, and I seriously wondered for a moment if he was going to throw me across his knee and spank me. "You're a smart woman, Quinn. You know it's stupid for you to stay here alone!"

I opened my mouth to argue, but he cut me off.

"You really didn't catch what the killer was telling you today, did you?"

I snapped my mouth shut, my eyebrows turning down.

"He's been watching you. He knows you live alone, and he also knows you frequent the gym."

Though I tried to recall the parts of the call that Trevor might be referring to, my brain was scrambled. I started to shake my head. "I don't—"

"Listen to the call again, and you'll pick up on it this time. But that's not what matters right now. What matters is making sure you stay safe. This guy is playing a very dangerous game with you, Quinn. These women aren't the mouse in his trap. You are."

My head was spinning. Had I really been so blinded by these clues and the things I had been forced to reveal that I hadn't even noticed that the killer had been slowly lowering a net over me?

Deciding it was better to trust Trevor's instincts rather than risk my life to protect my pride, I relented. "Fine." I nodded. "I'll stay at Dispatch until this is over."

Trevor shook his head. "No. You need some distance from that place for your own mental well-being. You're not permitted to sleep there anymore, and I'm going to start limiting how many hours you spend there."

My eyes widened again, and I shoved off from the counter to stand in front of him until my bare feet met his boots. "You can't do that! What if I miss a call from him? He was livid today when he had to wait *a few minutes* for me. Imagine what he'll do if I'm not there at all!"

"I've already taken care of that." Trevor reached into his back pocket. "I've informed all of the dispatchers that if he calls when you're not there, they are to forward the call to your cell phone immediately." He grabbed my hand and turned it over, placing a small rectangular device in my palm. "Use this to record the calls so we can continue to collect them as evidence."

I stared down at the recorder, trying to think of another argument, but he had thought of everything already.

"Quinn, you've seen enough of the evidence to know what this man is capable of. Do you really want to take the chance that you'll end up like one of his victims?"

I looked up into eyes that were so blue and electrifying it was difficult to look away. Then I allowed my arguments to die on a sigh. "All right. I'll go pack a few things."

I was halfway to my bedroom when the next words out of his mouth caused my steps to stutter.

"Do you want to follow me to my place or ride with me?"

Slowly, I turned and cocked my ear as though I hadn't heard him correctly. "I'm not staying with you, Trevor. I'll go to the motel."

I resumed the trek to my bedroom and, once inside, pulled a duffel bag from a high shelf in my closet and began shoving some clothes into it. The next thing I knew, Trevor walked into the room with a look on his face that said he was ready for round two. Or were we on round three at this point?

"You're not staying at the motel for the same reason. You'll still be there alone, and there are too many times where you'll be vulnerable coming and going."

I scoffed. "Well, you're just going to have to learn to live with a compromise."

Trevor folded his arms, and the mischief in his eyes made my stomach squirm.

He reached into his back pocket and pulled out his cell phone. After running his thumb up the screen a few times, he placed the phone to his ear as he cast his eyes around the room and smirked.

"What?" I snapped, planting a fist on my waist while the other hand held my half-full duffel.

His eyes danced. "Never thought I'd see the day when I was in your bedroom."

I growled and gave him a scowl that could singe the hair off a cat. "It's the first and *last* time."

He started to chuckle, but then whoever he was calling answered, and he turned his attention to the call.

I continued to pack, only half listening to his charming small talk with someone named Maggie—no doubt one of his many bedfellows. After exiting the closet, I went into the bathroom and pulled my toiletries and small makeup bag from below the sink.

I was in the process of dropping my hair dryer into the duffel when Trevor said, "Mags, I have a favor to ask." He paused. "I have a friend who is going to insist on renting a room from you, and I want you to turn her down."

Slowly, as if the forces of darkness had just taken possession of my body, I turned around and walked back into the bedroom. Trevor's eyes were on me, glinting with anticipation.

"Yeah, her name is Quinn Martin. She's five feet seven and has long, dark curly hair and a pissed-off look on her face." He laughed. "Yep, that's the way of it." His smile grew in response to whatever this Maggie person was saying. "Thanks, Mags. You're the best." Then he disconnected.

I was still standing on the threshold between my bathroom and bedroom, staring at him and trying to decide whether I could move the body by myself if I killed him.

Trevor shoved his phone into his back pocket. Then he folded his arms and widened his stance. "Looks like you don't have much of a choice."

CHAPTER 23

Quinn

I TIGHTENED my grip on the steering wheel, the sound of the leather creaking beneath my palms the only accompaniment to the drone of my tires as I navigated through town. A light summer shower had started, sprinkling my windshield with raindrops that magnified the yellow lights of oncoming traffic.

Stopping at a red light, I glanced in my rearview mirror, cursing the headlights of the truck behind me. Trevor, insisting that he wasn't going to let me out of his sight, had been on my tail since I'd pulled out of my garage. I couldn't stop him from following me, but I was still headed to the Emeline—the only one of the two motels in town where I didn't fear catching some kind of disease.

After Trevor had ended his call with Maggie, he confessed that she was the proprietor and night agent of the Emeline. That hadn't deterred me. In fact, it had given me hope. If she was the owner of the property, then at the end of the day, she was a businesswoman. And no businesswoman in her right mind would turn down a good paying customer with law enforcement credentials to back them up.

I turned in to the motel's parking lot a few minutes later and parked in the space adjacent to the entrance. Grateful for the white hoodie I'd changed into before leaving the house, I exited my car and pulled the hood over my loose curls. Then I skittered inside, trying to avoid as much of the rain as possible.

When I entered the lobby, a bell tinkled overhead, and a petite woman with short gray hair who looked to be in her sixties greeted me with a warm smile. "Hello, dear. How can I help you this evening?"

Trevor wasn't the only one with charm, and boy, could I turn it on when I needed to. I offered a grin infused with youthful innocence in return. "Hello. I would like to book a room, please." I pulled out my wallet and removed my ID and a credit card and set them on the counter. "And I'm probably going to be here for a while, so I hope that's okay." With any luck, she would hear that, and dollar signs would flash in her vision.

The woman's gray eyes scanned me, and I had the distinct sense she was sizing me up. "You must be Quinn."

Shit.

I cleared my throat. "Um, yes, I am. I assume you're Maggie?"

Maggie's laugh was raspy but easy. "I sure am, honey. And if you know who I am, then you also know that I can't rent you that room."

The bell over the door tinkled behind me. I didn't need to turn around to know who had just walked in, but I did anyway. Trevor offered a cocky smile as he leaned against the doorframe, crossing his arms and ankles like he was content to wait all night if he had to.

I glowered and returned my attention to Maggie, my diabetes-inducing smile back in place. "Maggie, please. I just need a safe place to stay for the time being. I would really appreciate a room, and I promise I will be the best customer you've ever had." I implored her with my eyes, hoping she would yield to the solidarity of womanhood.

Maggie tilted her head to the side and frowned, her gaze sympathetic. "Oh, honey, I'm sorry, but the answer is no."

Her response shocked me to the point that I forgot to maintain my beguiling facade. Instead, I banged my fist on the counter, my eyes wide as my voice rose an octave. "You're really not going to rent me a room?"

She pressed her lips together and shook her head.

"You're in business to make a profit. How can you say no?"

Maggie's features lifted as she glanced at Trevor. "Trevor helped me out in a big way a while back. This is the least I can do to show my gratitude."

A small growl escaped before I muttered, "He's got this town wrapped around his little finger."

Maggie chuckled. "Yes. Yes, he does. Been that way since he was a boy. Must be those dimples he gets when he turns on the charm."

"I wouldn't know. I've never seen his dimples. I've only ever seen his horns." I scowled and turned my back to the desk to find Trevor grinning from ear to ear.

"Well," he said, "looks like you're down to two choices. That roach-infested place down the street that rents rooms by the hour or casa de Ryan. What's it gonna be?"

I folded my arms and eyed him with malice as I pulverized my molars and considered my options.

I could call Shelby and ask to stay at her place. But knowing the kind of problems she and Josh were experiencing, I didn't want to add a third wheel to their situation. Not to mention that the last thing Shelby needed was to stress about why I was having to stay somewhere other than my house in the first place.

Trevor, apparently realizing I was still doing my damnedest to figure out another solution, sighed and unfolded himself from the door, taking a step toward me. "Look, by staying with me, if a call from this guy gets forwarded to your phone, I'll still be there to listen in and help if you need it. It'll also give us more time to work the clues and the evidence together without having to be at the department all day and night." He glanced at his watch. "We've only got twenty-six hours left."

Damn that man and his ability to win an argument, but I

couldn't ignore that it was more important for us to get back to work than to spend all night trying to figure out where I was going to sleep.

My shoulders slumped, and I dropped the scowl. "Fine. But it's going to be *temporary*"—I pointed a finger at him to drive home the point—"until I figure out other arrangements."

He smiled, stepped to the side, and pushed the door open and waited for me to walk through. I hesitated, unwilling and unable to accept that I had just agreed to sleep at Trevor Ryan's house. *What the hell went so wrong that my life has become unrecognizable in a matter of two weeks?*

Trevor raised his eyebrows, questioning the holdup. With a growl, I got my feet moving and nearly elbowed him in the gut when I passed him on the threshold and caught him throwing Maggie a triumphant wink.

Five minutes later, I parked my car on a remote side street and climbed out, looking around to ensure no one was watching. Trevor pulled up behind me, his headlights allowing me to see what I was doing as I reached into the back of my SUV to withdraw my duffel and purse. When I emerged, he was already standing beside me. Without a word, he gently took the duffel from my shoulder and carried it to his truck while I locked my car then climbed into his passenger seat.

"All set?" he asked.

I nodded, putting my seat belt on.

Trevor pulled away from the curb and aimed his truck in the direction of his house. "Think you could have picked a spot a little farther away?" he asked.

I turned to look at him and noted his bemused smile.

We came to the end of the street, where he stopped at a red light. The rain had lessened to a mere sprinkle, and I inhaled deeply, taking a moment to enjoy the sight of the golden street lamps reflecting off the wet pavement. There was something about a summer rain that just seemed to wash everything clean.

"So, that situation with the cop in Vegas..."

My stomach somersaulted. *Is he really going to bring this up again?*

"That would have been what? Five, six years ago?"

I pulled my lower lip between my teeth and bit down on the soft tissue as I cursed the traffic light that refused to change. "Mm-hmm."

In my peripheral, I could see his contemplative nod. "And that situation... that's why you stopped dating?"

I crossed my legs and pressed my hands between them, uncomfortable in my skin and unsure of how to respond to his questions.

"Sorry. I didn't mean to make you uncomfortable." His tone was so empathetic, so genuine that I felt a crack in the armor I had kept in place all those years.

We sat in silence as I considered whether or not to answer. After all, he and everyone else had already heard the worst of it. And something about the way he was asking felt as though he was asking for *my* benefit rather than to cast judgment or because of a lust for gossip.

I relaxed my posture a bit and kept my eyes focused on the still-red traffic light. "Yes, that's why I stopped dating. Well..." I shifted in my seat. "I've *dated* since then, but it never goes beyond one or two dates. Lately, though, I'm just not interested in trying anymore."

Trevor looked at me. "Why is that?"

Never having really pondered that, I thought about it for a minute. "I just can't let myself trust someone enough to allow them to get close."

He nodded and scanned our surroundings. "And you had no idea that the guy was married?"

I whipped my head around. "Of course not!" I was horrified that he even felt the need to ask.

But then he looked at me again, and there was nothing but sympathy and a desire to understand reflected back at me.

I took a deep breath and forced my raging emotions to quiet. I was tired of running from this thing. Tired of trying in vain to pretend that it had never happened. Tired of the weight that had settled on my chest and pressed down on me with every breath. It was pointless to wish that I could change the past or erase that entire period from my life until it was nothing but a blank spot in a tapestry of memories.

My sigh was one of resignation. "It was a big call center, and I didn't work many shifts with who I now know to be his wife. Even when she and I *did* work together, I never saw him come in to visit her." I shrugged and looked out my window. "Apparently, they didn't have the best relationship."

"You don't say?"

Trevor's playful tone drew my gaze back to him, and I couldn't help but laugh at his sardonic grin. "Yeah, go figure, huh?"

Trevor's smile broadened, and in that moment, in a dark truck cab on a rainy summer night, I suddenly didn't feel so sad anymore. My breath came a little easier. The ice block around my heart felt a little less frigid.

The light turned green, and Trevor made a left. I watched him out of the corner of my eye, noting his relaxed posture—the way he just leaned back, one hand on the steering wheel, the other arm draped over the center console. What was it like to be that at ease? To have the kind of confidence that allowed you to be exactly who you were and not give a damn what anyone thought of it?

"You said you moved out here because of a friend." Though we hadn't seen another car or person for quite some time, his eyes were still alert and scanning. "I'm assuming that was Shelby?"

I nodded. "Yes. She moved out here to be with Josh after we graduated. After the situation with Trent—"

"The douchebag," he interjected.

I laughed. "Yes. The douchebag. I just needed to get away and clear my head. There wasn't a friendly face left in Dispatch after word got out, and all day long, people were whispering about me as I passed by." The pain resurfaced as the emotions of that dark time pumped through me and brought the memories back to life. "Where I had once stood out as a hard worker and someone who did the job really well, I was suddenly nothing more than a pathetic badge bunny and homewrecker." My eyes prickled, but I refused to let the tears fall. I had cried enough over what had happened. I took a deep breath, and like the tide pulling away from the shore, the sadness and shame began to abate. "For a young woman who wasn't very experienced with men or how cruel the world can be, it was a painful lesson."

"Ah." Trevor gave me the side-eye and a wry grin. "Hence the reason you insisted on parking in the next county just to keep your car from being spotted near my place."

Smiling sheepishly, I shrugged. "I was stupid. He toyed with me, and I fell for it. It won't happen again."

Trevor's gaze swept my face, but it was impossible to guess what he was thinking.

A moment later, we turned in to his neighborhood, and I directed my attention out the window again, noting the cute yards and front porches decorated with rocking chairs and potted plants. I'd known generally where he lived, but I had never actually been to his house. Part of me was expecting to walk into something that resembled a frat house, complete with kegs and pictures of naked girls pinned to the walls.

"So," Trevor continued, "you came out here to clear your head and decided to stay?"

"Pretty much. I left Las Vegas Metro without knowing what my next move would be. Shelby and I have been best friends since we were little girls—a lot like you and Gabe." I glanced at him, and he smiled, the affection for his best friend as clear as day. "She convinced me to come stay with her and Josh until I figured things out. I saw the opening for a dispatcher with Eden Falls PD, and the rest is history."

"Their loss, our gain." Trevor pulled into his driveway, and I leaned forward to get a better look at the house. The windshield still bore a few water drops, but the rain had stopped, giving me a clear view of the single-story dwelling, which was dark gray and accented by natural wood elements that included the front door, the pillars of the porch, and the garage doors, which we were parked in front of. The lawn was neatly manicured, and though there were no flowers, the flower beds were lined with small shrubs. The whole appearance was aesthetically pleasing, but it was most certainly a house without a woman's touch.

We climbed out of the truck, and I waited for Trevor by the grille as he retrieved my bag. When he joined me, I started to turn away to head for the front door, but he placed a hand on my arm to stop me. I glanced down at where our bodies touched then looked up at him, my brows coming together in question.

As we stood inches apart, Trevor gazed at me with eyes that were soft and reassuring. "I'm sorry you've had to sacrifice so much for this case." He brushed his thumb lightly over my skin, making goose bumps erupt everywhere he made contact. "For what it's worth, I respect the hell out of you."

I didn't know what to say. I didn't know how to express what it meant that he understood what the case was costing me and that, despite knowing my darkest secret, he still respected me. What was more, I didn't know what to make of all the ways Trevor was proving to be someone other than I had thought.

Time stood still, and the world went silent as I got lost in that moment, completely and utterly captivated by him. It wasn't just that he was good-looking. It was the way he *wore* those good looks; the twinkle of mischief in his blue eyes; his crooked grin; and the way he leaned in and looked at me as though I was the most interesting thing he'd ever seen. Something about him drew me in until all else disappeared, and the only thing my mind could comprehend was him.

Trevor released my arm, and I couldn't deny that I wished he hadn't. The loss of his warmth and that connection hit me harder than I was prepared to consider. Then his mouth curved into a fiendish grin, and the butterflies in my stomach were beating down the doors again. "Time to get back to work..." He clipped my chin with a finger as he walked by and called over his shoulder, "*Quinny-baby.*"

I tried to fight the smile working its way up my face as I watched him saunter away, but it was a losing battle. So I turned to follow him, and for the first time, I didn't mind the nickname.

CHAPTER 24

Trevor

THE MORNING LIGHT filtered through my blinds, dragging me from sleep, though I was far from having had enough. I swung my legs over the side of my bed and propped my elbows on my knees, studying the carpet fibers as I contemplated the grueling task Quinn and I had ahead of us that day.

With a groan, I stood and scrubbed my hands up and down my face in an effort to banish the fatigue still pulling at my senses. My footsteps were barely audible as I padded to the dresser and pulled out a pair of sweats. Quinn probably wouldn't appreciate my walking around in my boxer-briefs.

My thoughts drifted to the gorgeous brunette asleep in the bed across the hall. We'd stayed up until three in the morning, trying to figure out the riddle to the next victim's identity. We hadn't made a lot of progress, but when her yawning had started to interrupt every other word out of her mouth, I insisted we call it a night, even if it was only to get a few hours of rest before we were back at it. She protested, as I'd expected, but in the end, I'd won the battle, gently pulling her from her chair and ushering her down the hall and into the guest bedroom.

Although I had practically been dead on my feet, I tossed and turned for God only knew how long, unable to stop thinking about the fact that Quinn was so near. I'd imagined what she might be wearing as she slipped between the cream-colored sheets. Did she like to sleep naked? I doubted it, especially since she was in an unfamiliar bed. She was more likely the type to wear sweats and an old T-shirt, something that was comfortable and, in her mind, could in no way turn a man on. Except that Quinn was in a league of her own when it came to beauty and sex appeal. I was sure it would have disappointed her to know she could walk around dressed as the Michelin Man and still give every man within sight a hard-on.

In the end, since it was *my* fantasy, I'd settled on an image of her in a lace camisole with matching panties and tried very hard not to think about how tempted I was to march across the hall and bring her back to my bed.

After pulling on my sweats, I trudged into the master bathroom and splashed some cold water on my face. My reflection told the truth of how many hours I'd been putting in. My eyes were bloodshot, and since I hadn't shaved for a few days, my beard had grown in enough to give me a roguish appearance.

As I went about brushing my teeth, my thoughts drifted to the details I had learned about Quinn the day before. The relief on her face had been unmistakable when I told her how much I respected her. It was only then that I realized why she had always been so uptight. She took pride in her work, and after the incident in Vegas and how *one* decision had ruined the reputation she'd worked so hard to build, she was determined to never again give anyone a reason to see her as anything but professional and the badass dispatcher she was.

Knowing that, I could understand why she'd always given me a wide berth. With my reputation and the way the dispatchers liked to gossip, even a friendly conversation between us would have turned into a rumor that had us in bed by the end of the day.

Still, I wasn't sure how we were supposed to go back to the way things were before the case after everything we'd already been through together. The fact that she had opened up to me the previous night, been so honest and vulnerable, proved that things had changed between us. And I liked it.

I smiled as I thought back on that night I'd dragged her to Rustlers. She'd been so pissed that I had refused to take no for an answer, but she had clearly enjoyed herself.

She wasn't the only one who was surprised by the outcome of that evening. I'd watched her with Liz and Alex while I played pool with the boys. Seeing her laugh and interact with my adopted sisters as though she had always been a part of their circle had stirred something in me, something that I couldn't even name. But it felt like a piece that had been missing from deep inside had finally found its way home. It scared the hell out of me, but the thought of losing it again scared me even more.

I dried my mouth with the hand towel by the sink then stared at my reflection. Quinn would never go for someone like me. She had made that clear loudly and often. And I wasn't the type of guy who could give her what she wanted and deserved. I was the guy a woman hooked up with when she wanted to have a good time and blow off a little steam. I wasn't the guy she could depend on to help her navigate the waters of life when they got rough. I didn't do serious. It wasn't in my wheelhouse.

But that didn't have to stop us from being friends. I cared about Quinn and had for a long time. And I would do whatever I had to do to get her through this shitty situation in one piece.

I turned away from the mirror, wanting to get started on breakfast so that it would be ready when Quinn woke. In nothing but my sweatpants, I headed down the hall toward the kitchen, rubbing a hand across my chest, but when my feet hit tile, I halted and did a double take at the kitchen table.

A smile spread across my face as I shook my head and sauntered over to where Quinn was drooling on the notes spread out beneath her. Her dark eyelashes fluttered with her dreams, a delicate blush tinging the cheek that wasn't squished against the table. I ran my eyes down her body, tilting my head to see the full length of her beneath the table. At least she had changed from her jeans and sweatshirt into a pair of flannel sleep shorts and a white tank top. Now, *that* was a sight I could get used to.

Bending down, I put my hand on her back and drew gentle circles. It took a few seconds, but then her face scrunched up, and a soft moan came from her pursed lips. She sat up slowly, stretching her arms overhead. Then she winced and dropped them abruptly. "Oomph."

I raised my eyebrows. "A little stiff?"

She looked up at me as much as she could manage with the kink in her neck, her golden eyes hazy with the fog of sleep. "Yeah."

I pressed a hand to the base of her neck and massaged, trying to loosen her knots. "Go take a hot shower, and get rid of some of those aches. I'll have breakfast and coffee ready by the time you're out."

Quinn still seemed half-asleep, but she nodded and trudged toward the bathroom at the end of the hall, her wild curls bobbing and bouncing with each step.

I chuckled as I watched her go. Then I redirected my attention to food. Once the eggs were cooking and the coffee was percolating, I stepped outside to a crisp morning. The sun was already high in the sky, its bright-yellow rays pressing in on the remnants of fog from the previous night's showers.

I bent to retrieve the newspaper at my feet and waved to my elderly neighbor across the street, who held his paper in one hand and doggedly picked weeds from his flower bed with the other. The paper rustled as I unfolded it and began scanning the headlines. There wasn't much that caught my attention until...

"Fuck." My eyes darted back and forth as I rapidly consumed details that shouldn't have been in print anywhere other than our police file. The situation got worse with each line.

Not only were the specifics of the last victim's death and disposal described in gory detail, but a large portion of the article was dedicated to Quinn's sordid history and her supposed failure to save the victim because of her *lust for the spotlight as well as for the lead investigator, Office Trevor Ryan.*

"Fuck me," I muttered under my breath.

I lifted my eyes to the pastoral scene around me, which completely belied the ugliness that had befallen our town. This was going to devastate Quinn. A breeze kissed my bare skin and ruffled my hair, but I hardly noticed as I contemplated how to tell her. She needed to know sooner rather than later. I would prefer she hear it from me than give those vipers in Dispatch a chance to catch her off guard.

Remembering that I had breakfast on the stove, I jogged back to the kitchen and threw the newspaper onto the counter before turning off all the burners. I had just killed the last flame when I heard the bathroom door open.

Quinn appeared in the kitchen a moment later, dressed in a pair of black slacks and a sleeveless emerald blouse, her hair wet and wavy.

I must not have done a very good job schooling my features, because the moment her eyes landed on me, she halted, her expression speculative. "What's wrong?"

Folding my arms, I shrugged. "Nothing. Just the same old bullshit."

She nodded slowly. "Uh-huh. What kind of bullshit?"

I studied the tile floor and ran my hand up the back of my head, my hair fanning my palm. Deciding that I might as well rip off the bandage, I met her eyes and opened my mouth, but before I could say anything, her phone rang.

Quinn held up a finger. "One sec." She went to where her phone was perched on the end of the counter and glanced to see who was calling then frowned. "That's weird. It's showing Unavailable." She tapped the screen and put the phone to her ear. "Hello?"

Quinn's face morphed from confused to stunned in a matter of seconds. "How did you get this number?"

I closed the distance between us and stood in front of her, my expression a silent question.

Her eyes bounced back and forth between mine, then her head swiveled toward the counter, her gaze aimed a short distance from where her phone had been. She brushed past me, and when I twisted to see where she was going, I uttered an oath as she snatched the paper off the counter.

Quinn frantically read the article that had ruined an otherwise nice morning. Then she spoke into her phone again. "No! And do not call this number again!" She punched the end-call button before she slammed the phone down on the counter, her face far too pale.

I moved to stand beside her and cupped her elbow. "Who was on the phone?"

Keeping her eyes on the article and a death grip on the paper, she said, "That asshole reporter who wrote this article. He had the nerve to ask me for a comment."

I pressed my lips together, regretting she had found out that way. "I'm sorry, Quinn. I was trying to tell you about the article when he called."

Quinn slammed the paper back down on the counter and covered her face with her hands. "Who is doing this?" she asked, her voice muffled.

I shook my head, even though she couldn't see me. "I don't know. But we're going to find out."

"It has to be the killer." She lowered her hands and looked into my eyes. "Humiliating and discrediting me is all part of the pleasure he gets out of this sick *game*."

My eyes danced over her features as I searched for the right words. "I know this is hard, Quinn. But the sooner we get this guy, the sooner *all* of this goes away. We'll deal with the articles, but right now, our priority is figuring out who the next victim is."

She studied me for a moment. Then slowly, the tension eased from her face and shoulders. She took a deep breath and nodded then returned to the table and the notes scattered about. Over the next several hours, we sat at that piece of wood and poured all of our energy and focus into the riddle the killer had delivered.

It was early evening when Quinn sat back and rubbed her temples. "I feel pretty confident that she used to be a nurse, but she does something else now."

"Why do you say that?" I glanced down at her scribbles on the notepad in front of her.

With both index fingers, she pointed at the first and second clues. "She is descended from the nightingale once but related twice, and she is guilty of stealing life force, but she no longer takes, having chosen to give power instead." Quinn looked up at me. "Florence Nightingale is considered the founder of modern nursing, also sometimes referred to as the *mother* of modern nursing. So one could argue that nurses *descend* from her." She tapped her finger on the second clue. "And life force often refers to blood. A nurse draws blood, but this one doesn't *take* life force anymore, so I think she must do something else now."

I thought about her reasoning for a moment and nodded. "Yeah, I think you're onto something." I jerked my chin toward her notepad. "What about the *related twice* part?"

Quinn pursed her lips, her brow furrowing. "I'm not sure about that part yet." She ran her finger under the second clue as she reread it. Under her breath, she kept repeating the phrase "having chosen to give power instead."

Turning the phrase over in my mind as I meditated on her chant, I braced my forearms on the table and laced my fingers together. "If the first part of the clue has to do with her profession, and he's speaking metaphorically, then it would make sense to assume that the second part of the clue fits the same pattern."

Quinn slanted her eyes toward me, waiting for me to continue.

"Metaphorically, knowledge is power," I said. "So maybe she imparts knowledge now—something like an educator or librarian or something."

Quinn's eyes dipped to the table, then she nodded slowly. "I think that's a thread worth following." She made a note next to the clue, her knee bouncing so frantically beneath the table that I could feel the vibration through the floor. Then she dropped her pen and tapped the face of her phone, making it light up to check the time. It was just past seventeen hundred hours. Quinn's expression tightened.

I tapped her paper where the third clue was written. "Let's move on to this one. We haven't made much progress on it yet."

Quinn read the clue aloud. "She used to be a real tigress. A queen with a court of her own. Though nothing like her namesake, who chose the Tin Man over the Lion." She exhaled forcefully and slumped back in her chair. "Well, the Tin Man and Lion are obviously *Wizard of Oz* references, so maybe her name is Dorothy or Judy."

I thought about that for a moment then scrunched my mouth to one side. "I don't know. It seems a little too obvious. Not to mention that Dorothy never chose the Tin Man over the Lion."

Quinn growled and propped her elbows on the table, dropping her head into her hands. "You're right." She shook her head without looking up. "We're running out of time, Trevor. How am I supposed to figure out who these women are with so little time and information to go on?"

"Have you ever considered that maybe that's the point?"

Quinn met my eyes. "What do you mean?

I leaned in. "This guy is a sadist, Quinn. Maybe offering up these clues, making you think you actually have a chance to save someone but never giving you enough to succeed, is part of what gets him off."

Her eyes widened, then she shook her head and looked away. "I can't afford to think like that, or I'm never going to figure any of this out." She grabbed her pen and began adding notes to those she had already made beside the third clue.

Deciding that, for the moment, it was best to drop the discussion surrounding the likelihood of our figuring out who the woman was—or who any of the women were—I continued to work the clues with Quinn, because hope was all she had to hold on to—hope that we could beat this guy at his own game and that at least one woman would be spared the fate he had in store for her. But as I watched Quinn's emotional state deteriorate with each passing hour, I worried that she would end up a different sort of victim of the game the killer was playing.

CHAPTER 25

Trevor

Midnight had once again come and gone, and we failed to identify the killer's next victim. Having had nothing else to go on and feeling pretty confident about the nurse angle, we spent the last hours before our deadline calling the hospital and private practitioners, trying to track down any current or former nurses named Judy or Dorothy. I even woke the principals of each of our schools to ask about any staff who had formerly worked in the medical profession. But our efforts had been in vain.

So we once again found ourselves in Dispatch, waiting for a call that no one wanted to answer. I glanced at Quinn, who was seated in her usual place across from me. She was slumped back in her chair, her eyes downcast and glazed over, like she was lost somewhere deep inside of herself. Her navy uniform polo, usually pressed and neatly tucked into her black slacks, was rumpled and hung loosely around her middle.

From the workstation against the far wall, Julia glanced over her shoulder at Quinn, as she had been all morning. Then, as she had each time before, she turned her worried eyes on me. I tried to offer a reassuring smile, but it was getting harder to pretend that everything was under control. We had never *had* any control in the situation.

Sighing, I leaned forward and propped my elbows on the desk. My laptop screen was open but forgotten. I let my gaze drift across the room, my vision losing focus as I contemplated the reality we faced. It was beyond frustrating that our investigation was turning up so little evidence. The killer was like a specter, able to slip in and out of places and never leave a single piece of himself behind. And it seemed as though he knew our town better than we did.

After withdrawing my cell from the chest pocket of my uniform, I tapped Gabe's number.

He answered on the second ring. "What's up, man?"

With my thumb and forefinger, I rubbed my eyes. "Can you call the lab and lean on them a bit? See if we can get those results back a little faster?"

"You got it."

"Thanks, brother."

I was about to disconnect when Gabe said, "You sound like shit. You doing okay?"

Glancing at Quinn again, I found that she was still lost in a stupor, but I lowered my voice anyway. "Things are just a little tense in here today."

Gabe read between the lines, understanding how hard it was to just sit there, waiting for another call from that asshole to tell us where to retrieve the body of another victim we had failed. Not to mention the lingering question on everyone's mind—*who is it going to be?*

"Yeah, I can imagine," he said. "How's Quinn holding up?"

Since I was a cop, reading body language and noting details about a person's appearance were second nature to me, and I didn't like what I saw when I looked at Quinn. Her face was pale. Her eyes were unfocused. And her movements—usually crisp and efficient—were sluggish, as if she didn't even have the energy to breathe.

I would give Gabe details later, but at the moment, Blair was watching me like a hawk and hanging on every word, so I simply said, "It's taking a lot out of her."

Gabe grunted and was silent a moment before he wrapped up the call. "I'll see what I can do about the lab. Keep me posted on anything else you need, and take care of our girl."

"I will. Thanks, man."

Several hours later, near midafternoon, the call we were all waiting for came. The killer didn't waste any time telling Quinn where we could find his latest kill. He seemed more interested in playing with her than drawing out the suspense of where he had dumped his victim.

"I have to admit, Quinn..." His voice was hardly more than a sinister whisper. "I'm a little disappointed. I expected you would be a more formidable opponent."

Quinn closed her eyes against his words. The bastard was mind-fucking her, reinforcing her fear that *her* deficiencies were costing the women their lives. And I knew her well enough to know that the reason she didn't respond was because she agreed with him.

The killer sighed regretfully. "You'll have another opportunity. Perhaps you've just been... distracted."

Quinn's partners were once again turned in their seats, unblinking and fixated on her. Apparently, they had received my message loud and clear the last time, because none of them had even dared to try jumping on the line. Another call came in, and Julia turned back to her screens and answered it.

The killer continued his diatribe in that same cold, disembodied tone. "You really didn't learn much from your unfortunate experience in Vegas, did you?"

Quinn's response was wary. "What do you mean?"

"I mean," he said, dragging out the last word, "that it would seem history is repeating itself."

Quinn tensed, her eyes shooting to mine. "I don't know what you're referring to."

"Hmm, perhaps we should ask Lead Investigator Ryan. I'm

sure he's figured it out." His macabre chuckle followed as fire rippled beneath my skin. The son of a bitch was going to make sure everyone thought Quinn and I were fucking.

It was so obvious what he was doing... what he had been *systematically* doing all along. He was dismantling Quinn piece by piece, slipping into her mind whenever he felt like it, sabotaging her from behind enemy lines. And he had read her well enough to know that she would fail to notice his trespasses because she would be too focused on what she believed were her shortcomings and failures.

The chief and most of the department may have been willing to sacrifice Quinn in this high-stakes game, but I sure as hell wasn't going to let that asshole destroy her. I had to get his attention off Quinn and give him someone else to target.

Before he could say another word to her, I unmuted my phone. "I'm right here, asshole. You wanna talk to someone, you can talk to me." I took a seat and leaned back, leaving the typing to Quinn.

The killer's voice took on an edge that I had never heard in his conversations with Quinn. *Good. Let the asshole play his games with a man for a change.*

"Officer Ryan. I have to say I don't think I'll enjoy talking to you as much as I do our lovely Quinn, but I'd be lying if I said I wasn't hoping for the chance to speak with you."

The promise in his tone set off my internal warning system. "Oh yeah? Why is that?"

"Does she know?"

"Who?"

"Quinn."

I lifted my eyes to find Quinn motionless and watching me over her monitors. She still had her phone pressed to her ear, but her line was muted.

"I'm not interested in playing your mind games, but if you've got the balls to show your face, let's see how you do against someone other than an unsuspecting woman."

The killer sneered. "You and I aren't that different, Ryan. We both hunt the same prey. We just fuck them in different ways."

"You and I are very different. I leave women satisfied. You only manage to leave them beaten and dead." My words dripped with condescension. I wanted the asshole to get pissed... to slip and hang himself with his own rope. "Is that why you do it? It's the only way you can get your hands on them?" I snickered. "Do they point and laugh when you try to impress them with your dick? Or are you just too fucking repulsive to even get that far?"

His voice began to quiver as the rage took hold. "What? I should be more like you? Debasing myself with the kind of filth that frequents *your* bed?"

My gut tightened. *Is he taking a shot in the dark, or has he been studying me as well?* I masked my unease with sarcasm. "You're right. I'm sure you're quite the catch. Better to force yourself on a woman than lower your standards."

His laugh was mirthless. "That's amusing. A small-town hack cop lecturing me about low standards? Maybe we should ask Quinn for her opinion on the subject. Tell me, Ryan, does she have any idea what a pathetic fuckup you are?"

He paused, and my eyes found Quinn again.

"Oh yes. I know all about you," he said, taunting. "I know you were destined for the NFL, but you *pissed* it away on a bunch of trash pussy and booze until you were kicked out of college and forced to come back to this shithole of a town with your tail between your legs. I know you went from being the golden boy to nothing more than this town's great shame. Good thing Mommy and Daddy didn't live to see that, hmm?"

I ground my molars so hard that it felt like they would crack. All too aware of the eyes on me, I kept my body relaxed and my attention fixed on the shadows across the room.

The killer snickered, his husky voice like claws scraping the inside of my brain. "You. Are. Nothing. Ryan. You aren't capable of anything more than giving orgasms to women who think the periodic table is a menses-tracking chart. And by the time my work here is done, you're going to realize what a fucking *joke* you really are."

He disconnected, the click reverberating in my head along with his words. Quinn's keyboard had gone silent somewhere along the way. She stared at me, her eyes wide and horrified. *How can I expect her to look at me any other way now that she knows the truth? The truth of what a waste of space I actually am.*

She swallowed hard but was otherwise frozen.

I threw the phone down on the desk and stood, grabbing my jacket from the back of my chair. Keeping my eyes down, I collected my things, unable to look at Quinn—unable to witness the disgust written plainly across her features. As I strode toward the long dark hall that led to the exit, I kept my gaze dead ahead and my voice neutral as I called back to her, "I'm headed to the crime scene. I'll touch base later."

I stepped into the saffron light of the sun. Its brilliance was fading under the menace of thick black storm clouds rolling in. I felt nothing of the day's remaining warmth as the cold breath of my demons licked down my spine, their claws tearing at my insides. But no one would know. I had gotten good at disguising my monsters in a jester's garb and silencing their voices with a warm body and a good time.

CHAPTER 26

Quinn

I PUSHED against the heavy door and ran into the night. Thunder roared so loudly that I could have sworn the buildings rattled. Lightning flashed in the distance as sheets of rain fell around me. Despite the storm, the night was muggy—too warm for my jacket, so I held it over my head as a makeshift umbrella while I sprinted to my silver Xterra.

The parking lot behind the station was half-flooded, and of course the flooding was on the side that bordered Dispatch. With no way to avoid the massive pool of water, I leaped from the curb and tried to ignore the way my shoes filled after I landed with a giant splash. Had I not volunteered to work late, I would have been home—well, at Trevor's—hours ago, warm and with a full belly.

Instead, I had stayed to fill in for a while after one of the night-shift dispatchers called out, leaving the center short-staffed during a savage storm that had kept our phone lines ringing off the hook for the past several hours. Fallen trees that had blocked roads, broken windows, and smashed cars along with power outages and numerous car accidents had kept us busy enough that I had, for brief periods of time, managed to stop thinking about the deranged killer terrorizing our town.

The rainwater squished in my shoes as I continued the jog to my car. Only about twenty feet away, I held out my key fob. The lights on my SUV flashed as I pressed the button to unlock the doors. Once I was inside, I tossed my sopping-wet jacket onto the passenger seat and swept my sodden curls off my face. After starting the engine to let the car warm up, I pulled my cell phone from my purse and called Trevor. His phone rang several times before going to voice mail. Frowning, I ended the call without leaving a message.

Though I couldn't see anything but torrents of water cascading down my windshield, I stared at the glass, chewing my bottom lip. I hadn't heard from Trevor all afternoon, and that fact had been distracting me, even amid the chaos in the center. I tried telling myself that he was likely just as busy as I was. The body of Jennifer Davis, our most recent victim, had been left outdoors at the waste-transfer station. So he and the rest of our personnel charged with processing the crime scene were undoubtedly working like fiends to preserve as much evidence as possible.

Still, when the units had cleared the scene hours earlier, and Trevor still hadn't checked in, the knot in my stomach tightened further. During the phone call, he had done a good job of hiding that the killer's blows were landing, but I knew Trevor well enough to recognize a lot of his tells. It had been clear to me by the way his jaw had tightened and he'd focused his gaze across the room that he was struggling to maintain his composure.

I called his number one more time, and when it went to voice mail again, I told myself that he was likely already home and had just left his phone in a different room—even if that *was* totally out of character. Since this whole ordeal had started, he'd made himself available to me at all hours of the day and night in case I needed him.

Releasing a deep sigh that caused the wet spirals around my face to sashay, I placed one more call, this time to Rustlers to order takeout. I was way too exhausted to cook, and I was willing to bet Trevor felt the same. Once the order was placed, I turned my windshield wipers and the heater on full blast and proceeded to make my way through the flooded streets of town. Though navigating proved difficult because I still couldn't see much through the windshield, and the lights from passing cars and traffic signals reflecting off the wet, dark surface of the road played tricks with my eyes, my thoughts still somehow managed to drift back to the phone call earlier that day.

Trevor's eyes had filled with pain when the killer referred to him as the town's shame, and my heart cracked at the sight of it. And when Trevor packed up his things and left, refusing to meet my eyes, I had to fight both tears and the urge to run after him to comfort him and tell him that all those awful things that were said weren't true. Trevor was an incredible cop. I had witnessed on many occasions how much he cared about our town and the people in it. And the town cared about *him*. It didn't matter how he had ended up back here. This was where he was meant to be. And he was doing exactly what he was born to do.

As I turned onto the road that would take me to Rustlers, the memory of our conversation from when Trevor had dragged me to the bar came flooding back. He talked about Rustlers and all those women as being a distraction. At the time, I'd thought he meant a distraction from the job, but now I wondered if all the one-night stands and acting like the life of the party were really just a way for him to mask the shame and pain of his past—a way to avoid having to face the things that perhaps he had been running from for years.

With that thought, a worse one formed. Maybe that was the reason Trevor wasn't answering his phone. Perhaps the killer had triggered him enough to send him right into the arms of some harlot he had speed-dialed in hopes of erasing the day and everything the killer had brought to the surface. My stomach twisted tighter with each passing minute as I grew more certain that was the reason Trevor had disappeared. Images of him with his lips pressed to some faceless woman's neck, kissing his way down her throat as his hands roamed over her body, filled my mind as completely as the bile coating my throat.

I gripped the steering wheel harder and glanced in the rearview mirror, mostly as a means of distracting myself, since I couldn't even see through the water pouring down my rear window. I wasn't sure what bothered me more—the possibility that he had turned to some other woman for comfort or that the thought of it was wrecking me. *When did Trevor go from being someone I couldn't even stand to be in the same room with to someone who consumed my thoughts and provoked the worst case of jealousy I've ever experienced?*

I turned in to the parking lot of Rustlers, dodging water-filled potholes, and parked beneath the neon sign on the front facade. After killing the engine, I grabbed my purse and pressed my mouth into a firm line. I didn't want to know what Trevor was up to or who he was with. If he wanted to turn to cheap thrills when the going got tough, then fine. I wouldn't let my heart get any more tangled with him than it obviously already was. Deciding that I would get dinner and go back to my place instead of his, I shoved open my door and let the rain engulf me, not even trying to outrun it this time.

Trevor wouldn't be happy about my returning to my house, but if I was right about what he was up to at that very moment, he wouldn't even notice, and by avoiding his place, I could avoid confirming the very thing that would blow a hole right through my chest.

It didn't take long for my eyes to adjust to the dim atmosphere when I stepped into the bar's entryway, and when I proceeded to the main room, I was surprised to see how dead it was, considering it was a Saturday night. Montanans were accustomed to severe weather, so it took a lot to keep them home when Mother Nature howled. I turned toward the bar, hoping the food was ready so that I could get the hell home and forget about my awful day, but I halted when my eyes snagged on a lone figure sitting hunched over near the end of the bar.

Trevor was dressed in a pair of blue jeans and a white T-shirt, his arms propped on the bar top and encircling several empty shot glasses and a half-drained pint of beer. His gaze was downcast, and he seemed not to notice the half-naked barflies flitting around him, making various pathetic attempts to get his attention.

I walked toward him slowly, hiking my purse up when it began to slide down my shoulder. As I drew near, one particularly territorial floozy glared at me but immediately withered when I squared my shoulders and gave her a look that dared her to try me.

I dropped onto the barstool on Trevor's left and waited for him to acknowledge me.

"You should be home," he said without looking up.

I nodded. "Yeah. So should you."

He gave a laugh that was devoid of humor then tipped his pint glass to his lips and drained the rest of the amber liquid.

"You didn't answer my calls," I said.

Trevor raised his finger to the bartender, signaling for another round. "I disappoint everyone. Why should you be any different?"

I made eye contact with the bartender and shook my head firmly. He set down the glass he'd been about to fill from the tap and walked to the other end of the bar, giving us some privacy.

Putting my hand on Trevor's shoulder, I leaned in. "Trevor, you're better than this guy. Don't let him do this to you."

He scoffed and turned his glassy eyes on me. "He's not *doing* anything to me, Quinn. Everything he said was true. I did this to myself."

Trevor, realizing he'd never gotten his next round, swiveled his head around. "Where the fuck did Scott go?"

I stood and wrapped my hand around Trevor's bicep, giving it a yank before he had a chance to call out to the bartender. "Come on. I'm taking you home."

Trevor shook me loose and propped both elbows on the bar, raking his hands through his golden locks. The action loosened his gel, causing several longer strands to fall across his forehead, and for a heartbeat, I was rendered immobile. The man was unbelievably handsome, and my body was taking notice. I squeezed my thighs together in an attempt to neutralize my libido then gave myself a mental slap and a firm reminder to focus on what was important.

I grabbed Trevor's arm again and leaned over his shoulder so that my mouth was pressed to his ear. "Trevor Ryan, you get your ass up and walk out that door with me, or so help me, I will make sure you get every piece of paper that fills our queue from here to kingdom come."

Trevor looked over his shoulder at me, a smirk-filled dare written in his features that quickly vanished when I gave his arm a yank that had more muscle behind it than he clearly thought I was capable of. I tugged him to his feet, pulling him off balance before he got his legs beneath him. He began to fall into me but then caught the bar top with his free hand and steadied himself, gazing down with a look that was equal parts shock and irritation. "You're really fucking stubborn. You know that?" he growled but finally started walking toward the door.

"Then I'm in good company," I said to his back as I followed him out.

His white shirt was soaked through seconds after we'd exited the bar. It was impossible not to notice his tan skin through the thin material, every peak and valley of his well-muscled torso on display. I put a hand on his back to guide him to my SUV and flexed my fingers against the warmth seeping from his body into mine.

Once Trevor was situated in my passenger seat, I ran around to the driver's side and climbed in, dinner long forgotten. All I wanted was to get him home and out of his funk.

The first few minutes of the drive were filled with a tense silence. Dozens of things that I wanted to say came to mind, but I discarded each of them, unable to find the right one. But it was Trevor who, surprisingly, spoke first.

"He's right."

I glanced at him then quickly returned my attention to the treacherous road. "About what?"

Trevor dropped his head against the seat as if the effort to hold it up any longer was too great. "It's a good thing my parents aren't alive to witness how I turned out."

My eyes shot to him again, but before I could respond, he continued.

"They both thought I was going to have a big football career. That's what everyone thought. Including me." He looked out his window, and his voice grew quieter. "Didn't even make it out of college."

I swallowed hard, not quite sure what to say. I wanted to encourage him to talk about it, about the things he had clearly never dealt with, but he was teetering on a cliff, and I was worried I would push him over the edge. Then I took a deep breath and reminded myself that I talked people off cliffs every day. "What happened?"

I half expected him not to answer, but after a long pause, he did. "I went to college on a football scholarship. My first couple of seasons couldn't have gone better, and the third was shaping up to be my best. I had a number of pro teams interested in me."

He fell silent again and continued to stare out the passenger window.

"And then?" I asked.

Sighing deeply, he turned his gaze to the windshield. "And then my parents died. Car crash."

I glanced at him, scanning his profile for signs of emotion, but from what I could see in the dark interior, his features illuminated only by the headlights of passing cars, his face was a mask of stoicism.

He shrugged. "After that, I started partying and sleeping around. My performance on the field got increasingly worse, and so did my grades. So they tossed me out of school."

I nodded pensively. "And that's when you came home."

He scoffed. "Yeah. Didn't have anywhere else to go." He

propped his elbow on the window ledge, fingering the weather stripping along the top of the glass. "Gabe was deployed, so I just came back and did odd jobs. Construction. Chopping wood. Stuff like that." He shrugged again.

"Didn't you have family you could have gone to live with until you figured things out?"

He pursed his lips and shook his head. "Nope. My parents were it. No other family."

My heart cracked again. His tone said he didn't care, but his body language told me the pain was still as strong as it had been back then. "You made something of yourself, Trevor. Despite everything you went through. That's something to be proud of."

He scoffed again. "Yep. I sure did. I'm a thirty-two-year-old frat boy. I spend most of my free time at the bar, shooting pool, and I've had more one-night stands than a gigolo." He looked out his window again. "Just a hack cop in a small town."

My vision blurred. I blinked frantically, trying to banish the tears before they could fall. It was then that I realized why Trevor was telling me all of this. He hated himself, and he was using the confession as punishment.

"You're right to think I'm beneath you," he said quietly. "That's why I never made a move. You deserve so much better than me."

We had just pulled in front of his garage. He shucked his seat belt and exited the car before I could even turn off the engine and was almost to the front walk by the time I caught up to him. Grabbing a fistful of his soaked-through T-shirt, I spun him around to face me. The rain was falling so hard that I had to squint as I looked up at him. "You don't get to walk away from me. From *this*." I shouted to be heard over the storm. "And you don't get to keep hating yourself for falling apart after you lost your parents, Trevor. They would never be disappointed in you for loving them *so much* that you went to pieces when they died."

Even in the dark, Trevor's eyes blazed like blue flames, smoldering with an intensity that went beyond words.

With the fabric I was still clutching in my fist, I shook him. "You are an incredible cop. You have a town full of people who love and respect you, and part of the reason they love you as much as they do is because you loved *them* first." I released his shirt and jabbed my finger into his granite chest. "And you *do* have a family. A family that would die for you. A family that you returned to when you were lost and alone. Gabe and Liz and Alex—they would do anything for you, just as you would for them."

Trevor continued to gaze down at me, his body and expression rigid and unreadable as the rain dripped from the end of his nose and chin.

I swallowed hard and gathered the courage to tell him the rest of what he needed to hear—the truth. "And I have *never* considered you beneath me. Do you aggravate the hell out of me sometimes? Yes. Often, actually."

The corner of his mouth twitched.

"Do I hate the way you flirt with anything in a skirt then dare to flirt with me afterward? Yes." I stepped closer to him, the heat from his body radiating against mine, both of us thoroughly drenched. "But that doesn't change the fact that I know you're going to be a hell of a catch for a *good* woman once you stop avoiding all the grief and pain you've been running from by distracting yourself with easy women and a good time."

My chest heaved with the force of my conviction. I stood toe to toe with him, tilting my head back so that he could see the truth in my eyes. The warm rain slid down my skin, plastering my work clothes to my body in the same way my hair fell in wavy strands around my face.

Trevor was silent for the longest time, the tension between us thick and crackling. Just when I was about to demand that he say something, he took my face in his hands and lowered his mouth to mine. I froze. But then his warm lips began to move slowly and demandingly, and my body melted into him. I gripped his wrists as he cradled my face. Then his tongue slid against the seam of my lips as he gently asked for more. With a whimper, I opened my mouth to him.

The scent of summer rain and damp earth enveloped us. The taste of tequila and beer lingered on his tongue. Trevor's hands slid from my jaw and traveled down to my neck and then my shoulders, slowly making their way to my hips. He pulled me against him, growling when our bodies made contact.

Our tongues tangled and dueled, taking and giving in equal measure. Without thought, I ground my hips against him, shivering as he took the kiss deeper. The sound of the rain was lost to the roar in my ears as electricity shot down to my toes and ricocheted back up every inch of my body.

Trever snaked his arms around my waist and turned us so that he was walking me backward toward the house. We stumbled up the porch steps, our lips never losing contact. When my back hit the front door, his hips ground into mine, and I hooked my leg around him. He slid a hand down to hold it in place. Only when he pulled away after several fumbled attempts to get his key in the lock did my senses return enough to make me pause.

Trevor noticed immediately and pulled back to look into my eyes. "What's wrong?"

I bit my bottom lip, the fear of being too vulnerable causing the words to lodge in my throat.

Trevor brushed a thumb across my cheek, softening his gaze. "Do you want me to stop?"

When I didn't respond right away, he said, "I don't ever want you to do anything you don't want to, Quinn. I don't want you to have any regrets when it comes to us."

The gentleness and honesty in his words made me feel safe enough to admit what I truly feared. "I don't want to be your next distraction," I said softly.

The concern cleared from his face, a small smile lifting the corners of his luscious lips. "You've always been a distraction, Quinn. Since day one." His smile grew, and I was surprised to realize I was smiling too.

Trevor brushed a wet curl from my face and placed his hands on either side of my jaw again, his eyes searching mine. I gave him a small nod. Slowly, he leaned in for another kiss, giving me the chance to pull away if I wanted to.

But I didn't want to. I rose to my toes to meet him, wrapping my arms around his neck. Then with a tenderness I hoped he felt all the way to the shattered pieces of his heart, I kissed him.

I was so lost in the feel of him and the way my senses were spinning out of control that I hardly noticed when he swept me into his arms and carried me across the threshold and closed the door on the raging storm.

CHAPTER 27

Trevor

Sunlight streamed through the kitchen windows as I pulled two mugs from a cabinet and filled them with coffee. Steam rose and swirled from the obsidian liquid, hypnotizing me with thoughts of the previous night's unexpected turn of events. I went to the fridge to retrieve the half-and-half, a smile tugging at my lips as the memory of Quinn's body beneath my fingertips sent my blood rushing south. I'd never thought in a million years that I would hold Quinn Martin in my arms or that her razor-sharp tongue could almost make me forget my own name.

Returning to the mugs, I poured a splash of the cream into Quinn's coffee just in time to hear the door to her bedroom open. Never in my life had I been so anxious to see a woman, but ever since I'd kissed her goodnight at the threshold of her room, telling her I would see her in the morning, I'd been counting down the hours until that promise was fulfilled.

I turned at the sound of her bare feet padding across the tile floor, and my gut tightened at the sight of her lovely face, which was glowing and flushed in the morning light. She had dressed in a green tank top that hugged her slender frame like a glove and set her honey eyes ablaze. And as per usual, she had her curls piled on top of her head, several of the obstinate coils escaping her bun and tumbling loosely around her face.

I smiled and reached back for the coffee on the counter behind me. "Good morning." I handed her the mug.

Quinn smiled back, her eyes dipping to the mug as she sucked her bottom lip between her teeth. That small action set every nerve in my body buzzing as I recalled doing the same to that lip last night.

"Good morning." Her words were quiet, and her eyes remained on the steaming liquid she held between both hands. Quinn started to raise her eyes but made it only as far as my bare chest before she blushed and dropped her gaze again, her long dark eyelashes hiding whatever she was thinking.

I reached back for my own coffee then leaned against the counter, crossing one ankle over the other as I waited for her to confess whatever it was she was struggling to say. Like her, I was barefoot and still wearing my sweatpants. The whole scene was so completely domestic. I was surprised to realize that not only was I *not* freaking out about it, but these mornings with Quinn, both of us in our lounge clothes and fresh from sleep, had become one of the best parts of my day.

Finally, Quinn's gaze rose to mine, and her blush deepened. The woman seriously had no idea how fucking adorable she was.

She cleared her throat and tapped a finger against her mug. "Do you, um, remember last night?" Her pitch rose slightly as she spoke, as though she feared what I might say.

I snorted and pushed off from the counter then sauntered toward her. "I'll admit I was fairly hammered, but I would have to have been dead not to remember making out with you, Quinn."

The blush in her cheeks quickly spread to the rest of her face and down to her chest until it kissed the bit of cleavage revealed by her low neckline. I reached for a curl and gently tucked it behind her ear, then I lifted her chin to look into her eyes.

I had a question of my own to ask. Though a part of me didn't want to risk getting the answer I feared, it was best to just rip off the bandage rather than drive myself crazy wondering. "Do you regret what happened between us?"

All the worry and uncertainty vanished from her eyes, leaving behind only the warmth that was so completely Quinn. She smiled and shook her head. "No, I don't regret it."

I started to breathe again, only then realizing I had stopped. Then I lowered my mouth to hers, loving the way she rose on her toes to meet me halfway. Her soft lips gently pressed against mine. I could kiss her all day and never get tired of it. I'd wanted to do a lot more than kissing and touching last night, but it was obvious Quinn wasn't ready, and she said as much when I'd suggested we slow things down a bit.

I dropped my hand to her waist and pulled back to look at her, flashing a devilish smile. "There's something we need to take care of this morning. Go get dressed, and we'll head out."

She furrowed her brow. "Where are we going?"

My smile grew. "You'll see."

She protested at first, demanding to know details, but finally relented when I threatened to tickle her until she obeyed.

Half an hour later, we were in my truck and headed for the west side of town.

"Is this work related?" Quinn asked, picking at some imaginary lint on the cream-colored sweater she had changed into.

"No."

Out of the corner of my eye, I saw her glare at me, and I laughed. "Just relax and enjoy the ride."

"It's kind of hard to enjoy the ride when I don't know what you have up your sleeve." She folded her arms and looked out the passenger window. "Besides, we should be working on the case."

I slid my sunglasses down my nose just enough to look at her over the rims. "We've been working night and day on this case. We don't have the clues to the next victim yet, and we're at a dead end with the evidence and waiting on lab results. This is the perfect time to take a short breather, and even more than that, after the day we had yesterday, it's necessary."

She was quiet for several moments then said, "I figured out the clues about Jennifer."

My eyebrows rose as I glanced at her.

"The dots were pretty easy to connect once I knew her name." Quinn sighed deeply and ticked the answers to the clues off on her fingers. "We were right about her having been a nurse and leaving that profession for a role in education. She was the director of education at the hospital. Being related to the nightingale twice was a nod to both her nursing background and her surname. Hans Christian Andersen wrote *The Nightingale*. Jennifer's maiden name was Andersen. The clue about her being a tigress and a queen with a court of her own was a reference to her alma mater. She attended Clemson University, home of the tigers, on a basketball scholarship. She was recognized as one of the best players on the court."

I nodded, impressed at Quinn's ability to have been able to piece all that together so quickly.

"The last clue gave me some trouble, because I was still so sure it was a *Wizard of Oz* reference."

"It wasn't?"

"No. Since he said she was *nothing like her namesake*, I finally did a search of the name Jennifer and learned that Guinevere is actually the original form of Jennifer. From there, I naturally considered the most famous Guinevere of all and realized the tin man referred to the knight Lancelot, and the lion—also known as the *king* of the jungle—referred to King Arthur."

Exasperated, Quinn released a breath and shoved her fingers into her hair. "He gave us a first and last name, for crying out loud! If I had been able to figure out those clues, we could have saved her."

"Don't do that, Quinn." I squeezed her knee. "Of course it's easy to figure it out *after* you know who the victim is. Those clues could have led to a hundred different places."

"Yeah," she said, her tone resigned. "I suppose."

She was quiet for a minute then angled her body toward me

and asked, "Did you guys find anything at the crime scene yesterday that could be helpful in identifying this guy?"

I shook my head. "No. The scene was a mess by the time we got out there. Trampled by a bunch of employees then turned into a lake by the storm."

"What about surveillance footage?"

"Pretty much the same thing we got from the footage at the bar. A guy dressed in all black with his face covered. He used a different vehicle this time. We're running the plates, but I'm not holding my breath. He no doubt did what he did with the last car."

She raised her eyebrows, and I realized I'd never filled her in on that little discovery.

"He steals a car then switches the plates with another vehicle of the same make and model. Then, once that car can be connected to him, like with the surveillance footage we collected, he dumps it and repeats the process."

Quinn pursed her lips and stared out the windshield. It was a beautiful morning, nothing but blue skies, puffy white clouds, and sunshine for miles. That time of year, though, everything could change in an instant. Storms like the one we'd had the previous night could roll in faster than Castroneves in the Indy 500.

"There's got to be something we're missing," Quinn said mostly to herself.

Not wanting to use the short time we had away from the case *talking* about the case, I let the conversation lapse until we pulled in front of the costume shop. I hopped out of the truck and went around to open Quinn's door. She slid to the ground, her eyes focused on the sign above the storefront. "What are we doing at a costume shop?"

Giving a fiendish grin, I replied, "Liz texted this morning. She said our costumes are in, and we have strict instructions to try them on so there's enough time to make alterations."

Quinn looked apprehensive, but she allowed me to take her

hand and lead her inside. Ten minutes later, I was standing outside the dressing rooms in my masquerade getup, waiting for Quinn to join me. For the men, Liz had settled on tuxes with tails and gold vests to match the black-and-gold masks that would hide the upper half of our faces. She wanted more variety for the women's costumes, though, and had decided that scarlet would be the theme that linked them all. I had the inside scoop on it because what Quinn didn't know was that Liz had allowed me a heavy hand in picking out Quinn's dress, and I could not *wait* to see her in it.

"You have *got* to be kidding me." Quinn's voice came from behind the dressing room curtain, and I barely managed to hide my laugh before she stepped out where I could see her. I'd known she would balk at the dress. I had selected it, in part, as a dare to see if she would go through with it. But all humor died the moment she came into view. She was exquisite.

A black corset with what Liz had called a sweetheart neckline was the centerpiece of the dress. It was laced tightly in the back, placing Quinn's gorgeous breasts front and center. Folds of silken crimson fabric wrapped from the sides of the stiff bodice around her back then draped like a waterfall from her waist to the floor. The dress left her shoulders and chest bare. Her skin was so creamy and soft that I had to clench my hands to keep from reaching out to touch her.

I was so lost in her beauty that I almost didn't notice the irritated look that accessorized the gown as she stood with her hands on her hips. Regaining my composure and hoping to all hell that she hadn't noticed the way she'd rendered me stupid, I gave her a shit-eating grin and shrugged. "What?"

She pressed her lips together in a way that made her nostrils flare. "I can practically motorboat myself in this getup." She swept a hand down the length of her. "Can we please opt for something a little less in my face?"

I burst out laughing, which earned me another glare. Quinn folded her arms to emphasize her displeasure, and I allowed myself a moment to admire what the gesture did for her figure in that corset. Following my gaze, she looked down to realize that her boobs were practically popping out of her dress. She dropped her arms and growled, which only made me laugh harder.

Quinn stomped over and punched my arm. "Stop that!"

I shrugged innocently. "What? You look amazing."

"No, I don't." She frowned as she tugged at the dress. "I look like a harlot."

Sobering, I stepped closer to her and placed my hands on her shoulders. "No, you don't. You're breathtaking."

She dared to meet my eyes, and that familiar blush tinged the apples of her cheeks. Then she smiled as though she didn't want to but couldn't help it. "Yeah, well, you look all right, too, I guess."

I chuckled. "Aw, Quinny-baby. You say the sweetest things."

The shop owner, a plump woman in her mid-fifties, beamed at us from the dressing room where she had helped Quinn into the gown. Then she lifted a crimson mask adorned with delicate flowers and lace from a small satin-lined box and brought it over to Quinn. Watching from a short distance as they fussed over details, I got lost in thought about how much I had enjoyed having Quinn around the past few weeks. The sound of her laughter, rare though it was under the current circumstances, was a balm to my restless soul. For years, I'd been running from all the things I didn't want to feel, numbing myself with sex and various other distractions. But when Quinn was around, the storm inside me seemed to settle, and I no longer felt like I needed to run.

Truth be told, my whoring had gotten worse the past several months, ever since Gabe and Alex had gotten together. I was happy for my friend. And Alex was like a sister to me. I'd given them a lot of space so that they could just enjoy being in love, but it had left me feeling more alone than ever. And when I was alone, my demons came calling. No matter how many women I had filled my time with or how many nights I'd spent at Rustlers, that restlessness had never gone away. It had only dulled a bit for a few wasted hours.

Quinn smiled as she did a slow twirl in front of the mirror to see the full effect of her costume, and that smile just about brought me to my knees. She'd been so sad, so consumed with guilt over the case. It felt good to be able to give her a moment of peace and even joy.

Then it hit me—the realization that I *wanted* to be the one who made things better for her. I wanted to be the one to wipe away her tears, the one to make her laugh so hard that she had to hold her belly. I wanted to be a rock for her, to be someone she could rely on in fair weather and bad.

I'd never had that desire before. I was the guy who hit the road when things got too serious. There was a reason I hadn't had a girlfriend since high school, why I kept things light and superficial where women were concerned. *So what is it about Quinn that has me wanting the good, the bad, and everything in between?*

Quinn turned and sashayed toward me, her layers of skirt swishing. "I've never seen you in anything quite this fancy," she said, her eyes slowly canvasing my body and making my blood heat up.

I tugged her to me until we were pressed chest to chest. "If the sight of me in this tux does things to you, I'll buy the damn thing and wear it every night." I wrapped her in my arms and pressed my mouth to her neck then dragged my teeth over the sensitive skin. She giggled and squirmed, evoking a rush of euphoria that was completely foreign to me.

I pulled back and bent my head to kiss her, but just as our lips were about to meet, her phone rang.

"Give me just a sec," she said as she dashed to the dressing room where she'd left her purse. She emerged a moment later, frowning at the phone. "I don't believe it."

"What?"

"It's that damn reporter again."

"You want me to deal with it?"

"No, I can handle this jerkoff." She tapped her screen and put the phone to her ear. "I told you to stop cal—"

Quinn's eyes grew wide, and her jaw dropped.

I was at her side in an instant, but just as I reached her, she ducked back into the dressing room.

Peering in, I found her dumping the contents of her purse onto a little bench until her fingers closed around the recorder I'd given her. With shaking hands, she pressed a few buttons on the device then put her phone on speaker so that I could hear the other end of the line.

When the familiar voice hit my ears, I glanced to the front of the shop, where the owner was busy tidying her merchandise, far enough away not to overhear the conversation. Then I stepped into the dressing room with Quinn and closed the curtain to give us a little more privacy.

The killer hadn't wasted any time on trivialities or toying with Quinn. He was usually slow and methodical, preferring to draw out the experience, but now he was rattling off the clues to the next victim as though daring Quinn to keep up. Every time she tried to ask a question, he steamrolled her and carried on as if she hadn't made a sound.

And his tactics were working. Quinn was flustered and trying to get her bearings, but he wasn't giving her the chance.

"She's my little hummingbird," he said. "So full of energy, flitting here and there all the time. You've had enough practice in our game by now, Quinn, that this should be of little challenge to you." The malice in his tone was tinged with a smile. "Therefore, you have until midnight *tonight* to save her."

The line went dead.

Quinn stared at me, her eyes wide and her phone still lying on her open palm. When she regained her senses a moment later, she looked at her watch then back at me. "That's only fourteen hours! How could he possibly expect me to figure out who the next victim is in that length of time?"

I shook my head somberly. "He doesn't. That's the point." I

jerked my chin toward her phone. "What did your caller ID show?"

She glanced at the black screen. "Unavailable. That's why I thought it was the reporter."

I nodded. "This is him keeping things interesting. Turning up the heat. The call wasn't forwarded from Dispatch, so he wants you to know he managed to get your personal number. He called you when he knew you weren't at work, and he's shortening the timeline by calling less than twenty-four hours after he told us where to collect the last body. Then speeding through the call the way he did—he's messing with your head again, creating a sense of urgency and panic."

Quinn turned back to her purse and hastily chucked the dumped contents back inside. "Well, it's working."

"Get changed," I said, ducking through the curtain. "We've got to get to the station."

As I swapped my tux for my street clothes, one thought stalked my conscience. Maybe the new twist was because of me. I'd pushed him—pressed buttons that had triggered his rage. He was teaching us a lesson by showing us what happened when we didn't play by his rules. And deep down, my instincts told me he wasn't done making his point.

CHAPTER 28

Quinn

I PLAYED THE RECORDING AGAIN. I'd listened to it so many times that I'd lost count. Though I hadn't captured the beginning of the call, I managed to press Record just as the killer had begun spouting off his unfathomable clues.

"*—grew up seeing life carved in stone. A reality that no doubt influenced her artistic spirit. She's so skilled that one could imagine living within her work. Bright on the outside, she yielded to the darkness within. Perhaps it was due to growing up surrounded by sin. I'll have a lot of fun with this one, though. She's my little hummingbird. So full of energy, flitting here and there all the time...*"

I stood before the whiteboard in the small room where I had spent countless hours endeavoring to solve the sadist's riddles. Just as each time before, the clues were written on the board, surrounded by my frantic scribbles as I attempted to draw connections.

I held the uncapped Expo pen in the same hand that pinched my lower lip with my thumb and forefinger. Lost in contemplation, staring at the marks on the board, which had long ago begun to swirl in my bleary vision, I tried to block out the *tick, tick, tick* of the clock on the wall as it mocked me with its relentless march of time.

"Carved stone... artistic spirit," I whispered into the silence.

The door to my little workspace was open, since there was no point in closing it. The station had been empty for hours. As soon as Trevor and I had arrived at the department, he informed Gabe and the chief of the call I'd received, and while I disappeared into the command post to get to work on the clues, Gabe and Trevor got busy calling in every officer we had and organizing a massive patrol.

After the department had issued a PSA encouraging all citizens to go straight home after work and school and to stay there, the officers had taken to the streets with instructions from Trevor and Gabe to keep an eye and ear out for anything that seemed even remotely out of place. The hope was that if I managed to solve the clues, they would already be mobilized and able to get to the identified victim quickly. Or with a lot of luck, perhaps we could even catch him in the act of abducting the woman. But if I failed—my stomach lurched at the thought—then there might still be a chance to apprehend the killer when he made his move to dispose of the body.

My cell phone buzzed in my back pocket. Trevor's name showed on the screen. "Hey."

"Hey." His honeyed voice poured into my ear, soothing the rough edges of my nerves. "How are things going on your end?"

There was no pressure, no undercurrent of frustration or dissatisfaction with my performance, just a reflection of my own weariness and strain.

I sighed. "It's going all right, I guess. If I had the time he's given me in the past, I'd be feeling pretty hopeful, but..." I glanced at the clock and immediately regretted it. Only three hours remained.

"Just keep working on it, Quinn. That's all you can do."

I nodded. "I know. It's just hard not to feel partly responsible for these deaths when the ability to stop them is in my hands. It's hard not to think that if I were just smarter—"

"Don't do that. You've sacrificed a lot to help these victims, Quinn. None of their blood is on your hands."

We fell into silence as I tried to convince myself that he was right. In the background of the call, static and radio traffic competed with the loud rumble of his patrol vehicle.

"How are things going on your end?" I asked. We hadn't spoken to each other since he and the other officers took to the streets.

"It's pretty quiet so far. We haven't had many calls for service, which means the units have mostly been able to remain within the quadrants Gabe and I assigned them. We've got the whole town locked down. The challenge is going to be if he already has the next victim and he remains outside the city limits for the body dump. We've got the sheriff's office and highway patrol out en masse, too, though, so there's not much else we can do."

Except solve the clues. He might not have said it, but I knew we were both thinking it.

"I'm sorry I can't be there with you." His regret was palpable.

"It's okay. You're needed in the field, leading the team. I'm fine here."

"Any thoughts on who the victim might be? Even a vague guess is better than nothing."

I sucked my lower lip between my teeth and studied the board. "Not yet. But I think I'm getting a handle on how he operates."

"What do you mean?"

"It's kind of like crossword puzzles. The more you do them, the easier they become because you learn how the puzzle maker thinks. With victims three and four, he included a clue about their profession and one about where they had lived. Then there was a wild card. With Cheyenne, it was her race. With Jennifer, it was her name and the fact that she played basketball with relative notoriety."

"So you're thinking the pattern will hold true for this victim, and you're trying to figure out which clues refer to her career and where she's lived."

"Yes, but I'm pretty confident that everything he told me pertains to those two things, with the exception of his reference to her as his 'little hummingbird'—that one is the wild card."

Trevor hummed but was otherwise silent, presumably thinking about the clue and what it could mean.

"It could refer to some kind of mascot," he said. "But since he already did that with the last victim, I don't think he'd be that obvious."

"I agree."

"What about a nickname? Or maybe it's a favorite animal, something that she has as a personal symbol or totem."

Before I could respond, his radio chirped to life with a unit raising his call sign. "Hang on," he said. I could hear the radio traffic and his responses plainly, so when he came back on the line a moment later, I already knew he needed to go.

After a few more words of encouragement from him and a promise to remain available in case I needed anything, we disconnected.

Over the next two hours, I utilized every available resource to cross-reference the various interpretations I'd managed to conceive of for each of the clues, hoping that a name would emerge. I had considered everything from local artists on display at the art gallery a few towns over to someone who grew up near Mount Rushmore to those who'd had contact with our department or the hospital for drug problems, prostitution, or mental illness.

And at the end of those two hours, all I had to show for it was a pounding headache, fingernails that were chewed to stubs, and a hole in my stomach lining that was growing by the second.

I sat at the table that was shoved against the wall, my elbows on its metal surface and my fingers laced through my hair as my head rested in my hands. Sighing, I leaned back, my eyes gravitating to the whiteboard. I stared at the words written there, rage and heartache rising from the darkest places within me. The answer I sought was nestled between those words, right there for the taking. I could *save* this woman if only I could see her within those words.

My eyes landed on *hummingbird*, and Trevor's words came back to me. *A personal symbol or totem.* Then I heard the killer's voice in my head. *She's my little hummingbird.*

It wasn't so much the words that were circling my brain but the way he had said it, almost like he was dangling it in front of my face.

Then another word on the board caught my eye.

Sin. My pulse quickened, and my eyes darted to the top line. *Carved in stone.*

Then they moved to the next line down.

Artist.

"No," I whispered. My heart hammered against my chest, my breathing so shallow that the room began to tilt.

My eyes shot to the last line again. *Hummingbird.*

I tried to swallow, but my mouth had gone dry. *It's not true.* I shook my head, refusing to believe it. I wanted to close my eyes, to shut out the words that rose above all the others and floated toward me as all else faded away, but I couldn't tear my gaze from the board.

It didn't matter how hard I tried to convince myself I was wrong—how hard I tried to rearrange the puzzle pieces until a different picture formed. I knew, as sure as the bile churning in my stomach, that I was not wrong.

I shot to my feet, and with a shaky hand, I jerked my phone from my back pocket, cursing the damn thing as my fingers fumbled it. "Come *on*!"

Once I finally managed to place the call, I put the phone to my ear. Each unanswered ring made my heart beat harder. My free hand went to my forehead. I barely registered the clammy feel of my skin.

"Come on. Pick up!"

Halfway through the next ring, he answered. "Hey, what's up?"

"Trevor! Trevor, I know who his next victim is!"

CHAPTER 29

Trevor

THE BEAMS of my headlights painted the asphalt gold as my cruiser crept through the desolate streets of Eden Falls. I swept my gaze back and forth across the landscape, searching for movement and finding none except for the boughs of the trees as they dipped and swayed in the restless wind. The night was muggy, as it often was that time of year, and given the menacing look of the clouds that crawled past the nearly full moon, I half expected that a downpour was in our near future.

My gaze zeroed in on a pair of headlights approaching from the opposite direction. I slowed as they neared. Only when the other vehicle pulled up alongside me was I able to discern the light bar on the roof and the black-and-white paint on the body. The cruiser stopped, and I followed suit, rolling down my window to find my best friend waiting, his arm hooked over the door.

"It's like a fucking ghost town out here tonight," Gabe said.

I nodded, scanning the barren streets again. "Yeah. Looks like everyone actually listened to that PSA we put out."

Gabe idly drummed his fingers against the department's crest painted on his door. He glanced at his computer screen on the passenger side of his unit then turned his grave eyes to me. "It's twenty-three hundred."

A pensive nod was my only response. Words were unnecessary. We both knew that at that point, the next victim was likely beyond saving. The killer already had her, tucked away God only knew where, and was torturing her as she begged for mercy. Our best hope was to catch the motherfucker as he dumped her body.

My phone rang. I glanced at the screen. "It's Quinn."

"I'll let you take that," Gabe said. "I'm gonna head over to the west side of town and check in with the units there."

I nodded and let my cruiser roll forward again as I answered the call. "Hey, what's up?"

The panic in Quinn's voice made every hair on my body rise.

"Trevor! Trevor, I know who his next victim is!" She launched into some jumbled nonsense that I had trouble tracking—something about hummingbirds and sin and caves with pictures. It wasn't what she was saying that alarmed me. It was that Quinn, who was normally the poster child for calm and composure, was completely losing her shit.

"Quinn!" I said forcefully.

Immediately, she stopped talking.

"Who is it, Quinn?"

Sobbing, she said, "It's Sh-Shelby."

My blood turned ice-cold, but I kept my tone firm and even so that Quinn could grab on to it and anchor herself. "Are you sure?"

Her sobbing became more anguished. "Yes! Yes, I'm sure!"

"What's her address?"

As soon I had the location of Shelby's house, I snatched my mic and raised Dispatch. "Control, this is Adam Four. Send a code-three response to 127 Harvester Lane to check and advise per Four-Eight-Three." I kept the transmission vague enough that anyone listening to our radio traffic wouldn't have a clue what I was saying, but department personnel would recognize Quinn's body number and put two and two together.

I switched on my lights and sirens, flipped a U-turn in the middle of the abandoned street, and gunned it toward Shelby's house. The sound of Quinn crying and struggling to breathe through her sobs still filled my ear and reverberated through my bones.

"Quinn, I need you to forward Shelby's and her husband's phone numbers to me and Gabe, then I want you to go straight to my house and wait for me there."

"Wh-What? No! I'm staying here s-so I can help."

"Quinn, I'm going to do everything I can for Shelby, but I need to know you're safe at home so I can focus on doing my job. That's the best way you can help her right now."

Quinn hesitated, her breathing still ragged. "Please help her, Trevor."

Those four words cleaved my soul in two. The muscles in my jaw jumped as I bit down on the rage of what that man had done to Quinn and the fear that I wouldn't be able to fix it. With the scant remains of my self-possession, I banished all emotion from my voice and simply said, "I'm trying, Quinn. Tell me you'll go home and wait for me."

In truth, I knew Quinn was just as safe at the station as she would be at my house. The killer was busy with someone else, quite possibly Shelby. But if Quinn was right about that, and we were too late to save her best friend, I didn't want her at the station when I delivered the news. I wanted her somewhere she would feel safe giving in to her emotions, someplace where I could hold her without her worrying about the rumors it might start.

With another shuddering breath, Quinn finally agreed but only after making me swear that I would keep her in the loop. As soon as she disconnected, I radioed Gabe and asked him to start a trace on Shelby's number the moment Quinn sent it to his phone.

If Shelby really was the killer's next target, the odds of finding her at home were slim, but we had to try. So I continued my race through town, the landscape tinged red and blue from my flashing lights. I prayed with everything in me that Quinn was wrong, and I would find Shelby at home in her pajamas.

Minutes later, I joined two other cruisers in front of a small single-story tract home painted white with light-blue trim. The horror of why we were there was a grim contrast to the charming wooden flower boxes beneath the front windows.

I killed the engine and exited my vehicle in one fluid motion then hustled up the front walk to where the door to the home stood open, amber light pouring onto the porch, where two of our uniforms were speaking to a man I recognized as Shelby's husband, Josh—the same man I had envied just a few weeks ago when I'd thought he was on a date with Quinn.

As I approached, the two officers parted, taking up a position on either side of the door.

"What's going on?" Josh asked, his blue eyes wide and made even bluer by the subtle sunburn that swept across his cheeks and forehead.

I didn't waste time with niceties. "Is Shelby here?"

His brow creased. "No. Why?"

"Do you know where she is?"

"No." Josh's eyes darted between the two other officers and me.

"When was the last time you talked to her?"

He gulped. "I... I don't know." Shrugging, he added, "This morning when I left for work around seven."

My eyebrows rose. "That was the last time you had any contact with her? Sixteen hours ago?"

Josh's Adam's apple bobbed, his eyes widening a little farther. "I tried calling her around lunchtime, but she didn't answer or return my call."

"Is that unusual?" I asked in the tone I used with suspects and people I needed to get answers from quickly and without issue.

Josh jammed his hands into the pockets of his faded blue jeans and began to shift his weight between his feet. I also didn't fail to notice another gulp. "Uh..." His eyes shifted to the officer on his right then back to me. After a long, tension-filled pause, his shoulders slumped, and his eyes dropped to his tattered brown slippers. "We've been having some problems," he said quietly. "Sometimes she doesn't come home until pretty late, and she won't answer when I call."

Finally understanding the reason for his cagey behavior, I felt sorry for the poor bastard having to stand there and admit to strangers that his woman no longer wanted him. I dialed down my hard-ass approach, since I felt pretty confident he wasn't hiding anything. "We have reason to believe your wife is in danger and need to search your house to determine if there's anything that will help us to track her down."

Josh's head snapped up, his eyes darting back and forth between mine as though he was hoping he would find evidence of a lie. "What? What do you mean?"

I grasped his arm and gently but firmly pulled him off to the side. We didn't have enough probable cause to enter his home without a warrant, so I needed to get him to let us inside. "I'll explain everything, but time is of the essence here. Will you allow my officers to start searching your home?"

Josh looked over his shoulder at the officers waiting to enter. "Yes. Yeah. Of course."

That was all the invitation they needed. As they entered the house, they were promptly followed by another unit that had just made it to the show.

While my officers canvased the house, I filled Josh in on the circumstances that had led us to his doorstep. His emotion seemed genuine. His eyes filled with tears, and his hair was mussed from running his fingers through it repeatedly as he begged for us to be wrong.

Just as I had taken Josh inside to sit him down on the couch, where I told him to hang tight, Gabe called to tell me that Shelby's phone had last pinged at a remote location in the woods about twenty miles north of town. He already had the sheriff's department headed that way, but the phone hadn't transmitted for a few hours. My last vestige of hope that Quinn had been mistaken in her understanding of the clues died with that news.

And when a sheriff's deputy called an hour later, informing us that they had found a vehicle registered to Shelby and Josh Johnson but found no signs of the driver or any personal belongings, I had to stop myself from punching a hole through the wall of their home—the home where their love had thrived then dimmed. Quinn had undoubtedly spent countless hours there, making memories that would be soiled by the blood of the woman she had loved as a sister.

I had to get out of that house. I couldn't take one more second of watching Josh as he sat on their cream-colored couch, his face buried in his hands and his body racked by sobs that were interrupted only by his whispered prayers.

After giving orders to my officers for two of them to remain with Josh and the third to rejoin the patrol, I got back in my cruiser, but instead of joining the hunt, I let the engine idle. I glanced at the clock on the dashboard: zero one hundred hours. I slammed the heel of my hand against the steering wheel then dropped my head against the seat and closed my eyes.

Shelby was dead. I knew it in my bones.

How the hell am I going to tell Quinn that her best friend has been tortured to death? How am I supposed to tell her I failed?

Rage burned in my gut, gathering strength until it became a tornado of gasoline and flame. Every violent, ugly part of me roared to life until the world was tinted red.

He had chosen Shelby for one purpose—to torment Quinn and ensure that I failed to protect the one person in the town she cared for most.

I stared out the windshield, my eyes losing focus on the shadowed shapes that lined the street. My engine continued to purr, and my radio crackled. Slowly, my rage began to change form, shrinking and condensing from its wild maelstrom into a ball of ice, tight and hard in my gut.

We still had a chance to get the guy. I might not have been able to save Shelby, but I could avenge her. I could ensure that he paid for the sins he had committed in Eden Falls.

The gears in my head came back to life, churning and calculating. *Where are you going to leave her?* I kept my gaze unfocused, allowing my subconscious to enter the game. Stepping outside of myself, I envisioned the nameless, faceless killer. I tried to become him—his thoughts, his desires, his urges.

If this kill was about Quinn, where would I leave the body? Always among the trash, where they belong. Somewhere Quinn will find her. Or maybe somewhere Quinn will never be able to go again without thinking of the mutilated body of her best friend—of her failure to save her.

I considered Quinn's habits and routines. She mainly stuck to town, which meant the body would likely be left in another dumpster. She spent nearly all of her time at work. When she wasn't there, she was at home or at the gym. He wouldn't risk dumping the body anywhere near the station, and all of Quinn's neighbors would be home. It was the kind of neighborhood where people looked after one another, the kind where they would notice a strange noise and a car that was out of place. He wouldn't risk dumping the body there, not with everyone on high alert. That left the gym.

A prickle at the back of my neck told me I was on the right track. The gym was on the south side of town, surrounded by nothing but other businesses that would be closed, and its dumpsters weren't visible from the street. Quinn rarely visited that place without Shelby, and it would be easy to access undetected, even with the beefed-up patrol. He would get off on that—slipping in and out while dumping the body right under our noses.

I sat up and threw my car into gear then flipped another U-turn and headed back toward the main drag. Keying my mic, I raised Gabe and Carlson.

Gabe answered, "Go ahead."

Knowing the killer could be monitoring our traffic, I kept my transmission vague. "I'm headed to where I gave Carlson a bloody nose. I want you two to back me."

"Copy."

Carlson also acknowledged. I took a left on Sixth and accelerated, the roar of my engine increasing alongside the pulse for vengeance that drummed through me. Every mile served only to solidify my confidence that I was right about the location. The question was when he would make his move.

Minutes later, I took a right on Birch and slowed. I was two blocks from the gym and didn't want the sound of my engine to give me away. I radioed Gabe and Carlson. "Adam Four. On scene. Approaching from the southeast."

Gabe answered first. "Adam Two. Ten-four. I'm one minute out."

Then Carlson responded. "Adam Twelve. I'm two away, approaching from the west.

The gym faced Birch, with an industrial bakery to its rear and the newspaper office taking up the entire east side of the lot. The space between the bakery and the back entrance to the gym was where the dumpsters were kept. Only a block away, I killed my lights.

Seconds later, I turned in to the empty parking lot. With the clouds shielding the moon, it was almost too dark to even perceive the outline of the buildings. I eased to the far side of the gym, my cruiser cutting a path through the shadows.

As I turned the first corner, my heart drummed against my ribcage, the familiar prickle of adrenaline spiking my blood with anticipation. The last corner neared. In a matter of seconds, the nose of my black-and-white would enter the alleyway.

When I turned the final corner, absolute darkness descended upon me. The buildings blocked what little ambient light the night could offer to the point that all visibility ceased. I reached for the headlight switch, the sound of my shallow breaths the only thing to pierce the oppressive silence. With a flick of my wrist, light flooded the narrow space, and thirty feet ahead of me, a figure dressed in black froze and stared back at me through the holes of a ski mask.

CHAPTER 30

Trevor

"MOTHERFUCKER!"

I gunned the engine, my patrol car burning rubber as it careened toward the dark-colored sedan. He must have left the vehicle running, because he threw himself into the open driver's door and closed the distance between us before I could cut him off. The sound of metal scraping and crunching rose in the night. The shudder of my vehicle as it was thrown into the brick wall of the gym and assaulted on the other side by the fleeing car echoed through my bones.

In my side mirror, I registered taillights disappearing around the corner. I swore and stomped on the gas, deciding it would be faster to circle back around to the front of the building than attempt a three-point turn in the narrow space. As I shot down the back of the gym, I snatched the mic from my car's radio.

"Adam Four to all units. I'm in pursuit of the suspect's vehicle." I rounded the building and scanned for the sedan. For one agonizing heartbeat, I thought I had lost him, but then a sliver of moonlight sliced through the clouds and glimmered on the chrome of a bumper that was quickly disappearing down Birch. "He's in a dark-colored sedan, no lights, headed west on Birch and passing Fourth."

I was already out of the parking lot and picking up speed by the time I finished my transmission. The voices of my partners, who were jumping on the radio to advise they were en route code three, faded into the background as I zeroed in on the car, which was now only a block ahead of me.

He must have realized I had eyes on him and was closing in fast, because his headlights flooded the dark street at the same moment the distance between us grew. I increased my speed as well but not enough to keep him from gaining a bigger lead. We were still within the city limits, and though it appeared that none of our residents were out and about, I wasn't about to risk killing some kid who had snuck out of the house and was completely oblivious to what was going on.

My partners continued to transmit their locations, and as we drew closer to the edge of town, I realized the next-closest unit was still several streets away. It was all on me. If that asshole managed to give me the slip, he would be gone for good.

I keyed my mic again. "Adam Four. Suspect is turning north on First. Dispatch, contact the sheriff's office. Get them to set up a roadblock on Highway 83."

That highway was the easiest way for him to disappear. It led out of town, and I had no doubt he was well aware of all the side roads and logging roads that branched off it—perfect for someone to get lost in.

Sure enough, twenty seconds later, he turned west on Main, which turned into Highway 83 at the city limit. I followed, and as we left Eden Falls in our rearview mirrors, I noted that I didn't see any of my partners behind me yet. Gabe and Carlson had to be close, but they weren't close enough.

The killer accelerated further, and that time, I kept pace. Glancing down at my speedometer, I watched the needle creep closer to ninety.

"Adam Four. We're westbound on 83, ninety miles per hour. Is SO in position?"

Dispatch answered, "Negative. They've been advised, but their closest unit is five minutes out."

Dammit. I glanced in my rearview mirror again and saw headlights in the distance. The guy was smart and wise to the ways of law enforcement. No way would he stay on the highway, where he was easy to tail, and it would be even easier to lay down some spike strips.

I'd barely finished the thought when the taillights in front of me glowed red and the car swerved violently to the right. I slammed on my own brakes and gripped the steering wheel tightly, fighting to maintain control. As soon as I had slowed enough to keep from flipping my cruiser, I spun the wheel, turning onto the same remote road the killer had just taken.

About a mile in, the road began to rise as it took on a serpentine form, twisting and winding through trees that pushed in on the two-lane road. The suspect's taillights kept disappearing from view, each bend in the road making my adrenaline ratchet higher as I feared that I would take a curve and find that I had lost him.

Every few miles, I updated my partners on our location. Gabe and Carlson were on the same winding road, but they were at least two minutes behind me. Two minutes could mean the difference between apprehending that asshole and his slipping through our grasp. It could also mean the difference between life and death, depending on how it played out.

The sedan disappeared around another bend. I continued to follow, but that time, when I rounded the corner, the road ahead was abandoned. My pulse slammed against my neck, my eyes darting frantically as I tried to find movement in the shadows.

Twenty yards ahead and to the left, brake lights flashed through the trees. I accelerated until I found a nearly hidden logging road and turned onto it. Rocks pummeled the underside of the cruiser, and my tires dipped in and out of potholes. I clenched my teeth to keep them from cracking as my entire body shuddered from the abuse of the rough road. I didn't have to go far. Half a mile in, I found the suspect's sedan blocking the narrow passageway, the driver's door thrown wide open and the engine still running.

Scanning the dense foliage, I looked for signs of an ambush. Easing my door open, I listened. It wasn't difficult to hear twigs and branches snapping up ahead. He was choosing speed over stealth, trying to put as much distance between us as possible.

I jumped out of my car and keyed the mic at my chest as I bolted past the suspect's vehicle and headed farther up the road. "Adam Four. I'm in foot pursuit! Incoming units can see my lights from the road."

Without slowing to register the response from Dispatch and my partners, I found where the suspect had entered the woods and took off after him, allowing his ragged breathing and muddy footprints to be my guide. In my ear, the radio traffic was incessant. Though Gabe would have sounded totally calm and in control to anyone else, I knew my partner well enough to know that the subtle tightness in his voice was because it was killing him not to be right beside me as I hunted the son of a bitch.

Rocks shifted beneath my boots, and branches reached for me, scratching my face and arms as I tore through them like they were cobwebs. But when I caught sight of a black figure weaving through the trees less than fifty yards ahead, I pushed harder, eating up the ground.

But I was glad he was running. With nothing but intermittent moonlight to guide me, the only reason I hadn't lost him yet was because of his constant movement and the trail he was leaving. My call sign reached my ear, but I ignored it. I couldn't afford to lose even an inch of ground, or he would get away.

My chest heaved, and sweat broke across my brow, but my eyes remained trained on my target. I used the burn in my thighs to propel me forward, gritting my teeth in determination. Vaguely, I registered Gabe and Carlson advising Dispatch that they were with my cruiser. Those two would run like the devil himself was chasing them until they caught up to me. All I had to do was keep the killer in my sights.

A percussive blast shattered the stillness of the forest along with the tunnel vision that had formed around my target so that all my senses came roaring back.

Another blast followed.

Son of a bitch.

"Shots fired! Shots fired!" I shouted into my mic.

The chatter in my ear continued but became more frantic, with units talking over one another, trying to get their traffic out.

Bang. Bang. Bang.

I wasn't completely pissed that the asshole was shooting at me. The muzzle flashes helped me to track him. Still, since I had to move from cover to cover, it slowed my pace just enough that I feared I would lose him. He was firing over his shoulder, so I wasn't too worried that he would actually hit me, especially with how thick the trees were. But I also wasn't about to pull some rookie mistake by getting too comfortable in a gunfight.

Then something shifted. I couldn't say what it was, only that my instincts were hammering against my gut. I slowed and listened then realized what it was.

Silence.

He'd stopped running.

I crouched, taking cover behind a large conifer, and scanned the woods ahead as I strained to pick up a noise that didn't belong.

Nothing came but the creak of a tree branch swaying in the tenuous breeze and the sound of small mammals skittering about the forest floor.

After several moments, I eased from behind the tree, cautiously stepping one foot over the other. He was out there, lying in wait. I paused to listen then took another step.

Bang!

My body whipped back. I grunted against the pain and dove for the nearest tree as another blast ripped through the muted woods.

CHAPTER 31

Trevor

I STARED down at the body lying at my feet, my jaw aching from how tightly I'd been clenching it. The left sleeve of my uniform shirt was still damp with my blood. B positive coated my hand where I clamped down on the wound, relishing the stab of pain. Vacant hazel eyes stared back at me as red and blue lights bounced off the brick walls in a space that felt too tight to breathe.

A hand gripped my shoulder. "You okay, brother?"

I dragged my eyes away from the body and tilted my face to the night sky. "How am I supposed to tell her that her best friend is dead and I let her killer get away?"

Gabe was silent for a moment. "You just tell her. And you do it before she hears it from someone else."

I blew out a breath I felt like I'd been holding for hours. After taking one more look at Shelby, silently begging her to blink or take a breath, to show some kind of life, I finally turned away, leaving her to the swarms of officers and crime scene techs busy working the scene.

Before I could take two steps, Bryan materialized in front of me. He was dressed in his navy uniform pants and his matching Eden Falls Fire Department T-shirt.

"I need to look at that arm, bud." His red hair almost

appeared blond in the moonlight, which shone without mercy, illuminating a scene I would rather have not witnessed.

I tried to brush past him. "Not now."

He placed an unyielding hand on my uninjured arm. "You got shot, Trev."

"It's a flesh wound."

"Doesn't matter."

My glare did little to get him to back down. Bryan, Gabe, and I went way back. He'd chosen to become a hose dragger, a decision Gabe and I had never let him live down, but it didn't change our history. We'd been rivals as much as we'd been friends, but when push came to shove, we would always have one another's backs.

His blue eyes stared back at me, unblinking and resolute.

I leaned in and bared my teeth. "Fine. Just pack it and wrap it. I have somewhere I need to be."

* * *

I HADN'T EVEN MADE it to the front porch when I looked up to find Quinn standing in the open doorway of my house, soft amber light illuminating her from behind. I slowed but continued my march toward what was sure to be one of the worst experiences of my life.

She was still dressed in the cream-colored sweater and jeans she'd worn to the costume shop, her hair down and wild, as though she'd been nervously running her fingers through it all night. Her eyes followed me as I made my way up the steps and came to a stop in front of her. The entire drive home, I'd been debating how to break the news to her. In the end, I'd decided Gabe was right. I just had to give it to her straight. But as I opened my mouth, those amber eyes glistening with faltering hope locked onto mine, and I hesitated. In that hesitation, I could clock the precise moment her prayers died and grief possessed her.

Quinn's face crumpled, and soundless tears slid down her

cheeks. One by one, they grew in number until an endless stream of suffering reflected the pale light of the moon on her sweet face. A harsh sob tore from her throat, and she began to fold in on herself.

I moved swiftly to her and caught her just before she fell to the floor.

Wrapping an arm around her back and the other behind her knees, I lifted her in my arms and moved inside, kicking the door closed behind us.

Quinn buried her face in my uniform shirt, twisting her hand in the fabric as her body shuddered. The sound of her anguish was the worst kind of torture.

I carried her to the couch, sat down, and settled her in my lap as I wrapped my arms around her and rocked back and forth. I whispered words of comfort, telling her that I was right there with her, that she wasn't alone. I encouraged her to keep crying and to let herself break as many times as she needed, because I was going to be there to hold the broken pieces.

Quinn pulled back to look me in the eye, but she continued to clutch my shirt. Her red, tear-stained face reflected a depth of pain that I had once known myself. "I should have figured out those clues sooner!" Her voice was tight as she fought against shuddering breaths. "It was so obvious!"

Pressing a kiss to her forehead, I whispered, "It wasn't your fault, Quinn. None of this is your fault. You didn't fail Shelby." Smoothing her hair, I continued to hold her close.

She buried her face in my neck and allowed the grief to take her.

I had no idea how long we remained like that—a woman with a heart freshly broken and a man who had never wanted anything more than to take her pain away. Eventually, Quinn's breathing slowed, her tears stopped falling, and her body, exhausted from the force of her grief, slackened against mine. I waited a bit to ensure she was truly deep within the folds of sleep before rising from the couch. With her nestled tightly against my chest, I carried her down the dark hall to my bedroom, laid her down on the king-size mattress, and covered her with the slate-gray sheets and plush comforter.

Then I went to the closet and pulled out a pair of sweats and a T-shirt and disappeared into the bathroom to wash away the blood and grime. When I emerged a short while later, Quinn was still fast asleep and curled on her side. The soft glow from the bathroom light fell across her angelic face, her long lashes fluttering with whatever dream had swept her away from reality.

After easing onto the bed, I remained on top of the covers and turned on my side to face her, inching closer until she was tucked against me, my arm draped over her waist. For the longest time, I simply watched her, memorizing every detail and hoping that her dreams were peaceful. I had never watched a woman sleep or held her while she dreamed. I'd never even lain with a woman without first having sex.

With a tenderness I didn't know I possessed, I brushed Quinn's hair back from her face and grazed her cheek with my knuckles before returning my arm to her waist. The feel of her pressed against me and her soft breath caressing my neck were a new kind of pleasure.

Quinn's brow furrowed, and her lips puckered, a soft moan emanating from her throat. Her body tensed for a moment before her features became smooth again, and her body relaxed into the mattress. I dreaded the moment she would wake, when the suffocating grief and the memories would come flooding back. I knew all too well the torture of waking after a living nightmare.

First would come the hope—that it had all been just a bad dream, that life really hadn't been forever altered, that there hadn't been a loss so profound that it would whisper in her soul for the rest of her days. Then with her next heartbeat, the realization that it hadn't been a dream would set in, and wave upon wave of grief and rage would crash down on her until she felt like she would never be able to take another breath.

I tightened my arm around Quinn. She would hurt, and it

would hurt for a very long time. But she was strong. She would survive it. And I would be beside her for every agonizing step forward. I would hold her as long as she needed, I would listen when she wanted to talk or scream. I would give her a safe place to cry. And I would brush away every tear that fell.

She was my Quinny-baby. I would do anything for her.

CHAPTER 32

Trevor

SHORTLY BEFORE DAWN, a stirring at my side pulled me from a sleep so deep that not even dreams could reach me. It took a moment for my eyes to remember how to open, but when they finally did, I found Quinn lying on her side, facing me, the reality of the previous night's events still haunting her features.

Faint light trickled in through the partially open blinds—not enough to banish the dark but enough to see something in Quinn's eyes that I'd never seen before.

I was still lying on top of the covers with my arm draped over her waist, where it had been when I'd fallen asleep. With her gaze locked on me, Quinn pulled her arm free from the bedding and gently dropped her hand on my chest.

My breath caught where her hand rested, my body frozen with the fear that if I moved, the spell would break, and I would wake to find that it hadn't been real. But when Quinn's hand began a slow descent, tracing the planes of my chest and abdomen, down to where she slipped under the hem of my shirt, my pulse quickened at her bare touch.

Her fingers lightly brushed my skin, their slow dance communicating the same desire that flashed in her eyes. I wanted to reach for her, to explore the curves of her body in the same way she was exploring mine. But I couldn't.

I knew what she really wanted. Quinn wanted to forget that her best friend had been murdered and to feel something other than grief and guilt. She wanted what I had wanted ever since I learned of my parents' deaths—to banish the cold, hollow pit of loneliness and loss by getting lost in the arms of another.

But I didn't want to be to her what all those other women had been to me.

I had fantasized about being with her too many times to count—imagined her hand stroking my chest, as it was currently doing, urging me to do the same.

Her lips parted, then she scooted her body closer to mine, her eyes never leaving me. I placed my palm on the side of her face and gently stroked her cheek with my thumb.

As I read the uncertainty in her eyes, the fear that I would reject her, my gut twisted. I wanted nothing more than to ease her pain, to help her forget it even temporarily, and to hold her close so that she would feel less alone.

But my greatest fear when it came to Quinn was hurting her more than she was already hurting. I didn't trust that I could be the man she needed—the man that she deserved.

Quinn pulled herself free of the covers and moved closer until our bodies were pressed down the full length of each other. She cupped the back of my neck as she brought her lips within an inch of mine. She was waiting to see if I would accept the invitation. My eyes slid to her full lips. Their color matched the bloom of desire in her cheeks.

My hand went to her waist again, my fingers flexing on her skin as I fought my want of her. The situation was complicated enough as it was. Throwing emotional, grief-driven sex into the mix was a bad idea, especially when I knew Quinn had never harbored fantasies of her own where I was concerned. If we crossed that line, she was likely to regret it. Once the fog of her pain lifted and reason returned, she would probably hate herself for sleeping with the likes of me.

I raised my eyes to hers again and found the silent plea still written in her gaze—a plea not to turn her away, and it brought me to the brink of my resolve.

My face crumpled with the pain of denying her. "Quinn—"

"Trevor..." My name on her lips was so fragile. "Please." It was more of a whimper than a word, and it shattered the last of my defenses. I couldn't say no to her. I couldn't be one more cut in her tender heart.

So I shoved my worries and fears to the back of my mind and leaned down, capturing her mouth with mine.

The salt of her tears was faint on her lips. And when she opened her mouth to me, the feel of her tongue sliding against mine drew a moan from my throat.

I pressed my body into Quinn's, turning her until she was on her back and I was on top of her. Her legs were bent, and she spread her knees wider so that I could settle in her sweet hollow. I ground my hips into her once. Her moan poured into my mouth with the same sultry melody of the voice I'd come to crave in my ear.

I slid my hand up to cup her face and dove my fingers into her wild curls as I deepened the kiss, our ragged breaths colliding until they were one.

Quinn lifted her hips, rubbing herself against the bulge in my pants, silently demanding more. I slipped a hand between our bodies and found her waistband. Without hesitation, I dove underneath. It took only a second for my fingers to find the soft, warm flesh that beckoned for their touch.

Quinn arched her back the moment I made contact, throwing her head back into the pillows and exposing the pale skin of her throat. I clamped my mouth over her artery and sucked hard, her pulse fluttering wildly against my tongue.

Her hips rose off the bed again as she gasped and clawed at my back. With excruciating slowness, I slid a finger down her wet folds. When I was over her entrance, I pressed deeper, slipping a finger inside. I watched Quinn for signs of hesitation, but there were none. As her body closed around me and my finger began a sinful dance inside her, she sucked her bottom lip between her teeth and closed her eyes, allowing herself to get lost in the pleasure.

I almost came right then and there, just knowing that I was the one making her feel that way.

Over and over, I slid my finger out and back in, at a pace that had her writhing beneath me. Then my thumb found the tender nub at the top of her sex, and I traced small circles over it, changing the pressure to match what my finger was doing to her.

"Trevor," Quinn moaned, "*more.*"

I smiled at the sound of her plea and the sight of the pink glow creeping across her skin. Slowly, I withdrew from her, earning a scowl and a grunt of protest that made me laugh.

Sitting back on my heels, I locked my eyes on Quinn and held her gaze as I grabbed the hem of my shirt and slid the material over my head then tossed it to the ground. Quinn's eyes shot to the bandage on my arm, a fresh wave of worry casting a shadow over her features.

I smiled reassuringly. "It's okay. Just a scratch."

She watched me for a moment, clearly trying to determine whether I was telling the whole truth. But I didn't give her any more time to think about it. Taking her hands, I pulled her to a sitting position then discarded her top in the same manner I'd done mine.

My gaze fell to her lacy blush-colored bra, which hugged the firm contours of her breasts. Her peaked nipples pressed against the delicate fabric and made my mouth water with the need to taste them.

I reached behind her and unclasped the bra, her breasts springing free as I pulled the garment away and added it to the growing pile on the floor. Though I could have spent the rest of the night just savoring the sight of her, I had more work to do before I would allow myself to taste her.

I moved my fingers to the button on her jeans, popped it loose, and drew the zipper down. Then I gripped the waistbands of her pants and underwear and began sliding them down as Quinn lifted her hips to help free herself of the barriers between us.

I allowed myself one gratuitous gaze down her body as I stood from the bed and shoved my own pants to the floor. Quinn watched. Her eyes widened when I sprang free, her mouth falling open in a silent gasp.

Placing my hands on either side of her shoulders, I leaned down to kiss her, my tongue darting through her parted lips and tangling with hers. When I sucked her bottom lip between my teeth and gave it a playful tug, she whimpered and squirmed, attempting to pull me back down on top of her. But I resisted.

Turning my attention to the bedside table, I pulled open the top drawer and retrieved a condom. Quinn watched as I rolled the latex down my shaft, her chest heaving with her growing desire. Fully armored and reaching the edge of my control, I rejoined her on the bed and settled between her open legs. The feel of her naked body squirming beneath me was ecstasy.

Lowering my lips to her breast, I captured a tight pink bud between my teeth. I sucked hard and groaned when she arched her back, pressing herself into me, her folds sliding against my erection. I moved my tongue in slow circles around her nipple, pausing every couple of laps to suck her into my mouth. Then I moved to the other breast and gave it the same attention while I slipped my hand between her legs again.

Quinn whimpered and clawed at my back, her mouth open and her head thrashing against the pillows. I entered her with my finger once more, and when I began to massage that small bundle of nerves with my thumb at the same moment I curled the finger that was inside her, she bucked wildly beneath me.

I dove for her neck, licking and sucking as my hand continued its brutal quest to give her more pleasure than she'd ever known.

Quinn screamed my name, her fingernails drawing a sting down my back as she continued to thrash against me.

Unable to delay my release any longer, I removed my hand and gripped her hips. My shaft found her entrance, and with one smooth motion, I thrust inside. The feel of her clamping down on me caused my entire body to shudder.

Gritting my teeth, I used every ounce of willpower to hold still so that Quinn's body could adjust to me. I waited until I felt her muscles relax and she began moving her hips, urging me onward.

Propping one forearm beside her head and gripping her bent leg with my other hand, I began a slow dance, sliding out of her until just my tip remained buried in her silken folds, then I plunged back in. With each thrust, I ground my hips against her, using the friction against her clitoris to take her pleasure higher.

Quinn quivered beneath me, her legs gripping my hips and lifting her to me. Her soft moans and her pounding heartbeat were the most beautiful symphony I'd ever heard.

As my body slid against hers and her arms held me close, I realized that I would never be able to let her go. I would never be able to let *us* go. Quinn had ruined me for any other woman. I realized that that had been true for a long time, but in that moment, with our bodies fused together as one, I understood that she was what I had been waiting for. She was the thread that had begun to stitch my torn and battered heart back together.

Quinn buried her face in my neck, kissing her way up the base of my throat before tracing the line of my jaw. I increased my pace, thrusting and withdrawing, gritting my teeth as I fought the release that beckoned at the base of my spine. The feel of her body tightening around me and my heart trying to beat its way out of my chest whisked me away to a place that was hazy and surreal, where nothing mattered outside of that moment, frozen in time with Quinn.

The pressure continued to build. I could feel Quinn's body starting to seize. She was right *there*. Then she cried out, her muscles clamping down on me, milking my rock-hard shaft. Before her scream died, my own release came. I rode the sweet wave of euphoria, letting my consciousness slip away.

When my breathing began to slow and the spots faded from my vision, I looked down at Quinn, afraid of what I might see.

But when her pink lips pulled into a small smile, and her eyes drifted shut while her fingers drew small circles on my back, relief as powerful as the incredible orgasm I'd just had washed over me. I brought my lips to hers and kissed her softly before withdrawing.

Once I had Quinn settled beneath the covers, I discarded the condom and returned to her side, pulling her against me. With her tucked in my arms in the early light of dawn, I found a peace I had never dared hope could be mine.

CHAPTER 33

Quinn

THE SLOW, rhythmic beating of Trevor's heart beneath my cheek was an anchor holding me steady in the squall of my emotions.

Shelby was gone.

A part of me still couldn't—wouldn't—believe it. She was my best friend, my champion, my sister.

The tears on my cheeks had dried long ago, but the void remained, and I didn't know how to feel about that. I hadn't cried enough. The tears should have flowed for days and days. But as I lay there with Trevor, my naked body pressed to his, my head resting on his chest as he idly dragged his fingers through my hair, there was not even a hint of a sting pricking my eyes.

I had no concept of time or how long we'd been lying there, but I had watched the morning light paint its way across the room until the entire space was awash in its canary glow. My gaze was fixed on the wall beside the open bedroom door, but my vision was unfocused. I no longer saw Trevor's bedroom. Instead, I was in the dispatch center, and a shadowy, faceless figure occupied an adjacent part of my mind, his voice—his mirthless laugh— echoing through every thought and every memory.

I had let him in, so busy guarding the front door that I'd left a back entrance wide open for him to stroll into my head. I had once again allowed myself to be manipulated by a man who had been able to identify and exploit my vulnerabilities without my even knowing it. And my lack of vigilance, my inability to truly see him for what he was, had cost the lives of five women, including my best friend. He had stolen a piece of me that I could never get back.

But with the loss, something had also been found—a craving for vengeance, to *destroy* another human being. I'd never thought myself capable of it, but I felt its tantalizing power as surely as I felt Trevor's hands on me.

My eyes narrowed on the gilded cream-colored wall. I might have failed to save the lives of those women, of Shelby, but their deaths were a debt that would not go unpaid. I didn't yet know how I was going to do it. That sociopath had been miles ahead of us the entire time. But he had a weakness, and I was going to find it.

Trevor kissed the top of my head, drawing my consciousness back to him and the bed we shared, his fingers still tangled in my curls.

"I need to shower and get to the station." His voice was raspy, the result of too many hours and the strain of the case. "Want to join me?"

I burrowed my cheek into his chest, not ready to relinquish his warmth and comfort but also knowing that the world would keep turning regardless of my need for it to stop, to freeze time for just a little while so that I wouldn't have to deal with the aftermath of everything that had happened. So I nodded and slid from the sheets.

Minutes later, the bathroom was filled with swirling steam as we stood beneath a hot stream of water. Trevor took the soap from a dish perched in the niche and worked it into a lather. Then he began to work the soap over my body, his touch tender and reverent. When he pulled me into the circle of his arms and massaged the suds down my back, I let my head fall to his chest, too depleted to hold it up a moment longer.

Trevor wrapped an arm around my lower back, holding me firmly against him while he used his other hand to massage my neck. I needed this. I needed *him*. And that realization scared me. I didn't know what I was to Trevor. I had no idea what this morning had meant to him, had no indication of where our relationship would go after everything was over. Hell, I didn't even know if I could call what we had a relationship. But at the moment, I was simply too used up to contemplate it any further.

Trevor took the shampoo bottle and squirted a generous amount of the jasper-scented liquid into his cupped palm. He then gathered my hair on top of my head and scrubbed my scalp with great tenderness as fluffy piles of white suds dropped onto my shoulders and chest.

My eyes drifted to the white bandage on his left arm, which he had covered with cling wrap before getting in the shower.

"How did you get hurt?"

His hands paused for a heartbeat before he continued his work, but I didn't fail to notice that he avoided my eyes. "It's really not a big deal. I was in the woods, checking out a lead. Wasn't paying attention." He shrugged. "Like I said, it's just a scratch, but Bryan wasn't going to let me leave the crime scene last night without doing his mother hen thing."

The crime scene. Shelby's *crime scene.*

My eyes dropped from the bandage and settled on something else that had left me with questions—questions that I hadn't had the emotional bandwidth to ask when they first arose.

"What does this mean to you?" My fingers gently grazed the tattoo over his left peck—two doves with wings intertwined. Whoever had done it was a skilled artist. The soft shading of the black-and-gray image created such exquisite depth I almost believed the birds could take flight.

Trevor used his body to back me up until I was directly

beneath the stream of water, tilting my chin up so that he could rinse the shampoo from my hair. "It's a tribute to my parents."

Strong fingers scrubbed my scalp then slowly worked their way down to massage my neck again. The sensation of his calloused hands working the slick soap over my skin was exquisite. I closed my eyes and dropped my chin to my chest, yielding to the pleasure.

"Why doves?"

"When I was a kid, we had this large tree in our backyard. In the summertime, my mom liked to get up early and sit out on our deck, sipping her coffee and enjoying a few minutes of quiet before Dad and I started pestering her."

The sad smile in his voice drew my eyes back to him.

"One year, when I was about ten, two doves nested in that tree. My mom was obsessed with them. She kept watch over the yard to make sure no predators came anywhere near that nest." He chuckled, the smile reaching his baby-blue eyes. "When the hatchlings took flight, she was so thrilled that you would have thought she had laid those eggs herself."

Trevor brought a finger to my cheek and brushed some stray suds aside. "Dad and I teased her mercilessly, but she gave as good as she got." He shrugged. "For several years after that, those doves returned, and Mom was always right there, helping to ensure those babies had the chance to fly."

He smiled again, and I was shocked to realize that I was smiling too. "After that first year, Dad realized how much it meant to Mom to give those birds a chance. He said Mom's big heart was what he loved most about her. So he joined her in keeping watch over the nest each season after that."

Trevor's voice strained against the emotion that fought to escape. But he swallowed and grabbed the shampoo again and that time worked the lather into his own hair. I watched, mesmerized, as suds and water traced a path over his shoulders and down his chest, then diverged along the contours of his well-defined stomach.

When I lifted my eyes, I found him watching me, hunger burning in his gaze. I reached for him, pulling him toward me until his body was pressed against mine. Trevor cupped my cheek then leaned down and captured my mouth with his. My lips parted the moment he made contact, a moan emanating from my throat as his tongue thrust into my mouth.

With his other hand, Trevor cupped my butt, pulling me in tighter, his hips grinding against me until the pulse in my core became unbearable. I whimpered against his lips as his tongue continued to ravage the inside of my mouth. When his fingers disappeared between us and massaged my sensitive bundle of nerves with expert precision, my body began to tremble with my need for him.

I wanted to feel him inside me again, to feel his thick shaft sliding into me with agonizing care. But instead, Trevor turned me around so that my back was pressed to his chest. His fingers circled my wrists and lifted my hands to the shower wall. Then his palms were on my breasts, massaging and squeezing, building the tension between my legs. His mouth was on my neck, his tongue flicking against my skin as he sucked and kissed his way to my shoulder.

One of his hands traveled down my wet torso, inching closer and closer to where I wanted him. I moved my hips in a serpentine motion, shuddering at the feel of his hard shaft rubbing against me. With his other hand, Trevor squeezed my breast again, then his fingers latched onto my nipple, pinching as his teeth nipped at my neck.

My head fell back against his shoulder, and when his fingers slid just inside my folds, I sucked steam-filled air through my teeth and pushed my hips forward, urging him to enter. For a moment, he just slid his finger up and down, teasing and coaxing, adjusting the pressure until the need was so strong that I grabbed his hand and pressed him to enter.

A sensuous chuckle filled my ear as his lips kissed along the shell. "Tell me what you want, Quinny-baby."

I swallowed hard, bursts of light flaring behind my closed eyes. When I didn't answer, he dragged his finger through my sensitive flesh once more. "I want to hear you say it, Quinn."

Then his fingers were on my clitoris, and he showed no mercy as he pressed against my nub, working in fast, hard circles.

I cried out, the pleasure almost too much to take. "I want to feel you, Trevor. I want you inside me." The words were hardly more than a groan, nearly drowned out by the water and the roaring in my ears. But that one confession was all it took.

Trevor's mouth latched onto my neck, sucking hard as two fingers dove into me. And just as he had masterfully built the ecstasy when we made love that morning, his fingers proved equally skilled. His thumb continued to rub my clitoris as his digits thrust into me over and over, slow at first then feverish as I neared my breaking point.

My head fell back against him again, my breathing ragged and my eyes closed as I got lost in the feel of him.

Trevor's voice was in my ear again, barely more than a strained whisper. "Come for me, Quinn. I want to feel you come for me."

When he thrust into me again, his thumb still pressed against my apex, the world shattered. Darkness exploded with light, and wave upon wave of unadulterated ecstasy crashed over me, my body shaking and my heart beating painfully against my chest.

With my eyes still closed and my breathing still fast but slowing, I leaned my forehead against the tiled wall and relished the euphoria that would be too brief. Trevor placed gentle kisses along my back and shoulders, his hands softly roaming my curves and sliding over my wet skin.

I turned to face him, closing my hand around his still-hard shaft. But Trevor gently gripped my wrist and stilled my movements. Then he kissed me. "We can get to that later if you still want to, but right now, I just want to take care of you."

I blinked at him, my mouth parting, but words escaped me. I hadn't had a ton of relationships, but of those I'd had, not once did any of those guys put my needs ahead of theirs, especially when it came to sex.

Trevor kissed the tip of my nose and reached behind me to turn off the water. When I followed him out of the shower, he held open a large towel and wrapped it around me. The plush fabric was luxurious against my skin.

We dried off in silence, the humid bathroom a cocoon of warmth and shelter from the outside world.

Trevor wrapped his towel around his waist and moved to the counter, where he proceeded to groom himself for work. "I don't know what time I'll be home today," he said, "but I'll check in on you throughout the day. If you need anything, and I mean *anything*, I want you to call me."

I wrapped my own towel around my body, tucked a corner between my cleavage to hold it in place, and leaned against the counter, my back to the mirror. "I want to go to the station with you."

Trevor paused in the process of gelling his hair, hesitation and concern staring back at me from his reflection. "That's not a good idea, Quinn. It's too soon."

"I can't just sit around here all day, alone with my thoughts."

"I can ask Alex and Liz to come hang out."

Shaking my head, I looked at my feet. "No. I don't want company. I just want to stay busy, and there is no better way to do that than helping to catch the guy who murdered my best friend." My tone had a hard edge that I hadn't intended.

Trevor rinsed his hands then leaned against the counter and crossed his arms. He chewed the inside of his cheek for a moment as he assessed me. When he spoke, it was with caution. "I get it, Quinn. I really do. And I want nothing more than to say yes to you, but I can't because I know that if I did, I'd only be agreeing to causing you more pain and risking the case. You're too close to it now. I can't allow you to continue your calls with this guy. It would be a conflict of interest."

I pressed my lips together to keep from biting out the first thing that came to mind. He had my best interests at heart, but that didn't stop my blood from turning to molten lava. I would not rest until I destroyed that psychopathic asshole. But I couldn't do that by sitting in Trevor's house all day, waiting for him to get home. I also knew that further arguing the point with Trevor was useless. So I took a deep breath and wiped all remnants of my thoughts from my face. "You're right." I pushed off from the counter and moved toward the door to the bedroom. "Promise you'll keep me posted on any progress?"

He smiled and gave a firm nod. "I promise."

I opened the door, absently noting the way the steam twirled and danced as it escaped captivity. One other thought came to mind. I paused on the threshold, twisting to look over my shoulder. "Trevor?"

"Hmm?"

I opened my mouth then closed it. Then I tried again. "Please don't tell anybody about us. About"—I waved my arm between us—"about *this*. I don't want history repeating itself."

Understanding softened his features, and he straightened. "What happens between us is nobody's business. You can trust me, Quinn."

I studied him for a moment, weighing and judging the sincerity of his words and body language. I wanted to trust him, and a big part of me believed that I could. The past few weeks hadn't been hell for me alone. Trevor had been dealing with his own stress and pressure, his own feelings of defeat and failure. Yet not once had he made that known. Every moment since I had become involved in the case, he shoved aside his feelings and needs to tend to mine. Still, it wouldn't be the first time I had been fooled by a handsome face and a few pretty words.

Trevor was still watching me, his gaze unwavering. So I offered a small smile and nodded before disappearing into the bedroom to plan my next move and prepare for Trevor's wrath.

CHAPTER 34

Trevor

I PARKED my truck at the rear of the station, among the other personnel vehicles, and climbed out then pulled open the back door to retrieve my gear. My actions were automatic, and my thoughts were on the woman I had left behind. All things considered, Quinn had seemed better that morning than I'd expected, but I knew from experience she could be hard to read when she had her walls up.

Visions of her naked body swam in my head as I made my way through the parking lot, the feel of her nails clawing at my back still palpable beneath my thin white T-shirt. Being inside of Quinn had been one of the best moments of my life, but I couldn't shake the knot that had settled in my stomach when I'd kissed her on top of her head and we'd said our goodbyes. She had stood at the door, arms crossed and eyes down, her expression indifferent, and all I could think was that she was regretting what had happened between us.

I kicked myself for letting things go that far then making it worse with that encore performance in the shower. She had been vulnerable, her world painfully and irrevocably altered, and what had I done? I'd stuck my dick in her, somehow thinking that *I* could actually be the one to make her feel better. *How could I have been such a damn idiot?*

Throwing open the door to the rear entrance of the station, I marched toward the locker room. Judging by the way administrative staff and officers alike were jumping out of my way, I must have looked as murderous as I felt.

When I reached my locker, I set my gear on the wooden bench in front of it. As I changed into my uniform, I continued to contemplate Quinn's demeanor that morning. Maybe I had read her all wrong, and our intimacy wasn't the issue. Maybe she was just having trouble dealing with everything that had happened. And that thought made me feel even more like a low-life piece of shit for leaving her to deal with it on her own.

I slammed my locker shut, the clang of metal reverberating off the walls and through the silence of the otherwise unoccupied room. Taking a seat on the bench, I dropped my head into my hands, digging my fingers into the hard spikes of my gelled hair. The last thing I wanted was to make the situation worse for Quinn. It had been a long time since I'd been serious about anyone, and that was if being serious about someone in high school even counted. I still wasn't sure I even knew *how* to be there for a woman.

But that didn't stop me from wanting to try—for Quinn. With a deep sigh, I rose from the bench and headed for the briefing room, where the chief and every officer working the case would be waiting.

Upon entering the room, I glanced at where the chief stood with his forearms braced on the lectern, one foot propped on the shelf near its base. As expected, six other officers, including Gabe, were already seated, chatting among themselves in unusually hushed tones.

It wasn't until Gabe, wearing a grave expression, nodded to the chief's left that I noticed the addition to the large evidence board that had been there, slowly collecting information, since the case's inception. At first, my brain only registered that something was wrong. A split second later, my stomach dropped.

"What the fuck?" I spat.

"We're going to get to that," the chief said, his icy-blue eyes narrowing beneath his bushy gray eyebrows.

I looked at Gabe, a nonverbal demand for an explanation.

Gabe sat relaxed, an ankle crossed over his opposite knee, but his dark eyes smoldered. "Photos and confidential details about the crime scene were published on the *Gazette*'s website early this morning."

I looked at the board again. Someone had printed the full article and pinned it up next to the notes and crime scene photos from the night before so that some of the pictures we had taken were side by side with those printed on the newspaper's website. They were identical.

The lid I'd been trying to keep on my temper was threatening to blow. I balled my hands into fists in an attempt to level out and slowly turned my gaze to the chief. "You know what this means." The low menace in my voice cut through the stillness of the room. Even Carlson, who never knew when to keep his damn mouth shut, sat silent with his eyes forward.

Scanning my partners, I tried to determine which of them had betrayed us. Those pictures were cold, hard proof that the press was getting their information from someone inside the department. *So who in the room is a damn turncoat?*

"Trevor." Chief Kelly waited for my attention.

I took my time giving it to him.

"Have a seat, son. We're going to deal with the leak now that we have proof the information isn't coming from the killer. But we need to discuss the case first."

I scoffed. "You really think that's wise when the person feeding information to the press is probably sitting in this room?"

Chief Kelly smashed his lips together, though the action was nearly obscured by his thick mustache. "At this point, the damage is done. I'm more concerned about nailing this asshole and preventing further murders. Besides, whoever is selling the information already has access to the details."

The chief nodded to an empty seat beside Gabe, who was situated in the last of three rows of cheaply upholstered chairs. I hesitated, but when Gabe gave me a subtle nod, I relented.

Chief Kelly relaxed his shoulders, maintaining his slightly bent position over the lectern. "Right." He looked between Gabe and me. "What do we know so far, and what information are we still waiting on?"

Gabe was the first to speak. "There's nothing out of the ordinary with any of the victims' financials, and interviews with family and friends indicate that at least some of the women were having marital difficulties, but outside of that, there were no grudges or threats against them."

The chief puckered his lips and offered a pensive nod.

I crossed my arms and picked up where Gabe had left off. "Cell phone records for each of the victims show a call from an unavailable number lasting between three and five minutes on the day they were killed, and there were no other calls placed or received afterward. It's worth noting that the call Quinn received from the killer on her cell was also from an unavailable number."

"We traced the victims' phones," Gabe said. "The last ping on each of them was in a remote, wooded location—but a different place each time. We've also located the first victim's car. It was called in by a hiker and found several miles from where her body was dumped, obscured by brush and wiped clean. I'm sure we'll eventually find the other victims' vehicles out there, too, but that's a lot of forest to cover."

I cut in again, offering up something I'd been considering but hadn't yet voiced. "The fact that we can place each of them out in the woods before their phones stopped transmitting along with that last phone call they all received makes me wonder if they're voluntarily meeting this guy."

Gabe, still sitting as cool as a cucumber, turned to me. "That would explain how he's still managing to get victims despite the public panic and all the PSAs we've put out telling people to stay home and keep away from strangers."

I nodded and worked my teeth back and forth as the cogs in my head spun. "Yeah, maybe they *do* know him."

"What are you thinking?" the chief asked. "That this guy is local?"

Carlson snickered. He sat opposite us with only a narrow aisle between and leaned toward his partner, Nash, on his left. "It's probably that creepy-ass janitor at the high school that all the female students complain about."

Ignoring Carlson, I shook my head in answer to the chief. "No, not local. I think he's a chameleon. He's a master at blending in and getting to know the people and the lay of the land."

I dropped my eyes to the chair back in front of me as a thought began to manifest. My words were slow to form as I kept pace with the ideas mashing together to create a partial picture. "Quinn figured out early on that he's picking his victims ahead of time. We figured he was stalking them, getting to know their routines, but maybe he's doing more than that." I looked at the chief again. "Maybe he is actually getting to *know* them. Infiltrating their lives somehow."

The room became deathly still until only the sound of the antiquated AC unit perched on the windowsill could be heard.

After a moment, the chief cleared his throat. "What else do we know?"

"This guy has mastered the art of getting away with murder," Gabe said. "He leaves very little evidence behind by killing his victims then disposing of the bodies somewhere else, in a way that contaminates any evidence left on the corpses." His lips turned white as he pressed them together and shook his head. "And as for the victim profiles, they're all over the place, even without considering the cases in other jurisdictions. White, Black, Native American, anywhere from twenty-three to forty-five. Some with kids, some without. Incomes ranging from twenty thousand to three hundred fifty grand a year. The only things they have in common are that they're all female, married, and living in Eden Falls."

"And the profile on the killer?" Chief Kelly asked.

I slid down in my chair a bit, letting my knees fall open. "From what I saw of him last night, I'd say he's about six feet and a buck ninety. He's got an athletic build, and with the way he took off through the woods, he's in good shape. The guy's narcissistic and considers himself highly intelligent, which"—I canted my head—"has proven to be the case so far. He also believes he's superior to law enforcement and likes to demonstrate how much smarter he is than any of us. And we know from things he's said, in addition to the several cases from other departments that I'm confident are related, that he has killed dozens of times before."

Gabe chimed in. "Speaking of those other cases, Trevor was able to determine a pattern. In each instance, the asshole killed seven women then just up and disappeared."

The chief's brow wrinkled. "Seven?"

I nodded.

"Any thoughts on why seven?"

Pressing my lips together, I shook my head. "No, but maybe when we figure that out, we'll also learn the significance of his killing at midnight."

To my left, Nash leaned forward to see around Carlson. His dark Puerto Rican eyes locked on me. "What's the deal with the lab results?"

Gabe answered. "Nada so far, but I'm not holding my breath."

The chief cut back in. "Why is that?"

I released a frustrated sigh. "Because there was very little DNA evidence in any of the other cases, and what they *did* manage to obtain returned to an unidentified subject."

Chief Kelly swore under his breath and turned his crystal eyes on the windows against the far wall. Golden light poured in through the filmy glass, highlighting the dust particles drifting through the air and the decades-old stains on the threadbare carpet.

Finally, the chief said, "Well, at least when we *do* get this guy, we'll be able to tie him to those other homicides and make sure he burns for them all."

Every head in the room bobbed up and down with silent agreement.

Straightening from his bent-over position at the lectern, the chief put his business face on. "All right. Ryan. McNeil. What's your next move, and what do you need to make it happen?"

Gabe and I exchanged glances, and he spoke first. "One good thing that came out of last night is that we now have one of the cars this asshole has been using, and we got to it before he could wipe it down. We were able to run the VIN and determine that it was stolen in Billings last week. We're working on getting surveillance footage from around the area where the car was taken. With some luck, maybe we'll finally get to see the son of a bitch's face."

Gabe had barely finished before I cut in. "I want Quinn off the case."

The room went silent again, all eyes turning to me.

I ignored them and held the chief's gaze. "She's been carrying too much of the burden of this case. It wasn't fair to put her in this position in the first place, and now it has cost her her best friend, and she blames herself. The toll it's taking on her is too high. It's not worth it."

Chief Kelly studied me, but before he answered, Carlson, with his frat-boy demeanor, laughed. "Sounds like the case isn't the only thing you've been working, Ryan."

A muscle in my jaw ticked as my eyes slid to him. Nash leaned into his partner and whispered something in his ear. All humor evaporated from the greenhorn as he faced forward and shut his trap.

"You're right," the chief said, and I turned my attention back to him. "It's time to take Quinn off the case, but keep in mind that that also likely means this guy is going to start killing without warning, and we won't have the opportunity to save any of the victims."

My voice carried a razor-sharp edge. "He never intended for Quinn to be able to solve any of those clues. This was not about a chance to save the victims. It was about torturing *her*, and we helped him do it."

Chief Kelly opened his mouth to respond, but the words died in his throat when his eyes flicked to the back of the room. The rest of us turned in our seats, and when I located the object of his distraction, my stomach hit the floor.

CHAPTER 35

Trevor

THE COLOR DRAINED from Quinn's face as she stared at the board, which told the full story of how her friend had died. It took me a moment to recover from the shock of seeing her there, but when my senses finally returned, I launched out of my chair and headed straight for her. Placing my hands on her shoulders, I gently turned her around and steered her out of the room and into one of the interrogation rooms.

"What are you doing here?" I asked as I shut the door and turned to face her.

Quinn was still pale, her eyes unfocused and aimed at the floor between us. With silent steps, I went to her and cupped her face in my palms. Soft chocolate coils brushed the backs of my hands as I stroked her cheeks with my thumbs, encouraging her to look at me. When she finally did, the heat of pain glowed in her golden irises.

"Tell me that wasn't what it looked like." Her voice sounded fragile.

"I told you to stay home, Quinn." The reprimand was soft, but it triggered her.

Quinn's features began to twist until rage supplanted shock. She placed her palms on my chest and shoved. "Tell me that the fucking newspaper did not publish photos of what that monster did to my dead best friend!"

My hands, hovering in the air from where they had cradled her face moments before, fell to my sides. I nodded, aware that my regret was written on my face. "The photos were published online early this morning."

Her eyebrows drew down as her cheeks turned a deeper shade of crimson. "How the hell did they get them?"

I took a step back and leaned against the door, crossing my arms. "I don't know. We were just about to discuss that when you walked in."

"Good. Let's go." Quinn charged for the door, looking determined as hell to toss my ass out of the way.

When she reached me, my hand shot out and braced against her stomach, bringing her to a sudden stop. She looked down at where our bodies met as though she couldn't believe I was getting in her way. Her eyes slid up to mine, sending me an unspoken threat to move or lose the appendage.

"You're going home, Quinn." My fingertips burned where they continued to press against her taut stomach, the ribbed material of her black tank top the only barrier between our skin.

Her matching leather jacket creaked as she ran an agitated hand through her loose curls. "I'm not going anywhere."

"Quinn—"

"This psychopath just killed my best friend, Trevor, along with four other women," she said through gritted teeth. "He's not going to stop unless *we* stop him. I'll be damned if I'm going to sit at home while he's out there choosing his next victim!"

She pressed her body into my hand, everything about her posture telling me that if I wanted her to leave, I would have to throw her over my shoulder, drive her home, and chain her to the heaviest piece of furniture I owned.

Recognizing that I was fighting a losing battle, I swore and dropped my hand. Without a word, I stepped away from the door and held it open for her. For a moment, she eyed me as though expecting a trap, then she promptly vacated the interrogation room and led the way back to the briefing.

All eyes were on us when we walked in. Or rather, all eyes were on Quinn, every officer in the room conducting a subtle threat assessment. Quinn didn't spare any of them so much as a glance. Instead, her focus was on Chief Kelly.

She squared her shoulders and lifted her chin. "I want to help, Chief. I'm okay to help."

Chief Kelly's gaze slid to me. Reluctantly, I gave a nod, and he mimicked the gesture to Quinn. Her shoulders dropped a little, and she allowed me to lead her to the seat I had occupied next to Gabe. Noticing that her attention was once again affixed to the evidence board, I promptly marched to the front of the room, spun the board around, then planted myself in the seat to her right.

Chief Kelly brought the meeting to an end, advising that he was going to maintain a beefed-up patrol until the case was brought to a close. After encouraging everyone to keep working the evidence and to wait and see what the lab could tell us, he dismissed the other officers but requested that Gabe, Quinn, and I remain.

Carlson made his way toward the door, running his mouth as usual. I hadn't been paying him much attention until he started talking about the events of the previous night.

"We're gonna be the ones to get this fucker," he said to another one of our newer officers. "Hell, if he hadn't managed to shoot Ryan while he was chasing the asshole through the woods last night, he'd probably be sitting in one of our cells right now."

A low growl emanated from my chest when Quinn's head snapped around to me. "For fuck's sake, Carlson, learn when to keep your damn mouth shut."

I glared at him over my shoulder, and when he saw the look on my face, he blanched. Then his eyes slid to Quinn, who was openly gaping, her attention shifting between Carlson and me. With the look of a child who had just been scolded by his mother,

Carlson ducked his head and shuffled out of the room, practically pushing people through the door.

Shaking my head at his stupidity, I turned my attention to the chief, who was still at the lectern, but I was all too aware of Quinn staring at my profile. I shifted in my seat, fearing what she was thinking now that she knew I'd had Shelby's killer in my sights and let him get away.

Once the room cleared, the chief left the lectern to shut the door then chose a nearby chair.

"Now"—he looked between the three of us—"let's discuss the issue of this leak."

I sighed heavily and tossed a hand into the air. "We've been keeping an eye on who's accessing the database. No one who doesn't have a valid reason to access the file has been in it."

"That means either the leak is someone who is working the case," Gabe said, "*or* someone who is working the case is being careless with evidence, and whoever they're sharing that information with is leaking it to the press."

Quinn scrunched her face. "Can't we just go to the newspaper office and threaten them for interfering with an investigation?"

I shook my head. "It wouldn't do any good. They're going to argue freedom of the press and refuse to give up their source. We could press the issue, but there are no guarantees we'd get anywhere. We're better off flushing out the source of the leak."

Chief Kelly ran a hand over his balding head. "How do you want to go about doing that?"

I looked over Quinn's head to find Gabe staring back at me. A lifetime of being thicker than thieves had given us the ability to communicate without words. He nodded, so I filled Chief Kelly and Quinn in on what we were thinking. "We'll start by interrogating everyone who's working the case, beginning with those who have accessed the file since Shelby's death."

The chief puckered his mouth and cast his gaze to the shiny toes of his boots. Then he nodded. "Keep me posted, and let me know if you need anything."

He surprised us all when he leaned forward and placed a weathered hand on top of Quinn's, which she had resting on her thigh. Their eyes locked, and the chief gently squeezed her hand.

Quinn's lip quivered, but her cheeks remained dry as she nodded her understanding. Then the chief stood and left the room.

I studied Quinn for a moment, watching for any cracks in her facade, but she was stoic—poised.

"Well..." Gabe stood and looped his thumbs over his duty belt as he caught my eye. "We've got some reports to go over. I'll get started."

He was referring to Shelby's autopsy report.

"I'll be right there," I said.

Finally alone, with the silence pressing in on us, I placed my hand on the back of Quinn's neck and brushed my fingers along her skin, trying my damnedest to figure out what she needed.

With her hands still in her lap, she fiddled with her fingers as her eyes went to the evidence board again. She stared at it as though she could see through to the pictures on the other side.

After a couple of minutes had passed, I was about to tell Quinn I would walk her to her car when she suddenly stood and looked down at me. "I'll be in Dispatch if you need me for anything."

She headed for the door but only made it a few steps before I was on my feet with my hand wrapped around her arm, preventing her from traveling farther. "You're going home, Quinn."

She looked down at my hand then up at me, her expression conveying that she was sure I'd lost my mind.

"I let you stay for the meeting, but now it's time to leave."

Quinn ripped her arm out of my grasp and backed up a few steps. "I have to be there to take his next call, Trevor."

I advanced, my features locked with resolve. "No. I'll be handling those calls from now on. We're done playing by his rules."

She started to argue, but I cut her off. "The chief agrees, Quinn. You're off the case." My tone was sterner than I'd intended, but I could see her digging her heels in.

Quinn stared at me for several moments, as though she didn't recognize me. Then her gaze hardened, and her mouth set into a firm line as she clenched her fists at her sides. "Fine," she said finally then immediately spun on her heel and was gone.

Twenty minutes later, as I sat at my desk, Gabe at his desk beside me, I was still distracted by the image of Quinn and the betrayed look on her face when I'd sent her home.

"You think he went after her to send a message?"

I glanced at Gabe, furrowing my brow. He jerked his chin toward Shelby's autopsy report, which was lying open in front of me.

"Yeah, I do." I leaned back, lacing my fingers behind my head, and swiveled back and forth in the creaky office chair as I thought about how fucked-up the whole situation had become.

Then I spun my chair to face Gabe's profile. "How the hell does this shithead roll into *our* town, torture and kill five women, and he's still walking free? Meanwhile, one of our own is selling his soul to the press and ensuring the public knows just how epically we're failing." The disgust in my words was weighted equally toward all parties involved, me included.

Gabe sat back and swiveled his chair in my direction. He propped an elbow on his armrest, partially obscuring his mouth with his hand, and was pensive for a moment before letting me in on his thoughts. "I don't know, man. We're doing everything we can, but this guy is good." His eyes locked on mine. "He's really fucking good."

I was about to respond when my phone vibrated against my chest. My eyes narrowed when I saw the caller ID. I answered immediately. "Ryan."

One by one, my muscles went taught as I listened. My grip on the phone tightened. I thought I might actually crack the damn thing. *Do not shoot the messenger. Do not shoot the messenger.* The mantra wasn't helping to ebb the flow of liquid heat coursing through me. I wasn't a guy who got pissed easily, but I was quickly burning through my last fucking ounce of control.

"I'm on my way." I ended the call without waiting for anything further and launched from my chair with so much force that the hunk of junk slammed against the desk behind mine.

Gabe's deep voice crashed against my back. "Where're you going?"

Already halfway across the bullpen, I wasn't even sure he could hear my growled response. "Probably to prison."

CHAPTER 36

Trevor

My blood hadn't cooled any by the time I marched into Dispatch two minutes after Julia had called to tell me that Quinn had, in fact, not gone home like I'd instructed her to but instead had her ass parked at her desk. The quiver in Julia's voice when she'd relayed Quinn's whereabouts to me along with what sounded like genuine concern for Quinn's emotional well-being had kicked my respect for the girl up a notch. I knew I made her nervous as hell, so the fact that she would call me for Quinn's benefit said a lot about her character.

I barreled down the dark hallway, drawn by the dim light of the main room ahead, all while entertaining visions of throwing Quinn over my shoulder and hauling her ass out to my truck, gossip be damned. I was momentarily struck by the realization that never in my life had a woman gotten me so bent out of shape that I had devolved to caveman status, but I banished the thought just as fast as it had come.

Reaching the end of the hall, I took a moment to size up the room. My eyes landed on Julia first. She was seated to the far right of the large open space, working the fire radios and wearing a pinched expression. When she saw me, her wide eyes darted toward the opposite side of the room. I followed the direction of her gaze and found Quinn at the center console, where she had been spending most of her time the past few weeks.

I took a step toward her then halted. Her frame was stiff. Her eyes were locked on the screen in front of her, and her knuckles were completely white where they wrapped around the receiver she held to her ear. Blair and Meredith were seated against the wall to Quinn's left, turned in their chairs and so captivated by Quinn that they weren't paying me any attention for once.

Altering my course, I angled for Julia instead. She leaned back as I bore down on her and seemed genuinely afraid. When I reached her desk, I snatched up her receiver and clicked onto Quinn's call, and only then did the girl start to breathe again.

The room was silent, aside from a few beeps from the monitors and the occasional squawk from the radios. It wasn't unusual for things to be quiet in the middle of the day on a Monday, but it still felt eerie, as though the whole of Eden Falls knew the call was taking place and waited with bated breath.

"I'm pleased that you decided to show up today, Quinn," the killer said in dulcet tones. "I'm sure there were plenty who told you to stay home, but that you didn't listen demonstrates how much our relationship means to you."

Deep shadows pooled beneath the hard cut of Quinn's cheekbones. They matched the ones under her eyes. For a moment, it seemed that Quinn wasn't going to respond, but then with a feral tone and moving nothing but her lips, she answered, "You mean *nothing* to me."

The killer *tsk*ed. "That can't be true, or you wouldn't be speaking to me right now. You would be home, mourning your best friend."

Quinn's expression darkened until she looked downright murderous. "Shelby wouldn't want me sitting at home, crying over her. She would want me *here*, finding a way to ensure you suffer every bit as much as she did."

A sinister chuckle came over the line. "You would have to

work very hard to make me suffer that much. She was a special guest, so I made sure to give her extra attention."

Despite the ghostly pallor of Quinn's complexion in the glow of her monitor, I could see the last of the color drain from her face. "Why Shelby?" she asked through gritted teeth. "I've done everything you've asked—played your sick game and followed your rules." Unadulterated hate punctuated each word she spat.

A bored sigh preceded his response. "You're making me the bad guy, Quinn, because it's *easy*. But even though Shelby fit, I couldn't have brought her into the game if she hadn't chosen to play."

Quinn's eyes widened, and her head retracted as though he'd just reached through the line and slapped her. But the reaction was gone almost as fast as it had manifested. She pulled the phone closer to her lips until they brushed against it. "How did you get to be so fucked up?"

Oh shit. The shift in Quinn was instantaneous, and I wasn't the only one who noticed. Blair's and Meredith's eyes were wide, and they were gaping at each other like a couple of largemouth bass, and beside me, Julia let out a little squeak and shifted nervously in her seat.

"I'm not the one who's fucked up, Quinn." The killer's intonation hadn't shifted in the slightest. "I'm doing the world a favor by taking out the trash."

"You *are* the trash, you sick fuck. But I'm guessing I'm not the first to tell you that, am I?"

What the hell is she doing? Quinn was falling off the deep end, and I didn't have the slightest idea what to do about it. I considered taking over the call again, but I had a feeling Quinn wasn't going to let that happen. She would fight me tooth and nail, and the last thing we needed was to give that master manipulator something more he could use against us.

"Careful, Quinn," he warned her.

"Or what?" Quinn shot back. "You think I'm scared of

someone who has to tie women up and beat them in a pathetic attempt to convince himself he has a modicum of power?"

I took a step toward Quinn, but the phone cord wouldn't let me get any nearer. My gaze bored into her as I willed her to look at me, but nothing existed to her outside of that call and the man on the other end of the line.

"You'd better shut your fucking mouth—"

"And what has shutting my mouth gotten me? A dead best friend and a psychopath using me as a one-eight-hundred number."

The killer's breathing accelerated. Quinn wasn't just playing with fire. She was splashing kerosene on the damn flames and enjoying it. I waved my arm in an attempt to get her attention. When her eyes lifted to me, I dragged my finger across my throat, but she immediately dismissed me and returned her full attention to the call.

"Why don't we have a little chat about Mommy Dearest?" Quinn's tone was saccharine, a maniacal smile spreading across her face but failing to reach her eyes, which were hard with hate.

"I said shut your fucking mouth."

Shit. This is getting out of control. Was she trying to make herself victim number six?

"She knew you were her biggest mistake, didn't she?"

A growl tore through the ragged breaths on the other end of the line.

"She didn't love you, didn't give a shit about you, because she knew you weren't worth the trouble. And you hated her for it."

"Shut up, you stupid cunt!"

"And if your own mother can't even find a reason to love you, what woman ever could?"

"I'm going to slice you from your pussy to your throat and leave you in the middle of town so that everyone can see you're nothing but a cheap, filthy whore!"

The roar of the killer's voice in my head made the sudden silence when he hung up even more jarring. My eyes were still on

Quinn, my gut twisting at the satisfied smile playing at her lips as she gingerly set her phone down.

What the ever-living fuck just happened? I wasn't the only one asking that question, judging by the looks on the other women's faces and the way their heads kept volleying back and forth between Quinn and me. If they expected me to have an answer for Quinn's complete personality change, they would be disappointed.

I set Julia's phone back on the desk and continued to stare at Quinn, so many things racing through my mind that I didn't even know where to start dealing with any of it. But as I watched the woman I was struggling to recognize, I began to realize what she was doing. I had done the same thing after my parents died. Only instead of channeling rage and taunting a serial killer to keep from having to deal with my grief, I had turned to partying and screwing around. And over the past few weeks, I had begun to understand what it had cost me. I didn't want that future for Quinn, a future in which she couldn't let anyone get close and she could no longer trust herself to deal with the hard stuff.

Quinn, I realized, was on the brink of shattering, and her rage was the only thing holding her together. She was a runaway train on an unfinished track, and I felt powerless to stop her. If, after all of those years, I still hadn't managed to face the things I'd been running from, the pain of losing my parents and the shame of what a disappointment I had become, how the hell was I supposed to help Quinn through it?

And after that stunt she'd just pulled, I was more terrified than ever that her face was going to end up on that evidence board next to Shelby's.

CHAPTER 37

Quinn

"Do you have a death wish?" Trevor asked before he skidded to a halt in front of me, barely restrained anger etched into the lines of his face. He cupped his hand around my elbow and pulled me from the desk then marched me across the room to a semi-secluded corner. "What the hell were you thinking pushing him that far?"

I crossed my arms and considered him coolly before answering. "When you can give me a good reason for chasing him through the woods without backup and getting yourself shot, I'll get back to you on that."

Trevor's eyes darted back and forth between mine, his lips pressed together as though he was holding back every dirty word he wanted to hurl at Carlson for letting me in on that little secret. Then, after a minute of obvious internal war, his shoulders slumped in silent surrender. "He was right *there*, Quinn. I had to go after him."

I understood how impossible it had been for him to watch the man who'd ruined so many lives fade into the night while Trevor was stuck waiting for backup, but the emotional side of my brain wasn't ready to forgive him for putting himself in that kind of danger then lying to me about it, calling a freaking gunshot wound a scratch. His recklessness had nearly cost me him in addition to Shelby and on the same night to the same man who had been torturing me and screwing with my head for weeks. So no, I wasn't going to let Trevor off the hook that easily—not yet. So I maintained my mute indifference.

Trevor swore and shoved a hand through his hair. I tried to ignore the way my stomach flipped at the sight of his disheveled strands.

Putting his hands on his hips, Trevor worked his jaw back and forth and studied me. "Quinn, I know how badly you're hurting, and I get that you want to hurt him as much as he hurt you."

I looked away, pulling my arms tighter against my chest.

Trevor lowered his voice. "But you're making things worse. I cannot focus on hunting this asshole down if I can't trust that you're not going to go off and take matters into your own hands."

My gaze swung back to him, my teeth creaking as I ground them together. "It's a good thing I took matters into my own hands rather than going home like a good little girl, or we never would have gotten him to give up two very valuable pieces of information."

His brow furrowed. "What information?"

"He *does* have something he looks for in these women, some common thread that we have yet to find."

Trevor seemed to search his memory of the call and came up empty.

"He said Shelby *fit*, Trevor. He said that even though she fit, he couldn't have brought her into the game if she hadn't chosen to play."

Trevor's attention was locked on me, so I took the opportunity to press the matter further. "And now we know that his mother is a trigger. We can use that to our advantage. Get him to lose that calculated control so that he makes a mistake."

Trevor growled and looked over my head. He was right on the verge of being exactly where I wanted him.

"We're missing something, Trevor. Something big. I can feel

it." I bit my lip, trying to determine whether he was ready for the next part. "And I'm going to figure out what it is."

Trevor's eyes flashed to mine. "No way. You're off this case, Quinn." He brought his nose down until it nearly tapped mine. "You have one more chance to go home of your own free will. After that, I will lock you in a damn cell until this is over if I have to."

I mashed my lips together until they started to tingle and rose onto my tiptoes to close the tiny distance that remained between our noses. "I. Am. Not. Going. Anywhere."

I fully expected him to drag me back to his house and chain me to the plumbing, so his unexpected reaction gave him the unfair advantage of completely knocking the fight out of me.

"Quinn..." His face softened as much as his words. "I can't lose you to this guy."

Until this case, I had never seen Trevor express an emotion other than devil-may-care and cocksure. So the fear and anguish rippling through every square inch of that beautiful face nearly shattered me.

With a heavy sigh, I let the tension slip from my frame. Using my body as a shield against the rest of the room, I clasped my fingers around Trevor's large wrist and squeezed. "You won't, Trevor. I know you think I'm playing a dangerous game, and maybe I am, but I haven't completely lost my good sense."

He raised his eyebrows to challenge that statement.

I rolled my eyes in return. "Trev, I *need* to be a part of bringing him down. I know you're worried about me, but doing something to stop him is going to be a lot more therapeutic than sitting at home, ruminating over my failures and Shelby's death. I know you can understand that."

Trevor looked as though he was struggling to decide between spanking me and giving me what I wanted. With a brush of my thumb against his wrist, he caved—reluctantly.

"Fine." He sighed. "You obviously already have it all planned out, so you mind filling the lead investigator in?"

"I want to have access to all the case materials. Every phone call. Every picture, autopsy report, and any other piece of evidence that's been collected."

Trevor looked skeptical. "Why?"

"I told you before—there is *always* a trail. I intend to find it."

CHAPTER 38

ONE HOUR LATER, I was holed up in the small command post Trevor and I had been using to work the victim clues. In the end, the chief had been easier to convince of my plan than Trevor, probably because I had Trevor's support, and that seemed adequate for the chief. The room was filled with boxes, manila folders stacked high on the metal table I had pulled to the center, and the whiteboard, which was wiped clean and patiently waiting for me to start marking it up again.

Sitting at the head of the table, I took a deep breath and pulled a tower of folders toward me. I was just about to flick open the cover on the first one when Trevor came in, carrying another box.

He set it on the opposite end of the table, flipped the lid off, and rummaged inside. After withdrawing a few pieces of glossy paper, he replaced the lid. "All right. That's everything."

My eyes went to the contents of his hand, which he was trying to obscure behind his leg. "What's that?" I pointed at the evidence in question.

"You get everything but these" was all he said.

"Trevor, we had a deal."

"Tough."

"Trevor—"

"Quinn, these are the photos of Shelby's body. You can have everything else, but there's no way in hell I'm letting you sear these images into your mind."

Before I could argue further, he moved to my side, leaned down to place a kiss on the top of my head, then cupped my cheek. "I'll be around if you need me." With those parting words, he took his leave.

I spent the rest of the day poring over the case files, combing through every detail of the investigation. Trevor had even made copies of his notes and theories, which provided surprising insight into the fact that though he might play the part of the cavalier playboy, he was actually incredibly astute.

A yellow legal pad sat beneath my wrist. The pen I'd used to mark up several pages was a blur as I feverishly tapped its end against the table. I glanced down at my notes, scanning my scribbles, but my mind remained blank. Nothing in the case files had stood out to me. The guys had been *very* thorough in their investigation, so if there really was a trail we had missed, I didn't think it existed between the pages of the case jackets.

After restacking the file folders, I removed a flash drive from one of the evidence boxes. Its label indicated that it memorialized the numerous phone calls I'd exchanged with the killer. After flipping to a clean page in my notepad, I opened the first file on the drive, closed my eyes, and allowed the killer's serenade to transport me back to a time when my best friend was alive and my biggest problem was that my application for a promotion had gone unanswered.

One by one, I worked my way through each of the calls. I'd had to listen to the last one, the call I'd taken at the costume shop, several times before I could detach myself enough to listen for what might be hidden rather than agonizing over how obvious the clues that had led me to Shelby too late had been.

By the time I finished with the calls, it was nearing twenty hundred hours. My eyes were bleary, and my body ached. I set my pen down on the notepad and rubbed my eyes.

"How's it going?"

I jumped at the sound of Trevor's voice and twisted to find him leaning against the open doorway behind me, his arms and ankles crossed. He looked like freaking James Dean, his biceps straining the fabric of his uniform shirt, and his lips, dressed with an easy smile, screamed "Kiss me!"

I growled and let my body slide down in the chair. "Not good."

Trevor came into the room and propped his hip on the edge of the table so that he was facing me. "Maybe there's nothing to find, Quinn."

"There is *always* something to find."

He watched me for a moment, his expression unreadable. Finally, he jerked his head in the direction of the employee parking lot. "Let's call it a day. You've been at this for way too long. You need a break."

I shook my head. "No. I'm good."

"Quinn—"

"Trevor, I'm good." The edge in my voice was sharp enough to cut steel. I took a deep breath and slowly let it out, simultaneously releasing the tension in my face. "I'm sorry. That... frustration was meant for me, not you."

He nodded slowly and continued to study me. Then he rose from the table and left the room. Guilt poured through me until I could hardly stand the feel of my own skin.

I was just about to go after him when the crinkle of paper and the smell of grease-laden french fries tantalized my senses. Trevor reentered the room, carrying a hefty brown bag with grease stains from one of the local burger joints in one hand and a chair in the other. Without a word, he took a seat beside me, shoving file folders and boxes out of the way, and proceeded to empty the contents of the bag.

My mouth began to salivate and my stomach rumbled. It was only then that I realized how long it had been since I'd eaten.

With a wry grin, Trevor placed a cheeseburger and fries on a napkin in front of me.

"I figured you'd put up a fight if I tried to get you to leave," he said, "so I brought plan B, just in case."

I didn't know what to say. I looked down at the food in front of me then watched as Trevor began to devour the first of the two cheeseburgers in front of him. Sauce dripped from between his fingers, and he ate with the same enthusiasm with which he made love.

A smile tugged at my lips, and in that moment, I realized Trevor was a much better man than I had ever given him credit for.

Trevor wiped his mouth with a napkin and glanced at my untouched food. "Come on, babe. You gotta eat."

Deciding that he had put up with enough of my tantrums and ultimatums for one day, I did as he said, and we ate our meals in silence. When we were through, Trevor cleaned up the debris and gave me a quick kiss. "I'm going to be here as long as you are, so if you need anything, I'll be close by."

My body registered the exact second his warmth left the room. A big part of me just wanted to go home with him and spend the hours of darkness wrapped in his embrace. But an even bigger part of me was crying for vengeance for every life that had been wrenched from the world at the hands of the sadist who had occupied my every waking thought.

So I shoved aside the siren song of comfort and threw myself back into the evidence, which lay in stacks before me.

Not until several hours later did I finally admit that my brain needed to rest for a bit. Opting for the cot in Dispatch over Trevor's sinfully decadent bed, I grabbed a few hours of sleep and returned to my self-imposed prison just after dawn.

True to his word, Trevor had remained at the station through the night, choosing to snooze in his truck for a bit rather than go home and leave me alone.

Over the next two days, we kept to a similar routine—my poring over every piece of evidence and research we had collected, and his keeping me fed and protected while he continued to work the case from his angle.

In the evening of the third day, my ears pricked at something I had heard at least two dozen times already.

I was relistening to all the calls between the killer and me, convinced that the thread that would unravel the entire enigma was buried somewhere within. With my mouse, I slid the time marker back ten seconds. My voice filled my ears.

"Considering we're going to be working together, and you now have my name, how about you give me your first name as well? A sign of good faith," I had prompted.

"I'm just an old fiend, Quinn. I don't provide faith."

I slid the cursor back and listened again. After it had played through once more, I picked up my pen, wrote the words *old fiend*, and circled them several times. I stared at the words, my mind clinking with the cogs that were turning the phrase over.

I recalled that it had struck me as an odd choice of words at the time, but then my attention had shifted to trying to keep him on the line, and the words had been forgotten.

I clicked on another call, the one in which he'd bargained to exchange clues for answers.

"Why would you have any interest in my personal life?"

"You've got to pay the piper, Quinn. That's how this game works."

I grabbed my pen again and jotted down *Pied Piper* next to *old fiend* and circled it as well then focused on the words.

He had made references to "paying the piper" several times after that. Each time he'd called with the clues, he had started by asking, "Are you ready to pay the piper, Quinn?" At the time, I'd thought he was being facetious, but suddenly, I wasn't so sure.

Out of curiosity, I opened a new browser page on my laptop,

typed in *old fiend* + *Pied Piper*, and began scrolling through the returns.

An article about a third of the way down caught my eye. I clicked on it and discovered it was an analysis of a short story by Joyce Carol Oates that had apparently been inspired by a serial killer in the sixties named Charles Schmid, otherwise known as the Pied Piper of Tucson because of his ability to lure victims to their deaths.

When I read on, I learned that the villain in the short story was a strange but captivating man who lured an innocent girl from the safety of her home. His name was Arnold Friend. I wrote down the name, and as the article suggested, I put a slash through the *R*'s. As I stared at the remaining letters, a cold tremor passed through me. I was confident I was on to something, but I wasn't sure how it factored in yet. After flagging the page, I pulled up the short story it referenced and gave it a read. Afterward, I was both creeped out and impressed by the author's ability to convey what it felt like to encounter true evil. But nothing else had stood out to me as potentially relevant to the case.

Not sure where to go from there, I was about to continue listening to the rest of the call, but something at the edge of my awareness prodded me to stay with my current stream of thought. On a hunch, I googled *Pied Piper* and was met with a slew of articles, fables, and other works that referenced the flamboyant mythical figure.

As I read through the first several returns, my instincts lit up. Nothing was coming into focus yet, but I could sense that something important was right in front of me.

The Pied Piper seemed equal parts folklore and historical fact. Without knowing if it would lead anywhere, I began to notate names, places, and dates contained within each major rendition of the Piper. When I was through, I scanned the contents of my full page of notes and scribbles.

My eyes returned to Charles Schmid. From my research, I had learned that he'd killed three women before he was captured. I didn't believe for a second that it was a coincidence that our guy was using phrases so closely linked to the story that had been inspired by Schmid. But it didn't make sense that someone who had killed so prolifically—if we were correct about the other crimes he was connected to—would take any sort of interest in someone who had killed only three times before being apprehended.

I shifted in my seat, growing antsy from the niggle in my gut. I knew the answer was right *there*—hidden within the marks on that hideous pad of paper.

My eyes slid over the page once more then focused on one particular scribble. *The Pied Piper of Tucson.*

The clock on the wall ticked loudly as voices began to fill the bullpen. It was time for shift change. I rubbed the back of my neck but continued to stare at that one line. Then my fingers froze where my neck began to tingle. Slowly, I straightened, widening my eyes.

Could that be it?

CHAPTER 39

Quinn

SCHMID WASN'T A GACY, Bundy, or Dahmer. If anyone mentioned his name to the average Joe, they would likely get nothing more than a vacant stare in return. *But...* if they asked some of the longtime locals around Tucson, they might actually get a different response. Stories like Schmid's often became local folklore—a ghost story that children told at slumber parties.

Knowing that serial killers often began their killing sprees where they were most comfortable—the places where they lived and worked—I pulled up the number for Tucson PD and gave them a call.

Five minutes later, I was speaking to a detective in their homicide division.

"You want me to do what?" he asked.

I winced. It was a big ask, but the case was too important to back down. "I'd like for you to search your records for any murders within the past thirty years that involve women being killed in the manner I described."

"Lady, do you have *any* idea how long that will take or the kind of resources it'll require?"

As someone who had conducted a lot of research for our

department, I did know. I puffed my cheeks and released an exasperated breath.

My eyes roamed the table and the piles of reports and crime scene photos stacked on top of it before coming to rest on my notes. I looked away then immediately returned to the notepad.

Straightening, I asked, "Actually, Detective, if I gave you a date to cross-reference, would you be willing to give it a try?"

There was a pause followed by a grumble and the sound of papers shuffling. "All right. What's the date?"

I bit my lip and infused my voice with the sweetness of a summer peach. "Um, if you could try July 22 and June 26, that would be great."

He sighed loudly. "All right. I'll call ya back when I've had a chance to look into it."

After giving him my phone number and really piling on the obsequious gratitude, I hung up and repeated the process with the Pima County Sheriff's Department, figuring that our guy might have killed in the area surrounding Tucson as well.

For the next several hours, I waited on pins and needles to hear back from both agencies. In the meantime, I continued to focus on the Pied Piper-and-Charles Schmid angle, going so far as to draw a giant mind map on the whiteboard, complete with all the details I'd drawn from both the Oates story as well as the literature that referenced the Piper.

It was nearing midafternoon, and I was about to call the Tucson and Pima departments again when my cell rang with an Arizona area code. My heart leaped into my throat as I lunged for the phone sitting ten feet away on the table.

"Hello?"

"Ms. Martin, this is Detective Schaeffer getting back to you." Without waiting for acknowledgement, he pressed on. "I didn't find any victims whose deaths matched the MO on the dates you provided."

My hopes sank faster than a rock-laden body being dumped

by the Mob. "Thank you for checking, Detective. I really appreciate it."

Just as I was about to hang up, he continued, "But one of our old-timers heard me talking about your request..."

That was code for *I was bitching about your stupid request and lack of respect for my precious time.*

"And he recalled a case he worked over a decade ago that reminded him a lot of what you described."

Detective Schaeffer filled me in on the details of that case, and I had to agree with his partner. The similarities were too many to be coincidental. I quickly jotted down the pertinent facts then thanked him again for his efforts.

Shortly after we hung up, Pima County called to report that they had come up empty, which wasn't a total surprise after the new revelation.

But something was bothering me about the Tucson case. The dates that the detective gave me meant that if Trevor had been right about the other cases he'd identified in ViCAP, Tucson wasn't our perp's first killing spree. It was still a good find, but it left me doubting that the killer was from Arizona.

I dropped unceremoniously into my chair and shot a puff of air at a loose curl hanging in front of my eyes. Turning my attention to the whiteboard, I reexamined each piece of information I'd captured there. Then I looked once more at the scattered pages of notes lying in front of me.

A piece of paper with Trevor's cop scrawl was sticking out from a stack of folders and caught my eye. Feeling as though I had hit another dead end, I summoned my abdominal muscles and scrunched forward to snatch the paper before falling back in my chair.

The page contained his chronological list of matching cases from the ViCAP system. I examined the dates written beside each entry and noted that Tucson was now the second-oldest case we were aware of. Of course, who knew how many other departments had dealt with the killer and, like Tucson PD, hadn't uploaded the information to the national database?

I eyed the first entry and puckered my lips. It was San Diego PD, and Trevor had written the name and phone number of a detective beside it. The ticking of the wall clock began to lull me into a state of hypnosis as I continued to stare at that one piece of data, allowing myself to succumb to the swirling mass of information tangling within my thoughts.

After several moments, something one of my professors had said in a long-ago criminology course came to mind. Just as most serial killers began killing in their hometown, many of them also knew their first victim.

Reinspired, I shot up in my seat and punched the San Diego detective's number into my phone.

He answered almost immediately. "Detective Alvarez."

I stood and began to pace. "Good afternoon, Detective. My name is Quinn Martin. I'm a dispatcher with the Eden Falls Police Department."

Alvarez's tone shifted from authoritative to congenial. "Oh, yeah, I spoke to one of your officers a couple of weeks back. Ryan, I think it was."

"Yes, I'm assisting on the case he's working."

Alvarez let out a low whistle. "You must be the dispatcher who's had the displeasure of dealing with the homicidal asshole he and I have in common."

I smiled at the blunt and very accurate summation of events. "Yes, that's me."

"You guys had any luck nabbing that son of a bitch yet?"

"No, but I'm chasing a hunch, and I was hoping you'd be willing to help me in that endeavor."

"Considering you've gone way above the call of duty to go after this guy, I'm at your disposal, Ms. Martin."

I filled Alvarez in on my theory and asked for his opinion.

"Well..." he said, the word strained and accompanied by a squeak that conjured an image of him reclining in his office chair.

"You're right that it's not uncommon for the first victim to be linked to the killer, but I have to say I don't think that's the case in this instance. If Officer Ryan's correct, and our case was this perp's first go-round, then Charlene Winslow was the first victim, and we were very thorough in investigating everyone close to her. None of them set off my Spidey senses, and they all either had an airtight alibi or passed a lie detector test with flying colors."

I frowned and bit my pinky nail on the hand that was pressing the phone to my ear. Then I turned to the whiteboard again. "Detective, what was the date of Charlene's death?"

"Hmm, it was fourteen years ago. Let me pull up the day." The clacking of his keyboard filled the silence as I continued to stare at the dates I'd written on the whiteboard.

Then Alvarez was in my ear again. "July 29."

That time, I didn't let the disappointment deter me. "Detective, if you'll humor me for a moment, I'd like to try something else."

"Go for it."

"Search homicides within the past thirty years, female victims, occurring on either July 22 or June 26."

"I know that tone. *Your* Spidey sense is going off. Give me a minute." He clicked away on his keyboard again.

I remained silent for the several minutes it took him to sort through all the returns. But I was rewarded for my patience.

"Well, hot damn," he said.

My heart skipped a beat. "What did you find?"

"We had a case, one year prior, dated June 26. Cynthia James. The details aren't exact, but it's close enough that I wouldn't rule it out as a contender."

My pulse threatened to blow a hole in my neck. "Could you forward that file to me?"

"Sure thing. Keep me posted?"

"Absolutely." I sounded like a kid trying to get Mom and Dad to get their butts out of bed on Christmas morning.

True to his word, Alvarez had the file in my department email in a matter of minutes. I was seated at my laptop, my knee bouncing up and down so fast that I could rival a sewing machine. As I scanned the details of the case, I noted the similarities and differences to ours. Alvarez was right. It wasn't an exact match, but my body was vibrating.

Two names stood out to me in the case file. After researching the first, I quickly discarded it. But the second had me digging further. Unable to find much, which was odd in and of itself, I opened my search engine again, entered the name, and selected images. I was presented with page upon page of faces.

I scrolled down, my eyes burning from having been at it for so many hours. Just as I was about to give up and try a different tack, one face caught my attention. I clicked on the image to make it bigger and leaned in. My eyes widened.

"Son of a bitch!"

CHAPTER 40

Trevor

"Then why is the system showing that you *did* access the case file later that morning?" My head was pounding, and I was trying very hard not to knock the two front teeth out of the guy sitting across from me.

"How the fuck should I know?"

"Because it was your login credentials that accessed the file, dumbass."

Moore rolled his icy-green eyes and flippantly tossed a hand in the air. He was among the first that Gabe and I had called in to interrogate with the intention of flushing out the leak, and he was making it clear that he didn't appreciate the treatment.

"Look—" He straightened in his seat. "Like I've said a hundred fucking times, I haven't been in that file since before the last victim."

The red creeping up Moore's neck told me how hard he was fighting to keep his temper in check in the presence of a senior officer. I took in the subtle details of his appearance and body language, noting everything from how the fluorescent lights cast a glare on the gel that held his longish dark hair perfectly in place to the way his shoulders were tensing beneath his uniform shirt.

He had the build of a swimmer, tall with broad shoulders and good definition, but he was a total preener—one who got laid a lot. Of course, he used the uniform and his badge to full advantage when it came to making panties drop.

We continued to stare across my desk at each other, me sizing him up and looking for signs of deceit, him trying to appear cool even though we both knew he was failing.

I had been vacillating between anger and confusion since the interview had started. If he was really sitting there, lying to my face despite the evidence staring back at the both of us, then he must have thought I was a huge fucking idiot. But I didn't know why he would deny accessing the database on the date and at the time in question if one, he had the right to access the file, since he'd been involved in the case, and two, he could easily explain it away by saying he needed to reference the information for his report.

Deciding to try a different angle, I leaned forward, placing my forearms on the desk. "Could anyone have gotten ahold of your login credentials?"

He shrugged. "How the hell should I know? I haven't given them to anyone, but it's not exactly like it'd be hard for someone to look over my shoulder from time to time when I'm working."

We once again fell into a silent standoff. The guy wouldn't budge, and though he was clearly fighting the urge to connect his fist with my face, he wasn't showing any signs of duplicity. Moore had been on the force for four years. In that time, I'd seen him flirt with the boundary between what a cop was legally allowed to do and what he wasn't. But not once had I ever seen him actually cross that line. And that was the only thing that was giving me enough pause to consider the truth of his claims.

My cell buzzed against the wooden surface of my desk. I glanced down at it and answered when I saw that the call was coming from the front desk.

"Ryan."

"There's a reporter here requesting to speak with you."

Margaret, our administrative assistant, sounded as though she had already gone a few rounds with said reporter.

I resisted the urge to growl. "Who is it?"

Margaret lowered her voice. "A pencil-necked weasel whom I highly doubt has ever been laid."

I clenched my teeth to keep from laughing. Margaret was like a grandmother to all of us, but she had a mouth like a sailor. Gabe and I had gotten a kick out of it when Alex came to refer to Margaret as Betty because the feisty old lady had reminded her so much of Betty White. Alex just didn't realize that the similarity went beyond looks alone.

"All right. I'll be right there."

I stood and pointed a finger in Moore's face. "Wait there until I get back."

He muttered something as I walked away, but I really didn't have the energy to bother to find out what it was.

When I shoved open the door that separated the front of the department, where the public had access, from the back, where all the actual police work happened, I grumbled and debated whether or not I should just turn around.

But Dierk Jensen saw me a split second before I made up my mind, so I figured I'd better just deal with it and pray that I still had enough self-restraint to keep from grabbing the dickhead by the collar and tossing him out on his wimpy ass.

"Ah, Officer Ryan." Dierk clicked his recorder on then met me at the corner of the long counter Margaret was situated behind. Thrusting the recorder in my face like a microphone, he adjusted his wire-rimmed glasses with the other hand. "I wanted to give you the opportunity to comment on the abhorrent lack of progress in solving the murders that have recently plagued our town."

A muscle in my jaw twitched, but that was the only outward sign of how much I hated the prick. "No comment."

His self-gratified smile grew, and I could have sworn I could see the slime dripping down his false facade. "Nothing to say about your total ineffectiveness and failure to protect those you are sworn to defend?"

My body temperature skyrocketed, the heat under my skin threatening to singe my uniform right off. Rather than repeating myself, I started to turn back toward the bullpen, but Dierk's nasally voice slammed against my back with a statement I couldn't ignore.

"Then perhaps you'd like to comment on your personal involvement with Quinn Martin and how it's affecting the case, not to mention the safety of our citizens."

I halted. With my back still to the journalist who had been responsible for sharing the confidential details of the case with the public, I closed my eyes and took what was supposed to be a calming breath through my nose. Before I was through, Dierk decided to push the matter.

"One of my sources informed me that the two of you were having a grand ol' time at the costume shop on the day that Shelby Johnson was savagely murdered. What say you to that?"

Slowly, I turned, and I knew by the way his Adam's apple bobbed that everything I wanted to do to him was written plainly across my face.

I stalked toward him menacingly. When the toes of my shined boots met his pretentious loafers, I folded my arms and glared down at him. "Speaking of sources, let's talk about the one who's selling you lies and confidential information in equal proportion."

Dierk quivered ever so slightly before raising his chin in defiance and false bravado. "I don't have to reveal my sources."

"Apparently, fact-checking is a thing of the past as well." I lowered my face a few inches closer to his. "What do you think is going to happen to your career when I provide your boss with all the things you've gotten wrong in the past two weeks? How many more lies and half-truths will I find when I comb through *every* article you've ever written for the *Eden Falls Gazette* once this case is over and I have the time to focus on a new asshole?"

Indignation replaced fear as Dierk sputtered and tripped over his words, his voice rising to a prepubescent squeal. "Perhaps I should stop wasting my time with the troglodytes and ask Quinn Martin to provide a good reason for fraternizing with *you* instead of actually trying to save the lives she was given a chance to save!"

I dropped my arms and pressed my body into his space, ensuring every inch of my six-foot-three frame swallowed his five feet, ten inches. His eyes bulged, and he began to backpedal as I marched forward as if he weren't even there. When his back banged into the double doors that led to the street, I stood close enough to keep him pinned to the glass and hovered my nose right above his. Then I lowered my voice and let the promise of bodily harm ring through it. "If I see you within fifty yards of Ms. Martin or catch wind of you having *any* kind of contact with her, my mugshot is going to be the next photo your employer gets to print."

I didn't think it was possible, but Dierk's eyes got even wider. "I-Is that a *threat*?"

"What do you think?"

Dierk's eyes darted back and forth between mine. He attempted to pull himself up to his full height, but when I narrowed my eyes, he faltered and began to stumble backward through the doors. Once on the sidewalk, he adjusted his tie and half walked, half trotted away.

"You know the next thing he prints is going to be an accusation of police corruption and a detailed account of how you threatened him, right?" Margaret asked from behind me.

I grunted and stalked back toward the bullpen. "Let him. That asshole's days are numbered."

CHAPTER 41

Trevor

I TOSSED my pen across my desk and reclined in my chair, interlocking my fingers behind my head. "Well, that was productive."

Gabe smirked and started stacking the paperwork on his desk in tidy piles. "We had to start somewhere."

We'd spent the better part of the past few days interviewing personnel and digging through our databases to determine who had accessed the information that had been shared with the press. Having just finished the last interview, we were no closer to nailing our rat.

Pressing my fingers against my eyes, I rubbed until I thought I might actually rupture an eyeball. "I'm fucking over this case, man."

Gabe grunted and continued to sort his desk.

Eyeing the neat stacks he'd just made, I seriously contemplated knocking them over just to get a kick out of his reaction. Things had been way too serious lately.

I opened my mouth to say as much when the sound of a door crashing against the wall had me on my feet and scanning for a threat.

When I turned around, I found Quinn running toward us,

her eyes wide and her face flushed.

"Quinn, what the—" I rushed toward her.

But she blew past me and called over her shoulder. "I need you both in the command post!"

I looked at Gabe, who was also on his feet, wearing a bewildered expression.

As Quinn approached the chief's office, she glanced back, and when she saw us still standing there, she yelled, "The command post. Now!" Then she banged on the chief's door and entered without waiting for a reply.

Unwilling to find out what she would do if we were still standing there with our mouths hanging open when she returned, I hastily made my way to the small room she'd occupied almost nonstop for the past three days, Gabe hot on my heels.

Not even a minute later, Quinn jogged into the room with the chief right behind her. I had to focus really hard not to laugh at the sight of his sixty-year-old body jogging behind her, his walrus mustache twitching at both the confusion and indignation of a subordinate demanding he follow her and not ask questions.

With the chief, Gabe, and me standing on one side of the table and Quinn on the other, we waited for her to explain her sudden psychosis.

Quinn tucked her hair behind both ears and took a steadying breath as she gazed down at the table, where several more piles of paper had accumulated since the last time I'd been in there. I tried to ignore that her navy department polo was rumpled and her slacks were hanging a little lower on her hips.

"I found something," she said, pausing as though she expected us to interrupt. When she saw that we were all waiting to hear what she had to say, she continued. "Okay. Let's start from the beginning. I was listening back to the calls between me and the killer, and I noticed a phrase that seemed out of place." She spun a notepad around so that it faced us then pointed at some words she'd circled. "He referred to himself as an 'old fiend,' but then I also noticed that he kept making references to the Pied Piper. So I searched those two phrases together and found a short story about a serial killer from the sixties."

Quinn proceeded to fill us in on the details of Charles Schmid and his brief killing spree in Tucson, Arizona.

"I thought it seemed odd," she continued, "that our perp would have focused on someone with so little notoriety. But then it dawned on me that someone who was born and raised in that area would likely have grown up hearing the horror stories about the local serial killer."

Gabe and I exchanged looks then returned our attention to Quinn.

She slid another piece of paper in front of us that had a bunch of scribbles and *Tucson PD* written across the top. "So I called Tucson PD and asked them to search their records for any murders that fit our MO, and they found a cold case that's a dead ringer for our guy. I was confident that meant he was from Tucson, but then I realized that the dates the detective gave me meant that this was the *second* location where he had killed." Quinn tipped her head. "It didn't rule out Tucson as his hometown, but it definitely made it less likely."

She held up her hands. "Okay, so hold on to that information for a moment." She moved to the whiteboard. "While I was waiting for Arizona to get back to me, I started researching the history of the Pied Piper. I just found it odd that he made so many references to him."

She pointed at a paragraph she'd scrawled on the whiteboard. "The Piper has been the inspiration behind several creative works, including this verse from a Goethe poem."

I read the lines she pointed at.

And then this many-sided singer is occasionally a girl-catcher; He's never arrived in any town, without captivating many. And however bashful the girls might be, and however prudish the women, all of them grow weak with love at the sound of magic lute and song.

Quinn held up a finger. "*But* I found that the Pied Piper may actually have been a real person." She moved to the other side of the board, where dates, places, and other figures were noted. "Centuries ago, in Hamelin, Germany, one hundred thirty children suddenly went missing. Theories abound as to what happened to the children, but the story of the Pied Piper asserts that the town had a rat infestation that was causing serious problems for the townsfolk. One evening, this flamboyant figure dressed in bright colors entered the town and claimed that he could solve their problem. Once he and the town council agreed on a fee, the man went to work, using his flute to charm the rats out of their hiding places, and they followed him into the river and drowned. But after the Piper remedied the town's problem, the council reneged on the deal and refused to pay him. So this savior of sorts turned sinister in an instant and took his revenge on the town by playing his magical song and luring the children away from their homes. The children were never seen or heard from again."

I raised my eyebrows. "What does this have to do with our suspect?"

Quinn smiled in a slightly maniacal way that had me a little concerned. "Well, everything I found seemed to revolve around the Piper. So I reasoned that maybe our killer identifies with him—maybe even sees himself as the Piper reincarnated or perhaps a two-point-oh version. Whatever it is, I considered the possibility that some important detail may be buried within the folklore of the Piper."

Quinn moved to the table and extracted a small stack of paper from one of the leaning towers of folders. "There were two main references that stood out to me. The first was a poem written by Robert Browning, which references the origin of the Piper story, but it claimed a date of July 22, 1376 for the alleged event. *Historical* records, however, recorded June 26, 1284 as the day the children were lost."

Then she moved to the other end of the table, tucked her hair behind both ears again, and held up her hands, palms facing us.

"Okay, so going back to Tucson and that it appeared to be the second stop in our killer's mission. Seeing that you"—she motioned to me—"listed San Diego PD as the first department that dealt with this killer, I called Detective Alvarez. I recalled from one of my classes that serial killers tend to have a personal relationship with their first victim, so I wanted to get his take on that."

I nodded slowly, agreeing with her train of thought.

"But Detective Alvarez felt strongly that wasn't the case in this instance. I still felt confident in my original theory, though—that the killer started out in his hometown. And if that was the case, and there was no connection to the first *known* victim, I considered that maybe that victim wasn't actually the first." Quinn waved her hands as she began pacing. "Which then begged the question—how can we figure out who the real first victim was? Since this guy seems to identify with the Piper or even *as* the Piper, I got an idea and asked Alvarez to check their records for homicides that fit our perp's signature." She stopped pacing and pointed at the two dates on the board again. "Occurring on either the date described in the Browning poem or the date listed in the historical records, and bam!" She smacked the board. "He got a hit."

My eyes widened, and my mouth fell open. I was surprised I'd even managed to follow all that, but I was even more impressed that Quinn had managed to put together an entire tapestry based on a few phrases that had struck her as odd.

"So who was the first victim?" I asked.

She smiled. "Cynthia James. White female. Thirty-four years old. Reported dead on June 26, one year prior to what we *thought* was the first case. I asked Alvarez to forward the report to me."

Quinn picked up a folder and flipped it open then slapped it down on the table in front of us. The grisly images of a woman who'd been beaten and strangled stared back at me. With the exception of a few details, she could easily have been one of the bodies we'd found in recent weeks.

Quinn then bent over the table, flipped to the autopsy report, and pointed at the things she wanted us to note as she filled in the remaining details. "The ME placed her time of death around midnight. She was lashed repeatedly with either a belt or something similar then strangled to death. One of the main differences between her case and those that followed is that the blood spatter indicated she was killed in her bed, and that is also where her body was found. She was also badly beaten by the killer's fists before he took the belt to her, and there's no mention of salt in her wounds. But she was dressed in cheap lingerie, just like our girls, and she had an oily substance on her body. The other major difference is that the killer never called law enforcement to report the body." Quinn's eyes lit up as she paused and leveled us with a hold-on-to-your-trousers gleam. "Except that he *did*."

I frowned. "Huh?"

Quinn flipped to another section of the file, which was a witness statement.

"The victim and her husband had separated three months prior. The husband was questioned and quickly cleared because he had an alibi. He was working the night shift at the warehouse where he stocked merchandise. The victim's sixteen-year-old son found her. He told the cops that he had snuck out the night before, and when he returned home in the morning, he found his mother murdered in her bed. He then called 911 to report the body."

I dragged my eyes from the report and found Quinn watching me expectantly. "You think the kid did it?"

She pressed her lips together and smiled, slowly nodding. "His name is David James. Apparently, he was very convincing at playing the role of the bereaved and traumatized son. The police never even considered him a suspect. But playing off my theory that the killer knew his first victim, when I read the report on Cynthia, her husband and her son stood out to me as the obvious suspects. And get this—they moved from Tucson to San Diego the year prior." Quinn shrugged. "Once I learned of the husband's alibi, I naturally zeroed in on David. I couldn't find much on him at first, but then I found this." Quinn picked up the file folder, flipped to a new page, then slapped it back down in front of us.

Chief Kelly, Gabe, and I all leaned in, and Gabe and I swore simultaneously. "No fucking way."

The chief snapped his head around, his eyes darting between us. "What? What am I missing?"

Gabe looked like he was about to murder someone, and I was confident my expression matched.

I stared at the picture of a young David James, noting the thin white scar above his Cupid's bow. "That asshole hit on Liz and Quinn when we were all at Rustlers a little over a week ago."

The chief's face turned crimson as he flicked his eyes to Quinn.

As we all returned our attention to the copious notes Quinn had made, which had arrows connecting various dots and circles highlighting the most crucial bits, Quinn's voice became very soft. "The game was never about figuring out who the victims were. Those clues were a sleight of hand meant to get us to focus on the wrong thing. While we were focusing on the victims, he was surreptitiously feeding me clues about *his* identity."

I stared at Quinn for a long time, her eyes meeting mine with a fire that made me fall for her even harder. "You're a genius, Quinn."

She smiled shyly and tucked her hands into her pockets.

"Right." The chief straightened and crossed his beefy arms "How do you want to play this?"

Gabe cleared his throat. "We start by getting warrants for his financials and phone records. See if any of it gives us an idea of where this prick has been hiding."

I nodded. "Once we have his current address, I want to tie in with the local PD and have them execute a search of his residence."

Gabe angled toward me, hooking his thumbs over his duty belt. "What do you think about releasing his photo?"

I considered the pros and cons before answering. "It would mean more eyes looking for him, and depending on how he's getting his hands on these women, it might make it harder for him to take any more victims." I tilted my head. "But at the same time, if he knows we're onto him, he could easily go underground, and we could lose our shot at him for good. He's intelligent enough to disappear."

Chief Kelly swished his mustache from side to side, his eyes locked on all the evidence. "We wait. Can't risk letting this asshole get away." Making a sweeping arc with his pointer finger, he added, "And since we still don't know who is responsible for the leaks, I want only you three working on this. And work fast. If we haven't gotten a lock on this shithead within forty-eight hours, we'll release his photo and label him a person of interest."

The three of us nodded our understanding, then Gabe and the chief left the room. After closing the door, I made my way to Quinn, who was still standing between the whiteboard and the table with her arms wrapped around herself. Despite the exhaustion pulling at her features, she was still the loveliest woman I'd ever laid eyes on.

I threaded my fingers through her long, dark curls, gently pushing them back over her shoulders. She tipped her face up and smiled, but it lacked the energy she'd had moments ago.

"You need rest," I said.

She nodded and let her head fall against my chest as she wrapped her arms around my waist. "We both do. But it's going to have to wait."

I pulled her tighter against me. "I'm really proud of you. You're a real badass."

She snorted. "Not badass enough. It took five people, including my best friend, dying before I was able to catch on to his game."

Stepping back, I cradled her face, urging her to meet my eyes.

"I called seven departments, all with cases that have been open for *years*. No one from any of those departments got even close to this guy. Now, thanks to you, we have a name and a photo."

In true Quinn fashion, she sidestepped the compliment. "Thank you for looking out for me. And even more importantly, thank you for recognizing how much I needed to stay on this case."

I smiled and kissed the tip of her nose. "It was either that and stay on your good side, or tell you no and risk losing an appendage I might need later."

Quinn laughed, and it felt so damn good to hear it. I took her in my arms again and lowered my lips to hers. As she melted into me, I waited for her lips to part, and when they did, I slid my tongue against hers in a sensual dance. A soft moan tore from her throat, and I wanted nothing more than to take her home and get her naked beneath me.

I gripped the back of her neck, and her curls wrapped themselves around my fingers. Quinn pressed her hips into me, where the bulge in my pants was growing by the second. Our tongues darted and tasted with increasing need. I had to get a handle on the situation, or we were both going to have a lot of explaining to do. Not that *I* would mind, but Quinn would be mortified if anyone caught us.

So with the restraint of a saint, I pulled away, immediately missing the feel of her. Still cradling her head, I brushed a thumb against her cheek and gave her a sinful smirk. "Come on, Quinnybaby. Let's go get this asshole. The sooner we get him, the sooner I get you back in my bed."

Quinn's thousand-watt smile locked back in place. As she stepped around me, I smacked her on the ass and followed her to the door.

Trevor

BY THE NEXT MORNING, our covert operation was full steam ahead. Gabe was working to get his hands on a warrant that would grant us access to David James's financials and phone records, and Quinn and I were busy tracking down the asshole's address. When she handed me a slip of paper a few minutes later, I grinned from ear to ear and thanked the Fates when I saw where he lived. Clearly, they wanted him locked up as much as we did.

I plucked my cell phone from the chest pocket of my uniform and pulled up a number I had hoped to have a reason to call again.

The line rang once. "Detective Alvarez."

"Alvarez, this is Trevor Ryan with Eden Falls PD."

A pause followed. "She figured it out, didn't she?"

I grinned again. "Yeah, she did, and we were wondering if you happen to know anyone who'd like to help us take the piece of shit down."

"Hell yeah, I do."

I filled Alvarez in on the details of how Quinn had connected the dots. He was silent, other than the occasional "son of a bitch" and "no shit," but I saved the best part for last.

"We're working on getting access to his cell phone data, bank statements, and credit cards, hoping that will give us some idea of where he's been holed up."

"How can I help?" Alvarez asked.

"Quinn was able to track down the guy's address. It wasn't easy. He's got it in a trust under a different name."

"The fucker's definitely not dumb."

"No, but his luck just might be turning to shit. Turns out he stayed close to home and bought a house that's smack-dab in the middle of your jurisdiction."

A sinister laugh filtered through the line. "Wasn't that thoughtful? Sounds like I need to take a little field trip."

* * *

OVER THE NEXT FEW HOURS, the records we'd been waiting for began to pour in. Gabe and Quinn were making quick work of sorting through them while I worked with Alvarez to orchestrate the search of James's residence.

The three of us had moved the command post to the briefing room, since it was much larger and gave us more room to spread out. Quinn and Gabe were currently seated at a low wooden table against the far wall near all the windows, and I was at the whiteboard, jotting down logistical details Alvarez was delivering over the phone.

Just as I was finishing up with what was probably my dozenth call with Alvarez, Quinn growled as she slammed a piece of paper down on top of a stack sitting beside her. Gabe squeezed her shoulder as he leaned back in his chair and used his thumb and forefinger to rub his eyes.

Capping the dry-erase pen I'd been writing with, I sauntered over to the pair of them and assessed the situation. Quinn's cheeks were flaming red, and her hair, which she was wearing down again, had doubled in size, and several curls were poking out at odd angles. She'd opted for dark blue jeans and a white T-shirt, which only made the blood rushing to the surface of her skin that much more noticeable.

Gabe was in uniform, as usual, but his dark eyes were bloodshot, and he had at least three days' worth of stubble on his face.

"Do I even want to know why the two of you look like you placed a bet to see which one could go the most rounds on the tumble cycle?"

Quinn glared up at me, pinching her lips together. Gabe, ever the levelheaded one, didn't bother to acknowledge my smartass remark, opting instead to fill me in on their obvious discontent. "We just finished going through all of James's records. His credit cards and bank statements haven't shown any activity for over a month, other than automatic payments to cover his bills."

I grunted. "So he's using cash."

Gabe nodded. "Yeah."

"What about his phone?"

He pressed his lips together and slowly shook his head. "Not much there, either, but we did get a small win on that front." Gabe shuffled through the stack of papers in front of him, selected a few, and handed them to me. "It looks like he's kept his phone off for the better part of these past six weeks, so we don't have much to go on, but on the few occasions he's turned it back on, it has geoverified to Eden Falls."

I scanned the records he'd handed me. That was something, at least. If nothing else, it further confirmed that we were on the right track and would only strengthen our case against him.

"So he was here for several weeks before he started killing," I said.

Gabe nodded again. "Yeah. He was probably doing recon. Getting the lay of the land. Infiltrating himself in the victims' lives and sizing up the police force."

Quinn spoke next. "He's always three steps ahead of us." She thrust her fingers into her hair, causing her curls to become just a little wilder. "He's arrogant enough to believe that he's never going to get caught yet smart and cautious enough to avoid leaving breadcrumbs just in case he does." She jabbed a hand toward the papers I was holding. "He's ensuring that if he gets busted, the evidence is circumstantial and tenuous at best. It would take our catching him in the act to nail a solid conviction."

The look of despair on Quinn's face made me itch to wrap my arms around her and promise that we were going to get the guy, but I'd been careful about how I acted around her, ensuring that no one would pick up on the change in our relationship, not even Gabe. But it had taken effort to keep it from him. The man was my partner, my best friend, and my brother in every way that mattered. Our entire lives, we'd shared everything with each other. I could recite the details of how he'd lost his virginity, of the shame and guilt he'd struggled with from what he'd had to do when he was deployed, and the exact moment he'd fallen in love with Alex. And with the exception of the demons I'd secretly battled since my parents' deaths, he could do the same for me. But Quinn had made her wishes clear, and after learning what she had endured at Las Vegas Metro when her relationship with that asshole cop was discovered, I understood her motives.

So I settled for words of encouragement instead. "We're going to get him, Quinn."

I said it as much for her as for myself. Because we *had* to get him. If we failed, it meant that he would disappear, and Quinn would spend every day looking over her shoulder. And I would spend every day waiting for him to return for her, fearing that I wouldn't be there to protect her.

And he *would* come back for her. So failure was not an option.

My phone rang in my hand. Alvarez's name came up on the screen.

"Yeah?"

"We're ready to go."

Alvarez kept the line open while they executed the search warrant so that we could hear what was happening in real time. The professional courtesy made me like the guy even more. Gabe,

Quinn, and I were seated at the table, and my phone lay in the middle as we all leaned in, anxiously waiting to hear that the boys and girls in blue at San Diego PD had found something that would help us ensure that David James would never again see the light of day, and no other woman would suffer and perish at his hands.

They arrived on scene, and Alvarez gave orders, directing his people to their positions. The guy was impressive, his years of experience and intellect evident as he coolly commanded the situation. But underneath it all, I could detect the unyielding hunger for justice.

We listened as they breached the house, our eyes trained on my phone as though we could will them to find the evidence that would secure a life sentence. After they finished clearing the house, they began the search. Alvarez reported that the suspect's only registered vehicle was in the garage, which wasn't surprising, since we knew he was using stolen vehicles to execute his crimes.

We continued to monitor the situation as room by room, they tossed the residence. So far, nothing out of place had been discovered. I glanced at Quinn, noting that the hope was slowly slipping from her face. When my eyes traveled to Gabe, he gave one solemn shake of his head, telling me that his concerns matched mine.

They *had* to find something.

My hope was on its last breath when Alvarez said something that kicked my heart into overdrive. "What the fuck is this?"

We leaned in farther as I cursed the fact that we only had audio.

A loud banging emanated from the phone. None of us dared breathe.

Then a crash came, along with the sound of a door being kicked in.

After several seconds of silence, Alvarez came on the line. "Ryan, we've got a problem."

CHAPTER 43

Trevor

"What kind of a problem?"

Alvarez expelled a forceful breath. "He knows we're onto him."

My eyes met Quinn's and Gabe's. Their expressions were pinched and their bodies taut.

"He's got hidden cameras in the house," Alvarez continued. "We just broke into the basement. He has a bunch of monitors. I can see where every one of my damn officers is. The system has remote access. He's probably watching us right now." He swore, and something shattered several feet from the phone.

I pressed my thumb and forefinger hard into my orbital sockets. *This is a disaster.*

Picking up my phone, I took it off speaker, then I moved away from the table. "If he knows we have his identity, he's going to disappear, and we're not going to hear from him until the bodies start to pile up again."

Or until he comes for Quinn. My shoulders were pressed to my ears, the tension in my body so strong that my muscles began to protest.

Alvarez's tone was calm despite the hint of frustration

beneath his words. "He's not going to disappear. Not yet. His urge to complete the cycle will be too much for him to resist."

The implication hung thick between us.

"So I've got the time it takes him to murder two more women. Then we're up Shit Creek for good."

Alvarez's weary sigh said it all. "I'm sorry, man. I really thought this was going to go down differently. We'll keep tossing the place. You have my word that if there's something to find here, we'll find it."

I hung my head. "Yeah. Okay. Thanks, man."

Taking a deep breath, I wiped the disappointment from my face before turning back to Quinn and Gabe. "They're going to keep searching. He'll let us know if they find anything."

Gabe glanced at Quinn then nodded. "I'll go update the chief." He clapped me on the back as he walked by.

I watched Quinn, trying to read all the emotions flashing across her face. Without thinking, I went to her, knelt down, and drew soothing circles on her back. "You gotta stay in the fight with me, Quinn. It's not over yet."

She turned her face to mine then nodded. Her movements were slow and labored, the exhaustion painfully apparent.

Growing voices drew my attention to the open doorway. A heartbeat later, Carlson and Moore appeared on the threshold. Their conversation came to a stop the moment they spotted us. A sly smile slid up Carlson's adolescent face, then he looked at Moore, elbowing him jocularly in the gut before they snickered and kept walking toward the break room.

I didn't think much of it until Quinn shrugged my hand away and stood. "I'm going to get some fresh air."

As I watched her retreating back, I couldn't help but wonder if she was beginning to blame me as much as I blamed myself for the fact that David James was still walking around a free man.

With Gabe briefing the chief and Quinn grabbing some alone time, I decided to distract myself by answering emails and returning phone calls while we waited to hear back from Alvarez.

Ten minutes later, Gabe took a seat on the edge of his desk, facing me. "The chief gave the go-ahead to release James's photo." He shrugged. "Might make him more likely to run, but since he already knows we're onto him, figured we might as well try. Maybe we'll get lucky and someone will spot him."

I chewed the inside of my lip and nodded, unsure if that was the right call. But it didn't really matter. The chief's orders trumped my preferences, so it was a done deal.

Gabe looked around the bullpen. "Where's Quinn?"

"Getting some air."

"She's taking it pretty hard."

"Yeah, not to mention she's hardly slept for three days."

Gabe squeezed the back of his neck and rotated his head back and forth. "We could all do with some shut-eye."

When I didn't comment or look up from my email, he pressed the issue. "There's nothing else we can do right now. Alvarez will call when they're done at the house. We're still waiting on the damn lab, and the son of a bitch hasn't called in with the clues to the next victim yet. This is as good a time as any to get some sleep, and it's been way too long since I've gotten my hands on my woman."

The corner of my mouth lifted. Sighing, I leaned back and rocked in my chair. "You're right. Who knows when we'll get the chance again?"

Gabe nodded as if to say, "Hell yeah, I'm right."

I glanced at the back door I was sure Quinn had disappeared through. "Can you take Quinn back to my place? I'm going to pick up dinner for us, but she's been running on fumes for days. She might feel better if she can go straight home, shower, and have a hot meal waiting for her when she gets out."

I couldn't tell what he was thinking, but Gabe grinned and slapped me on the shoulder. "Sure, buddy. I'll see ya in the morning."

When I called to place the pick-up order at Quinn's favorite restaurant, they informed me it would be ready in twenty minutes. Since it would take me only two to get there, I decided to continue clearing my email while I waited.

Fifteen minutes later, I made my way to the employee parking lot and almost groaned when I came within sight of my truck.

Blair was standing ten feet from it, tossing her short black hair with her usual attitude. She spotted me within seconds, and her face broke into a grin. "Hey, Trev."

I gritted my teeth to keep from telling her that only my friends called me that. "Hi, Blair." I kept my eyes locked on my truck and marched purposefully toward it.

Blair bit her lip and glanced left then right.

Almost there. Do not *engage.*

Blair began to dance in place, all the while chewing her bottom lip and looking around as though she thought someone might jump out at her at any moment.

Ignore her. Ignore her. Ignore her.

"Dammit." She spoke as though I wasn't meant to hear her, but clearly, she was trying to get my attention. And clearly, I was a damn idiot, because even though I knew that, I was incapable of ignoring a lady who appeared in distress—even if Blair barely met the category requirements.

I took a deep breath, sensing that I would seriously regret the question I was about to ask. When I drew even with her, I stopped. "Anything wrong, Blair?"

She pulled her lips in and tucked her hands into her pockets, her shoulders riding high. "My car is in the shop, so Meredith gave me a ride this morning, but she had to leave early."

I nodded but didn't respond.

Blair waved a hand. "Anyway, it's not a big deal, but I haven't been able to reach anyone else to get a ride home."

Shit. Rescuing Blair was the last thing I wanted to do. All I wanted after the longest three weeks of my life was to pick up our damn takeout, get home, shower, and have a nice dinner with the woman I *did* want to have as company.

My shades were on, but I met Blair's ardent stare. Swallowing the growl that was trying to claw loose from my throat, I jerked my head toward my truck. "Get in. I'll give you a ride."

Blair gave a triumphant smile. "Thanks! You're my hero!" She walked to the passenger door with way more bounce than was necessary and climbed in.

Her commentary was nonstop as we drove to her house, interrupted only by her giving me directions. I heard all about the highlights she was thinking of putting in her hair and the hideous bridesmaid dress her cousin was forcing her to wear, because apparently, she was insecure when Blair was around to steal the show. And of course, she didn't miss the opportunity to bemoan how incompetent the other dispatchers were.

When we finally reached her house, I noted how long five minutes could feel.

Blair unbuckled her seat belt and twisted toward me. "You want to come inside?" She bit her lip and stuck her chest out farther, a small smile playing at her lips.

I turned my attention back to the garage doors I'd parked in front of and kept my hand on the wheel of my idling truck. "No, thanks."

"You sure?"

"Yup."

She sat there watching me for ten very awkward seconds. Finally, she reached for her purse on the floorboard, but instead of picking it up and getting the hell out of my truck, she rummaged inside for a moment then messed with something near the base of her seat. Sure that she was stalling to give me time to rethink my decision, I fought to keep my expression neutral.

When she finally straightened, with bag in hand, she glanced at me one more time. I turned my attention to the scene outside the driver's-side window and waited until I heard the door open and felt the truck rock as she climbed out.

"Thanks again for the ride." She beamed. "Let me know how I can pay you back." Then she shut the door and wiggled her ass up to the front porch.

I put the truck in reverse and waited just long enough to ensure she made it inside safely before gunning it out of the driveway.

When I walked through my front door thirty minutes after I'd left the station, I was cursing the fact that Quinn had probably long been out of the shower and hungry for dinner.

Setting the food down on the kitchen counter, I cocked an ear, realizing that it was far too quiet, no sounds of the television or noises from the bathroom or anywhere else.

Gabe would have brought Quinn straight to my place and made sure she'd gotten inside safely, so I made my way down the hall and ducked my head into each of the bedrooms and bathrooms but found no sign of Quinn. There wasn't even a pile of dirty clothes to signal she'd come home.

Beginning to panic, I made my way into the living room, thinking maybe she was on the deck, enjoying the evening sun. An orange glow streamed through the French doors that led to the backyard, and my steps faltered once I was halfway across the room. There, in the gilded rays of the dying day, Quinn lay on the couch, curled up on her side, fast asleep and still wearing the clothes she'd had on for two days.

I knelt beside her and gazed at her peaceful face. It was the first time in weeks that it had been free from the lines of worry and self-reproach. My gaze slid down her body, and I noted how vulnerable and young she looked in that position. I considered carrying her to bed but decided against it. She'd had so little sleep lately that I didn't want to risk waking her.

So I kissed her gently on the temple and placed a blanket over her before heading down the hall to shower, hoping that I would soon join her in her dreams.

CHAPTER 44

Quinn

"YOU PEOPLE ARE SO *FUCKING* incompetent! If I have to call about this *one* more time, I'm going to sue the whole department and make sure every single one of you is relieved of your positions!"

I closed my eyes and took a deep breath as the line went dead. Then I took another and consciously willed my blood to cool from a boil to a simmer. A call-taking screen was open on my monitor, and I promptly typed the details of the call I'd just taken from the irate soccer mom who still believed she had the right to personally police the parking situation around the soccer field. That time, I hadn't been relieved that it was her calling instead of the killer.

Once I sent the call to Blair to dispatch to the units, I flopped back in my chair and ran my fingers through my hair. I rarely wore it down at work, but lately, I just didn't have the energy to bother much with my appearance.

"Why did she even take the call from this stupid bitch?" Blair spoke quietly to Meredith, who was seated beside her.

I debated whether I should let the snarky reply that was locked and loaded in my throat have its day in the sun. Ultimately, I decided that getting into it with Blair over the undoubtedly perfectly coiffed and overly pampered soccer mom just wasn't worth my remaining energy.

My eyes went to the queue holding all the calls that hadn't yet been dispatched. There were quite a few waiting for officers to become available. It had been a busy morning, which was not unusual for a Friday, but it felt especially chaotic because we were down a dispatcher. Julia had called in sick that morning, and since we didn't have any more leads on the piper case, I had volunteered to work my usual shift to keep the dispatch center from getting too overwhelmed. Maybe I'd been too generous.

With another deep sigh, I reached under my desk and extracted my notebook from my bag. Since things were quieting down, I wanted to take another look at my notes on the piper. Though a big part of me believed it was an exercise in futility. Even when we'd thought we had finally gotten one step ahead of him, he was still the one to secure the checkmate.

Every part of my being whispered to me to just give up, to accept that the monster was too powerful to fight. But it just wasn't in me to give in to evil, no matter how much easier it seemed. At the end of the day, even if we lost, at least we would lose with our integrity intact, knowing that we had gone down swinging. And that was the mentality I *had* to hold on to, because when he called next, I was confident it would be ugly. Things had shifted in our twisted relationship the moment I dared to challenge his power and humiliate him by forcing him to show his weakness.

I was using a pen to guide my eyes down a full page of notes, when I became distracted by Blair's commentary as she shuffled through the huge bag she always brought to work. "Dammit. Where the hell is it?"

Meredith's brow furrowed, the gesture calling even more attention to the way her horrific blond dye job clashed with her naturally dark eyebrows. "What's the matter?"

Blair growled. "I can't find my phone."

"When did you have it last?" Meredith asked in a lilting voice, her desire to please the queen bee by being helpful disgustingly apparent.

Blair scrunched her mouth to the side and flicked the long side of her bob over her shoulder. Everything about her actions read like a bad acting job. After a few seconds, her pucker turned into a wicked grin. She spun in her seat and reached for her landline, punching in a number she knew by heart.

I squinted at my notes, trying to block out whatever drama my partners were engaging in, but with Blair's next words, it was impossible for me to pay attention to anything other than her phone call.

"Hey, Trev."

My skin crawled at her flirtatious tone.

"I think I might have left my phone in your truck last night. Could you check for me, please?"

Meredith's dark eyes grew four sizes, her jaw dropping as she began to dance excitedly in her seat. She whispered something to Blair, who shooed her away with her free hand.

"Thanks, Trev," Blair continued. "I'm just lost without it. I've probably got a million messages by now."

My chest grew tight, the nausea churning in my gut making it difficult to swallow.

As soon as Blair hung up her phone, Meredith pounced. "Oh em gee!" She bounced up and down. "Why is your phone in Trevor's truck?"

Yeah, that's what I'd like to know.

Blair smirked and examined her bloodred fingernails. Their tips were filed to points that reminded me of cat claws. She shrugged a shoulder.

"Oh, come on," Meredith whined. "Give me the dirty details! Did Trevor finally bury his sausage in your bun?"

My mouth went dry. I couldn't bear to hear anymore. Images of Trevor and Blair naked and taking pleasure from each other's bodies flashed in my mind, the assault so intense that the room began to spin.

Blair glanced at me, her smirk deepening, before she returned her attention to Meredith. "Let's just say he gave me a ride I'll never forget."

Meredith squealed and stomped her feet repeatedly against the dingy carpet. "I knew he'd be amazing in bed. I mean, the man can *move*. Even the way he walks is enough to make me wet."

Blood rushed to my ears until Blair and Meredith sounded far away. I couldn't breathe. The room was closing in around me. *Could I really have been stupid enough to let this happen again? Did I really walk right into the waiting arms of another player who'd just run the best con I'd never seen coming?*

Trent. The piper. And now Trevor. How many men would manipulate and violate me before I finally had enough sense to see them for who they truly were? To see the games they were playing with me?

I revisited the previous night's sequence of events. Gabe had met me outside and said that Trevor wanted him to take me home. He'd said that Trevor was going to pick up dinner, and he would be right behind us. When I made it back to the house, I contemplated taking a long-overdue shower but decided against it, thinking that Trevor would be walking through the door any moment, ready to eat. So I emptied the dishwasher instead. By the time I was through, he still wasn't home, so I sat down on the couch to wait for him. Another ten minutes passed. I considered calling him but didn't want to come across as a needy woman who couldn't be alone for five minutes, so I just continued to wait. Eventually, the pull of sleep had become too strong to resist, and I'd woken up on the couch in the morning. Trevor had clearly come home at some point, but I had no idea how late he had stayed out or who he'd been with.

Until now.

When Trevor entered the comms center a few minutes later, the heat emanating from me was enough to challenge a five-alarm fire. He glanced at me as he strolled toward Blair, his eyebrows drawing together when I didn't return his smile.

"Found it." He handed Blair her phone.

She clutched it to her heart and sighed. "Thank you so, so much. I can't believe I didn't notice it was missing until now."

In my peripheral, I saw Trevor glance at me again, but Blair wasn't about to relinquish his attention. She stood and placed a hand on his arm, her fingers disappearing beneath the short sleeve of his uniform shirt. "Thanks again for last night." Her coquettish smile and the way she batted her ridiculously fake eyelashes at him conjured some pretty creative ideas about how I could cause her maximum pain.

"No problem."

Trevor disentangled himself from her grasp and came over to me. I kept my eyes trained on my screen, willing my phone to ring. When he reached me, he placed a hand on my shoulder and squeezed. I clenched my teeth as I fought the urge to launch myself out of my chair and accuse him of every dirty thing for which I'd already condemned him.

Like an answered prayer, the phone rang. I snatched it up and shrugged Trevor's hand off my shoulder. He hovered as I processed the trespassing call, but when I hung up and still refused to acknowledge him, he finally left, looking back over his shoulder just once before he disappeared down the dark hall that would lead him out of that godforsaken place.

For the next two hours, I was forced to listen to Blair giving vague details to Meredith, who simply could not leave the juicy piece of gossip alone. On days like this, I absolutely hated my job and questioned all my life choices. When the officers had issues with their partners, they were able to drive away and keep their distance for the better part of the day. When a dispatcher had issues with her partners, she was forced to sit and stew in it.

Just a few more hours, I reminded myself. *After that, I can go home—to my home—and close the door on this shitty world.*

The phone rang, and I quickly picked it up, desperate for a distraction—for someone other than Blair and Meredith to listen to. I would even take that godawful soccer mom over the two of them. "Eden Falls Dispatch."

Heavy breathing came over the line.

"Hello?"

Nothing.

Fear licked its way across my skin. "David?"

His dark, humorless laugh slithered from the phone, into my brain, wrapping sinister tentacles around me until only cold and darkness remained. "It was you who figured out my identity, wasn't it, Quinn? You were the one who led the police to my doorstep."

After a brief hesitation, I replied, "Yes."

"I knew you were a worthy opponent. From the moment we met, I knew you were... different."

Silence followed.

Movement in my peripheral drew my attention. I turned my head to find Blair and Meredith clicking onto my call. Without Trevor there to threaten them, there was nothing I could do to stop the intrusion.

Instead, I did my best to focus all of my attention on the piper. "We know everything there is to know about you, David. It's only a matter of time before we track you down, but things will go better for you if you turn yourself in."

He snickered. "Will they?"

"Yes. The prosecutor will be more willing to make a deal if you cooperate. You have information about your victims that we want. You can use that to your advantage."

"That's not how the game works, Quinn. You may have figured out my identity, but it's not all that hard to start over as someone else."

My gut twisted. He was right, of course. Someone like him would have zero trouble vanishing into thin air and popping up with a whole new identity somewhere far away.

"Then why are you calling? To give me the clues to the next victim?"

"Oh, no, Quinn. Not at all. You won't be getting any more clues."

My heart leapt into my throat. "Why not?"

"Because you broke the rules of the game."

"No, I—"

"You decided that you held a certain degree of power in this situation. You don't. And I am going to make that quite clear. Thanks to you, the poor woman rotting in the back of a refuse truck never had a prayer of being saved. Had you not chosen to challenge me, she might have had a chance."

My nose burned as my eyes filled with tears for our sixth victim. I clamped my mouth shut and fought the emotion.

"Her blood is on your hands as much as it is mine, Quinn."

I could feel the scorching heat of Blair's and Meredith's eyes on me. My fingers gripped the phone, as I was desperate to anchor myself to something. He was right. No one had been looking for that woman. She undoubtedly knew that no one would be coming to save her. And it was all because I had decided to go all in on a losing game.

In that moment, alone in the fight and surrounded by enemies, I realized Trevor had been right. The piper would not end our game until he claimed me as his final victim. Whether in body or spirit, he would ensure that the woman who had answered his call all those weeks ago was dead. Perhaps she already was.

"And victim seven?" Despite my effort to mask the effect he had on me, my voice was thick with grief.

"You'll find her soon enough."

I closed my eyes as a tear slid soundlessly down my cheek.

CHAPTER 45

Quinn

I STEPPED into the late afternoon sun, the piper's voice still reverberating against my skull, and turned my face to the soft breeze, willing it to cleanse me of the rot that was growing inside. Wrapping my arms around myself, I drifted past the picnic table on our small swath of grass and came to a stop only once the cool bark of our towering hickory scratched against my bare arms.

Soon, officers would pour out of the station. They would climb into the patrol cars that were lined up like perfect soldiers, and they would depart in search of a body that no longer sheltered a soul. It wouldn't take long to find her. Eden Falls was too small to harbor more than a few garbage trucks.

As if conjured by my imagination, the back door to the station flew open, and a string of uniforms marched into the parking lot. I tucked myself closer to the tree, grateful for the shade that hid me from view. I didn't want to see anyone. And I didn't want anyone to see *me*—the once-calm, levelheaded dispatcher who had cost a woman her life because she'd failed to keep her emotions in check.

The low murmur of half a dozen voices carried on the breeze, but one rose above the rest. I searched the pack for the source and found Carlson near the rear.

"That's our boy!" he howled, his face ruddy with amusement, "plowing his way through the dispatchers!" Carlson cocked an elbow on Nash's shoulder as they walked side by side, leaning in close enough that he could have kissed his partner on the cheek if he'd wanted to. "Blair—now, that's not a huge victory or anything. She's pretty easy to get into bed. But Quinn?" His voice rose with my name. "I mean, *damn*, now that takes a fucking genius. You've got to be the smoothest motherfucker who ever lived to bang that one!"

Nash shrugged Carlson off and cut away toward his cruiser, but the others all joined in to voice their awe and admiration of Trevor, several of them even going so far as to make comments about pleasuring me and what it would be like to have my legs wrapped around them while they rode me hard.

My cheeks burned, and tears fought the last vestige of my control as it hit home how badly Trevor had betrayed me. He had looked me in the eye and promised that our relationship would remain private. But not even a week after we'd made love, he had not only humiliated me in front of everyone we worked with, ruining the reputation I had worked so hard to build, but he had also moved on to someone else. To *Blair* of all people—the woman who had sought to make my life hell for years and one of the least classy women in town.

The door to the station swung open again. That time, Gabe and Trevor exited. The two had their heads bent toward each other, appearing engaged in a conversation meant only for them. I fisted my hands at the sight of the man who had stolen my heart and shattered it beyond salvation. My body vibrated with the force of my hatred. I fought the urge to go to him and say things to him that I hoped would cause him as much pain as he had caused me. But what I had to say wouldn't hurt him. Because for it to hurt, he would have to actually care about me.

Before I even realized that I was moving, I found myself halfway across the parking lot with eight sets of eyes on me, including a pair that were as blue as the Montana sky in July.

When Trevor noticed me, a small smile ghosted his lips. He angled toward me but then stopped almost immediately. His eyes were alert as they swept across my face and body, as though he registered a threat but couldn't make sense of what his instincts were telling him.

Gabe noticed something was up too. He held back a few steps, his gaze wary and his body rigid.

I maintained an aggressive pace, my eyes locked on Trevor, until the toes of my shoes kissed his boots. "You son of a bitch." The words were quiet as they slipped between my clenched teeth.

Trevor's eyes narrowed. "Quinn, what the hell—"

I poked my finger into his chest. It hurt me more than it hurt him, since he was wearing his bulletproof vest, but I didn't care. The pain felt good. That kind of pain I welcomed. It made the rest dull just a bit. "You fucking no-good liar!" I roared.

Trevor's head snapped back, his eyes growing wide. He reached for me, but I slapped his hands away.

"Don't touch me!" My vision filled with tears, his beautiful form morphing into a wavy blur, but no way in hell would I let one single drop fall. A caustic laugh I barely recognized as my own filled the stunned silence around us. "You're good, Trevor. I'll give you that. Looking back, it's as clear as day to me what an idiot I was for not seeing who Trent really was. But someday, when I look back on *us*, I don't think even then I'll be able to find the cracks in your disguise or the obviousness of your lies."

Trevor glanced around at our spectators then in hushed tones asked, "Quinn, what the hell are you talking about?"

I scoffed. "I'm talking about the way you bragged to all of your buddies about how you got me into bed!" I leaned in closer, my lips pulling back from my teeth as my voice turned low and lethal. "I'm talking about how you spent last night."

I heard the words tumbling from my lips, and a distant part of me was mortified that I was laying the private details of his betrayal and our affair out in the open for all to hear and judge. But an even bigger part of me just didn't give a shit anymore. All of my secrets had been blasted across town for the past three weeks. It didn't matter what I said. I was already ruined. My reputation had been reduced to ash. My best friend was dead. Not only had I failed to catch the piper, but I had made the situation worse. There was a body in a garbage truck ready to prove it. And I had finally opened my heart to someone only to end up as the running joke of the locker room all over again.

Trevor tried to reach for me again, confusion on his face, but I wasn't buying it. I would never believe another word that came out of his mouth. He would never touch me again. And he would never bear witness to another second of my pain.

With that vow, something shifted. The raging inferno became a wall of ice. I took a step backward out of his reach then another. "Truly impressive, Trevor." My words were dull. I could feel the fight draining from my body, leaving behind a pain so unbearable that I wondered how my heart was still beating. "Your record remains unblemished."

Trevor's arms dropped to his sides, his lips pressed into a grim line. Encircled by his friends, their eyes darting between us, we stared at each other. He stood perfectly still, as did I. And I could have sworn I could hear the last piece of my heart break.

I took another step back then spun and marched away, allowing just one more tear to fall.

CHAPTER 46

Trevor

I watched Quinn stalk toward the dispatch center, her back ramrod straight, her hands fisted at her sides. I had no idea what had just happened, but I'd had a bad feeling all day, ever since I'd returned Blair's phone to her, and Quinn had given me the cold shoulder.

The guys shifted awkwardly around me, their gazes jumping from one another to me.

Gabe finally broke the tension. "All right, what the fuck is everyone standing around for when we have a crime scene to process?" he barked.

That was one thing about my partner. He could be downright scary when he wanted to be. Apparently, our partners agreed, because they jumped to life and couldn't get out of there fast enough.

Gabe pulled up to my side, bumping his shoulder against mine as he crossed his arms. He watched Quinn for a moment then turned a side-eye on me. "Well?"

I tore my eyes away from Quinn long enough to scowl at Gabe. "Well, what?"

"Are you going after her?"

Still trying to make sense of the whole situation, I was silent. When I finally answered, resignation filled my tone. "No."

Gabe angled his body toward me and dropped his arms. "What do you mean, '*no*'? You're really just going to let her think you betrayed her?"

I thrust a hand toward Quinn, who had just reached the outer edge of the comms center. "You saw her! She won't listen to me. What the hell do you want me to do?"

Gabe's voice rose to meet mine in a borderline shout. "Tell her you didn't betray her!"

"How do you know I didn't? I'm not exactly shy about sharing my conquests."

Gabe didn't say a word. He just waited me out while his dark eyes drilled a hole in my face.

I growled and shoved a hand through my hair as I turned away. "This was going to happen sooner or later. I knew it was only a matter of time before she woke up and realized she deserves a lot better than me."

"What the hell are you talking about?"

I turned back to Gabe and threw my arms out at my sides, a sardonic smile on my face. "I'm just the good-time guy, brother! Everyone knows that. If a chick wants a good lay, I'm her man. But no woman in her right mind would tie herself to me and expect that life was going to be roses ever after."

Gabe took a step forward and punched his pointer finger at me. "That's a fucking cop-out, and you know it." He pushed past me, shoving my shoulder with his, then climbed into his car and took off.

I stared at the door of the comms center, where Quinn had disappeared, and thought about what Gabe had said. He was probably right. I should go after her and clear up this mess, but I knew that I wouldn't, because the truth was I'd been waiting for this moment ever since Quinn and I had slept together. Something that good was never meant to be mine.

Running my hand through my hair again, I released a harsh

breath. With one more glance at the comms center, I strode to my car and reminded myself this was why I didn't do relationships.

* * *

BILLIARD BALLS CRASHED against each other as Carlson started a new game. He'd been trying for the past hour to get me to join in, but I was content to watch, not that I was really paying attention anyway. The day had turned out to be the shittiest one I'd had in a long time. My balls had still been aching from the verbal kick to the nuts Quinn gave me when we finally located the sixth victim and pulled her broken body from the back of a dump truck only to process another nearly worthless crime scene. As if that hadn't all been enough to make me want to go home and drink until I blacked out, I returned to the station only to be called into the chief's office, where he'd promptly removed me from the case.

Apparently, he'd heard the same rumors Quinn had, and he determined that our relationship was too much of a distraction. Out of concern that our personal business would cloud our judgment and we—or someone else—would pay the price, he felt that it was best to give us some distance from each other. Since Gabe and I had both taken point on the case, and the killer was only willing to talk to Quinn, I was the logical sacrifice.

A pair of double D's rubbed against my chest, and I looked down into a set of eyes that were not the color of sun-kissed honey. The blonde who was doing her best to hold my attention batted her fake eyelashes, which could have whipped up hurricane winds. Her painted-on red dress left nothing to the imagination, its spaghetti straps straining to support her augmented assets. She was attractive in that quick-fuck porn-star kind of way, but lately, I had found that the girl-next-door vibe was the only thing that really did it for me anymore.

That didn't stop me from trying to get my head in the game with the willing distraction, who, at the moment, was ensuring I could feel her hard nipples caressing my chest through my thin white cotton tee. I smiled and threaded a hand through her hair then gripped the back of her head and used my tongue to trace the outer shell of her ear.

But even as I went through the motions, my mind was someplace else. As much as it chapped my hide that I wasn't going to get to see the case through to the end, to be the one who slapped the cuffs on David James as I took delight in telling him about all the wonderful experiences that awaited him in a max-security prison, it bothered me even more to know how badly I'd hurt Quinn.

I'd been at a total loss as to what had caused her feelings for me to change so suddenly—until Nash pulled me aside after I left the chief's office and filled me in on the details everyone else had. When I asked him how everyone had found out about my relationship with Quinn, he said his best guess was that Carlson had noticed she and I were getting close, and knowing my history with women, he'd speculated that there was more going on and had shared his theory openly until rumor became fact in everyone's mind.

But it was the part he'd told me about Blair that had gutted me most. That cunning bitch had spread the word that she and I had hooked up after I took her home. It was only then that I realized why Quinn had given me the cold shoulder that morning. Blair had no doubt already planted the rumor in Quinn's ear, then when I, like a stupid son of a bitch, returned Blair's phone to her, it was just further proof in Quinn's mind of what she already feared was true. For her, it was history repeating itself, and I had played right into Blair's hand, helping her reopen Quinn's deepest wounds.

The busty blonde—Samantha, I thought her name was—pressed herself against me and buried her face in my neck, where she proceeded to suck and lick as if her life depended on it. Out of habit, my eyes raked the room, assessing each of the patrons packed into Rustlers. The yellow light was dim, the jukebox was loud, and everyone seemed to be having a good time, enjoying the start of their weekend. When my eyes landed on Carlson with his Cheshire grin as he leaned on his pool stick, eyeing my companion and me, my mind started working on my plot for revenge. I had every intention of kicking Carlson's ass, but I was smart enough to be strategic about the timing and opportunity. Until then, I would continue to play it cool and let him think we were good.

Withdrawing her face from my neck, the blonde stood on her toes and pressed her mouth to my ear, relaying in vivid detail all the filthy things she wanted me to do to her. There had been a time when a woman like that would have excited the hell out of me. But all I could think about was that hers wasn't the face I wanted to look at, and it certainly wasn't the body I wanted to hold.

Why didn't I just go after Quinn instead of letting her walk out of my life thinking that I would ever betray her that way? How could I let her think she got herself played like that again?

The answer came to me without effort. Gabe was right. I'd copped out. I was so damn afraid that I was going to screw things up with Quinn that it was easier to just let it happen rather than continue to be afraid of the day that I would inevitably disappoint her beyond repair.

The blonde reached between us and squeezed my cock. I fisted her hair and tilted her head back. As I looked into her eyes and questioned whether she was really what I wanted, the energy in the air shifted. Like a magnet, I felt pulled by some inexplicable force that drew my attention toward the entrance of the bar on the opposite side of the room.

The moment my eyes landed on Quinn, my gut twisted, and my lungs ceased to work. Her eyes were wide, her mouth slightly open in a look of horror and total disgust. At first, her gaze ran down the length of the woman cradling my dick, but then our eyes locked, and her face began to crumple. She turned so abruptly that she ran into the barrel chest of the mountain man behind her. He reached out to steady her, but she scurried around him, then she was gone.

My head dropped, and I closed my eyes. I could still see Quinn and the unadulterated pain on her beautiful face. It was an image that seared my soul and could never be scrubbed away.

When I opened my eyes, I gazed at the woman in front of me. If there had been even a small chance that I could have set things right with Quinn, it had just gone up in flames. There was nothing to stop me from going home with the blonde and losing myself in her body for a few meaningless hours. Fucking and avoiding things I didn't want to feel was what I knew how to do. I knew what waited for me at the end of that road. I had traveled it many times.

But for the first time, I saw another road laid out before me. It was rocky and rough and full of unknowns. It meant facing more than a decade of pent-up grief, anger, and self-hatred. It meant letting go of the safe but shallow existence I had built and risking everything to possibly end up with nothing.

The blonde smiled up at me and ran her tongue around her candy-apple-red lips. I'd made it this far on cheap thrills and had learned to live with the man I'd become. For some of us, life would never be more than empty.

CHAPTER 47

Quinn

I RAISED my eyes and canvased the room before glancing back down at the newspaper I was concealing under my desk. The front-page article that I had already read more than once revealed details about the sixth victim and my part in her death in equal measure. Dierk Jensen, the journalist responsible for the article, was certainly no fan of mine.

Having returned to work the previous day after my little display of aggression with Trevor, I already knew that the piper's latest victim was Janelle Parker, a forty-six-year-old beauty with long silver-blond hair and a lithe body that brought a lot of business to her Pilates studio. I had taken Janelle's classes on and off for years and had always been a little bit in awe of her. She was one of those women who seemed to have life figured out. Her business was thriving. She had two beautiful children, both of whom had successfully launched and were excelling in college. Her husband of twenty-four years was as kind and generous as they came. And though Janelle and Stephen had separated shortly after their youngest left home, the two weren't ready to call it quits and had been working toward reconciliation.

Dierk had done a masterful job juxtaposing Janelle's beautiful soul with mine, which was apparently tarnished and beyond redemption. A profound sense of guilt washed through me as I read the final paragraph once more.

Janelle Parker's death will undoubtedly leave a hole in the heart of Eden Falls, and as our community mourns this woman, who was every bit as exquisite on the inside as she was in appearance, we have to ask ourselves: how many of our own could have been saved if Dispatcher Quinn Martin had put as much effort into the opportunity she had to protect these women as she did in bedding a badge? Even the killer himself, who has now claimed six lives in our once-great town, informed Ms. Martin that "her [Mrs. Parker's] blood is on your hands as much as it is mine."

Closing my eyes, I tossed the newspaper back under my desk. I wanted out of there. I couldn't stand another day of being cooped up in that dispatch center, waiting for the piper's final call. What was the point? He wasn't going to give me a chance to save any more victims, and after he killed the next, he would vanish. Then one day, he would pop up someplace else. There would be more victims, more families and communities thrust into a cycle of grief and fear.

My hands flew to my face then raked through my hair. I'd had the chance to stop him, a chance that no one else had ever been given. And we had gotten *so* very close. I felt the weight of not only the deaths in our community but also of all those who had come before and all who would come after.

My skin crawled with the need to move, to run away, to be left alone. I eyed the hallway to the exit and considered that I could just leave and never look back. The temptation became more acute when, in the next moment, Blair's radio crackled with a voice I couldn't bear to hear.

"Twenty-Five Adam Four. I'll be on foot in the Lakeview area."

I didn't think I was imagining the extra-breathy response from Blair as she answered Trevor. My cheeks heated, and my fingernails dug into my palms as I fought the urge to march over to her and wrap the cord from her damn headset around her throat.

After I had accomplished that, maybe I would do the same to that slut who had *literally* coiled herself around him last night. The pain of Trevor's betrayal, the images of him with Blair and that blonde, piled on top of the grief, humiliation, and guilt that had been eating away at me for weeks. The weight of my emotions grew heavier until my lungs constricted, and it was difficult to take a full breath. Then my heart began to thrash against my ribcage.

It's just a little panic attack. You're fine. I closed my eyes and tried to inhale through my nose, but my chest was too tight. Everything was falling apart. My career had been my identity, and I had managed to screw it up all over again. No way could I remain in Eden Falls after everything that had happened. *And how the hell am I supposed to explain to another department why I'm suddenly picking up and starting over somewhere else for the second time?*

And Shelby—my ride or die—was gone *forever*. I hadn't even begun to process that loss. I'd distracted myself so that I wouldn't have to—told myself that I would deal with it when this was all over and lives no longer depended on me. Well, that time had come sooner than I had expected, and the loss threatened to destroy me.

I glanced around the room again. Julia had her back to me at the fire console, but she peeked over her shoulder in my direction, a look of sympathy on her face. Blair and Meredith, seated to my left, had their heads bent toward each other. In my fight to hold myself together, I hadn't even noticed that they were talking about me and not bothering to hide that fact.

"I'm just glad everyone is finally seeing her for who she really is," Blair said in a stage whisper.

"I know." Meredith's head bobbed up and down. "They all thought she was so smart, but her little act finally bit her in the ass. At least Dierk is willing to tell the truth."

My blood heated to a boil in the span of a heartbeat, its warmth spreading up my chest and into my neck until it flooded my face. The sting from my fingernails sinking into my palms only fueled the rage that was building.

Blair snorted. "And once again, she spreads her legs for the wrong guy and screws up yet another job." She shook her head. "What a joke."

For the first time in my life, I discovered my breaking point. I shot to my feet. "I don't know what makes you think you can comment on *my* sex life, Blair, when half the town's male population has crawled up your snatch!"

Julia spun around in her chair at my sudden outburst, her eyes wide and her jaw halfway to the floor.

"And here's a little tip, Meredith. If you want people to think you're smart, start by getting your own brain rather than sharing the half a brain that belongs to Blair."

The two women stared at me as though I had completely lost my mind. That was fair. I had.

Blair's chin bobbed up and down as she attempted—and failed—to form words. I shot them each a look that promised bodily injury if they so much as squeaked. When they snapped their mouths shut and leaned back, trying to put as much distance between us as possible, I considered my job done and marched out of the dispatch center but not before I caught a glimpse of Julia grinning from ear to ear and offering a firm nod of approval as I went by.

When I burst out the door seconds later, I plopped down at the picnic table and dropped my face into my hands. I waited for the regret and guilt to come, but it didn't. Instead, I felt just a bit lighter. I could breathe a bit more easily.

Lowering my hands, I put my focus on the mighty mountains in the distance. I wanted to disappear in those mountains—to get lost among the pine trees and winding, gurgling rivers. Out there, all alone, perhaps I could finally find some sense of peace. Perhaps I could forget the images of nearly naked bodies beaten beyond recognition. Maybe I could forget sky-blue eyes and golden skin. I could forget that, for a short while, I had truly believed I might be able to find happiness after everything was said and done.

I inhaled deeply, savoring the feel of cool, clean air filling my lungs, and when I released it, a little more tension slipped away.

"Alex gets that look about her when she's up to her neck in shit and assholes."

I whipped my head around to find Gabe walking toward me, wearing a weary smile. He took a seat across from me and folded his hands on top of the table and waited.

I chuckled. "Well, it seems there's never a shortage of either, so I guess I'll be wearing this look for a while." I dropped my gaze to the table and traced the grain in the wood with my eyes.

"Unfortunately, that's true."

Gabe paused. When I didn't say anything, he pressed further.

"You've had a lot of weight on your shoulders these past few weeks, Quinn. It's okay if you've cracked a little along the way."

I snorted. "I think it's safe to say I cracked more than a little."

"We've always relied pretty heavily on you. Everyone knows you're the brains of our operation."

I raised my eyes to him, and he shook his head. "What we asked of you this time wasn't fair. It was too much."

Biting my lower lip, I gazed over his shoulder at the mountains again. "I should have been able to do more. I should have figured out who he was sooner. If I had—" I shrugged a shoulder.

"No." The way he said it left no room for argument. "We were *all* responsible for stopping this asshole. Every cop who has ever worked the piper case is responsible. We all failed, Quinn. But you gave it your all, and there isn't a soul in the department who doubts that." One corner of his mouth lifted. "Except for maybe a couple of your less charming partners, as Trevor tells it."

I smiled, but it withered immediately at the mention of Trevor's name.

I could feel Gabe's eyes on me. He was assessing me with his cop stare. "It wasn't him."

My forehead creased. "What wasn't him?"

"I don't know how people found out about the two of you, but it didn't come from Trevor."

I studied *him* that time as I contemplated whether or not I wanted to go down that rabbit hole. My desperate desire to believe him won out. "How do you know?"

"Because Trevor tells me *everything*. Except he didn't tell me about the two of you. And if he didn't tell me, he didn't tell anybody."

Gabe allowed me to digest that before he continued. "I normally don't get involved in other people's business, but I've seen a real change in Trevor these past few weeks. A change for the better. And I think that has a lot to do with you."

I searched Gabe's eyes, wanting desperately to believe what he was telling me.

"You're good for him, Quinn. And"—he shook his head like he couldn't believe what he was about to say—"and I think he's good for you too."

I looked away, the image of Trevor with that other woman coming to the forefront of my mind. "It's too late for us."

Gabe offered a half smile. "Nah. It's not too late."

My lips folded in on themselves. Even they didn't want to relive the details. But after a long pause, Gabe raised his eyebrows. So with a sigh, I told him what he was waiting to hear. "I went to Rustlers last night to pick up dinner after work. Trevor was there." I looked down at my hands in my lap, where I was picking at my cuticles. "He was there with a woman. Some blond Betty Boop wannabe. They had their hands all over each other."

I cleared my throat and raised my chin, pushing back against the tears that seemed always at the surface lately. I would *not* be the woman who cried over a man who had done her wrong. Been there, done that.

"Anyway," I said, "given Trevor's history, I'm sure the two undoubtedly had a very busy night."

Gabe, whose face had been stone as he'd listened to me,

smirked. "Let me tell you something I learned the hard way. It never pays to make assumptions when it comes to relationships."

My brow furrowed.

His smile deepened. "Trevor didn't spend last night with anyone other than you."

My head snapped back. Clearly, I wasn't the only one who had lost my marbles. "Trevor was *not* with me last night."

Gabe's dark eyes danced with amusement. "Yeah, he was. You just didn't know it. He was worried about you being alone with David James still on the loose, so he camped out in his truck all night, which was parked in front of *your* house."

I tried to find the words to respond to that revelation, but all I could manage were a few squeaks. Entirely too many feelings had flooded my system of late. I was certain that at some point, my body was going to shut down and refuse to power up again.

Not only had he not gone home with that second-rate Jessica Rabbit, but after all the horrible things I had said to him in front of his partners, he had still chosen to fold all six feet, three inches of himself into his truck so he could keep watch over me all night.

I was still trying to process that new and incredibly confusing information when Gabe asked, "So, can I count on seeing you at the masquerade ball tonight? 'Cause you know that if you no-show, Liz is going to send my ass to your house, and she won't let me come back unless you're with me and fully decked out."

I chuckled at the visual. "Sorry to make your life harder, but I'm just not in the mood for a party." Even if Gabe was right about Trevor, and there was a sliver of a chance we might be able to salvage something, the fact remained that the rest of my life was in shambles. The case would be over in the very near future, one way or another. At some point, I would have to face everything that had happened and begin putting pieces back together.

He nodded knowingly. "Ah, well. That's okay. I'll just have to make sure the punch bowl keeps getting drained and the streamers keep falling so she has something else to worry about."

We fell into an easy silence, enjoying the stillness of the afternoon. Birds chirped a joyful song in the tree, which shivered with the soft breeze above us. In that still and quiet moment, a whisper of something pecked at the deepest crevices of my mind. Like the Piper's flute, I coaxed and summoned until it began to crystallize.

Gabe, never missing a thing, raked his eyes over me. "What is it, Quinn?"

"He likes to play games," I whispered.

Gabe looked at me like I'd just gone off the deep end.

I sat up straighter and leaned in, my breathing shallow. "The piper. He likes to play games, especially when he gets to prove how much more clever he is than those who are chasing him."

Gabe nodded slowly. "Yeah. Where are you going with this?"

I gave him a wicked grin. "I know how to find the piper."

His eyebrows shot to his hairline. Before he had a chance to ask questions, I barreled full steam ahead. "He's going to be at the masquerade ball."

"Why would he show up to an event where everyone, including the entire police force, is going to be?"

"That's exactly *why* he'll be there! It's the kind of game he likes to play. He knows that we know who he is and what he looks like. But at a masquerade, he can hide and hunt right under our noses." I slapped my hand on the table. "He *will* be there, Gabe, relishing the fact that the killer we've been chasing is right there in our midst while we're completely clueless and having a good time. All the while, he'll be selecting his final victim, preparing to snatch her right out from under us."

Gabe eyed me as he pinched his bottom lip. After several moments in which I could see him mentally sorting information, he finally nodded. "You're right."

"And that's why I'm going to be there."

"No. Definitely not." He shook his head as if that were the end of it.

"I need to be there, Gabe. I know him better than anyone else. I know his *voice*. I'll hear it in my head for the rest of my life."

He shook his head again. "It's too dangerous. He's fixated on you. He's already targeted you indirectly by killing Shelby."

I tried to ignore the ache in my chest at the mention of Shelby's name and instead kept my single-minded focus on the vengeance I *would* claim. "Can you think of any place safer than a ballroom full of cops?"

Gabe kept his eyes trained on me, his expression stoic. He couldn't argue that fact. And as soon as he admitted it, I was going to get to work setting up the dominos that would end the piper once and for all.

CHAPTER 48

Quinn

I DID A SLOW TURN, taking in the exuberant crowd and the ornate atmosphere. Liz had certainly outdone herself. The masquerade was unlike anything I'd ever seen. The large, open space of the community center's common room had been transformed into a Venetian ballroom fit for the royal class. Dull-yellow bulbs that were once housed in the recessed lighting had been replaced with soft white and blue bulbs that made the room glow like a moonlit night. And the silver disco balls hanging from the ceiling could have been reminiscent of a tacky eighth-grade dance, but instead, they sparkled like starlight amid the white tulle that had been artfully draped around them.

To further add to the enchantment, thick billowing fog rolled sensuously from the stage and poured onto the dance floor, where a mass of people gyrated to the siren call of the band that was playing. My gaze drifted to Emmy, the town's sweetheart and the badass lead guitarist of Reprisal. I knew from having seen the group of teenagers perform at Rustlers that she also had a mean set of pipes on her.

Tonight, she dazzled in a cream-colored sequined gown with a ruffled skirt and a small train. Her mask matched the dress perfectly and covered her nose and eyes, a long white feather attached to the side creating an elegant sweep away from her face. The look was made even more stunning by the way it contrasted with the long-tailed tuxedos and black masks worn by the boys in the band.

No one would know it by looking at Emmy, but the girl had moxie. By day, she was the sweet, kind of shy, straight-A student who volunteered at the retirement home, tutored on the weekends, and never missed a church service. But when she was up on that stage, she absolutely transformed. The only girl in the five-member band, Emmy captured the show, even when she wasn't center stage and singing lead. Her round face, rosy cheeks, and cornflower-blue eyes gave the impression that she belonged on a shelf alongside a row of porcelain dolls. But I had seen a side of her that I wagered most hadn't.

I recalled all those months ago when she had shown up at the police department, flushed from running and rambling about Jace Maloy being kidnapped. One of my partners had done her best to soothe the girl, but Emmy refused to back down, promising to raise absolute hell until we got Gabe on the phone and relayed everything to him that she had told us.

Emmy stepped to the front of the stage, the enraptured notes of her Gibson rising above the rest of the music in a solo that echoed with the grace of her soul. Even with the mask, the rhapsody of the music was reflected on her angelic face. When she finished the solo, the crowd went wild. Emmy smiled in return, but it didn't quite reach her eyes.

Something had changed in the girl the past year, but I hadn't been able to put my finger on what it was exactly. She had once smiled and sparkled with all the enthusiasm of a young girl who still believed in fairy tales and the endless adventures that awaited. But her eyes had come to hold a little less shine, and her smile was a little less bright, as though she was no longer housed in the protective, naive bubble of youth but had instead been introduced to a world where dragons were fiction and the prince didn't come to save the day.

With a sigh, I returned my attention to the room, reminding myself that I was supposed to be tracking a killer. We only had *one* more chance to catch the piper, one chance to stop him from claiming his seventh victim and so many more once he left Eden Falls—and one chance to ensure I wouldn't spend every moment of every day looking over my shoulder, waiting for him to return for me.

Yet knowing how much was riding on tonight hadn't been enough to keep me focused on the task at hand. Ever since my conversation with Gabe earlier that afternoon, my thoughts and emotions kept swirling around the man who had stolen my heart when I wasn't looking. Even as I'd worked with the chief and the rest of the squad to quickly formulate a plan to ensnare the killer at the ball, I ached with the desire to go to Trevor—to do what I should have done in the first place, which was have an actual conversation with him rather than run away because I'd been so afraid he was going to betray me.

The truth was that deep down, I had known that Trevor had the power to hurt me worse than anyone else ever had, because I cared about him more deeply than I had ever cared about another man. And that had terrified me to my core. I'd already decided that when everything was over, I would give him the chance to have that conversation—if he wanted it. But for the moment, our personal lives would have to wait.

Slowly, I weaved my way through the crowd around the dance floor. My objective was simple. Make the rounds, act normal, and listen to every conversation I could in an effort to identify the piper by the sound of his voice. I tried to recall how his tone and speech had differed the night I'd met him at Rustlers, all the while keeping an eye out for tall, athletic-looking men who were either standing by themselves or appeared to be in the company of a new female acquaintance.

As I completed another full lap around the room, I spotted Alex and Liz standing to the side of the stage and decided to join them for a few minutes.

"Hi, ladies." I smiled and cast my eyes down the length of them both. "You two look stunning."

Liz beamed and did a slow twirl. "Thank you very much. I could say the same of you."

As Trevor had described, Liz had unified the three of us women with accents of scarlet. Alex's floor-length dress hugged her like a second skin and had a slit up to her midthigh. It was mostly black with a sweetheart neckline, but crimson sequins lined the top of the bodice and matched the belt that hugged her slim waist. Her mahogany hair was half-up, with large curls cascading down her back like a waterfall.

Liz's petite frame was draped in layers of chiffon. The flowy ensemble had a strap over one shoulder and was deep crimson at the top and faded into black toward the bottom. The look matched her feisty personality perfectly, and her ebony mask made her violet eyes pop, even in the dim light.

"I'm so glad you decided to come, Quinn." Alex gave a warm smile, but her eyes held a glimmer of sympathy. Gabe had undoubtedly shared the details of what had gone down between Trevor and me, but ever the lady, Alex wouldn't comment on it or ask any questions.

"Thanks, Alex. So am I." I frowned and looked around the room. "So, Liz, when I am going to meet this husband of yours?"

Alex's smile dropped, and her eyes shot to Liz.

Liz pursed her lips and shook her head. "Not tonight. That's for sure."

I looked questioningly at Alex, who tilted her head and shrugged. When Liz caught the exchange, her shoulders slumped. "He said he had to fly to Washington for work. I asked him to let it wait until morning. He knew how important tonight was to me, but—" She pressed her lips together and shook her head again.

Seeing the raw disappointment and hurt on Liz's face had me at a loss for words. As I was struggling to think of what to say, Gabe came up behind Alex and wrapped his arms around her waist. When he pecked her on the cheek and playfully nuzzled her neck, drawing an effervescent chuckle from the beauty, my heart squeezed. The two were made for each other. Even a blind man could see it. And the way they lit up in each other's presence made me yearn to experience the same. And just like that, my mind was on Trevor again.

Gabe hung around only long enough to make sure Alex was good. With another quick kiss, he broke away from his fiancée and strode toward me, stopping once we were shoulder to shoulder and facing opposite directions. He leaned in and lowered his voice. "You good?"

"A bit edgy, if I'm being honest."

"That's normal when you're the bait. Just keep your eyes peeled and your ears open, and stay where we can see you."

I nodded. "Copy that."

Gabe squeezed my arm then disappeared into the crowd.

To get a better vantage point, I moved to Alex's right and stood with my back to the stage. Liz and Alex were engaged in conversation about wedding planning. I half listened as my gaze skated back and forth across the room. I was about to turn my attention back to the two women when a dark figure in a far corner caught my eye.

Though he was almost entirely obscured by shadow, there was no mistaking that tall frame and those broad shoulders. His slightly mussed hair glowed gold, even in the low light, and matched his tuxedo vest. An obsidian mask enveloped his glacier eyes, which were locked on me and burned with the familiarity and desire that only existed between a man and a woman who had become a part of each other.

After the fight we'd had and considering the chief had removed him from the case, I hadn't expected him to come. But there he was, as solid and imposing as always. My heartbeat quickened as the music and chatter that surrounded us became a muted hum. The people and the decorations faded to a blur. All I could perceive was *him*. And though the sight of him had unleashed a thousand butterflies in my already-churning stomach, just knowing he was there, watching, made me feel safe, even as I attempted to lure a savage killer to me.

Perhaps it was the shadows playing tricks with my eyes, but I could have sworn Trevor's mouth quirked with a hint of that panty-dropping grin he was so good at. My mouth parted, and my breaths grew shallow, something that I was sure he noticed, since my sky-high corseted breasts emphasized every rise and fall of my chest. His smile grew, simultaneously confirming my suspicions and initiating a painful throb in an area that literally ached for him.

"Quinn?"

My name sounded distant as it met my ears.

"Quinn?"

The spell shattered, and my head snapped around to Liz. "Hmm?"

She glanced at where Trevor stood, a sly smile slipping up her face. But if she'd realized I'd been standing there drooling over him, she didn't say as much. Despite my embarrassment at having been caught practically undressing a man with my eyes in the middle of an active sting operation, I was grateful that she'd brought me back to reality. As much as I wanted to try to fix whatever had been between Trevor and me, it would have to wait. I had to ensure that at the moment, the only man on my mind was the piper.

CHAPTER 49

Trevor

It seemed as though the whole town had turned out for the masquerade. Dozens upon dozens of people pressed in on one another, the heat from all those bodies making the room stuffy.

I didn't like having so many people between Quinn and me. It was hard enough to keep an eye on her from the shadows with the artificial fog and low lighting, not to mention the stupid mask that was obscuring most of my peripheral vision.

But since I was off the case and most definitely not supposed to be there, the mask was a must, as was the dark corner in which I'd taken up post.

That being said, when Gabe had gone above the chief to fill me in on their partially insane plan, I had determined that not even an act of God would keep me away, not while they were dangling Quinn in front of a psychopath.

So far, Gabe and Quinn seemed to be the only ones who had noticed me, and the latter was currently watching me from across the room. I hadn't failed to notice the way her corseted bosom heaved harder and faster at the precise moment she'd registered my presence.

Witnessing the way her body still responded to me was a

major turn-on, and it gave me hope that maybe the thing between us wasn't over.

Quinn's eyes were still locked on me. I slid my gaze down her body, admiring the way that not even a gown could conceal that mouth-watering figure. The black corset made the creaminess of her pale skin even lovelier, and the rich folds of scarlet that wrapped around the back and draped to the floor emphasized the blush in her cheeks. She had pinned most of her curls in an elegant updo but left a few hanging loose down her neck and around her face.

As my eyes traveled back to hers, I threw her a hint of a smile that I hoped made it clear that I was busy picturing what it would be like to yank on the ties of that corset and watch as the gown fluttered to the floor.

Yeah, keeping an eye on Quinn definitely topped the charts as *best assignment ever.*

When she suddenly snapped out of the moment we were lost in together, turning her attention to Liz, I immediately felt the absence. All night, I'd been fighting the desire to go to her, to make things right and do what I should have done the moment she left me standing in the middle of the station parking lot with my heart and my pride in a puddle on the asphalt.

I'd been a coward, and it had cost me the only woman who had ever felt like home—the only woman who had ever made the cracks in my soul begin to seal.

If I went to Quinn and laid my soul bare, there was every possibility she would tell me to go to hell. And that was her right. If she decided she wanted nothing to do with me, I would respect her decision. But I couldn't live with knowing that I hadn't done everything in my power to fix things between us. Before the night was over, Quinn *would* hear the truth from my lips, and she would, after all these years, know the extent of my love for her.

Tearing my gaze from Quinn, I did another quick scan of the room. My instincts had just about been convinced that everything was code-four until a man and a woman on the edge of the room caught my attention. The man was decently tall, but it was hard to get a good look at his build with the way his tuxedo-clad form blended into the darkness around them. Their heads were bent toward each other in confidence except for the moments when they glanced around the room as though in fear of drawing attention.

A moment later, the pair moved toward the side exit, and the prickle at the back of my neck urged me to follow. With one more glance toward Quinn, convinced that she was safe while she was engaged in conversation with Liz and Alex in a room full of cops charged with keeping eyes on her, I made my way around the edge of the room until I reached the door the couple had disappeared through. Easing the door open, praying that the sound of the raging party within masked the rusty hinges, I poked my head out and scanned the area. There wasn't a soul in sight.

On a hunch, I stepped outside and kept my back to the wall as I moved toward the rear of the building. Sure enough, two voices became audible and grew in volume as I got closer. One of the voices, I recognized right away. The other was familiar, but the identity of its owner skipped around the edge of my consciousness. When I reached the corner of the building, I halted and continued to listen.

"I was just sitting there, doing my job, and she attacked me for no reason," the woman said.

"You mean physically?" the man asked.

The woman sputtered. "Well, she came at me like she was going to, but then she just flipped out and ran off. She has completely lost her mind!"

"It sounds as though the department has been derelict in their responsibility to ensure their officers and dispatchers don't present a threat to the community," the man said with so much pomp and righteous indignation that his identity finally clicked.

"Have you heard any more from the killer?" he asked.

"No, not since the last call when he made it clear that so much of this is Quinn's fault."

"When can you get the crime scene photos from the last vic—"

Even behind his mask, I registered the unadulterated fear in Dierk's face the moment I stepped into view, his russet-colored eyes swallowed by white.

At his sudden change in behavior, his female accomplice turned around, her expression matching his when she saw me.

I crossed my arms and spread my legs wide, waiting and letting them simmer in the fear and possibilities of what I was about to do to them.

Dierk's Adam's apple began to bob. Blair, on the other hand, wove her arm around his and plastered on a fake smile. "Trevor, we were just enjoying the moonlight," she said as she rubbed her breasts against Dierk's arm.

Dierk didn't seem to appreciate the gesture but appeared more concerned with me than getting Blair off of him. Obviously not having learned his lesson the first time, he lifted his chin and stuck out his prepubescent-looking chest. When he opened his mouth with what was surely going to be a haughty protest, I cut him off.

"If you know what's good for you, you'll shut the fuck up and accept that both your asses are grass."

Dierk snapped his mouth shut, but his beady eyes simmered.

"Here's what's going to happen," I said, focusing on Dierk. "I'm going to make good on my promise. First thing in the morning, I'm going to have a chat with your boss, and I'll lay out all the false statements you've reported about this case. I will put the fucking proof that you couldn't be bothered with a little thing like fact-checking in his hands. And while I'm at it, we're going to have a little conversation about the unethical lengths you went to to gather sensitive information about an ongoing investigation— an act that put the public you're meant to serve in greater peril, not to mention that, thanks to you, Quinn Martin has a strong case for libel against the paper."

Dierk shrank little by little until he practically disappeared against the backdrop of night.

I turned my attention to Blair. "As for you, consider your career over."

She started to argue, but I didn't give her the chance.

"The chief won't be able to fire you fast enough once I fill him in on the source and extent of our leak, and no other agency will let you within a ten-mile radius of their department. You're done, Blair."

I turned my back and left her standing there with her mouth flopping like a fish that had just been caught. I would finish dealing with the two of them later. At the moment, the most important thing for everyone to focus on was keeping Quinn safe and drawing the piper into the open before he got his hands on another woman.

As I reentered through the side door, the music and chatter swallowed me once again. My gaze went to where I'd last seen Quinn. She was no longer standing with Liz and Alex. My pulse quickened just a bit as I canvased the room for her black-and-crimson dress. Then I spotted her just as she disappeared around the corner to where the bathrooms were.

CHAPTER 50

Quinn

EMMY'S BAND played the final notes of one of their most popular songs, the driving beat of the drums creating pure ecstasy on the dance floor. When the piece concluded, silence fell, punctuated only by restless chatter. Emmy moved to the microphone at the front of the stage, her slim fingers wrapping gently around the stand. She kept her eyes downcast as her bandmates began to weave a familiar melody.

I was still standing with Liz and Alex, engaging in small talk while I used my dispatcher skills to eavesdrop on the conversations around me.

But as Emmy's achingly sweet voice, a rich mixture of caramel tones, piercing clarity, and just a hint of rasp, filled the room, my two companions and many of those around us abruptly ended their small talk and turned their attention to her. She began the first verse of "Eternal Flame" with a tenderness that captured the nostalgia of the piece, but when she reached the chorus, Emmy closed her eyes and raised her face to the heavens, unleashing the full power of her God-given gift. Goose bumps erupted across my skin as her voice filled the hollow places inside of me. The lyrics were everything I felt for Trevor but didn't know how to say.

My gaze drifted to the corner, where Trevor had stood in the shadows. When I found it empty, I swept the room. I could easily pick out nearly a dozen officers, all of whom brought their attention back to me at regular intervals. But Trevor was not among them.

I stepped toward the dance floor but stopped when my phone buzzed in my black sequined handbag. The device continued to buzz in my hand as I withdrew it from the clutch. My body went rigid when I saw the screen. *Unavailable.*

Taking a deep breath, I answered the call.

"Hello?"

"Hello, Quinn."

My blood ran cold at the sound of his vainglorious voice. In an attempt to drown out the overwhelming noise of the room, I pressed my finger against my unoccupied ear.

"What do you want?" Attempting to hide my growing excitement, I tried to infuse as much hostility into my voice as I could muster. I knew he wouldn't be able to resist executing his coup de grâce at the masquerade. Our plan was going to work. We were going to end him. *Tonight.*

He hummed in a lazy sort of way. "So many things, Quinn. But isn't that true of us all?"

With my finger still pressed against one ear and my phone pressed to the other, I surveyed the room. Women in opulent, sparkling gowns of varying colors laughed and prattled on with men who all seemed to be slightly altered replicas of one another. Their only differences were the colors and designs of the masks that obscured their faces.

"I'm through playing your games, David. If you've got a point, get to it. Otherwise, I'm done."

He sighed wistfully. "Apparently, I must remind you of what happened the last time you tried to take control of our game. Do not attempt courage, Quinn. There are still plenty of people to torture and kill in your name."

My gut twisted. He wouldn't hesitate to slaughter the entire town to make his point. When I spoke again, I replaced the challenge in my tone with complacence. "All right. What would you like from me?"

I scanned the room again, this time looking for Gabe so that I could signal to him that the piper was making contact.

"I'll get to that in a moment. But first, you're going to need to stop looking for your backup."

I froze. Then my phone buzzed against my ear.

"Look at it," he said.

When I glanced down at the screen, a text was waiting for me. I opened it and was greeted with an image of me in my masquerade gown. It had been taken when Gabe was standing shoulder to shoulder with me, telling me to keep my eyes open and to stay where everyone could see me.

I swallowed against the lump in my throat and pressed the phone to my ear once more.

"You really do look fetching this evening, Quinn."

My eyes resumed their hunt. "Thank you. I'd love to return the compliment, if you'd be so kind as to point yourself out."

He chuckled. "Ah, now there is the Quinn I know and love."

My nerves tingled beneath my skin. *He's here. Watching me.* He was *playing* with me.

When I didn't respond, he continued, "I have another proposition for you. Are you interested?"

Yeah, 'cause that worked out great the last time.

"Yes."

My phone buzzed again. I pulled it away, and my heart went into overdrive. He'd sent a picture of a young Hispanic woman bound to a chair and gagged, mascara running down her cheeks. She was Yardley Williams, the gym teacher at the elementary school and a regular in my kickboxing class.

I put the phone back to my ear. "What's the proposition?"

His voice a purr, he said, "I'm going to give you one more chance to achieve what you've wanted all along. I'm going to let you save her life."

My chest heaved in the tight corset as my breathing accelerated. He obviously wasn't going to have me figure out her identity, since he'd already shown me who she was.

"Let me guess," I said. "You're going to give me clues, and if I'm smart enough to decipher them, they'll lead us to wherever you have her tied up."

"No. I'm going to do even better than that."

It was getting harder to hear him. The band was playing a fast-paced song with a lot of percussion, forcing the conversationalists in the room to shout in order to be heard. I pressed my phone harder to my ear, until pain reverberated through the delicate tissue. Making my way toward the edge of the room, where I would be farther from the band, I said, "Whatever it is, I'll do it."

The dark laugh that knocked against my eardrum echoed with the whispers of hell. "I'll take you instead."

My brow creased, and I tucked my chin in an effort to block out some of the noise. "What?" I shouted.

"Tick-tock, Quinn. You have exactly ten seconds to decide. Remain at the ball, where you are safe and being watched by a dozen pairs of eyes. No one will ever know you had the chance to save her but chose yourself instead. It'll be our little secret. *Or* agree to take her place and die knowing that she lived because you were willing to sacrifice. It's up to you. Four seconds."

Four seconds? Four seconds to decide my fate and someone else's. Four seconds to decide whether I would have a future—a home, a husband, children—or if I would give that future to another.

"Two, one—"

"I'll do it!" The words were out of my mouth before I had consciously chosen them.

The room began to sway. The music pumped, and people laughed, but it all became the backdrop of a living funhouse. My mind swarmed with all of the things I would have done differently that day if I had known when I'd awoken that it would be my last day on earth. At that moment, all I could think about was Trevor. My eyes raked the room for him again but were left wanting. I would never get to make things right with him, never get to apologize for failing to give him the credit he deserved for being the man he was, never get to kiss his soft, sensuous lips again. I would never again get to fall asleep and awaken in his arms.

"Listen carefully, Quinn. When we hang up, you will proceed to the restrooms. Once there, keep walking until you reach the rear exit. You will get into your car and drive to Buckley Trailhead, where I will then give you further direction."

Buckley Trailhead was a good thirty-minute drive southeast of town. That would surely give me enough time to raise some kind of alert—maybe find a way to get the guys to track my phone.

As my mind raced through various possibilities for rescue, the piper kept talking. "Do *not* attempt to alert anyone to the situation. I have demonstrated that I have eyes on you, and that will not cease to be true. If you do anything to involve anyone else, our beloved Mrs. Williams will suffer a slow and excruciating death. I have already proven what I am capable of, Quinn. Whatever you think of, I will have thought of it first and prepared accordingly. It is entirely up to you whether her blood will be added to what is already on your hands."

The line went dead.

I placed my palm against the cool wall and took a deep breath. My eyes slid to the figures surrounding me. *So many people.* So many opportunities for help, yet help couldn't be further from my grasp. After pushing off from the wall, I made my way toward the corner where the bathrooms were, careful to keep my pace and movements ordinary.

When I slipped around the corner, I bypassed the lines filled with people bouncing and shifting from side to side as they waited to purge their bladders. The exit at the back of the event center was nearly engulfed in darkness, but the faintly glowing red sign above the door marked the first signpost on my journey toward death.

I passed through without issue and made my way to my car, which wasn't far. The sultry night air wrapped itself around me, drawing a sheen to my skin despite the chill that had settled in my bones. When I reached my silver Xterra a moment later, I glanced around the parking lot in search of my homicidal companion. There was only one row of parking spaces on that side of the building, so it tended to be less traveled. *Nice going, Quinn. Park where there is the least amount of foot traffic when you're acting as bait for a serial killer.* "And the Darwin Award goes to *me*," I whispered as I opened the driver's-side door and climbed in, tossing my purse onto the passenger seat.

The side street I pulled onto a moment later was as desolate as the parking lot had been. My engine roared as I slowly increased my speed. Now that I was on my way, I had nothing to think about other than what fate awaited me at Buckley Trailhead, and the reality of the situation finally sank in. I was literally driving myself to my own execution, offering myself up to be tortured and murdered, to have my naked, mutilated body scrutinized by the same people I had worked alongside for the past five years.

I fought to shove those thoughts from my head, choosing instead to focus on the facts. I wasn't dead yet, and no way in hell would I go down without a fight once Yardley was in the clear. The piper said he would keep eyes on me. *But how closely can he really be watching at this particular moment?*

My eyes went to the rearview mirror as I searched for head-lights. The view behind me was dark—too dark, I realized. My skin prickled. Blood rushed to my ears. I screamed, but it was cut short by the serrated blade that flashed in the moonlight before it bit into my throat.

CHAPTER 51

Trevor

I PRESSED my back into the wall as I crossed my arms and melted into the shadows. At some point while I was outside dicking around with Blair and Dierk, Liz had added strobe lights to what was already the worst possible atmosphere for a stakeout. The white lights bounced off the fog that continued to billow its way through the mass of bodies bouncing and gyrating around the dance floor. The contrast between the strobe and the otherwise-dark room was wreaking havoc on my eyesight, and I was pretty sure I felt a seizure coming on.

Other than the moments when I allowed my gaze to travel the room in search of anyone who looked and moved like David James, I kept my eyes glued to the corner where Quinn had disappeared several minutes before.

"Remind me how we ended up at an eighth-grade dance, dressed in these stupid costumes." Gabe took up a spot on the wall beside me, adopting a pose similar to mine.

I smirked and spared an appraising glance in his direction. "We're chicken shits who can't say no to Liz."

He pressed his lips together and gave a firm nod. "Right."

I went back to scanning the room, noticing that he was doing the same. "I found our leak."

At that little tidbit, Gabe whipped his head around.

"It's Blair."

He swore under his breath. "It figures. That woman always did need a lot of attention. Guess when she realized she was never going to get it from you, she decided to get it elsewhere and scandalize you and Quinn in the process."

I nodded. "At least none of us is going to have to deal with her conniving ass anymore." And I didn't just mean the leaks. It hadn't taken long after the blowup with Quinn and learning about the rumor Blair had started about me fucking her to put two and two together. In hindsight, it was so obvious that Blair had fooled me into giving her a ride home just so that she could plant her phone in my truck to add credence to the rumor and create doubt about me in Quinn's mind.

"How did she even get her hands on all that information without leaving a trail in the system?" Gabe asked.

"Moore."

I could feel Gabe's eyes on me. "You think he gave it to Blair, and she passed it on to Dierk?"

I shook my head. "Blair and Moore were fuck buddies a few months back. Remember? She came and sat in the bullpen with him while he worked on reports."

Gabe nodded and returned his gaze to the partygoers. We had both been annoyed by her nearly constant presence toward the end of shift when we were trying to bang out our paperwork. She sat next to Moore while making eyes at me.

"My theory," I continued, "is that she stole a glance at his login credentials and has been helping herself to whatever information she wants."

"Moore is gonna piss himself when he realizes that woman almost cost him his badge. He'd have a hell of a time getting laid without it."

My face split into a bigger grin than it had given in a long time. We fell into silence as he studied the crowd, and my eyes darted toward the bathrooms again. With still no sign of Quinn, I figured the lines for the restrooms must be massive and joined my partner in assessing the room. There were way more people than any of us had expected. I surmised that Liz must have worked her charms on the neighboring towns and tripled the proceeds by bringing in fresh blood. That woman was a force to be reckoned with, and that was why she was put in charge of community events. No one could raise more money for charity and get people to love opening their wallets than Liz Matthews.

Noticing that Gabe's eyes had locked on something, I followed his line of sight and grinned when I realized what had captured his attention. Alex was standing halfway across the room, her mahogany hair draped down her back in long curls, the black dress that Liz had picked out hugging the curves of her tall frame. She was engaged in conversation with Liz, absently running her hand down her thigh. Gabe's eyes tracked the movement, and I thought he might actually stroke out.

I laughed and nudged him with my elbow. "Careful, partner. You look more like a lovesick pup than a dashing prince in a tux."

He angled his body toward me and dipped his chin as he looked up at me. "Guess you've seen it in the mirror enough lately to know what it looks like."

I snickered and looked away. Both of us knew I couldn't deny it.

Gabe smirked and said, "You never should have let her walk away. Don't make the same mistake twice." Then he punched me in the shoulder before disappearing into the crowd to make the rounds.

"Not planning on it." He was too far away to hear, but the words weren't meant for him.

My gaze returned to the corner where I'd been waiting for Quinn to emerge. There was still no sign of her, and my gut tightened a bit. I knew women took longer in the john than men, and the elaborate gowns probably wouldn't speed things up, but still. It had been a good ten minutes since she disappeared, and she was hungry to catch the piper. I had a hard time imagining that she would stay away from the main floor for long when she knew that our best chance of capturing him was her ability to pick out his voice in the crowd.

My restlessness grew with each second that passed, the prickle on the back of my neck becoming more persistent. Unable to ignore my instincts any longer, I shoved off the wall and made my way to the restrooms. When I arrived, I found what I expected—two very long lines of antsy partygoers. I ran my gaze along the line of women until I found one I recognized despite the costume.

"Margaret—"

"Hey-ya, honey! What's shakin'?" Our front-desk watchdog beamed up at me.

Margaret's short white hair was styled in big curls and dotted with small pink rosebuds that matched her feathered mask and lacy gown.

"Hey, darlin'. I need you to do me a favor and check for Quinn in the bathroom. It's urgent."

Margaret's smile dropped, her expression becoming all business. She gave a nod and elbowed her way up the line, women jumping left and right to get out of her way. When she emerged less than a minute later, she pressed her lips together and shook her head solemnly.

I cursed and sprinted back into the main room in search of Gabe. It didn't take long to pick him out of the crowd, and I descended upon him in a matter of seconds.

He took one look at me, and his body went rigid. "What's wrong?" he shouted over the music and voices.

"Quinn's gone!"

"What do you mean, she's 'gone'?"

"I can't find her. I saw her heading toward the bathrooms about ten minutes ago, but she never came back, so I had Margaret check the ladies' room, and she said Quinn's not in there. Something's wrong, Gabe. I can feel it."

Gabe and I had worked together long enough to know that it was stupid to question the other's instincts. Without hesitation, he jumped on his radio and asked the other officers if anyone had eyes on Quinn. I didn't even need an earpiece to know the answer. It was written all over his face.

"Fuck!" I spun toward the place I had last seen her then turned back around to face Gabe. "How the hell does she go missing in a room full of cops whose sole purpose is to keep eyes on her?" I was shouting loudly enough that several people in our vicinity turned and watched me while taking several steps back.

Gabe didn't answer. Instead, he got back on the radio and started barking orders at units to set up a perimeter and search for Quinn to confirm she really wasn't on the premises. While he was coordinating officers, I ran toward the back of the building, recalling that I'd seen Quinn's car parked in the rear lot when I searched for a parking space earlier.

I blew through the back exit and ran down the line of parked cars, my stupid dress shoes slipping on the pavement and nearly sending me face-first into the asphalt. When I reached her parking space, I swore and ripped my cell phone out of the inside pocket of my tux.

Gabe answered immediately. "Yeah?"

"Her car is fucking gone!"

CHAPTER 52

Quinn

"Keep driving until we reach Main," the piper directed. My eyes flashed to the rearview mirror, where I could see his face floating next to mine, though the rest of his body was invisible in his dark clothes.

We reached Main Street moments later, and I fully expected to turn right, since that was the direction of the Buckley Trailhead.

"Take a left."

I hesitated, my eyes darting to the rearview mirror again and locking onto his.

He bared his teeth and pressed the blade deeper into my throat, the sting of torn flesh drawing a gasp from me as I winced against the pain. "I will slice your pretty throat from ear to ear, Quinn. Do not test my patience."

I made the turn.

"Good. Now stay on Main until I tell you otherwise."

Gulping against the lump in my throat and wincing again when the action caused the knife to dig in even deeper, I fought to bring my panic under control.

Breathe, Quinn. Remember your training.

Whatever I was going to do, I needed to do it before we

reached our destination if I wanted any real hope of getting out alive.

I glanced at my purse in the passenger seat and pictured my cell phone nestled inside.

"Give it to me," he said, his lips brushing my ear.

When I didn't respond, he pulled the blade tighter against my throat as he wrapped his other hand in my hair, grabbed a fistful of curls, and yanked back. The pain of having my hair wrenched out by the root along with the deepening gash in my skin caused me to cry out and jerk the wheel until we were careening across the road.

I took my foot off the gas and spun the wheel back and forth, trying to bring the vehicle under control. When we were once again gliding down the stygian street that headed straight out of town, the piper pressed his lips to my ear again, his breath hot on my skin. "Last warning, Quinn. Next time, your warm blood will spill down my arm before you even have the chance to think about disobeying me. Now, give me the purse."

Stiffly, I reached for the purse, trying to keep my upper body still to prevent further damage to my throat. My fingers clawed at the sequined satchel until it slid close enough for me to grasp. Once I had it in hand, I passed it to the piper.

Releasing the hold he had on my hair, he snatched the purse, then he rummaged through it. The sultry summer air poured into the car as he lowered the back window. I watched in the rearview mirror, but it was too dark to determine what he was doing. A moment later, silence returned to the cab as he raised the barrier between us and the outside world back into place.

We approached the edge of town, and I eased the car to a stop at a red traffic signal. When it turned green, I began to proceed through the intersection, but the piper grabbed my hair again and yanked. "Take a right."

I did as he said without qualm. Over the next forty-five minutes, he proceeded to lead me through a complicated network of back streets and forest roads until we were well north of town and headed east, with Eden Falls fading in the distance. I wasn't exactly sure where we were, as the mountains and trees far outnumbered the sporadic homes and structures we passed, but I knew that we were nowhere near Buckley Trailhead. I wondered if he had given me that destination as a failsafe in case I'd found a way to get word to one of the officers.

With the towering evergreens pressing in around us, I squinted against the darkness that nearly swallowed the luminescence of my headlights.

"There's a dirt road just ahead on the right. Take it."

My stomach churned with acid. Not once during the entire labyrinth had he slackened his hold on that damn knife, which was still searing my raw flesh. And we were about to enter his lair —the domain in which he had all control.

The road manifested at the edge of my high beams. I hit the brakes to avoid passing it and spun the wheel hard, my Xterra bouncing ferociously over the rough-hewn road until a warm trickle of blood cascaded down my throat.

Several minutes and a pint of blood later, a small fishing cabin came into view. It was nearly impossible to make out through the copse of trees that blocked the full moon, but an amber glow emanated around the edges of the windows. I brought the car to a stop in front of the weathered porch, which was in desperate need of repairs.

"Unbuckle your seat belt."

I did as I was told. Then the knife was gone from my throat and pointed at my heart, its tip pressing against the edge of my breast. "I will gut you, Quinn, then bathe in your blood."

I swallowed against my rising panic, but I was determined not to let him hear the fear in my voice. "I've done everything you've asked me to. All I want is Yardley home and safe."

Apparently, I was convincing, because he removed the knife and exited the vehicle before opening my door. With the knife, he gestured for me to get out. Then he grasped the back of my neck and propelled me to the front door. Vaguely, I registered the sound of rushing water and realized just how close we were to the river.

With a flick of his wrist, the door swung open, and the cabin stretched its mouth wide for me. It didn't take long for my eyes to adjust once we were inside, since the interior was nearly as dark as the world beyond.

An orange glow flickered about the small room as flames leaped and danced in the rock-faced fireplace that took up residence in the center of the far-right wall. A kitchenette sat immediately to the right of the door, and a full-size bed was located on the left wall. Farther down on the right was an open door that I assumed was the bathroom.

Noting the layout of the cabin was more a distant musing than a conscious act. My sense of smell had my instincts spinning out of control. As soon as we'd entered the dwelling, a strong metallic odor assaulted my nostrils and drew my eyes to the opposite side of the room. There, crumpled up on a large plastic sheet, was the figure of a young brown-skinned woman. Her back was to me, but the overwhelming scent of blood and lack of movement upon our arrival sent my stomach plummeting to the floor.

My feet were glued to the splintered planks beneath my high-heeled shoes, my eyes riveted to the undoubtedly lifeless body of Yardley Williams.

He half growled, half chuckled behind me. Then his hand slithered around my waist and pulled me against his body as his mouth met my neck. "Yes, Quinn. She's dead."

Bile rose in my throat, and I bit down against the nausea that began to build. His fingers curled into the corset at my middle, as though my torment and fear were turning him on.

"It was noble of you to sacrifice yourself for her. But it was also stupid. You should know me at least half as well as I know you by now. And if you did, you would have known that I would never have let her out of here alive."

My eyes were still riveted to Yardley's bloodstained corpse, a tear rolling down my cheek. He was right. Only an idiot would have trusted that he would ever have given me any chance to save one of his victims. He had proven that time and time again, yet I had walked willfully into the net he'd laid out before me. A true piper, he had played his demonic tune, and I had followed.

A shove at my back had me moving toward the bed, where a tangle of rope awaited.

"Hold your hands out," he instructed as he snatched up the rope.

He deftly bound my wrists with knots that only tightened as I struggled against them. Then he roughly spun me around, and there was the sound of thread snapping as he used the knife to cut away the crimson fabric of my dress. When the last bit of threading gave way, the heavy layers of my gown fell to the floor, leaving me in nothing but my black corset, matching lace underwear, and high heels.

"Get on the bed," he growled.

When I refused to comply, he placed a hand in the center of my back and shoved until I was bent over the bed with my face smothered in the quilted cover. He grabbed my ankles and hurled the rest of my body onto the mattress before walking away.

With some effort, I turned onto my back and tried to shimmy closer to the headboard. The piper moved to a narrow door opposite the bed, between the fireplace and the bathroom. When he opened it, a small closet appeared. He pulled something from the single shelf that sat high in the otherwise empty space.

My eyes tracked him as he returned, the glow of the fire glinting off something silver. The piper grabbed my bound wrists and hoisted them above my head. Then I saw some kind of metal cuff. He wrapped it around the rough rope, which was eating away at my wrists, and secured it to the log bed frame. Then he moved to the foot of the bed and grabbed my ankles, yanking me farther down the mattress and parting my legs so that I was spread-eagle. He reached under the bed and withdrew two more coils of the abrasive rope before securing each ankle to the lower bedposts.

After carelessly removing my high heels, he tossed them, and they slammed against the wall and came to rest beside Yardley's body. Still standing at the foot of the bed, the killer took a few steps back and extracted a cell phone from his pocket.

He aimed the device at me. "Smile pretty, Quinn."

I gave him my best *screw you* face.

With a sinister laugh, he snapped a picture then began tapping away at the screen.

CHAPTER 53

Trevor

WET BLADES of grass clung to the shiny surface of my black dress shoes as I stared down at the lock screen on Quinn's phone, which showed a picture of her and Shelby cheek to cheek and beaming at the camera. With my flashlight, I painted an arc of light around the desolate yard where we had traced Quinn's cell. I hadn't actually expected to find her with her phone, but with nothing else to go on at the moment, I'd hoped I would find some other clue that could point me in her direction.

I gritted my teeth as I canvased the yard, looking for something that I was beginning to realize I wouldn't find. I hated the feeling of being completely helpless while my girl was out there, likely caught in the clutches of a psychopathic killer who was obsessed with her. There was no other explanation. Quinn would never have left the masquerade ball without notifying someone unless it was against her will or she felt she had no other option.

When my light failed to reveal anything I might have missed the first three times, I growled and clicked it off. A slight breeze brushed past me, rustling the silver leaves of the Russian olive trees that dotted several of the yards bordering Main Street. I glanced down at Quinn's phone a second time. The screen lit up again, and I gazed at the honey-colored eyes that had always had a way of seeing right through me.

The trouble was I didn't know if the cell phone was a breadcrumb or a diversion. I raised my eyes to the road and traced its path until it dipped fully into darkness. It all came down to whoever had tossed it into the yard. Quinn could have left it knowing that we would trace her cell the moment we realized she was missing. If that was the case, the phone marked her direction of travel.

Again, I studied the road. It led directly out of town. It was also the direction that asshole had fled the night I pursued him after he'd dumped Shelby's body in the dumpster behind the gym. *Coincidence?* It came back to the question of who had tossed the phone. If David James had left it behind, I was certain he had taken Quinn in an alternate direction and left the phone as a false clue. Even if he had simply discarded the phone as a means of preventing us from tracking their movements, there was no way he would be dumb enough to flee in that direction twice then leave a tracking device along the same route. He would essentially be pointing in the general direction of wherever he'd been hiding out.

A desperate breath rushed from my lungs as my eyes traced a path across the distant mountains that circled Eden Falls. She could be anywhere. Nothing short of a miracle was going to get me to Quinn in time.

A ping came from my tuxedo pocket. I shoved my hand into the satin fabric and extracted my phone, praying that it held the miracle I needed. My brow creased when I looked at the screen and registered a text from what appeared to be a ghost number. My heart stopped when I opened the message and saw Quinn staring back at me, dressed in nothing but a black corset and panties, with her wrists and ankles bound to the posts of a log bed frame. Her gaze was fierce despite the tear tracks running down her cheeks. I zeroed in on the rivulets of blood cutting jagged lines down her throat and pooling in her cleavage. Then I focused on the two words written beneath the image and embraced the hellfire that ripped through me and ravaged my control.

You lose.

CHAPTER 54

Trevor

THE MOOD around the station was as black as a moonless night. Officers still dressed in their tuxedos milled around the bullpen, keeping their voices low and hanging their heads even lower. Most of them had known Quinn for years—at least, as much as she would allow anyone she worked with to know her. But we *all* respected her abilities and her tireless efforts to keep us safe and provide us with what we needed to succeed. She had always been the calm voice on the radio, an anchor during some of our toughest times, and like a lighthouse, she had guided us through the storms.

Alex and Liz, desperate to provide whatever support they could, had joined us in the bullpen and were busy brewing and serving endless pots of coffee, knowing it was going to be a long night. I watched them as they weaved their way through a sea of black, their gowns swishing with each step. Then my eyes grazed my partners. Several of them were casting furtive glances in my direction, but it was what I saw etched into the lines of their faces that bothered me most. The knowledge that we would be putting one of our own into the ground shone from their eyes as clear as a summer day.

Unable to look at any of them for another second, I leaned

forward in my chair, put my elbows on my knees, and let my face fall into my hands. Gabe, who was seated on the corner of my desk, grasped my shoulder and squeezed.

"I have never failed anyone worse than I failed Quinn," I said, my voice muffled by my hands.

"We were *all* responsible for keeping eyes on her, Trevor." Gabe's tone was firm but gentle.

I raised my head and looked up at him, all too aware of the sting in my eyes. "But she was *mine* to protect."

Gabe pressed his lips into a hard line. Then his eyes darted to Alex, who was making her way over to us with Liz at her side, and I knew he understood what I meant.

When the ladies reached us, Alex cast a pained glance at me then sidled up to Gabe. He wrapped an arm around her slender waist and pulled her close, as though he was afraid she would disappear too.

Liz stood in front of me and took a moment to sweep her violet eyes among the three of us. Then she put a fist on her hip, and in a let's-pick-our-asses-up-off-the-ground-and-actually-*do*-something-about-this tone she said, "There has got to be something we're not thinking of." The coffee in the half-filled pot in her other hand sloshed in answer to her agitated movements. "People don't just vanish. There is *always* a trail of some sort. We just have to find it."

A half smile crept up my face as I looked at my shoes and recalled Quinn saying the same thing when she'd been sure we had missed something that was buried in the evidence. And she had been right.

Quinn always found the needle in the haystack, the loose thread that would unravel the whole damn thing. If she were with us, she would probably have her nose in some obscure database or case file, finding the exact information we needed.

That got me thinking. *What would Quinn do? If the situation were reversed, how would she find me?* Liz had the right idea. We had to rally. Quinn had fought for each of those victims until the very last grain of sand had run out. And she would get the same from us. I shot to my feet and scrubbed my hands up and down my face. Then I looked around the room. With my voice filled with a battle cry as I set out to rally the troops, I said, "Liz is right. There has to be some way to figure out where he took her."

I locked my focus on Gabe but was aware of the bodies in my peripheral slowly moving closer.

A muscle in Gabe's jaw jumped as he crossed his arms and shook his head. "We're trying to get all the surveillance footage from around town to track her car after she left the community center, but you know that's going to take time—time we don't have. Besides, it's not likely this guy does his thing in a well-populated area. So other than a general direction of travel, the footage isn't going to give us much anyway."

I shoved a hand through my hair and started to pace within the small space next to my desk.

Alex spoke next. "How about checking all the rental houses within a fifty-mile radius?"

I stopped pacing and stared at her, Liz and Gabe following suit.

Alex swallowed, self-consciously darting her green eyes around the group. Then she offered a little shrug. "You said he's not from here. So he must be renting some kind of vacation home or something. And you said he texted you that photo of Quinn less than an hour after she went missing, so he can't be that far away. If you can somehow check the addresses of the rental houses that are currently occupied within the immediate area, he's got to be in one of them." She flung her open palm out to the side. "He's not exactly going to be able to take these women to a motel, and you already know from the marks on their wrists and that photo he sent of Quinn that he ties them to a bed, so it's not like he kills them in the middle of nowhere."

I turned to Gabe, who was also looking at me, each of us silently communicating in the way we had since we were boys raising hell.

After a heartbeat, Gabe stood. "It's not a bad idea. I don't know how long it'll take to compile that kind of information, but it sure as hell beats sitting here and doing nothing." He pulled his cell phone from his pocket and started to move toward an empty corner of the room. "I'll call Dispatch and see what we can do to get to work on that list."

Nodding, I placed my hands on my hips and let my eyes lose focus as I got lost in my thoughts about where Quinn was and what she might be enduring.

"There has got to be some way to track them," Liz said, still brandishing the coffeepot. "OnStar or something!"

Alex gave her soon-to-be sister-in-law a half-hearted grin and shook her head.

I started pacing again. "Her car doesn't have anything like that." Then my steps faltered, and my eyes widened as I turned to Liz.

Reaching into my back pocket, I retrieved Quinn's cell phone and punched in the code I'd seen her enter a hundred times. My heart began to gallop as the home screen appeared. I flicked my thumb across the screen again and again, scanning it. Then I stopped and stared at the device. "No freaking way."

CHAPTER 55

Quinn

THE PIPER MOVED about the cabin in a methodical fashion. He'd come and gone a few times, never absent for more than a minute as he did God only knew what outside, but it was clear his ritual had begun. His movements were sharp and efficient. They were the movements of a man who had enacted this scenario many times over.

My eyes tracked him as he moved to a large duffel bag along the wall that looked like the kind soldiers carried. Something crinkled as he extracted it from the bag, and when he turned toward me, the firelight illuminated a large plastic sheet. He proceeded to lay the plastic out on the right side of the room, careful to ensure there were no creases or bumps. When he was satisfied with the arrangement, he disappeared into the tiny bathroom.

I took the opportunity to pull against my bonds, but just as it had each time before, the rope held fast, and nothing gave but the delicate tissue around my wrists, which were becoming a slick and bloody mess. A cabinet slammed shut, and David returned a few seconds later, setting a bottle on the bedside table to my right. He then stepped outside again, and I stole a peek at the bottle, surprised to realize it was massage oil.

My mind conjured an image of the case files I had read on

each of our victims. One line of typed text in the ME's notes that had been consistent with each victim jumped off the page. *Unidentified oil-based substance was found on multiple areas of the body.*

A fresh surge of reality crashed down upon me, and the urgency to find a way out of the cabin intensified. My gaze swept the room as I searched for something that could be used as a weapon, but the space was practically empty, with the exception of a few bags dotting the perimeter. I was all too aware of the huge disadvantage posed by the situation. Not only was David James taller and stronger, outweighing me by a good sixty pounds, but he was also the only one with knowledge of what was in those bags. What were the odds that I could find what I needed to fight him off before he got his hands on me?

Okay, Quinn. Calm down and think. There is always a way out.

A weapon wasn't important until I found a way out of the bonds. Fighting every urge to avoid looking at Yardley, I forced myself to take in the details of her bloodied corpse. Red spatters covered the plastic sheet beneath her—the same kind of sheet that was laid out and waiting for me on the other side of the bed. Her body was still positioned on its right side, facing the wall to my left. She was dressed in what appeared to be a green negligee that was in tatters and clinging to her body by only a few stubborn threads.

Open gashes across her back, neck, and legs had begun to crust with dried blood around the edges of the wounds. Her body glistened as the firelight played across her skin, no doubt an effect of the massage oil that sat within reach. A deep ache bloomed in my chest as I imagined what her last few hours had been like. *Did she reach the point of praying for death? Or did she hold out hope that she would see her husband and children again?* Perhaps she had simply retraced the precise series of events that had brought her to this place and put her at the mercy of a devil concealed by flesh.

Closing my eyes, I inhaled deeply through my nose. I couldn't let it be personal at the moment. I had to detach, to look at the situation analytically, or I didn't stand a chance of escaping the same fate. When I opened my eyes, I tucked my emotions away, forcing them to disappear into the same black hole in which I stored everything I didn't have the luxury of feeling when I was at work and doing everything in my power to help people through the worst moments of their lives.

I brought my gaze to the top of Yardley's head and slowly worked my way down her body, assessing everything I saw. It was on that second pass that I found the answer to my first problem. The images from the autopsy reports flickered to life in my mental library. One after the other, I saw the corpses—saw the lash marks that had torn flesh away from bone—and realized that every single one of them, including Yardley, had those marks on both the front and the back of their bodies.

Whatever the piper used to inflict that kind of damage, he had to have released them from their bonds first. Otherwise, there would be no blood spatter on the plastic beneath Yardley, and the wounds would have been on only one side of the body. Hope sparked to life.

I would have only a split second to act, to catch him by surprise, but the moment he released my bonds would be my one chance to turn the tables. That brought me back to the second problem. Without a weapon, I didn't know how I could possibly hope to fend him off long enough to get out the door. *And even if I did manage to make it that far, then what?* I could run to my car and pray that the keys were still inside. He'd been in and out of the cabin several times since we'd arrived. He might have taken the keys. My car was my best bet for putting enough distance between us to get away, but if I took that chance only to discover the keys were gone, I would lose my lead and my only opportunity for survival.

Perhaps running straight into the woods was best—except that I was barefoot and my feet would be shredded in seconds. I wasn't confident that I could run far enough and fast enough with injured feet to outpace him. Even Trevor, who was in phenomenal shape, had said the guy could move. But I really only had to get far enough to hunker down somewhere and hide. It was summer. I could survive through the night outside, no problem.

The door burst open without warning, and I jumped. David didn't even spare me a look as he returned to the duffel from which he'd extracted the plastic and began rummaging inside. When he found what he was looking for, he rose and went to the plastic sheet beside the bed. It was then that I saw the black whip dangling from his hand. But it was different from other whips I'd seen. It had a thick handle wrapped in what looked like black leather, and instead of one long cord emanating from the handle, there were several shorter cords, each of which contained a series of knots.

David knelt beside the plastic and placed the whip at its edge, straightening the handle so that it was perfectly parallel to the protective covering. He then proceeded to adjust each of the cords until they were also straight and evenly spaced. His dark hair fell across his forehead as he worked. The glasses he had worn at Rustlers, which had given him such a suave and dashing appearance, were nowhere in sight. And at some point while he'd been outside, he had discarded his black clothing and was now dressed in tattered and faded blue jeans that rode low on his hips and a snug white T-shirt that conveyed the strength of his body.

He turned his head to look at me, a smile curling his lips and stretching the small white scar above his Cupid's bow. When he stood, it was with feline grace, as was the way he prowled toward me. Slowly, he lifted the hem of his shirt, revealing a sheathed knife on his right hip. With one hand, he deftly removed the knife from its covering and leaned over me, placing a hand beside my head on the pillow.

He brought the tip of the knife to where my breasts billowed above the corset and used it to trace my cleavage. The rope around my wrists and ankles bit into my skin as I tried to inch away from the blade. And when he dragged the steel down the stiff fabric of my bodice, descending toward where my skin was visible just above my panties, the scratching sound it made crashed against the silence. David's eyes met mine as he brought the blade to my navel and traced lazy circles around it, a sensuous smile touching his lips.

My breathing became even shallower and more frantic as I sucked my stomach in, attempting to pull away from the blade. He gave a low, dark laugh as he savored my struggle. Then he brought the blade to my throat. His pressure was less than it had been in the car, but I winced against the pain of the steel digging into the already mangled skin.

When I opened my eyes, his face was inches from mine, the delight he experienced at the sight of my pain and fear all too easy to read. I forced myself to slow my breathing and to hold his gaze. He could take my life. I was powerless to stop him. But I would not feed him another ounce of my fear.

David's grin widened. His mouth was so close to mine that his breath kissed my lips. "I knew from the beginning you were different. All the others cried and begged for their lives the second my steel touched their skin."

I remained mute but torched him with my eyes. He continued to hover above me, the two of us locked in a silent standoff as the air between us crackled with our mutual hate. Finally, he pulled back, placing the knife on the bedside table, then sauntered to the closet beside the bathroom. My eyes shifted to the abandoned blade—the solution to my second problem. All that remained was the courage to execute my plan and a decision to either run to my car or into the heart of the wilderness. I didn't like the odds of either, but that wouldn't keep me from giving it everything I had left. If I died, I wanted to die fighting.

David reached for something on the top shelf of the closet. Then he walked to the foot of the bed and brought a Polaroid camera to his face. He snapped another picture of me. The camera whirred as the photo slid from the device into his grasp. After giving the image a few shakes, he looked down at it and smirked. Then he put the camera back on the shelf and set the Polaroid on the bedside table between the massage oil and the knife.

Placing his hands on the bed, he trapped my chest between his arms and brought his face close to mine again. "Let's get started, Quinn."

CHAPTER 56

Trevor

I HELD my breath as I tapped my thumb frenetically across the face of Quinn's phone.

"What?" Liz moved closer, the corners of her eyes crinkling as she scowled at the phone.

When I didn't respond, she closed the remaining distance between us until she stood directly in front of me. "Trevor, what *is* it?" she demanded.

She tried to get a peek at the phone sandwiched between our bodies, but she was too short to get a good look. When I still didn't answer, she twisted to peer over her shoulder at Alex, who was standing silently at the corner of my desk, then she turned back to me and opened her mouth in what was sure to be one of her infamous ass-chewings, but I was gone before she got the chance.

I broke into a sprint, heading for the double doors at the front of the station, grateful that I had parked on the street rather than in the back.

Keys in hand, I wrenched the driver's-side door open and dove inside. As soon as the engine roared to life, I put the truck in drive and punched the gas. While keeping one eye on the road, I pulled out my phone and tapped Gabe's contact. It barely rang before he answered.

"Where the hell did you go?" he barked.

"I found Quinn."

"What? How?"

"Well, I found her car, at least, but given the time frame between when she went missing and when that prick sent me the picture, I doubt he switched cars. Even if he did, I'm willing to bet he did it closer to wherever he's holding her rather than run the risk of doing it in town with everyone out for the ball."

"How the hell did you find her car?"

The light ahead turned red. I swept my gaze across the intersection. Seeing that it was clear, I increased my pressure on the throttle and blew the light. "You remember that day at the gym when Quinn asked if I'd been tracking her LoJack?"

"You're shitting me."

"I accessed the app and got a lock on her car. It's deep in the mountains north of town."

Another red light appeared. That time, a white sedan entered the intersection. I swore and smashed my foot down on the brake, drawing a squeal from my tires. As soon as the car cleared my path, I punched the gas again, narrowly missing its bumper.

"You should have fucking waited for backup."

"Would *you* have waited if it was Alex?"

Gabe was silent for a split second. Then he breathed a curse and started shouting at the other officers, telling them to gather around. "Can you send me the coordinates?"

"Yeah, as soon as you stop jabbering in my ear."

When I finally reached the edge of town, the sidewalks disappeared, and the rural highway stretched wide, beckoning me to let my horses run. I answered the call and slammed the gas pedal to the floorboard, relishing the vibration in the steering wheel and the growl of the engine.

"I'll mobilize the units and fill them in on the way," Gabe said. "Just *don't* do anything until we get there."

"No promises, brother."

He tried to argue, but I silenced him by ending the call then exchanged my phone for Quinn's. I was already climbing the winding mountain road and doing my best not to wreck as I took a screenshot of her car's location and sent it to Gabe, noting that her vehicle hadn't moved.

I pushed my truck to its limit as the incline steepened, the yellow glow of my headlights mixing with the ghostly pallor of moonlight.

My mind once again asked the question of how Quinn's phone found its way into my hand. *Did she toss it in hopes that I would remember her offhand comment about the LoJack system? Or did the piper use it in an attempt to send us in the wrong direction and unwittingly give us the very thing we needed to find them?*

A feral grin crept up my face. I hoped it was the latter. That was a poetic kind of justice.

My eyes darted to the clock on my dashboard—quarter to eleven. I tried to reassure myself that we had time. We were going to get to Quinn before midnight.

But the uneasy feeling in my gut intensified. Quinn wasn't just another one of his victims. And nothing about her involvement in the case had been typical of David James's MO.

What if he kills her just to beat me—to prove that he's smarter and better than me? Even if he did plan to wait until midnight to kill her, the thought of what she could be enduring that very second was more than I could handle.

Images of the decimated remains of our victims played across my mind and ended with a vision of Quinn bloody, broken, and lying in a heap of garbage with her body on display.

I shoved a hand through my hair and leaned forward, willing the truck to gain speed. That was *not* how our story would end.

When I glanced at her phone again, the location of her car was unchanged. My gaze settled back on the road just in time to see a ninety-degree curve approaching at a dangerous speed. Without slowing, I whipped around it, using all of my skill to keep the tires on the pavement.

Hold on, baby. Just hold on. I'm almost there. I sent the message into the universe and prayed that God would carry it to her.

CHAPTER 57

Quinn

IT'S FUNNY, the things your brain focuses on when your life hangs in the balance, like how one man's hands can feel so different from another's. Goose bumps rose on my skin when another glob of cold oil hit my flesh. Hands, soft and without the telltale signs of hard labor, began to work the oil up my thighs, and all I could think about was a calloused touch that had made me feel more in one night than I had felt in a lifetime.

My skin shimmered where the oil captured the firelight as the piper's fingers squeezed and cajoled my legs into submission. His eyes roamed my body, a faint smile the only indication of how much he was enjoying it.

"It was my mother who taught me how a woman likes to be touched," he said as though he were someplace far away. His fingers moved farther up my thigh, mere inches from my womanhood. "She would come home late at night, reeking of booze and cigarettes and sex." He tilted his head to the side, watching his hands work. "But it was always me she wanted most."

My gaze shot to vacant eyes that were the color of milk chocolate. His movements were mechanical as he reached for the massage oil on the bedside table and poured a dollop on my other leg. "Even though I could smell the seed of another man on her, she'd change into that tacky lingerie, pull me from bed, and lead me down the hall to her bedroom. It was easier once my father moved to the other part of the house. Easier still when he left altogether."

I swallowed against the bile in my throat. I didn't want to hear his story. I didn't want to feel sorry for this monster. As I looked at the face that had been the last thing so many women had seen before death, there was nothing of the sadistic genius who had kidnapped me and tied me to the bed. Instead, I could almost see the little boy behind the demonic presence.

He began to massage my other thigh, his attention focused on the task. "She'd lie down in bed, and I was supposed to take the massage oil from her nightstand. I'd start with her feet and work my way up to her neck. The whole time, she would purr and groan like it was the best thing she'd ever felt."

I studied his body language, trying to determine whether I should engage or keep my mouth shut. If I spoke to him as a mother figure, someone who was warm and loving, rather than the abuser he had known, perhaps he would show me mercy, seeing in me the thing he had always craved but had never been given.

"And that made you feel good?" I asked, my tone kind and soothing.

He ignored me. "As I rubbed the oil into her body, she'd squirm until her negligee rode up her thighs and the straps fell down her arms."

His expression began to shift. The little boy was receding as the monster emerged. "She'd watch for my body to react, and when it did, she'd point and laugh like she'd won some game." His voice was no longer distant. It held an edge that brought more goose bumps to my skin.

But then his gaze traveled up my body until his eyes met mine. For a moment, he just stared at me. Then he moved to the head of the bed, trailing his fingers from my thighs, up my abdomen, then to my breasts. He leaned over me, one hand beside my head and the other tracing the upper curve of my breasts with just his fingertips. He searched my face then settled on the hair spilling over my shoulders.

With a gentle touch, he lifted a curl and stared at it as his thumb stroked the soft tendril. "My mother wasn't what a mother should be. She wasn't like you, Quinn. She was ignorant and happily so, and she'd spread her legs for any man who had a few pretty words for her."

His affect shifted suddenly, his skin turning a subtle shade of crimson as his eyebrows lowered and his lips thinned. He brought his nose closer to mine, his gaze burning through me. "I can almost forgive your whoring with that cop. After all, you've been under a fair bit of stress, and he is very good at getting women into bed."

A dark hum rumbled from his chest. "He made decent competition, actually. Night after night for weeks, I watched him seduce one woman after another. They were *begging* him to take them home. Then"—he dropped my curl and straightened—"one night, he just... stopped."

He stared at me for a moment. Then he gripped my chin until pain radiated from his fingertips. "You're a bit of a piper yourself, Quinn." His lips smashed against mine with bruising force. "Yes, I can *almost* forgive your whoring this once. But not quite. In the end, even you are a disappointment."

His affect shifted again to apathy as he casually took the massage oil in hand and squirted the gelatinous substance into his other palm. After rubbing his hands together, he rested them on my stomach and resumed the massage, sliding his fingers beneath the corset then under the waistband of my panties.

My skin crawled at his touch, my toes curling as I fought to keep from showing him how much it sickened me.

"Tell me about Charles Schmid," I said, hoping it would distract him from fondling me.

He scoffed. "Schmid was a fraud, pretending to be some

master seducer who led his victims to their demise. He was sloppy and wore his deviance like a costume. He didn't deserve the title. A true piper can hide the evil within—appear as the man every woman dreams about while he weaves his spell until she willingly marches to her death."

"He didn't deserve the title. But you do?"

"Yes, Quinn. I do." His laugh was charming that time, full-bodied and ringing with delight. "It was so easy, even from the start, to lure them into my trap. But their deaths were their own doing."

His fingers slid beneath my panties again, far enough that he grazed the dark curls that covered my sex.

I took a shallow breath and tried to focus on the conversation. If I had a prayer of getting out alive, it would be my intellect, not brute force, that freed me. "What do you mean, that it was 'their doing'?"

His eyes rose to mine for a moment before they settled back on his work. "I've never killed anyone who was innocent, Quinn. I simply take out the trash."

Perhaps I was pushing too hard, but I couldn't stop the question that followed. "What were they guilty of?"

He snickered as his fingers worked their way beneath the bottom edge of my corset, squeezing and clawing at my slick skin. "They were dirty whores, Quinn. Every last one of them."

My brow creased as I stared at the orange and yellow flames leaping in the rock fireplace. I conjured the memory of the phone call I'd had with him after he murdered Shelby. He'd said that she *fit*. He'd said that he couldn't have killed her if she hadn't chosen to play the game.

"Shelby wasn't a dirty whore." I watched him for a reaction.

His fingers paused, and he studied me. Then he placed a hand on either side of my chest and caged me with his body as he leaned in close. "It was her own sin that killed her, Quinn. Just like all the others. I took her to bed, then I took her life."

My eyes widened, and my chest heaved with my rapid breaths.

"You're a liar! She would never have slept with you! She loved Josh."

His eyes crinkled as his grin grew. "It's hard to resist the piper, Quinn, but Shelby practically jumped on my dick. She didn't love Josh. She was miserable and wanted to feel alive again. Just like all the others. I have a particular knack for finding the ones who are dissatisfied with their marriages, the ones just like my mother, who would go out on the town and fuck anyone who made them feel special while their men sat at home like chumps."

I couldn't breathe. The walls pressed in around me. His touch was sandpaper scraping over a third-degree burn. *How could Shelby have been that far gone and I hadn't known?* Then I remembered the night I met David James, the piper disguised as the man. Shelby had been there. And she had disappeared right after Trevor ran him off.

"It was that night at Rustlers, wasn't it?"

His lips twitched, but he didn't answer. Instead, he began to massage my chest and shoulders.

"Answer me, you son of a bitch! Was that the night you seduced her?"

He squeezed the tops of my breasts and met my eyes. "Like I said, it's their own sin that kills them. Your friend with the short dark hair, she was my intended target. After hearing her complain about her husband and his secrets, I was sure she would jump at my proposal."

Liz.

"Truthfully, I was impressed by her resistance. It's rare for a woman to say no to me." He slid his fingers up to my throat, wrapping them around my neck and gently stroking. "But then I saw that shiny ring on Shelby's finger and the fuck-me eyes she was giving me, and I knew I wasn't leaving empty handed." He watched his fingers work and shrugged. "She had her usefulness, though. I learned quite a lot about you by enduring her incessant chatter."

Nausea roiled in my stomach as all the what-ifs flooded in.

What if I left with her that night? What if I pressed her to talk to me about what was going on when I realized she was there without Josh? What if I had been more focused on helping her through her problems than chasing a promotion and playing the piper's game? Would my friend still be alive?

Having confirmation that that was the night Shelby had been marked for death, it raised another question. "Why did you wait to kill her?"

He looked at me like it was a dumb question. "I never kiss and kill on the first night. That would be sloppy and stupid, and we both know I am neither. If I were seen leaving with a woman who turned up dead the next day, I would have been caught long ago."

"So how does your little game play out, then?"

"So full of questions, Quinn. Your inquisitiveness is one of the things I love most about you." He was practically purring, clearly enjoying the opportunity to dazzle me with his cunningness.

Fine. I would stroke his ego if it got me answers. All the better to hang him with later. "I may hate you, but I can't deny how clever you are. We've been in this together long enough that I would hope you'd be willing to sate my curiosity."

He chuckled and took a seat on the bed next to my hip, his jean-clad thigh brushing my waist. I knew he was aware of what I was doing, but I also knew he wouldn't be able to resist the chance to impress me.

After an appraising look, he answered, "The first night is everything they hope it will be. Orgasm after orgasm. Whispers of their beauty and how sexy and irresistible they are. I leave them panting and begging for more. And when I kiss them good night like a proper gentleman, they watch me walk away and wonder if they'll ever see me again."

With a tender touch, he brushed a strand of hair back from my face. He was masterful in his disguise. Had I not known what lurked in the darkness of his soul, I would have seen sitting before me the charismatic Prince Charming all those women had seen. He truly was the Pied Piper. His sultry voice and chiseled body were his flute.

"After a few days of leaving them to fantasize about me while I collect the details of their personal lives and their routines, I call them. They're always thrilled to hear from me, of course, their pussies dripping with the memory of our last encounter. It's easy to convince them of another rendezvous—somewhere remote. Private. Somewhere no one would see us and report back to their husbands." He grinned. "I'm considerate like that."

So that was how their cars wound up in the middle of nowhere.

I filled in the rest for him to confirm. "So they drive themselves to an isolated place of your choosing, and that's when you attack."

He nodded.

But none of his DNA was ever found in their cars. "You drove them here in one of those stolen cars that you later abandoned then returned after the fact to hide their vehicles and eliminate every trace of you."

Grinning again, he said, "That's my clever girl."

He rose from the bed, holding eye contact as he slowly dragged the hem of his shirt up to reveal washboard abs with a smattering of dark hair that disappeared beneath the waistband of his low-slung jeans.

My heart began to gallop when he tossed the shirt aside. I knew that none of the victims had been sexually assaulted, but I also knew I was an outlier. David had never had the satisfaction of seducing me, of being inside of me before he killed me. He'd never been obsessed with those other women, courting them with his guile and intellect for weeks before bringing them to the cabin. And he had already completed his seven kills. When it came to guessing his intentions for me, all bets were off.

Out of desperation, I blurted the first thing that came to mind in hopes that it would distract him. "Why seven victims?" The words tumbled out in a near shout.

This time, his grin was feline. "It's my lucky number."

Before I could ask any more questions, his fingers curled over the waistband of my panties. My mind raced. I had to get him to release the bonds. It was my only hope of surviving the night.

The rise and fall of his chest became faster as he slowly tugged the black lace farther down. My panic climbed until all thoughts ceased except for the fear of what he was going to do to me.

There's always a way, Quinn. I forced myself to go inward, to stop feeling his hands on me, to stop hearing his ragged breaths. My eyes darted to Yardley again, my earlier thoughts echoing in my mind. *He releases them when he's ready to beat them. When the seduction is over and the hunger for the kill cannot be resisted.* I had to make him hungry for the kill.

"You murdered your mother because you couldn't satisfy her. Didn't you?"

He froze. His eyes widened, and a slow but palpable vibration began to take over his body.

"That's why she laughed at you. Because you were so stupid that you actually believed you could be man enough for her. That she could ever *want* you."

"Shut your fucking mouth." The words were quiet and strained.

"But she rejected you. She *laughed* at you. How many women have laughed at you, David?

"Shut up!" he roared, his face scarlet, the veins in his neck bulging. His hand snaked out, curled around my throat, and squeezed until I began to gasp. "You want to know why I do this?"

He released his hold long enough to slap me across the face, the sting of his hand drawing a throb that only intensified when he cut off my air supply again. "For *years*," he said through clenched teeth, "I fantasized about what I wanted to do to her. Over and over like a movie in my head, I saw it. I planned it out perfectly. Waited for everything to align. I knew she'd come for me that night." Spit flew from his lips, and a maniacal gleam entered his eyes. "I let her think that it was just another night like all the rest. She didn't know about the belt I'd hidden beneath her bed earlier that day. She didn't know that when my dick got hard, it wasn't because I wanted her. It was because I knew what I was about to do. The fear on her face when I punched her until she was nothing but a bloody slab of meat was the best fucking high."

I writhed beneath his touch as black spots formed in my vision.

He growled. "I almost came with the first blow of that belt. I whipped her until her flesh tore open and blood oozed over every inch of her body."

My heart slammed against my chest, and tears leaked from the corners of my eyes. The sounds of my gasps were so distant that I wasn't even sure it was me they were coming from. I thrashed as much as I could with the ropes binding me in place. And when my bulging eyes locked on the man stealing the life from my body, the animalistic snarl in his features convinced me that I had pushed him too far. *This will be the moment of my death.* Not peaceful after a full and satisfying life but brutal, caught in the throes of pain and fear with a lifetime's worth of regret for what would never be. My vision narrowed to a pinprick, and I prepared myself for the blackness of death.

But as the world grew far too quiet and my senses gave way to nothingness, a cold wash of air rushed into my lungs, and I felt life return. It took a moment to realize that the piper's fingers were no longer wrapped around my throat. And though the pain from where his bruising force had met with lacerated flesh was considerable, the rush of sweet oxygen felt too good to think about the pain or what might come next.

But when David's hand went to the knife on the bedside table, the fear returned. He brought the blade to my belly and pressed down.

I sucked in a breath and braced for the feel of flesh tearing open and warm blood spilling over my skin. For several agonizing heartbeats, he held the knife perfectly still. With effort, I tore my eyes from the steel that could gut me with ease and lifted my gaze to the man who held my life in his hands. I was startled when I realized he was watching me, waiting.

As soon as my eyes met his, he held up the knife, moved to the foot of the bed, and continued talking as if he hadn't just brought me within a whisper of death. "Can you guess when I did come, Quinn?"

The blade slid between my ankle and the rope, the cold feel of the steel barely registering as I tried to track the conversation and his movements. With a violent slash, the rope snapped and fell loosely around my ankle. He repeated the process on the other side before moving to the head of the bed.

Stretching over me, he severed the rope from my wrists, leaving it to dangle from the silver cuff that had tethered me to the headboard. Then he wrapped his hand around the back of my neck and squeezed so hard that I froze. "It was the moment I wrapped my hands around her dick-swallowing throat and felt her body shudder beneath me with her dying breath."

He slid his hand into my hair, grabbed a fistful, and yanked so that I was propelled from the bed, several of my bobby pins tinkling when they hit the floor. With a violent thrust from the piper, I followed their descent and sprawled on the plastic sheet. He gazed down at me with a sensuous hum. "You'll get to experience it for yourself tonight, Quinn. When I strangle you to the brink of death then bring you back over and over."

He bent and retrieved the whip he'd laid out beside the plastic. Sprawled on my belly, I had only a second to glance over my shoulder and witness him return the knife to the nightstand before a searing pain ripped across my back.

Even with the corset in place, the pain was excruciating. It was only a matter of time before he laid my body bare before that whip.

I tried to crawl toward the nightstand, forcing myself to think only of the knife. I'd barely made it an inch before he brought the lash down again with a loud grunt.

I screamed as my skin broke open, the force of the lash pressing me to the floor as the room began to darken.

CHAPTER 58

Trevor

My truck swerved off the road and dove into the tree line. Once it was fully concealed in the small clearing I'd spotted from the road, I killed the engine and the lights and took another look at Quinn's phone. If I had judged my location correctly, her Xterra was only about a mile away. Since I had no idea if she and that asshole were with the vehicle, I'd decided to approach from a distance to keep the element of surprise.

I hopped out of the truck, opened the back door, and pulled the duffel I used for work across the seat. My movements were smooth and efficient as I stripped out of my white tuxedo shirt and pulled a black T-shirt from the bag and put it on. Next, I retrieved a flashlight and two fully loaded magazines that I clipped to my waistband, opposite the gun already holstered on my other hip. Then I jogged into the woods.

Moonlight filtered through the trees and painted the forest floor in swaths of iridescent white. Nothing but the sound of my breathing and the scampering of tiny mammals reached my ears, but I kept my eyes peeled for movement captured by the lunar glow.

It was well after eleven. I could feel Father Time breathing down my neck and the Grim Reaper whispering in my ear.

Though I had been in some pretty hairy situations before, I had never feared for my life the way I feared for Quinn's.

My legs ate up the ground between me and that damn dot on her phone, but it still didn't feel fast enough. Once I judged that I had covered a little more than half the distance, I stopped behind the cover of an old pine and pulled my cell phone from my rear pocket.

I slowed my breathing as I tapped out a quick text to Gabe to let him know where I'd left my truck and that I was continuing on foot, but when I hit Send, the message failed to deliver. When I checked the bars on my phone, I realized there weren't any.

Shit.

I glanced around. There was still no indication that anyone else was nearby. So I decided to try calling instead.

No dice.

Unwilling to lose another second, I pocketed my phone and set off at a run, careful to avoid snapping branches and announcing my arrival. A few minutes later, I caught a glimpse of something through the trees and pulled up, taking cover behind another column of bark.

Through a thick tangle of timber, I glimpsed a sliver of yellow light. With a few deep breaths, I scanned the woods but saw no movement and heard no sounds except for the hoot of a distant owl and the rushing rapids of the nearby river. I crept closer, keeping my body at an angle as I stepped one foot over the other and reached for my gun.

Leather creaked as I tugged my Glock free of its holster and savored the heavy weight of cold metal in my hand. Inching closer, I soon realized that the light was coming from a small structure, but it only appeared in thin strips that formed right angles. Whoever was in that cabin had taken care to cover the windows until nothing but the edges of light were visible.

The structure sat in a small clearing, and not a hundred yards from me was Quinn's Xterra, bathed fully in moonlight.

I stopped just short of the tree line and retrieved my phone.

Still no signal. I swore and raked my gaze across the structure and the area that surrounded it. Then crouching low, I darted to the nearest wall. Just left of a window, I rose slowly, keeping my shoulder pressed to the log facade, and tried to get a peek inside. But it was no good. Whatever was covering the windows clung to the glass, preventing gaps.

Soundlessly, I circled the perimeter, checking each window as I had the first. None of them divulged the secrets inside, but I had determined that there was only one way in or out without crashing through glass. But what bothered me more was the total silence. Aside from the thrashing river, I hadn't heard a peep since I'd arrived, and that had my gut twisted in knots.

I had no indication of what I was about to encounter, no way of knowing whether I was going to find Quinn alive or the piper bathed in her blood and standing over her lifeless body.

With my back against the cabin, the door to my left, I tried my phone one more time, theorizing that the killer had sent that photo of Quinn from inside, so there must be some kind of connection here.

One bar appeared. I pulled up the text I had tried to send to Gabe, but before I could fire it off, a bloodcurdling scream came from inside. The phone dropped from my grasp as I lunged for the door, adrenaline flooding my system. When the door wouldn't open, I stepped back and gave it a thunderous kick. Wood exploded. Splinters flew in every direction. Light spilled past the threshold.

I was inside before the debris finished falling, and my blood went ice-cold as the scene came into focus.

Quinn was sprawled on her stomach on a plastic sheet, wearing nothing but her corset and underwear. Her hair was falling down in tendrils around her mascara-streaked face, and the skin across her shoulders and upper back was bright red and covered with lacerations. Blood oozed from them and stained her pale skin. Her wrists and ankles were branded with thick bands of red-and-purple bruising.

Standing over her was David James, a dead man walking. He was shirtless, his chest covered in a sheen, a cat-o'-nine-tails swinging from his hand. His face was contorted with the depth of his hate and rage as he glared down at Quinn before turning his attention to me.

Mere seconds had passed since I'd busted through the door, but finding Quinn like that had brought everything into slow motion. My heartbeat thundered in my ears. A tear slid down her cheek. A body covered in the same lacerations that marred Quinn's back lay crumpled on the far side of the room. My instincts noticed the details, and my brain narrowed my senses.

But the moment my enemy threw his weapon at me, time sped up and the sounds of the universe crashed against my ear drums. My hands shot up to guard my face from the legs of the lash as they snapped across my skin. In nearly the same moment, a shoulder drove into my solar plexus. I grunted from the impact then grunted again as I slammed against the wall behind me with a hundred ninety pounds of muscle pinning me in place. The force of the tackle had sent my gun sailing from my grasp. Vaguely, I registered its thud against the floor somewhere to my right.

James's fist connected with my face before he landed several blows to my middle. The fucker was fast.

In a calculated move, I exposed my ribs to his violent punches and wrapped my arm around his neck, pulling him tight against me so that his blows lost power. He struggled and grunted under my grasp. Having his sweat-slicked skin against my bare forearm made it difficult to hold him. With my free hand, I drove my fist into his face as I kept him in a headlock with my other arm.

My knuckles came away bloody. I wasn't sure if the blood belonged to him or me, but I really didn't give a shit. As I was about to deliver another nose-crunching punch, the prick hooked his fingers under my nostrils, yanking my head back and making my eyes water. My grip around his neck loosened for just a moment, but it was enough for him to escape my grasp and ram his fist into my temple. The room was still spinning from the blow to my head when his other hand jabbed my windpipe.

When he stepped back and drew his knee to his chest, aiming for my kneecap, I spun to the side just in time to avoid the blow, causing him to strike the wall instead. With him directly behind me, I drove my elbow into his face. His head snapped back as a satisfying grunt flew from his lips.

Lactic acid and adrenaline flooded my body until I both burned and vibrated with the primal satisfaction of the fight. My breathing was ragged, my heart beating so fast that it slammed into my chest nearly as hard as some of those punches I'd taken.

James was feeling it too. His chest heaved as his lungs dragged in oxygen, and his skin was no longer coated in a mere sheen. Rivulets of sweat cascaded down his tanned skin, dipping into the crevices of his muscled torso.

Before he could recover, I slammed my fists into his face one after the other, driving him back toward the door. After a few solid hits, he managed to rally and dodge the last. The maneuver left my right side open. He ducked his head and drove his body into mine again, wrapping his arms around my torso, holding me so tightly that I couldn't land a good hit. We wrestled on our feet, each of us wrapping the other in a bear hug. The struggle went on, the two of us grunting and panting—him fighting for his freedom, me fighting for the love of my life and for every woman the asshole had destroyed.

In the melee, I ended up with my back to the wall once more. James continued to press his body into mine, but he freed a forearm and brought it to my throat, baring his teeth in a demented grin. He opened his mouth to speak, but before he managed to breathe a word, a guttural scream pierced the sounds of our struggle. I watched in confusion as James's eyes widened and his mouth slackened.

The pressure on my body evaporated as he staggered backward. When he twisted to gaze at the large hunting knife sticking out of his right flank, I saw Quinn standing behind him, trembling and holding her bloody hand away from her body. Her amber eyes were huge, her mouth hanging open, as she stared at the evidence of what she'd done.

James's face warped from shock to rage as his eyes traveled from the knife to Quinn. In one more act of inhuman strength, he lunged for her. She took a step back, but he would never have gotten his hands on her.

My hand shot out and gripped his throat. I squeezed until his eyes bulged then pulled his face close to mine. "*You lose*, motherfucker."

I shoved him with so much force that he fell straight back, driving the knife even deeper into his liver. Blood gurgled from his lips as he struggled to speak. Within seconds, his eyes became glassy and his head lolled to the side.

His dying gasp drew a sob from Quinn. She covered her mouth with the back of her unbloodied hand and stared down at the man who had reduced her life to tatters. Fresh tears streamed down her cheeks, her body trembling even more violently than before.

I went to her and pulled her to me, tucking her face against my neck as I stroked her hair.

"I-I k-killed him," she sobbed.

Though she had dealt a killing blow, straight through the liver with a knife big enough to cut it in half, a soft heart like Quinn's couldn't handle the thought of having ripped someone from life. It would cause a fissure in her soul that would never close. "No, baby. You just wounded him. If I hadn't made him fall on that knife, he would have gotten out of here alive."

She clutched my shirt and gasped for air between sobs. Several minutes later, when sirens blared through the silent night and red and blue lights danced with the fire's glow, we were still locked in our embrace, her face buried in my shirt and my arms around the woman I would never let go of again.

CHAPTER 59

Trevor

WITH MY ARMS crossed and a glower on my face, I stood beside a red-and-black medic rig, the words Eden Falls Fire Department on its side, as I watched Bryan gingerly apply some kind of salve to Quinn's mangled wrists. She was sitting on the end of the stretcher, just inside the ambulance, her palms turned up and the backs of her hands resting on her knees. Aside from the corset and panties I'd found her in, she was wrapped in a sheet I'd grabbed from the bed and had pulled around her just before Gabe and the rest of the guys joined the party.

Bryan pulled some gauze out of a bag he had beside Quinn and began to wrap her wrists. When she winced, I got the overwhelming urge to revive David James just so that I could kill him again. My body language must have given my homicidal thoughts away, because Quinn turned worried eyes on me and bit her lower lip.

Bryan took one look at her, followed her gaze, and gave me the once-over before he said, "She's going to be okay, Trevor. Our girl's made of some pretty tough stuff."

My jaw tightened as my eyes slid to his profile. *Our* girl?

Bryan glanced over his shoulder again, wearing mischief like makeup as he confirmed that his comment had struck the right chord. If he wasn't careful, I was going to beat the ginger out of his hair.

Quinn, always worried about everyone but herself, did what she did best as a dispatcher—defused the situation. "Trev, I'm good. Really. Why don't you check on the guys while Bryan finishes up here?"

And just like that, the sweet lilt of her voice and the gentleness in her golden eyes quelled the urge to pound my fist into someone's face and brought me back to an even keel.

My lips turned up in a soft smile as I stepped to the back of the rig and captured her face between my hands. As I brushed her velvet cheek with my thumb and my gaze swept over her features, I told myself repeatedly that I hadn't lost her. She was safe. And she was mine.

The tips of my fingers tangled in her mostly fallen curls as I pulled her forehead to my lips. She wrapped her hands around my wrists and squeezed as though the contact were a lifeline.

When I pulled back, I said, "I'm going to check on the progress inside."

She nodded and released her hold on me.

Then I turned to Bryan. He was dressed in his usual navy shirt, the Eden Falls Fire Department logo on the left breast, and his navy uniform pants. "I'm riding to the hospital with her. Let me know when she's ready to go."

He gave a curt nod. "Will do."

Then I leaned in closer and bared my teeth, speaking low enough that Quinn wouldn't be able to make out the words. "And make sure your hands don't touch anything that isn't broken or bleeding."

Bryan struggled to keep the grin off his face, but in an unusually intelligent act of self-preservation, he managed to rein it in and gave another nod.

When I entered the cabin a moment later, I stopped just inside the threshold and scanned the space, finally able to absorb every detail. Across the room, Yardley's body was still being photographed and processed. A couple of officers were in the bathroom, taking inventory and collecting evidence. Several other uniforms milled about the bed, taking notes and discussing their findings.

Gabe stood near the foot of the bed with his back to me. Taking up a position on his left, I crossed my arms and opened my stance as I dragged my gaze along the bed, pausing at the sight of severed ropes dangling from the bedposts. The rage began to churn and rise from the pit of my gut again. I took a slow, deep breath through my nose and tried to detach from the situation. It was a lot harder to put your investigator hat on when all you could see was the love of your life practically naked and tied to a bed while some other man touched and tortured her.

"You good?"

Gabe's quiet words brought me out of my head and back to the room. I glanced in his direction and found him giving me the side-eye. I nodded. "Peachy."

He smirked but turned his attention back to the officers who were busy collecting DNA off the bedspread. No doubt we were going to find remnants of each of our victims—and Quinn—on that damned thing.

I tore my eyes away and focused on the area surrounding the bed instead. My gaze snagged on the nightstand against the wall to my left. On it sat an open bottle of massage oil and a squat lamp with a dingy yellow lampshade. Vaguely, I recalled the slick feel of Quinn's skin beneath my fingertips when I'd held her against my chest as the cavalry arrived. I hadn't thought anything of it at the time, but as I stared at that massage oil, it was the only thing I *could* think about.

The urge to go for a long, hard run took over. In my restlessness, I squeezed the back of my neck. I closed my eyes and tilted my face to the ceiling as I fought once again to rein in my emotions. Recognizing that I wasn't going to be any help, I began to turn toward the door, intending to leave the crime scene to Gabe and our partners while I returned to Quinn. Just as I angled away, I caught sight of something white that had fallen between the nightstand and the bed.

Without taking my eyes off of the item, I slapped the back of my hand against Gabe's arm. "Hey, give me a glove."

He reached into his back pocket and extracted a blue latex glove and handed it over.

As I pulled it on, I went to the bedside table and took a knee, then I reached my index finger and thumb into the narrow space beside the bed and extracted what felt like a thick piece of paper. When I held it up, I saw that it was a Polaroid picture. I flipped it over and gazed at an image of Quinn stripped to her black corset and matching panties, her wrists and ankles bound to the bed and already turning purple. Mascara streaked down her cheeks, but her expression was feral. The photo was similar to the one he'd sent to my phone. *Why the hell would he have taken a Polaroid?*

"What is it?" Gabe asked.

I rose to my feet and handed it to him. Gabe took one look at it and swore before handing it back.

Then Nash called to us. He was kneeling in front of the small closet opposite the bed. "Hey, McNeil, Ryan, you're going to want to see this."

Nash's back was to us, his dark head bent as he looked down at something. Though we had turned on every light in the dingy cabin, the fire still roared to his right, turning his coppery skin a lighter shade of bronze.

Once we were positioned at his back, I could see what he was looking at. He pointed at a black hole in the floor. "Found a loose floorboard. He was using it as a hiding place."

"A hiding place for what?" I asked.

Then I noticed a large book sitting in his lap. He picked it up, his hands masked in the same blue latex I still wore, and handed it to us. Gabe took the book, flipped it over, and examined the cover. It was sable and marred by various marks and dings, as if the book had traveled far and wide.

Balancing it in one hand, Gabe flipped the cover open, and we swore in unison.

One by one, he flipped through the pages. The contents were nearly identical with every turn.

"It's a kill book," Gabe said under his breath.

The photo album was filled with the piper's victims, women of all different races and ages. And for every victim, there were two Polaroids placed side by side. The first photo looked just like the one of Quinn. The women were bound to a bed, wearing nothing but skimpy lingerie, their faces filled with terror. In the second, their lifeless, bloody bodies were spread on a piece of crimson-smeared plastic.

"Before and after shots of his handiwork," I said.

Gabe, his lips pressed together, nodded as he continued to study each face.

My stomach turned as I stared at the evidence of how close I had come to losing Quinn. I had found her on that fucking plastic, bloody and fighting for her life. She had come so close to that *after* shot.

Gabe snapped the book shut and called for an evidence bag. "Good work, Nash." He thumped our partner on the back before handing the book off to be logged and preserved.

Then he removed his gloves and clapped me on the shoulder. "Let's get some fresh air."

I nodded and followed him out of the cabin. We stopped just a few feet away from the dwelling.

"Well," Gabe said, "one good thing that came out of all of this, aside from sending that motherfucker straight to hell, is that we'll be able to bring closure to all those victims and their families."

I nodded again, my eyes on Quinn in the back of the medic rig. It looked like Bryan was just about done. He said something that brought a smile to Quinn's lips, but they were too far away for me to hear what it was. She still had the sheet wrapped around her, holding it under her arms. Her dark curls were pulled over one shoulder as Bryan dabbed at her back.

I thought of the officers and detectives across the nation who were finally going to be able to close all the cold cases that the piper had left in his wake. They were finally going to be able to go to the families of his victims and tell them that the man who had stolen their mothers, daughters, and sisters from them had been laid to rest. Then I thought of Alvarez and the case that had haunted him for most of his career. The ghosts of failure and souls without justice that kept him up at night, that plagued every case and his waking thoughts, could now become a memory—all because the dark-haired beauty sitting thirty feet from me had had the courage to challenge a killer and the brains to beat him at his own game.

Epilogue

THREE MONTHS LATER . . .

"Eden Falls Police Department. How may I help you?" I glanced at the screen with the caller's information, noting the familiar number.

"Do you have *any* idea how many times I've had to call about people parking in front of the soccer field when they don't have kids who play soccer?"

I rolled my eyes and smiled, thinking back to a time when I would never have thought calls like this would delight me. "I'll let the officers know, Mrs. Wallace. You have a nice day."

After disconnecting, I sent the call for service through to Julia, who was working our main law channel. The ding from her computer notified me that it had arrived.

She snickered. "I'm sure they'll get right on top of that." Then she spun in her chair to face me. One foot was folded beneath her opposite leg, which was dangling from the elevated seat. She always liked to jack it up as high as it would go. "What are you still doing here, Quinn?"

I leaned back and scrubbed my hands over my face. It was stuffy in the center, which wasn't unusual through the summer and fall. But winter would soon be upon us. "I just want to make sure you guys are really good before I take off."

"We're fine!" Julia flapped a hand at me. "It's only an hour until shift change. Things are quiet. And even if they don't stay that way, we can handle it until the night shift gets here."

I glanced at Meredith and our newest dispatcher, April, both of whom nodded enthusiastically.

"Yeah," Meredith said, her chubby cheeks forcing her eyes shut from the breadth of her smile. "You need to get ready for your party. We'll see you at Rustlers in no time!"

I still couldn't believe the change in the woman. Ever since Blair had been disgraced and relieved of her duties, Meredith had done a one-eighty after a few days of licking her wounds and realizing that perhaps she hadn't chosen her company wisely. She'd been an exemplary employee since and was even quickly becoming a friend.

Though Trevor and the chief got the kudos for kicking Blair to the curb, I had done my own share of cleaning house after *finally* getting promoted to supervisor—and taking over Blair's previous assignment. It had been a tall order, but I had thrown myself into the work with a renewed sense of purpose, insisting that any dispatcher who remained with the department was expected to maintain a professional attitude and a spirit of teamwork.

After months of team-building exercises, unofficial lunches and hangouts, and a few friendly office competitions, like the upcoming pumpkin-carving contest, the entire atmosphere had changed, and we were finally all on the same side, helping one another and the department to succeed.

I smiled at the insistent faces staring back at me and put my hands up in surrender. "Okay. Okay. I'm outta here."

After collecting my bag and telling the girls I would see them in an hour for the birthday party they had planned for me, I stepped into the late-autumn sun, sliding my sunglasses into place. The golden light infused my skin with its warmth. The meandering breeze carried the scent of pumpkins and hay bales, courtesy of the fall decorations we'd placed around the comms center.

It only took a few minutes to make my way across town to the football field sandwiched between our elementary and middle schools. When I parked my car and stepped onto the green grass, I shielded my eyes against the sun and located the tall man with golden hair, broad shoulders, and a narrow waist who just so happened to occupy my every fantasy.

"That's it, Aiden! Nice!" Trevor clapped then hollered to another kid. "Get after it, Kyle! Hustle, hustle, hustle!"

I smiled as I came to a stop beside my Pee Wee football coach, my shoulder grazing his arm.

He looked down at me, and even with his shades in place, I could feel the heat in his gaze and read his thoughts in his smile. "Hey, beautiful."

"Hey, Coach."

Trevor snaked his arm around my waist and pulled me to his side. Feeling his body against mine never got old.

"What are you doing here?" he asked. "Thought you'd be getting all gussied up for your party."

"I'll head out in a few minutes. Just couldn't wait that long to see you."

His thumb stroked my side, sending shivers up my spine and back down into my toes.

I watched for a moment as the young footballers scrimmaged. "They've really come a long way this season."

Trevor smiled like a proud papa bear. "Yeah, they have. These kids have got talent. They just needed someone to help bring it out."

And Trevor had been perfect for the job. He'd never said it outright, but the kids had done a lot for him too. Somehow, the demons that had stalked him all those years with what he had thought were failures and disappointments to others had turned into blessings and a purpose he'd never seen coming. He had confessed to me once, while we were lying in bed, our arms around each other, utterly sated from our lovemaking, that he realized he was where he was always meant to be, doing what he was always meant to do.

Shaping the next generation of athletes and protecting his beloved town had filled the holes in his heart and given him a reason to like what he saw in the mirror, and I'd never been so proud of someone in my entire life.

I curled into him tighter and placed my hand on his chest, the faint red marks circling my wrist catching my eye. A wave of sadness washed over me as the marks conjured memories and thoughts of how much our town had lost—of how much *I* had lost. But they also served as a reminder of how much I had gained.

I now knew that I was not an easy adversary and that I would fight for my life and for the lives of the innocent until my last breath. I had also proven to myself that I was capable of enduring the worst that life could throw at me. And while it might have cost me the person I had been, I had risen from the ashes and been built anew—stronger.

And not least of all, I had gained a partner and a love that would last a lifetime, and he had already proven that no matter how bad things got, he would never stop fighting for me and for us.

I smirked. Yes, Trevor Ryan was the man I hadn't seen coming, and somewhere along the way, he had become the man I couldn't live without.

Trevor leaned down and nuzzled my ear. "How long do we have to stay at the party tonight?" he asked in an impish tone.

I chuckled and smacked his chest playfully. "Long enough to avoid being rude. It's very sweet that the girls wanted to throw me a party."

He looked out at his players, his lips turned down in a slight pout.

Again, I laughed. "I promise our sheets are going to see plenty of action tonight."

With that, he waggled his eyebrows and turned his brilliant smile on me, the one that made him look like some bronzed god backlit by the afternoon sun.

After enjoying another few minutes of watching him interact with his players, I was about to take off so that I could shower and change before all eyes were on me, but Trevor's phone rang before I could kiss him goodbye. So I waited.

"Hey, brother. What's up?"

Trevor's body went rigid, and his grasp on my waist tightened. I whipped my head around to search his face for answers, but his eyes were unreadable behind the sunglasses.

"What do you mean, 'he's missing'?"

The creases in Trevor's brow continued to deepen in response to whatever Gabe was conveying.

"Okay. I'm on my way," he said with urgency in his words.

The second he pulled the phone away from his ear, I demanded answers. "What? What's going on?"

Trevor shoved his sunglasses on top of his head, and my stomach clenched at the worry in his sky-blue eyes. "Mark is missing."

"What do you mean, 'missing'?"

He shook his head. "He was supposedly on a business trip back east, but Liz hasn't been able to get ahold of him, so she tried to track him down through the hotel where he told her he was staying. They had no record of him. Same with the airline. He was never booked on the flights he gave her."

I tried to swallow, but my mouth had gone dry.

Trevor ran a hand through his hair and forced out a breath as his eyes scanned the field and his players, though I doubted he was really seeing anything in front of him. His mind was with his family.

"Go. I'll stay with the kids until their parents arrive then meet you at Liz's."

"Are you sure?" I could tell he was torn between leaving me and being there for his sister.

I nodded firmly. "Yes. It'll give me a chance to call Julia and ask her to cancel the party. I'll be there before you know it."

He pressed his lips together then kissed me on the forehead and took off at a sprint toward the parking lot.

I watched him go, his form growing smaller as the knot in my stomach got bigger. I had become close friends with both Liz and Alex the past few months, and Liz had openly shared her concerns about Mark and their marital problems. But I had never gotten the impression that Mark was the kind of guy who would just disappear on his family. Still, if my time with the piper had taught me anything, it was that people could wear all kinds of disguises, and those disguises could conceal all sorts of secrets.

But all my years as a dispatcher had honed my instincts to a fine point, and the niggle in my gut told me something much more sinister was at play.

He's beautiful and dangerous. And he's convinced I have something they want. Now I'm his captive, and we're alone in the frozen Montana wilderness with nothing but each other and our mutual hate to keep us warm. But as circumstances shift like the surrounding snowstorms, I soon realize my only hope of staying alive is to trust the man who was sent to kill me.

Zach

As an enforcer for a ruthless cartel, I've got no problem getting my hands dirty. But when I'm sent to retrieve the *one thing* that could destroy the cartel's entire operation, I'm confronted by a blue-eyed beauty whose tongue is as sharp as her aim, and she's a temptation I can't afford. Because between the cold nights and the scorched sheets, it's *my* secrets that might just get us killed...

Love This Book?

I am sincerely grateful to you for reading *When Midnight Strikes*. Creating stories has been a lifelong passion of mine, and people like you are a part of making the dream a reality.

If you enjoyed this book, please consider leaving a quick review. Reviews help other readers to find the book and take a chance on it, and they are one of the best ways you can support an author.

You can jump to the review page by scanning the QR code below.

With gratitude, Riley.

About the Author

With a passion for justice and a heart for people, Riley is a former emergency dispatcher living out her dream to write stories that exemplify the healing power of love and the eternal battle between good and evil.

Riley holds a bachelor's degree in criminal justice and master's degrees in counseling and forensic psychology. Her education, professional experience, and slightly macabre mentality set the stage for her novels and fuel an imagination that sends tingles tripping down her readers' spines.

Living in Montana with the man who stole her heart, and the two rescue pups who took a piece as well, Riley is hard at work bringing love, passion, thrills, and chills to all who dive into the pages of her books.

Subscribe to Riley's newsletter by scanning the QR code and receive *exclusive* bonus content, updates on book news, and behind-the-scenes shenanigans!

Also by Riley Skov

EDEN FALLS MONTANA SERIES

When Shadows Fall

When Midnight Strikes

When Secrets Kill